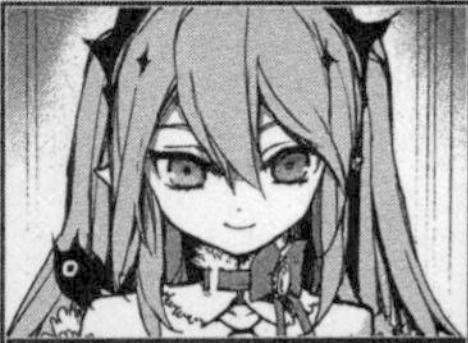

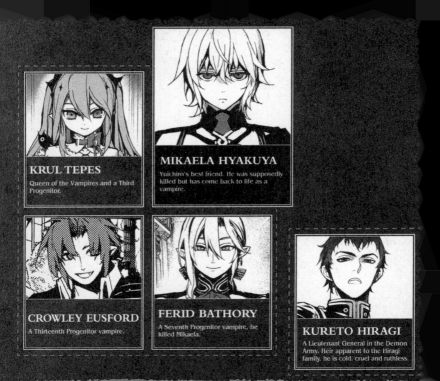

KRUL TEPES

Queen of the Vampires and a Third Progenitor.

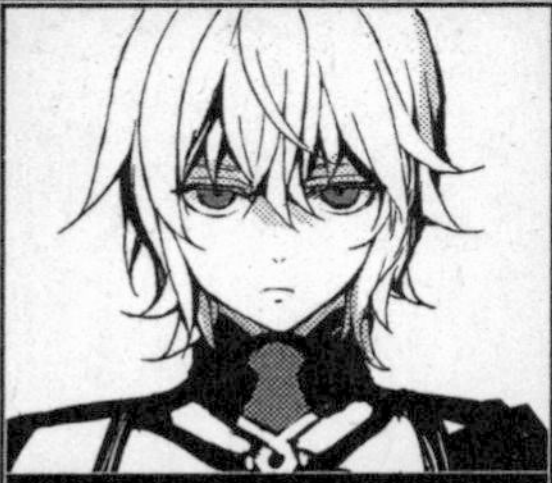

MIKAELA HYAKUYA

Yuichiro's best friend. He was supposedly killed but has come back to life as a vampire.

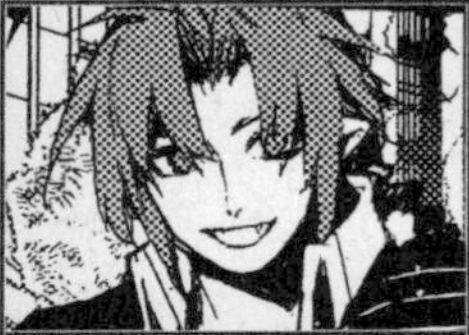

CROWLEY EUSFORD

A Thirteenth Progenitor vampire.

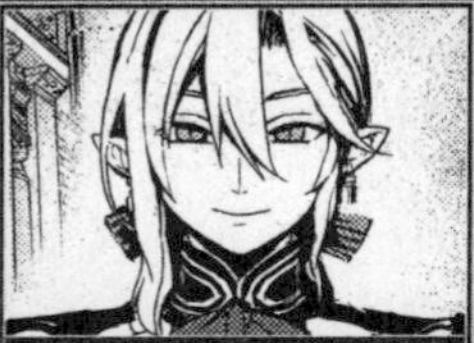

FERID BATHORY

A Seventh Progenitor vampire, he killed Mikaela.

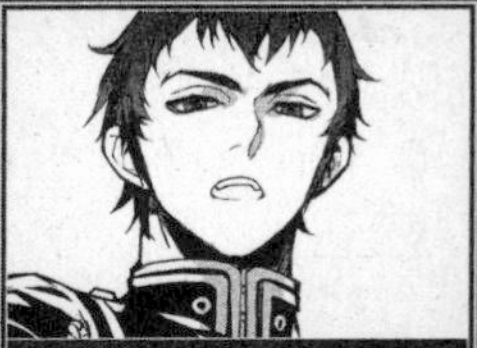

KURETO HIRAGI

A Lieutenant General in the Demon Army. Heir apparent to the Hiragi family, he is cold, cruel and ruthless.

STORY

A mysterious virus decimates the human population, and vampires claim dominion over the world. Yuichiro and his adopted family of orphans are kept as vampire fodder in an underground city until the day Mikaela, Yuichiro's best friend, plots an ill-fated escape for the orphans. Only Yuichiro survives and reaches the surface.

Four years later, Yuichiro enters into the Moon Demon Company, a Vampire Extermination Unit in the Japanese Imperial Demon Army, to enact his revenge. There he gains Asuramaru, a demon-possessed weapon capable of killing vampires. Along with his squad mates Yoichi, Shinoa, Kimizuki and Mitsuba, Yuichiro deploys to Shinjuku with orders to thwart a vampire attack.

In battle against the vampires, Yuichiro discovers that not only is his friend Mikaela alive, but he also has been turned into a vampire. After, Yuichiro undergoes further training and grows stronger as a fighter, becoming much closer to his squad mates.

Under Kureto's orders, the Moon Demon Company attacks a vampire enclave in Nagoya. Yuichiro and his squad succeed in assassinating the vampire noble Lucal Wesker, but the squads sent after Crowley Eusford fare much worse, with almost twenty of their number being taken hostage. The surviving squads plan a desperate rescue attempt, but Crowley is just too strong. The hostages are freed, but Guren is captured. Shinoa and the others attempt a desperate escape, only to run across Mikaela on the way out...

Seraph of the End

—VAMPIRE REIGN—

Seraph of the End

—VAMPIRE REIGN—

CONTENTS

10

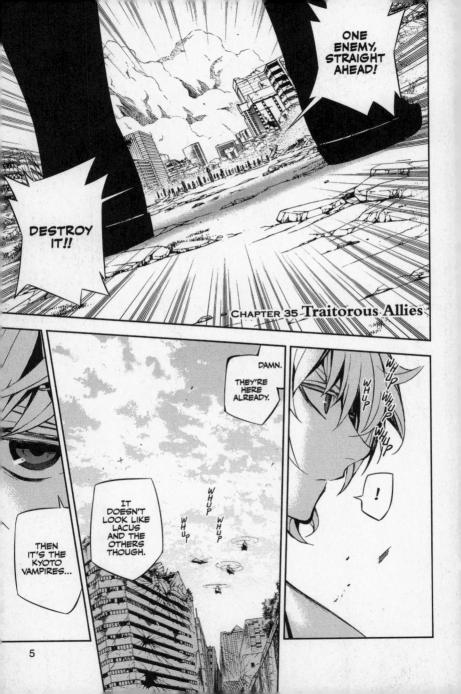

ONE ENEMY, STRAIGHT AHEAD!

DESTROY IT!!

CHAPTER 35 Traitorous Allies

DAMN. THEY'RE HERE ALREADY.

WHUP WHUP WHUP WHUP

!

IT DOESN'T LOOK LIKE LACUS AND THE OTHERS THOUGH.

WHUP WHUP WHUP

THEN IT'S THE KYOTO VAMPIRES...

CHAPTER 35
Traitorous Allies

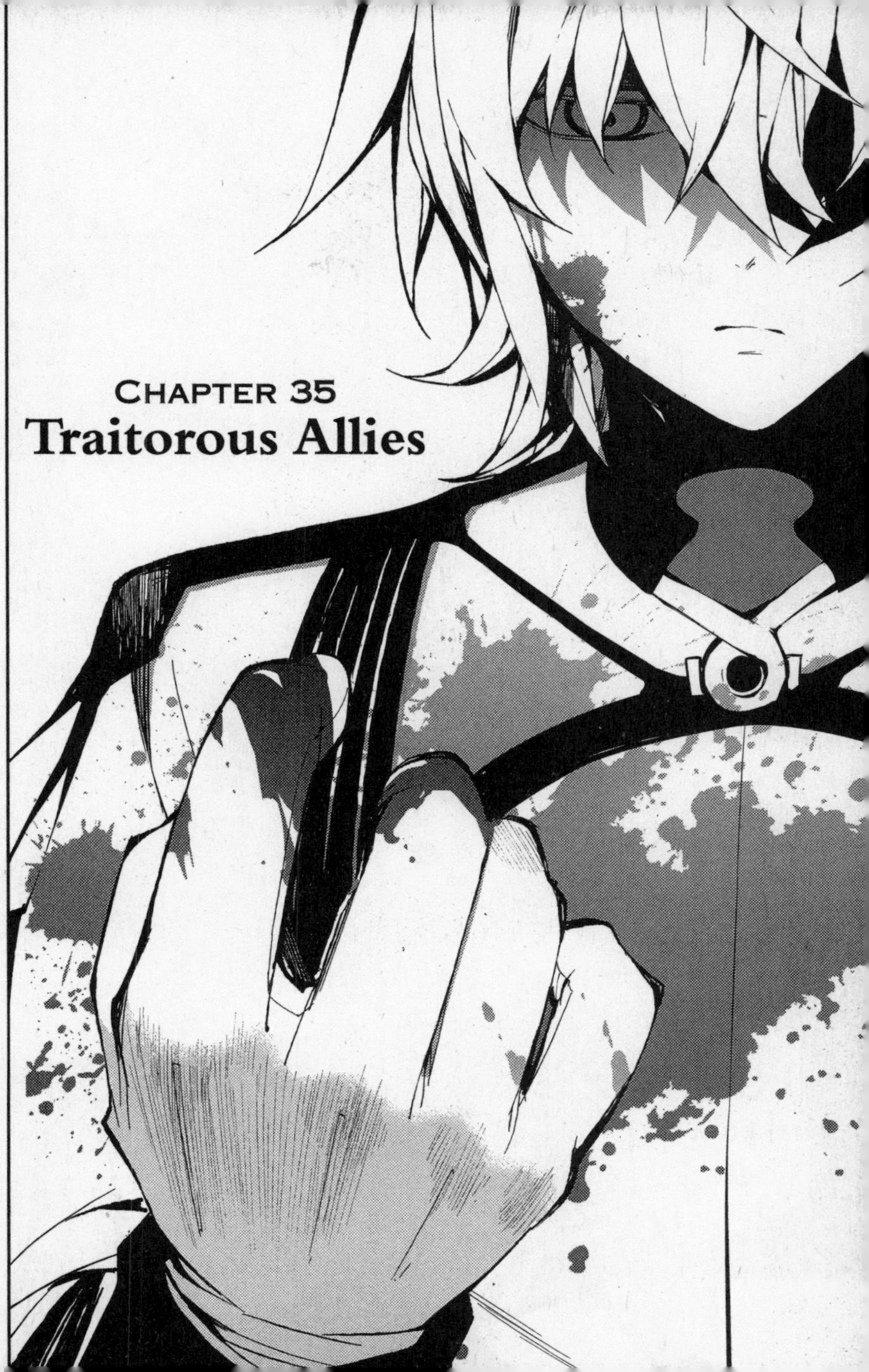

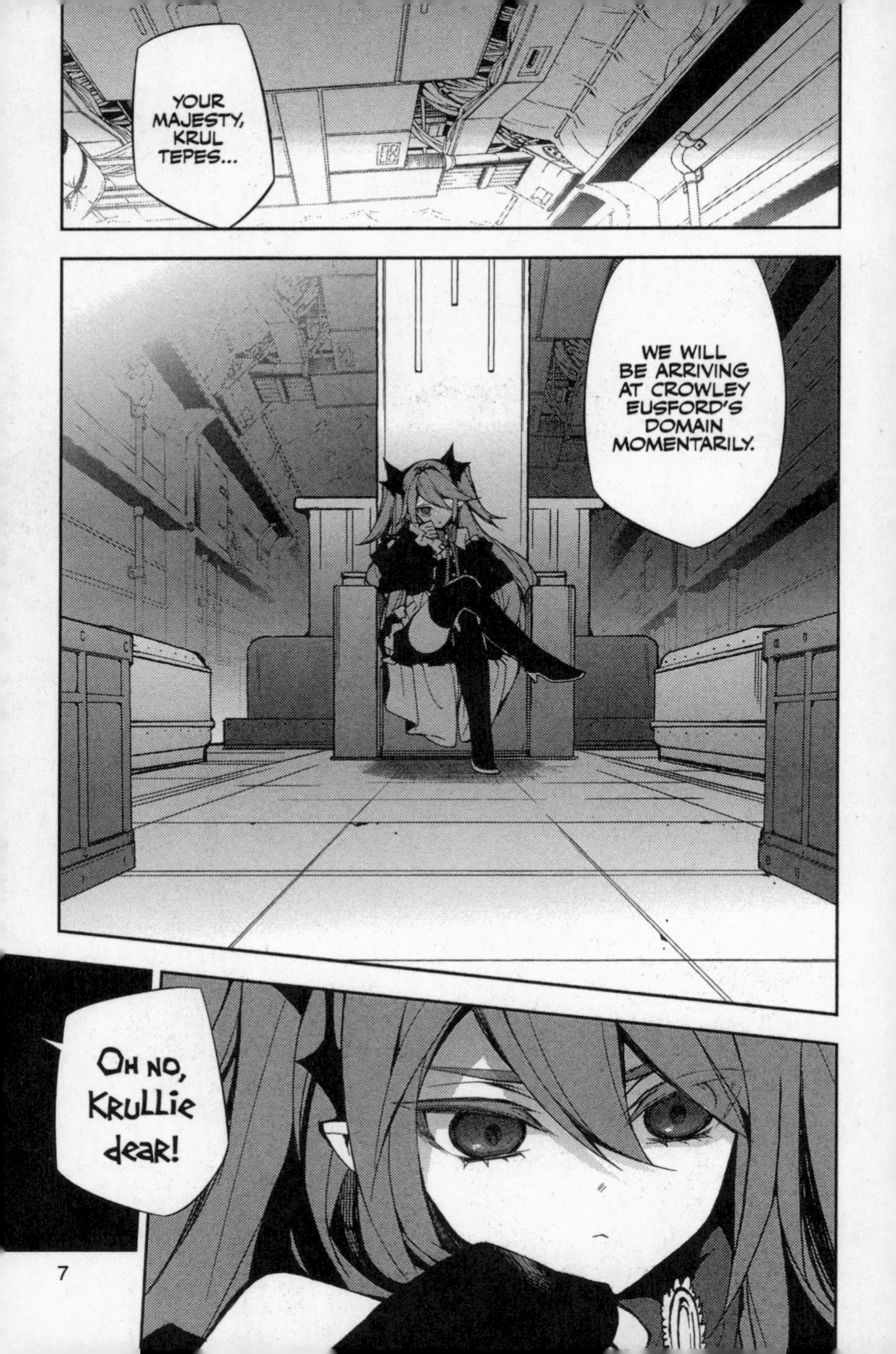
YOUR MAJESTY, KRUL TEPES...
WE WILL BE ARRIVING AT CROWLEY EUSFORD'S DOMAIN MOMENTARILY.
OH NO, KRULLIE DEAR!

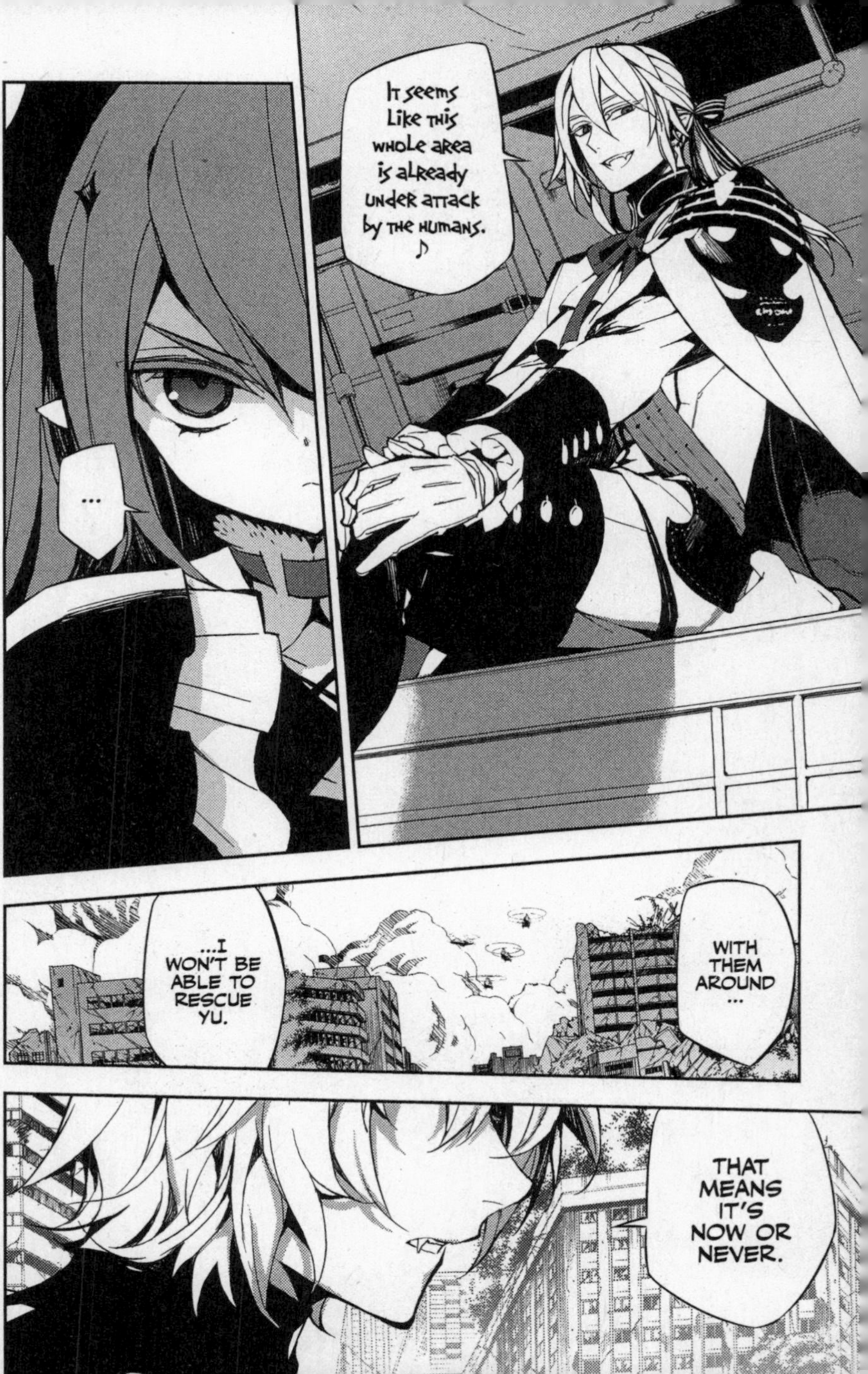
It seems like this whole area is already under attack by the humans. ♪
...
WITH THEM AROUND...
...I WON'T BE ABLE TO RESCUE YU.
THAT MEANS IT'S NOW OR NEVER.

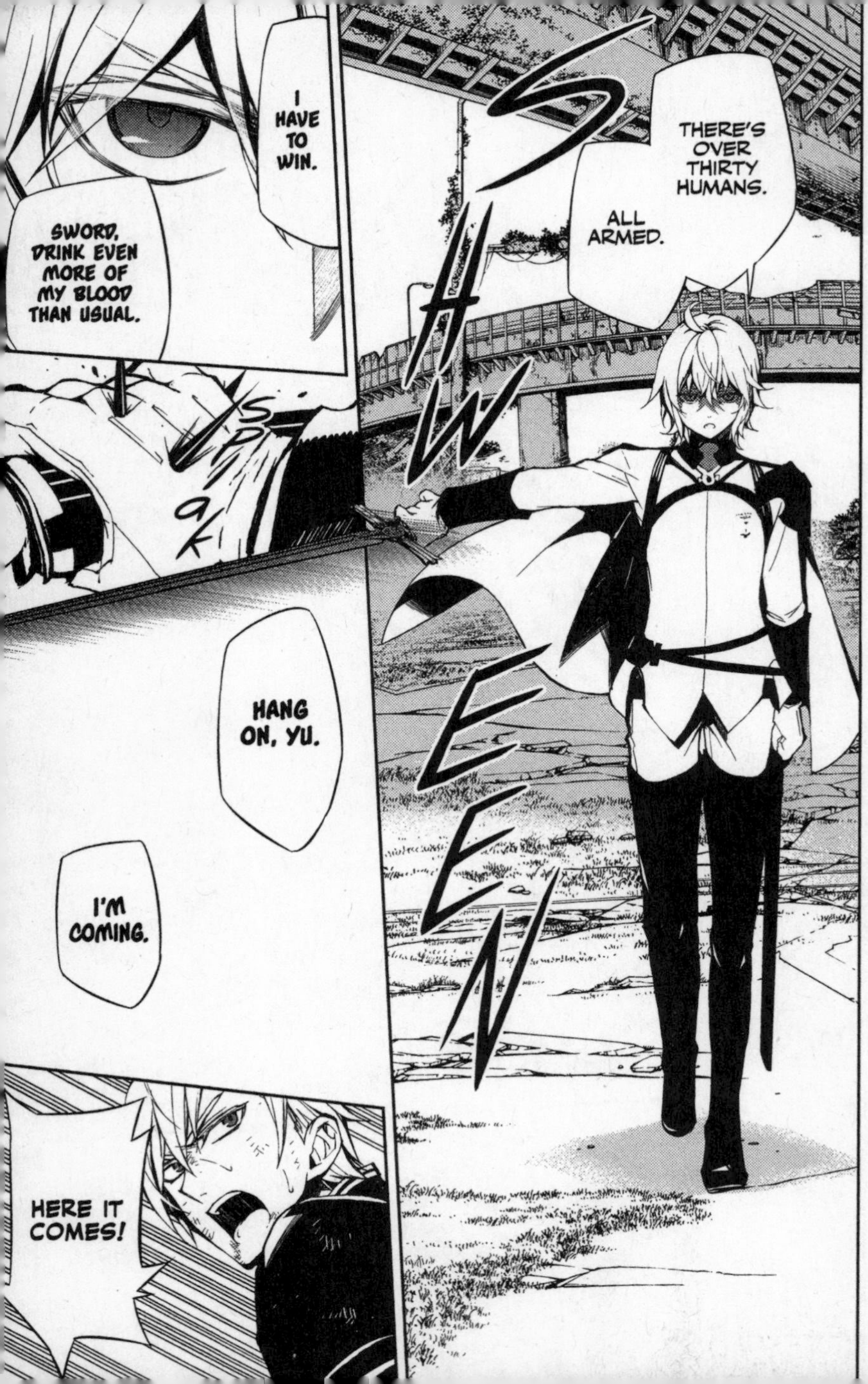
THERE'S OVER THIRTY HUMANS.
ALL ARMED.
SHWEEN
I HAVE TO WIN.
SWORD, DRINK EVEN MORE OF MY BLOOD THAN USUAL.
SPLAK
HANG ON, YU.
I'M COMING.
HERE IT COMES!

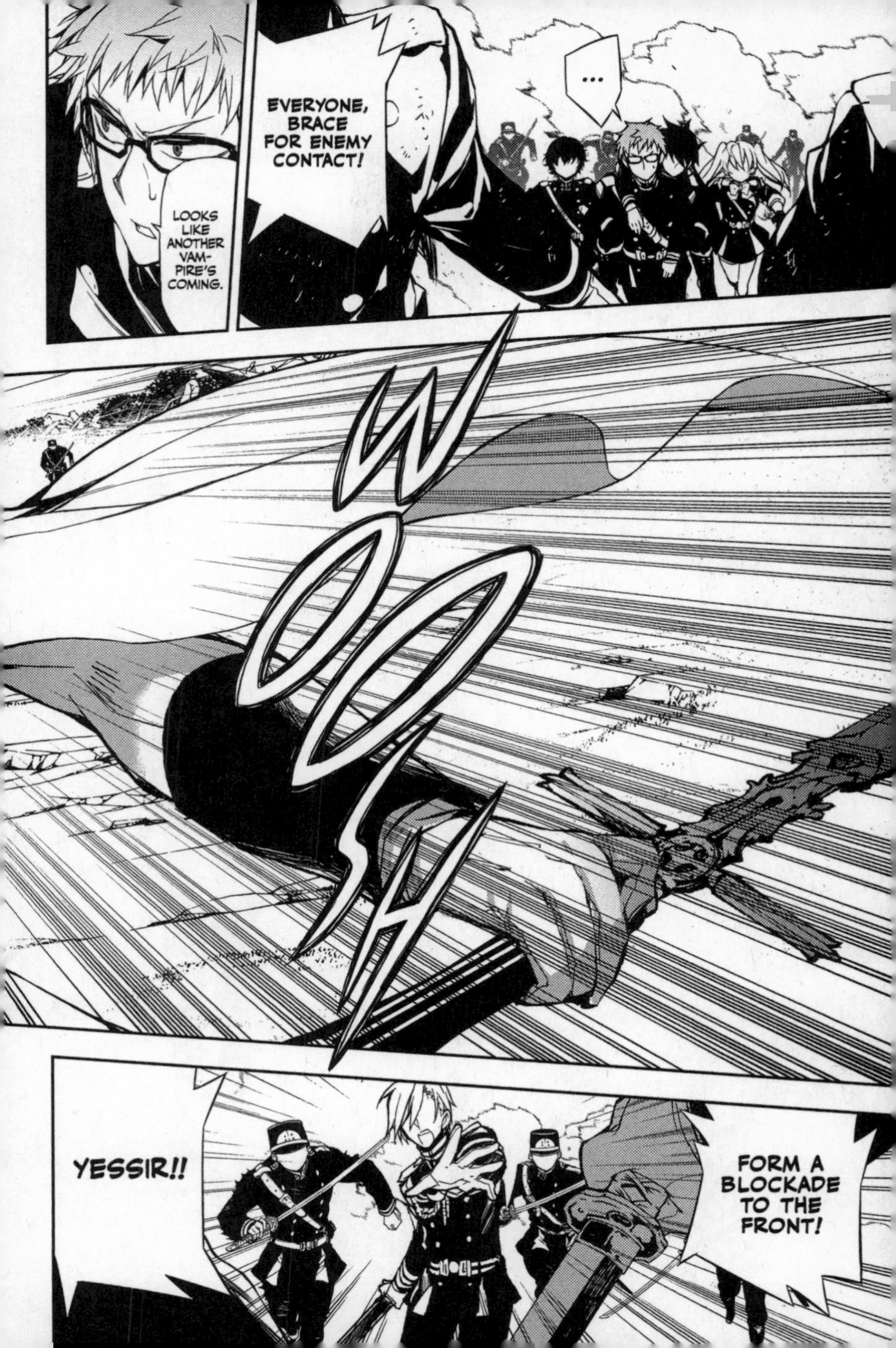
...
EVERYONE, BRACE FOR ENEMY CONTACT!
LOOKS LIKE ANOTHER VAMPIRE'S COMING.
WOOSH
FORM A BLOCKADE TO THE FRONT!
YESSIR!!

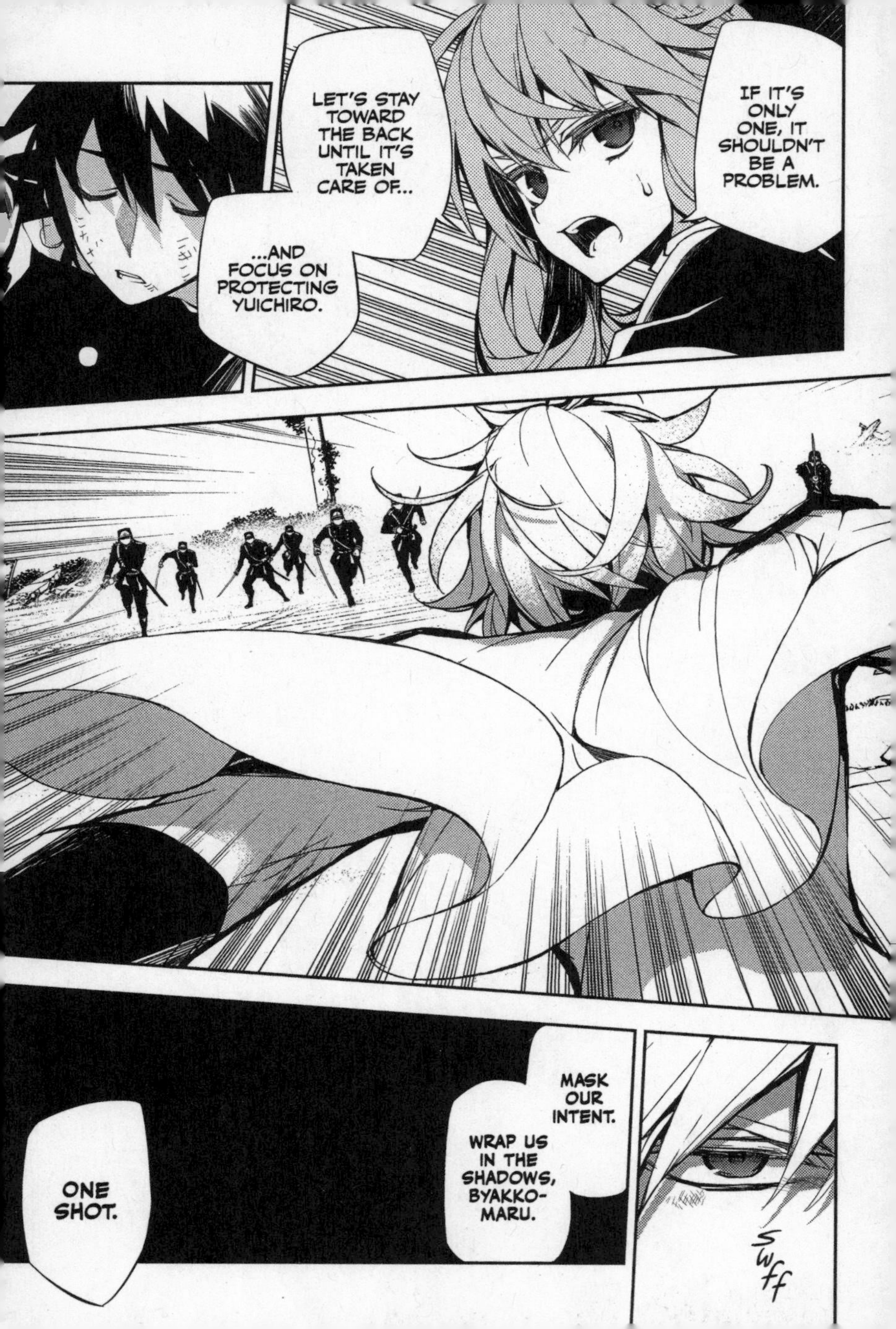
IF IT'S ONLY ONE, IT SHOULDN'T BE A PROBLEM.
LET'S STAY TOWARD THE BACK UNTIL IT'S TAKEN CARE OF...
...AND FOCUS ON PROTECTING YUICHIRO.
SWFF
MASK OUR INTENT.
WRAP US IN THE SHADOWS, BYAKKO-MARU.
ONE SHOT.

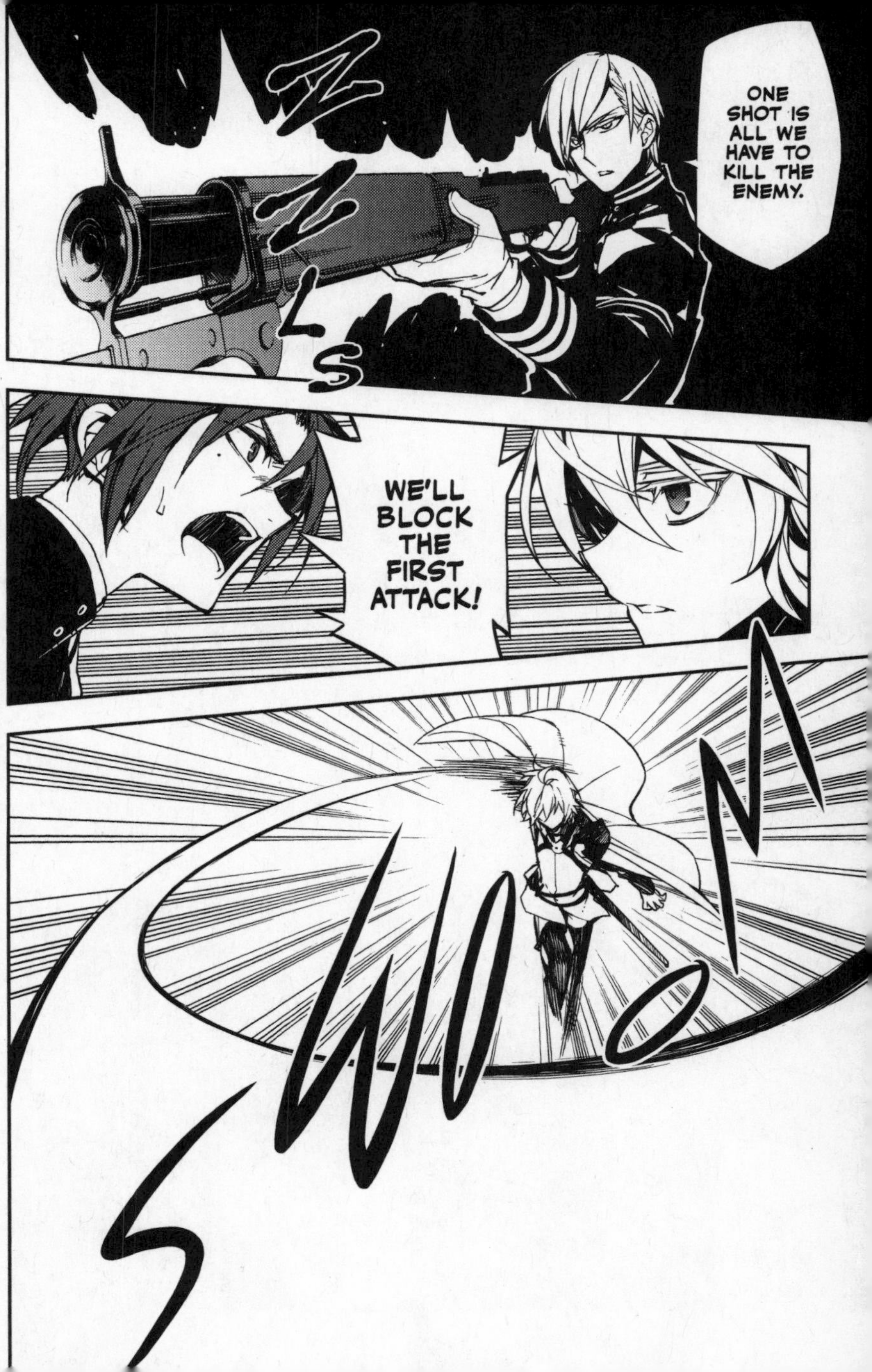
ONE SHOT IS ALL WE HAVE TO KILL THE ENEMY.
ZNZNLS
WE'LL BLOCK THE FIRST ATTACK!
SWOOM

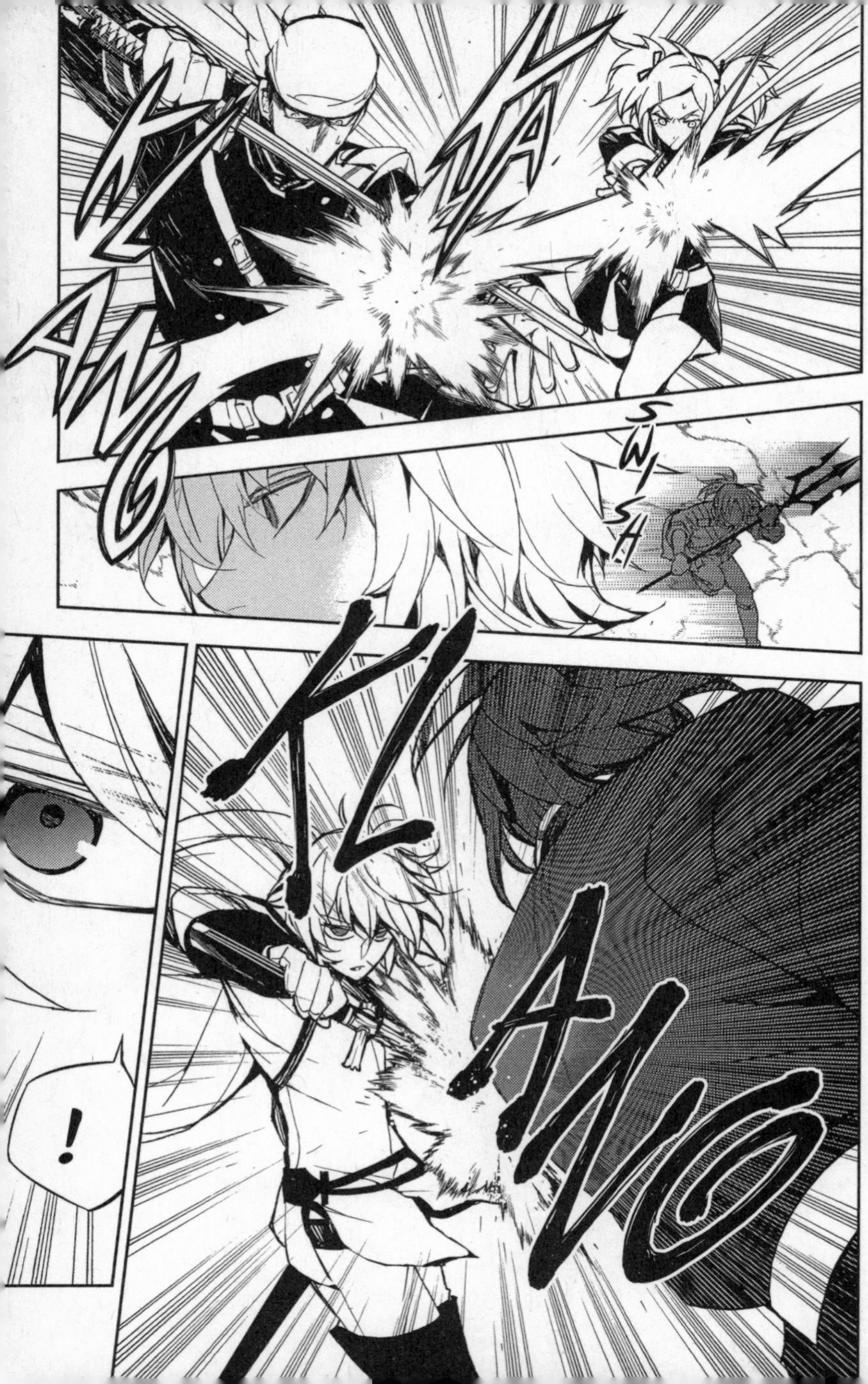
KLANG
SWISH
KLANG
!

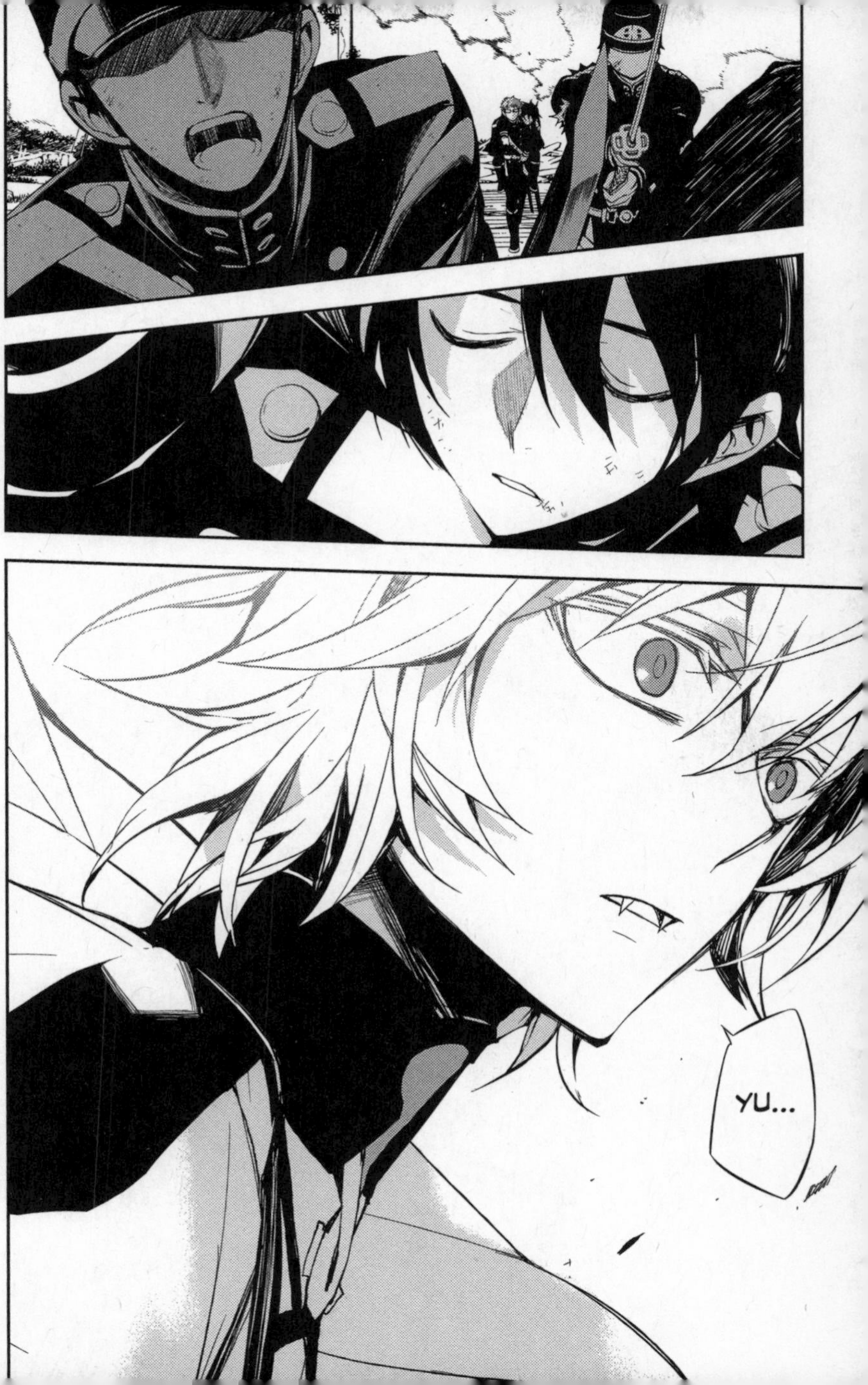
YU...

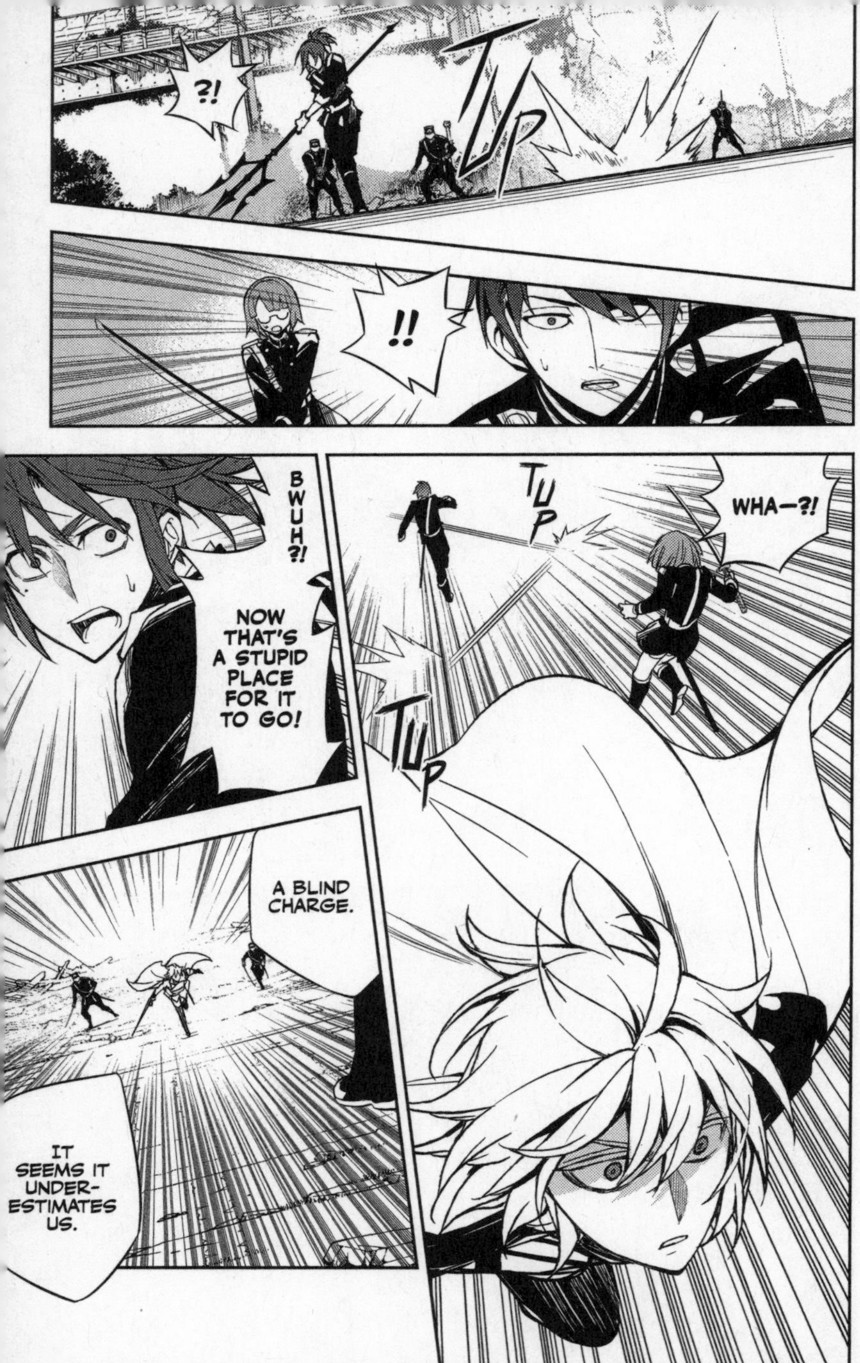
TUP
?!
!!
TUP
WHA—?!
TUP
BWUH?!
NOW THAT'S A STUPID PLACE FOR IT TO GO!
A BLIND CHARGE.
IT SEEMS IT UNDER-ESTIMATES US.

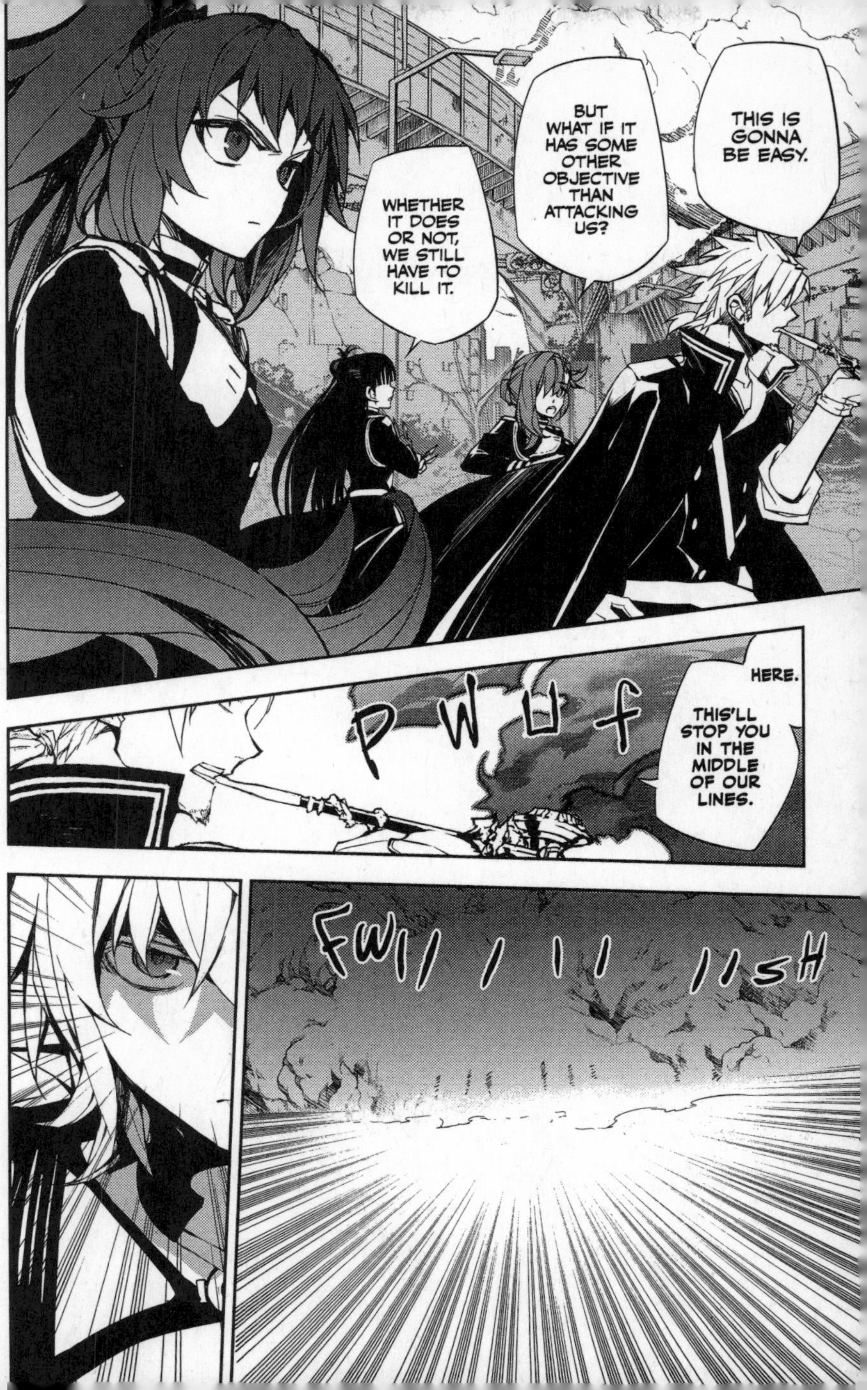
THIS IS GONNA BE EASY.
BUT WHAT IF IT HAS SOME OTHER OBJECTIVE THAN ATTACKING US?
WHETHER IT DOES OR NOT, WE STILL HAVE TO KILL IT.
HERE.
THIS'LL STOP YOU IN THE MIDDLE OF OUR LINES.
PWUF
FWIIIIIISH

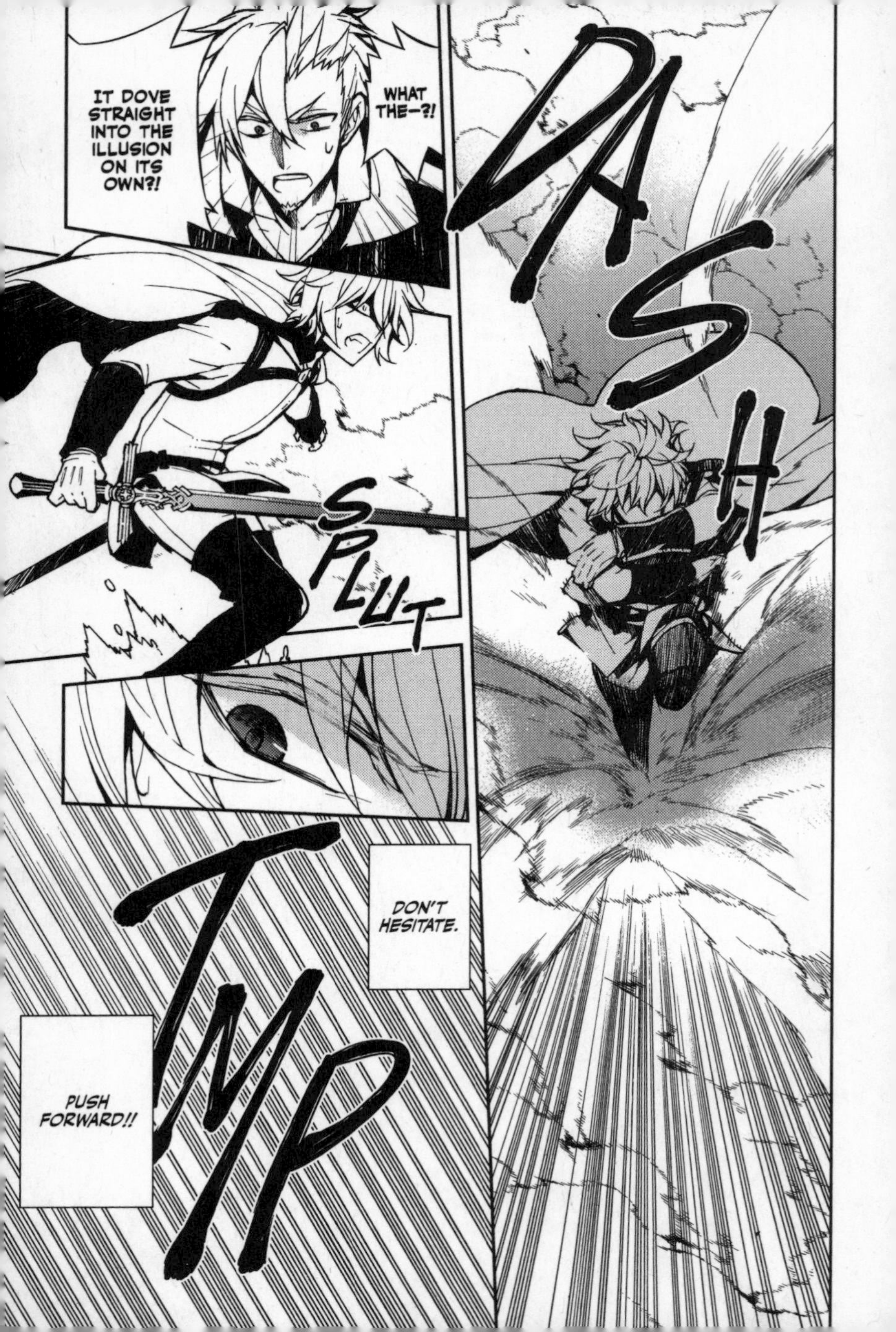
DASH
WHAT THE—?!
IT DOVE STRAIGHT INTO THE ILLUSION ON ITS OWN?!
SPLUT
DON'T HESITATE.
TMP
PUSH FORWARD!!

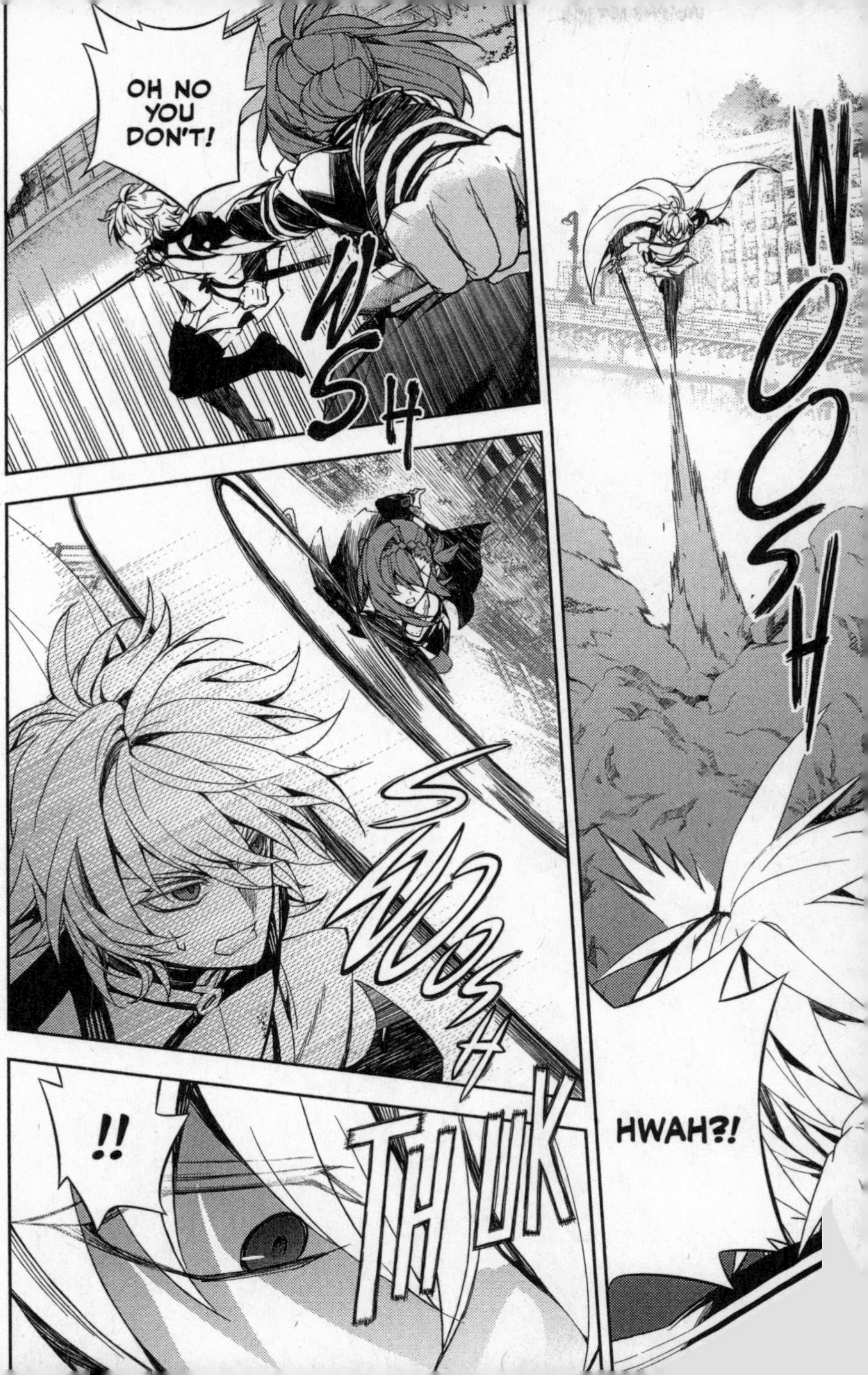
WOOSH
HWAH?!
OH NO YOU DON'T!
WHSH
SWOOSH
!!
THUK

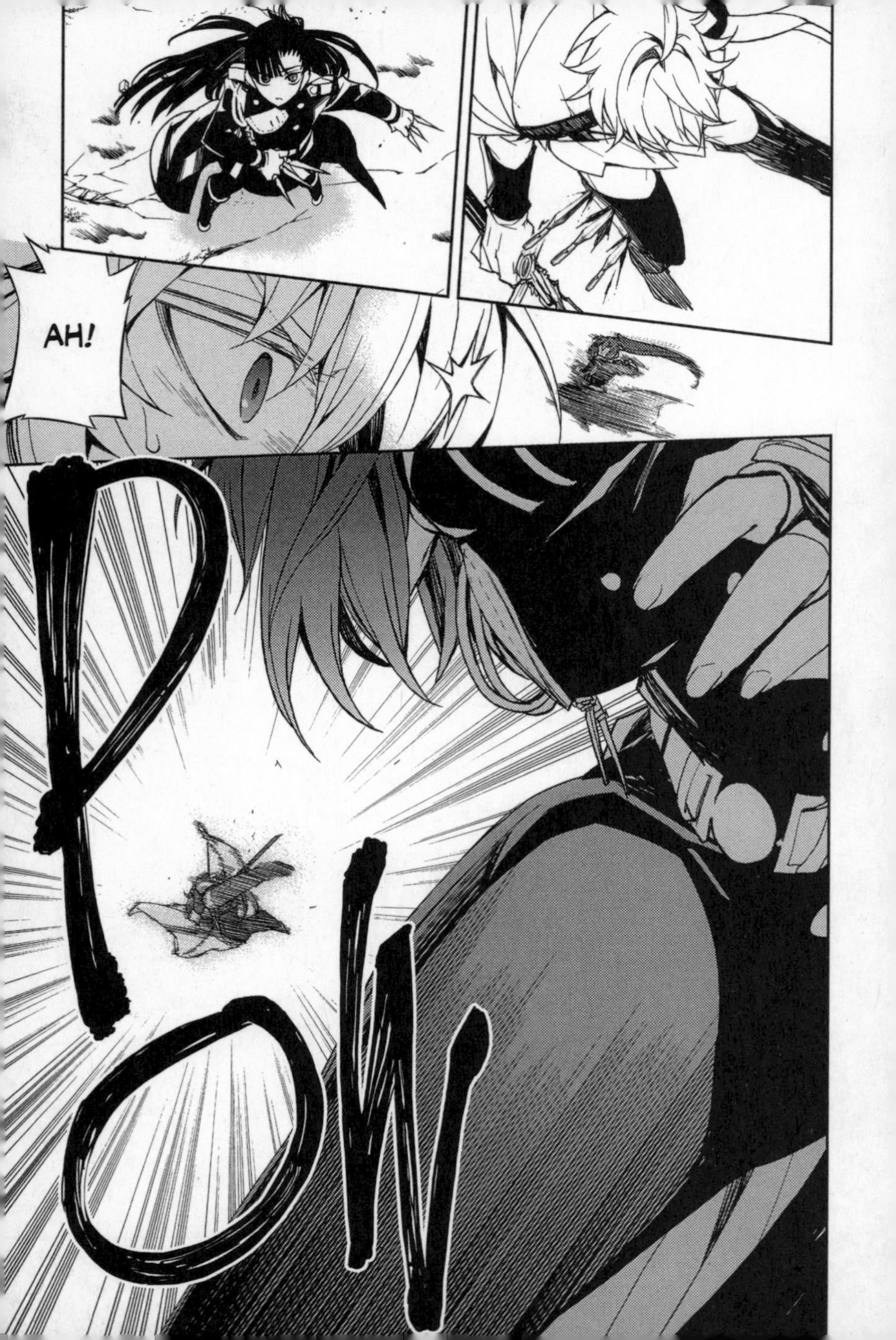
AH!
POW

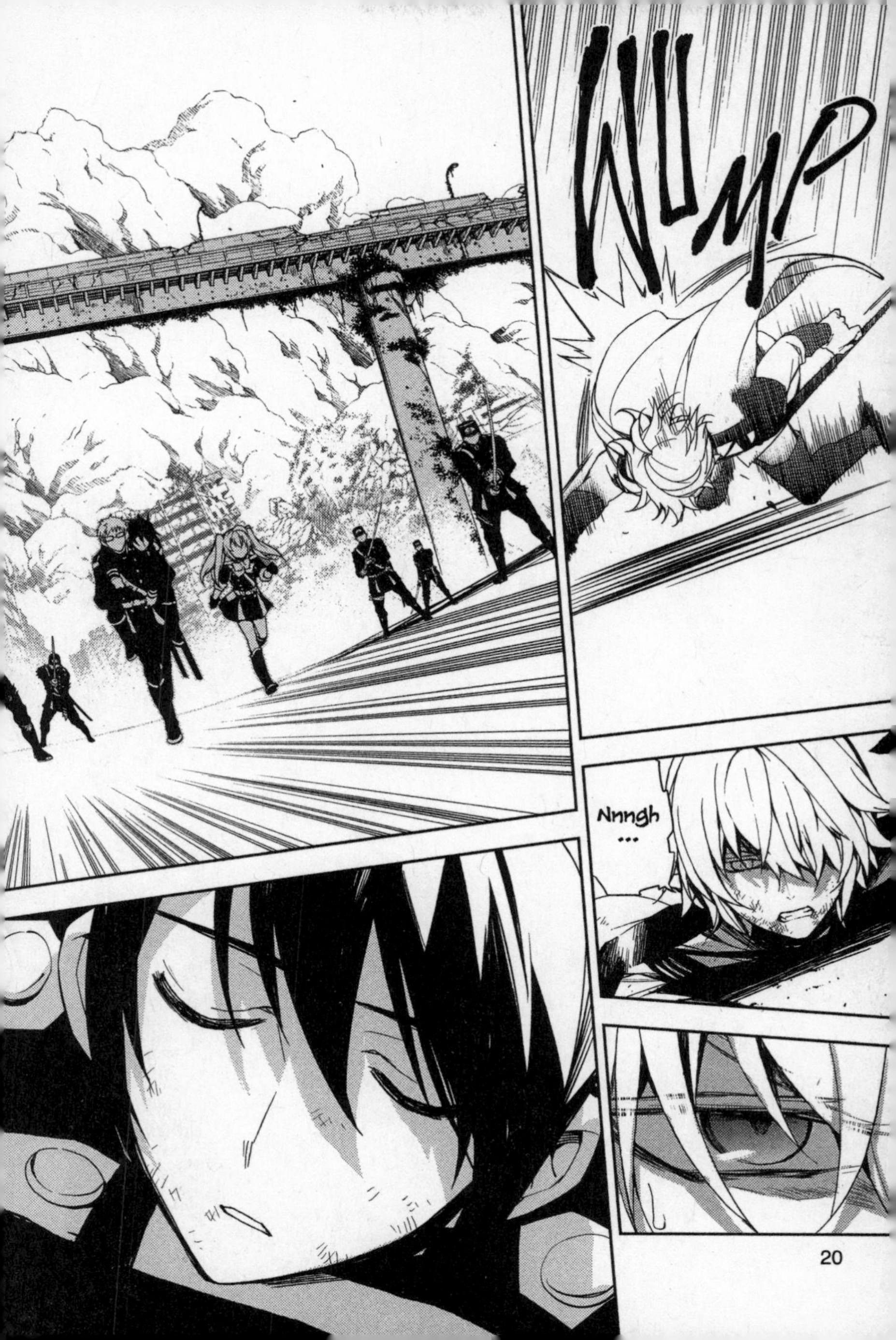
WUMP
Nnngh
...

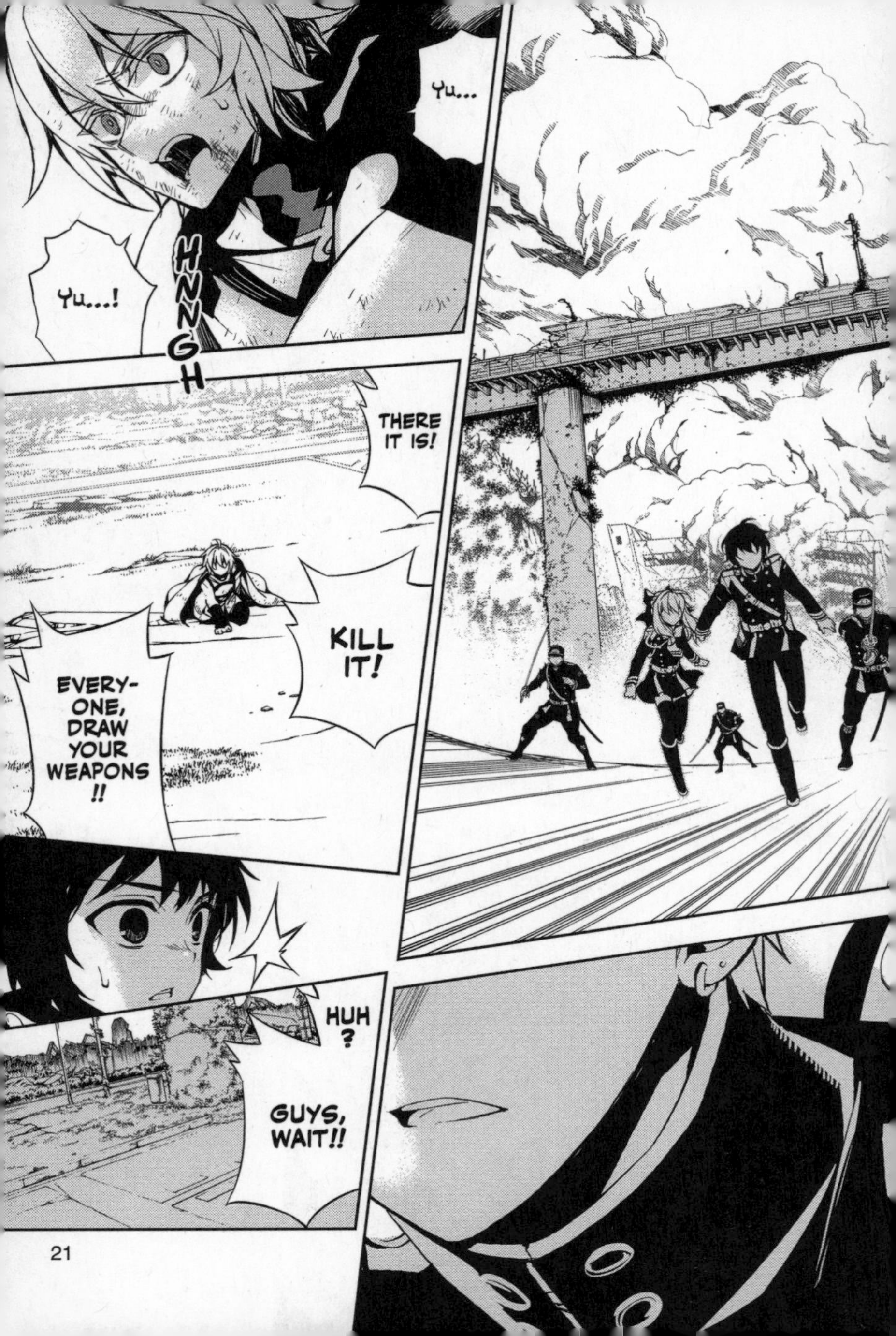

Yu...
HNNNGH
Yu...!
THERE IT IS!
KILL IT!
EVERY-ONE, DRAW YOUR WEAPONS!!
HUH?
GUYS, WAIT!!

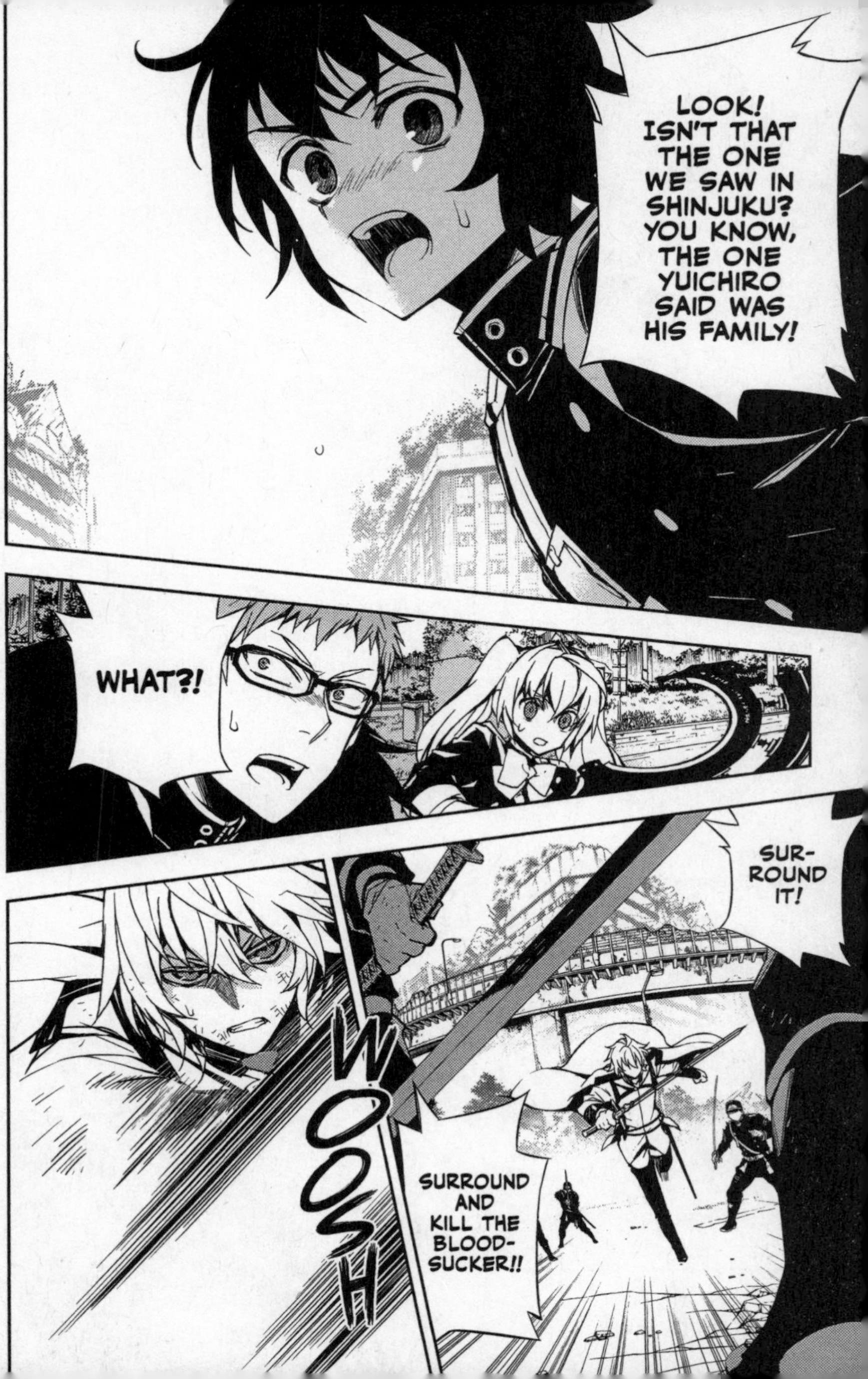
LOOK! ISN'T THAT THE ONE WE SAW IN SHINJUKU? YOU KNOW, THE ONE YUICHIRO SAID WAS HIS FAMILY!
WHAT?!
SUR-ROUND IT!
SURROUND AND KILL THE BLOOD-SUCKER!!
WHOOSH

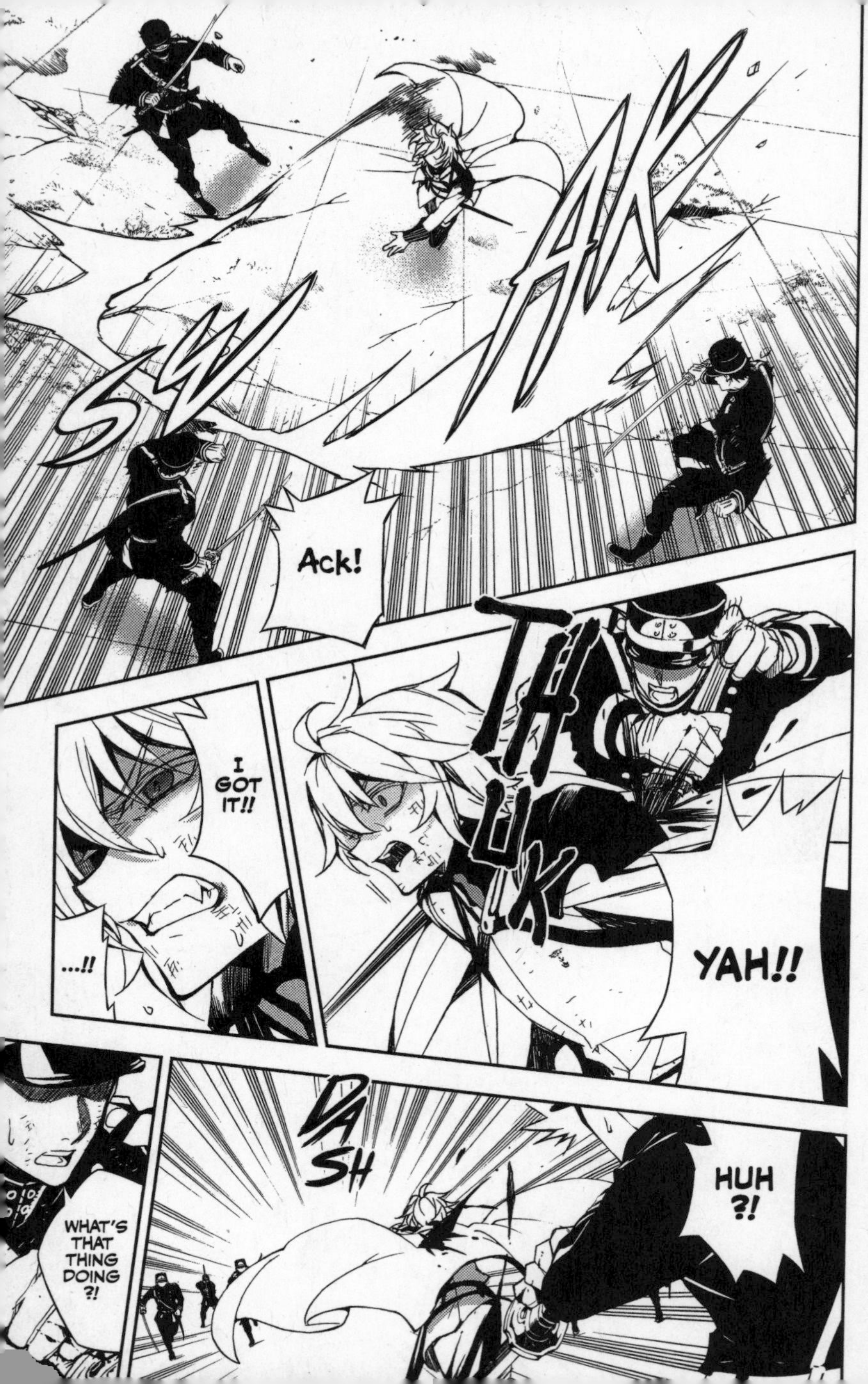
Ack!
YAH!!
I GOT IT!!
...!!
DASH
HUH ?!
WHAT'S THAT THING DOING ?!

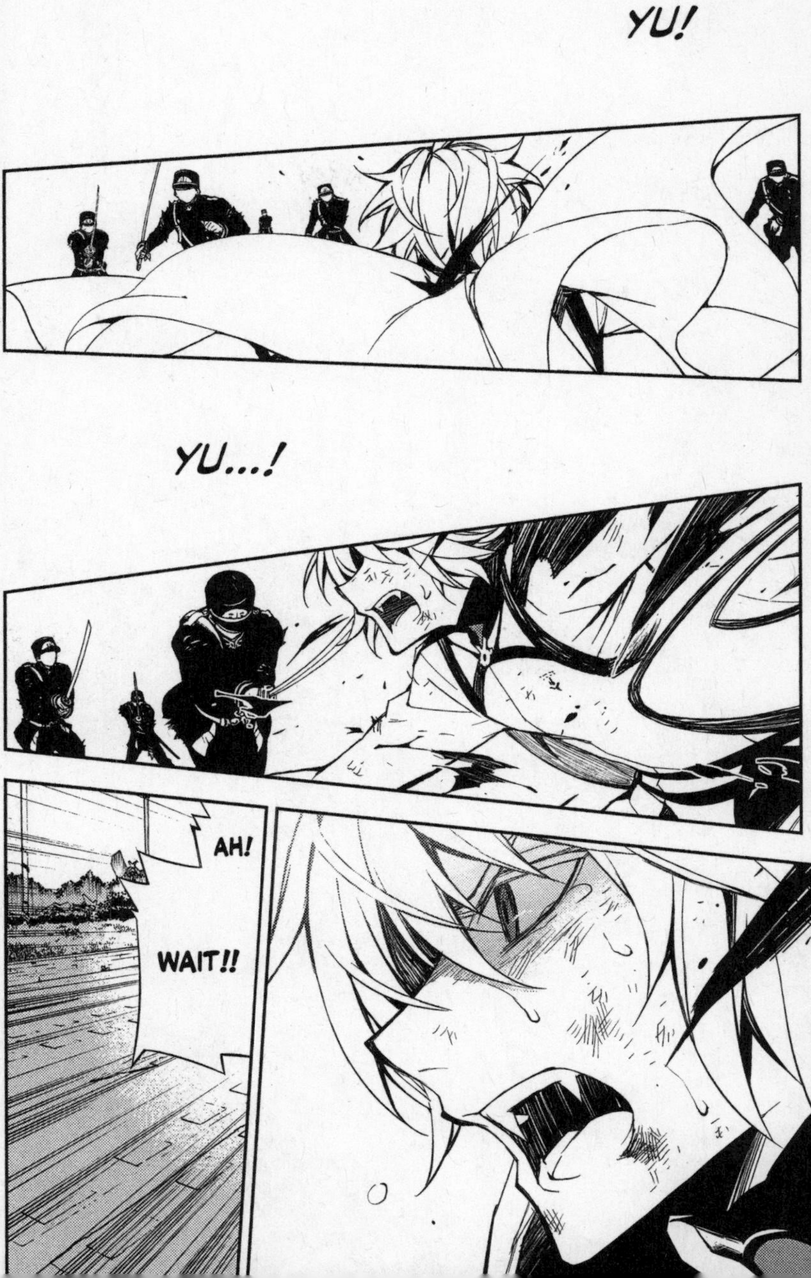
YU!
YU...!
AH!
WAIT!!

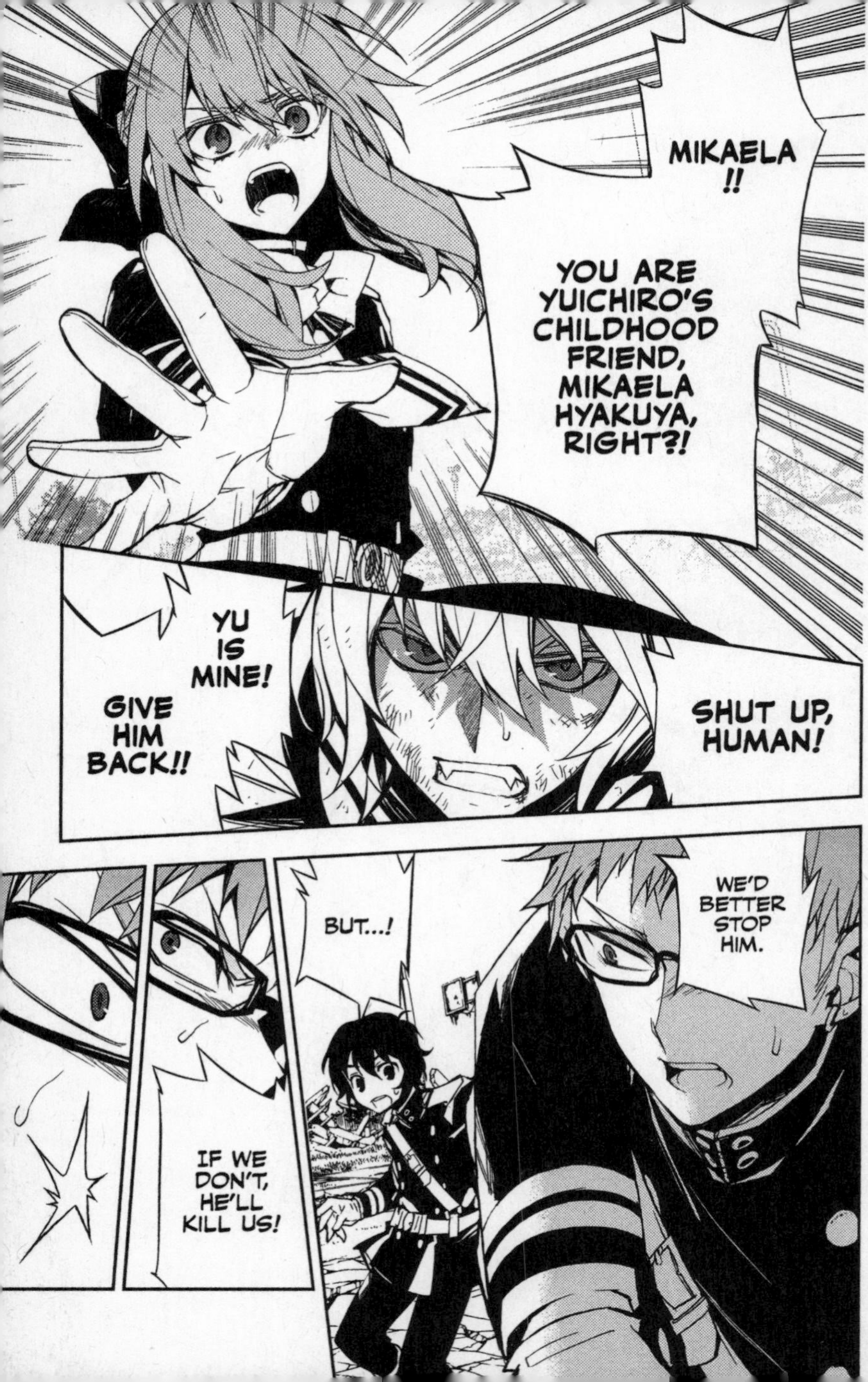
MIKAELA !!
YOU ARE YUICHIRO'S CHILDHOOD FRIEND, MIKAELA HYAKUYA, RIGHT?!
SHUT UP, HUMAN!
YU IS MINE!
GIVE HIM BACK!!
WE'D BETTER STOP HIM.
BUT...!
IF WE DON'T, HE'LL KILL US!

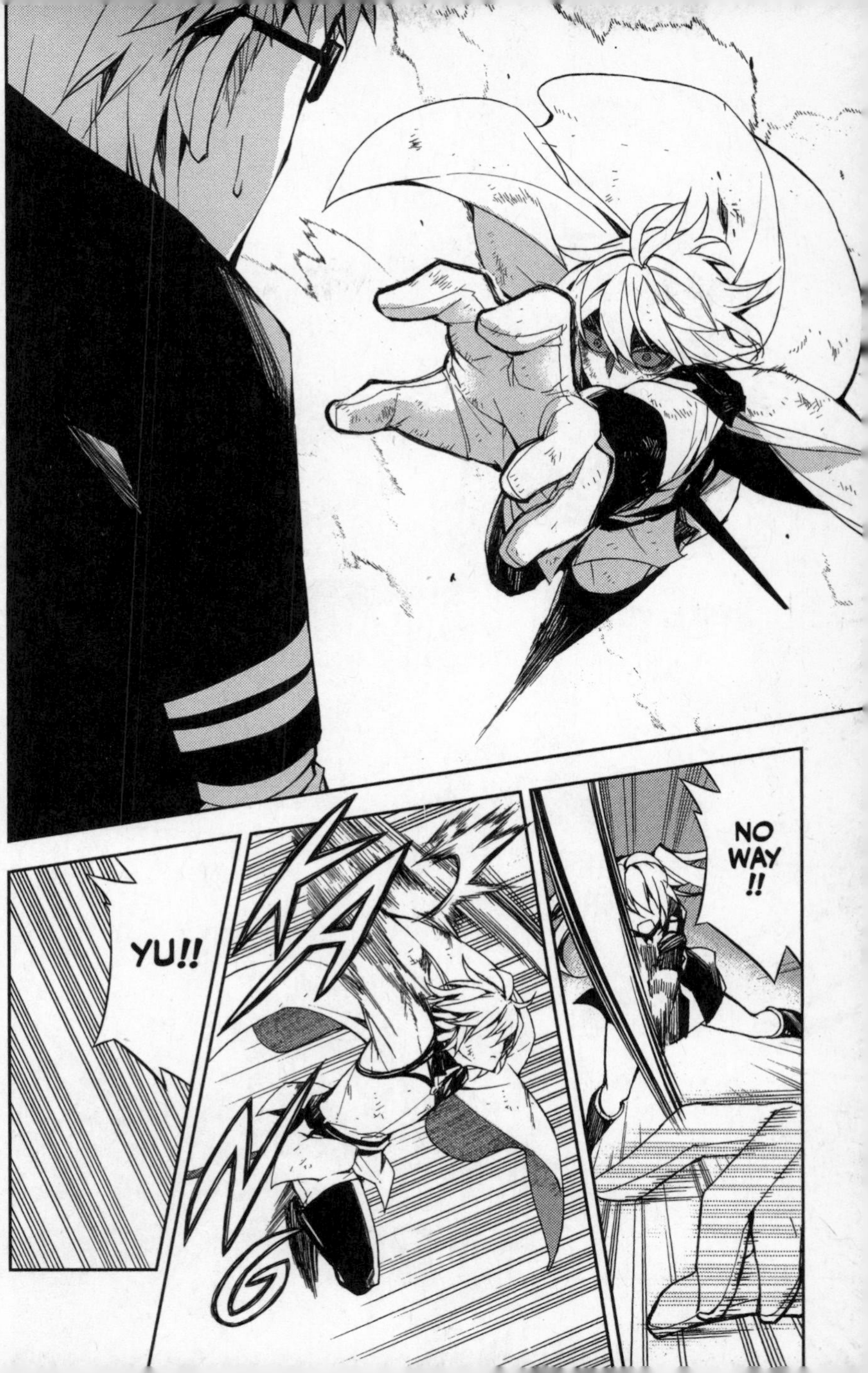
NO WAY !!
KANG
YU!!

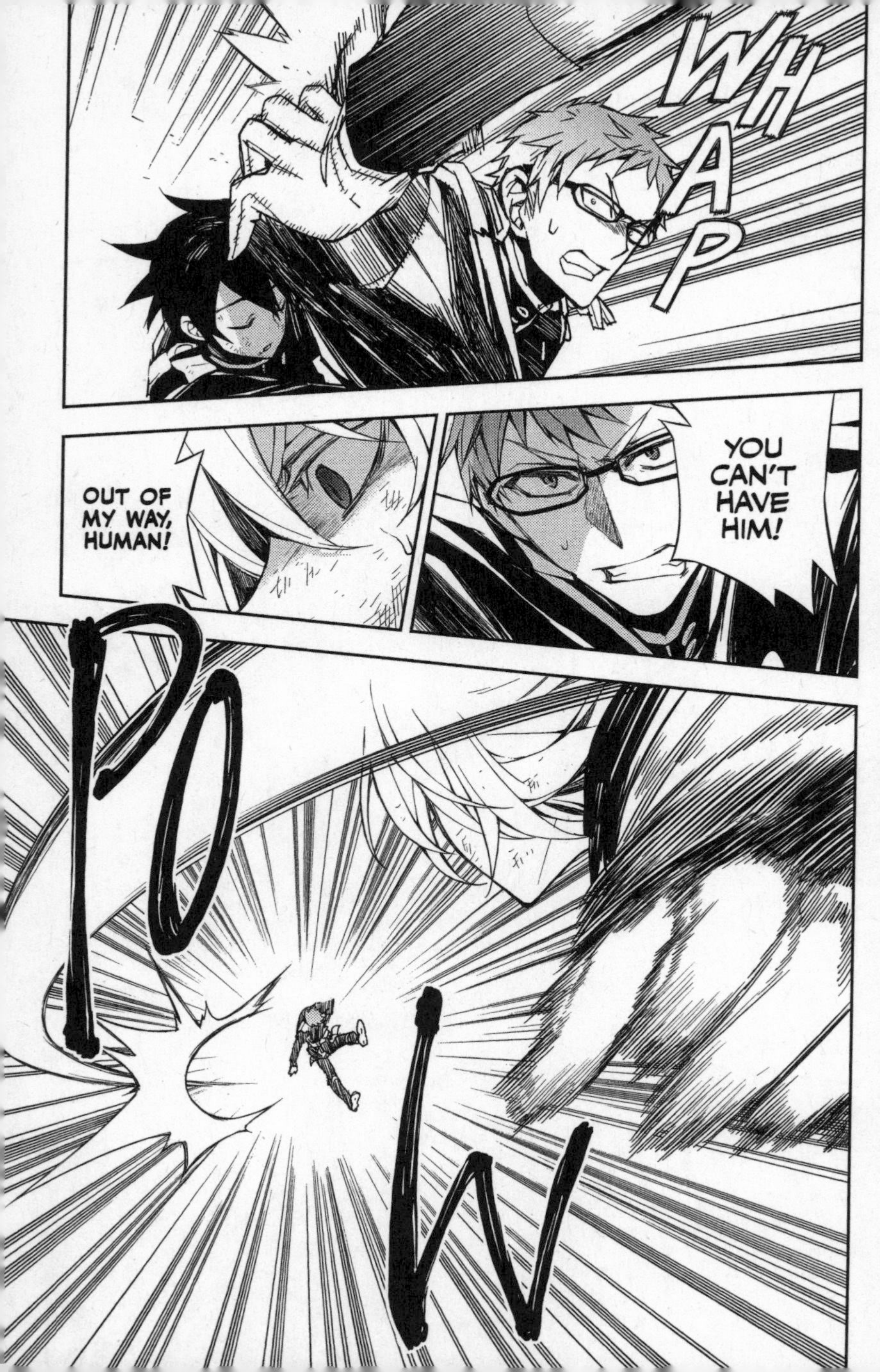
WHAP
YOU CAN'T HAVE HIM!
OUT OF MY WAY, HUMAN!
POW

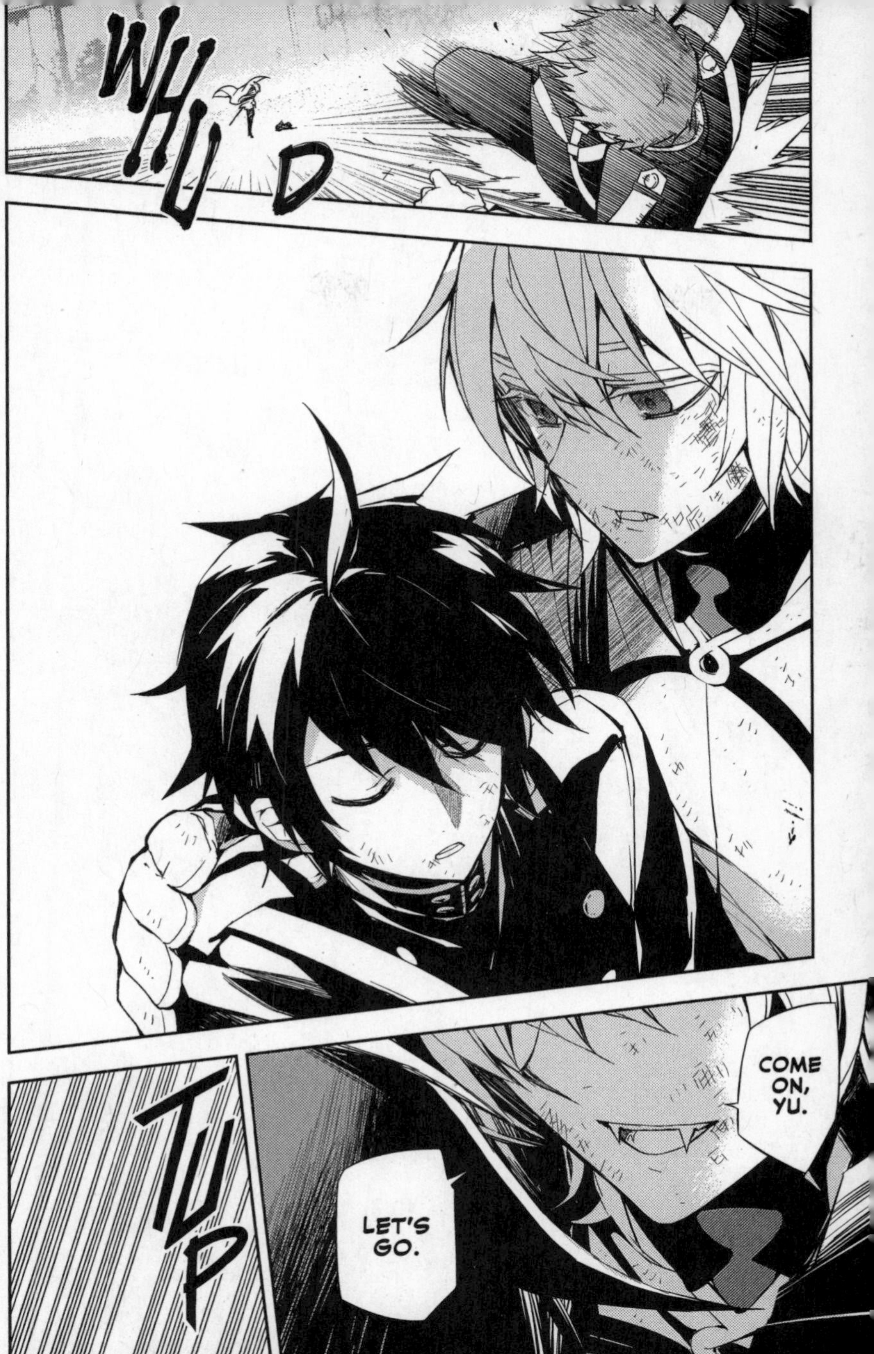
WHUD
COME ON, YU.
LET'S GO.
THUP

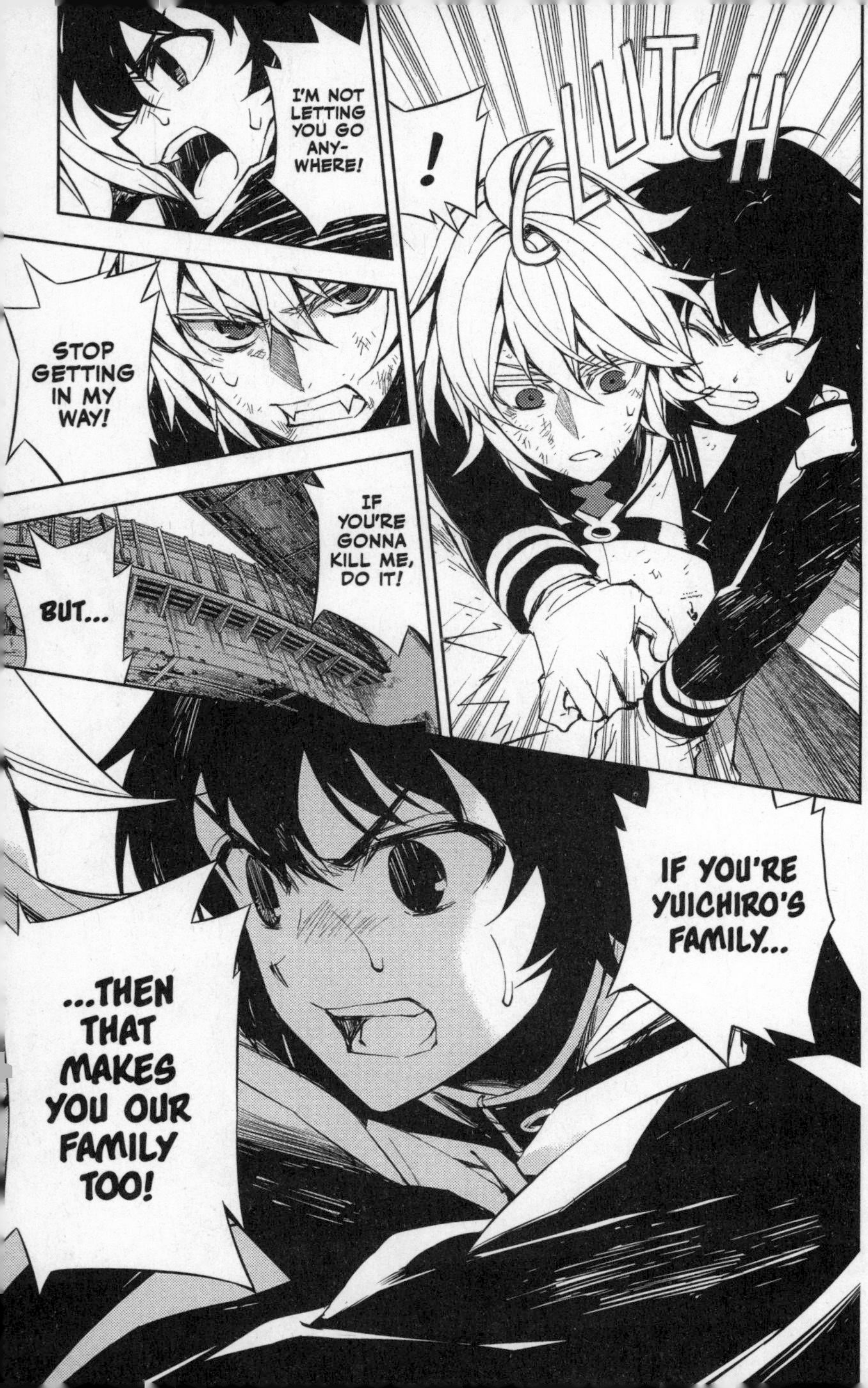
CLUTCH
!
I'M NOT LETTING YOU GO ANY-WHERE!
STOP GETTING IN MY WAY!
IF YOU'RE GONNA KILL ME, DO IT!
BUT...
IF YOU'RE YUICHIRO'S FAMILY...
...THEN THAT MAKES YOU OUR FAMILY TOO!

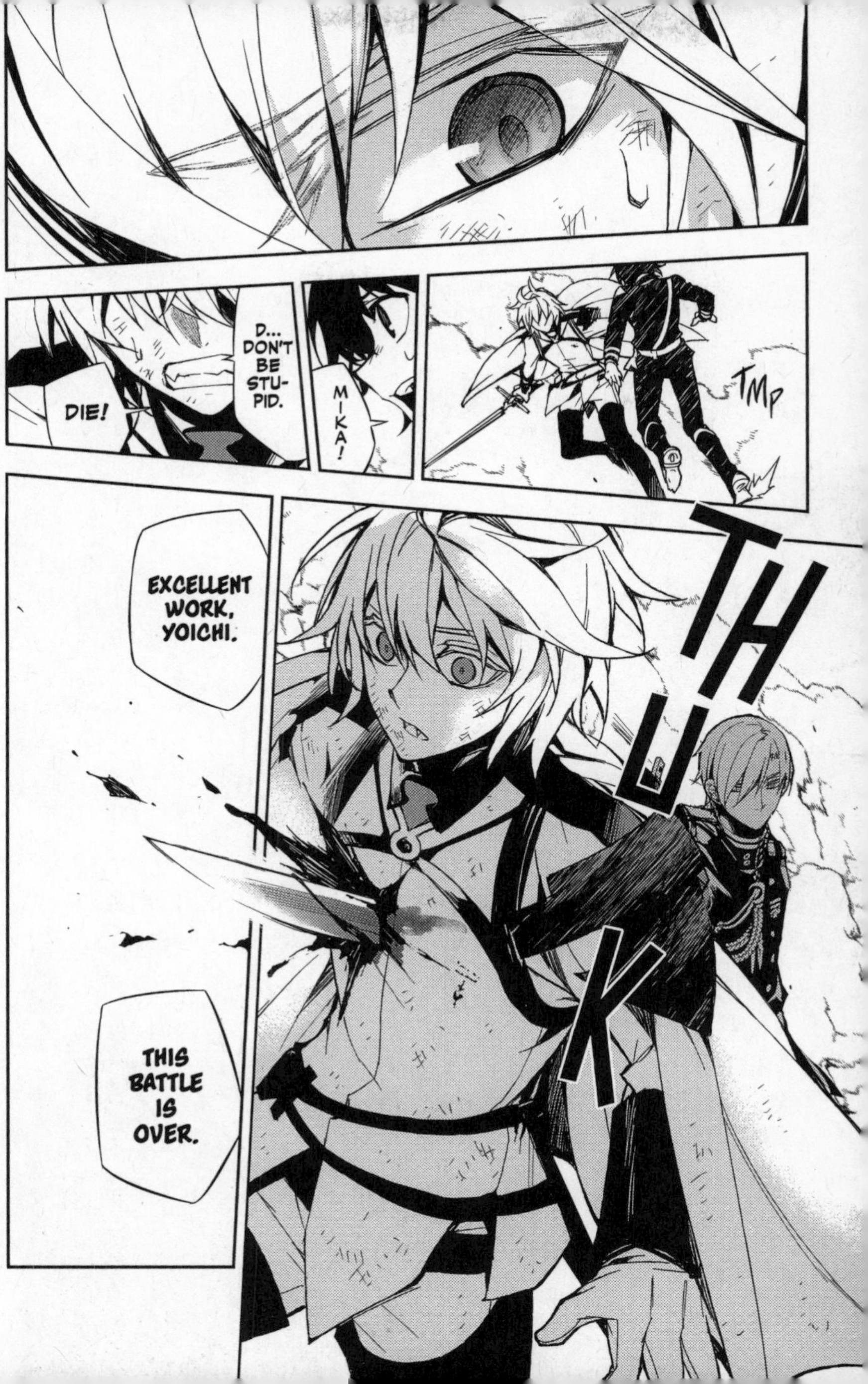
TMP
MIKA!
D... DON'T BE STUPID.
DIE!
THUK
EXCELLENT WORK, YOICHI.
THIS BATTLE IS OVER.

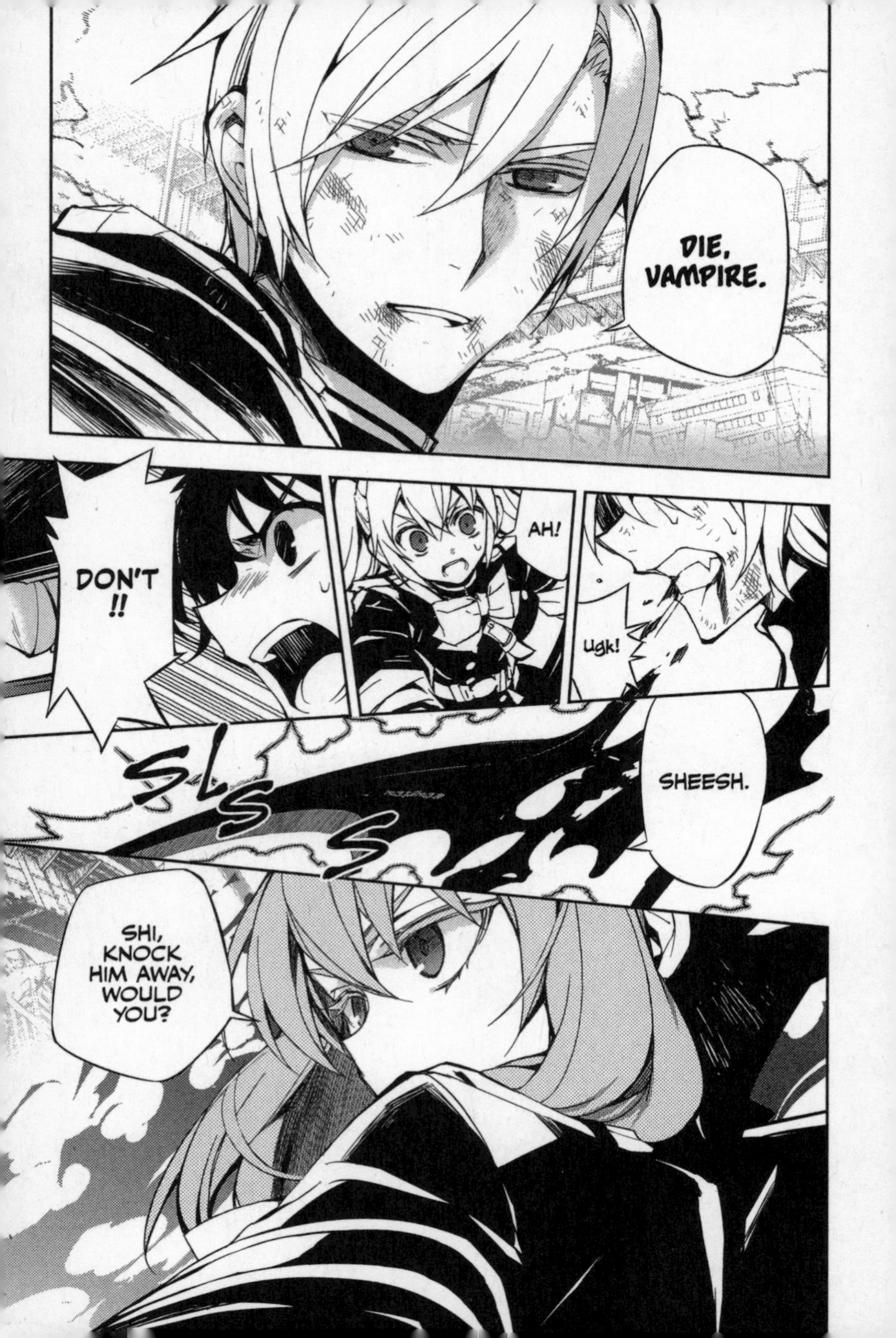
DIE, VAMPIRE.
Ugk!
AH!
DON'T !!
SHEESH.
SSS
SHI, KNOCK HIM AWAY, WOULD YOU?

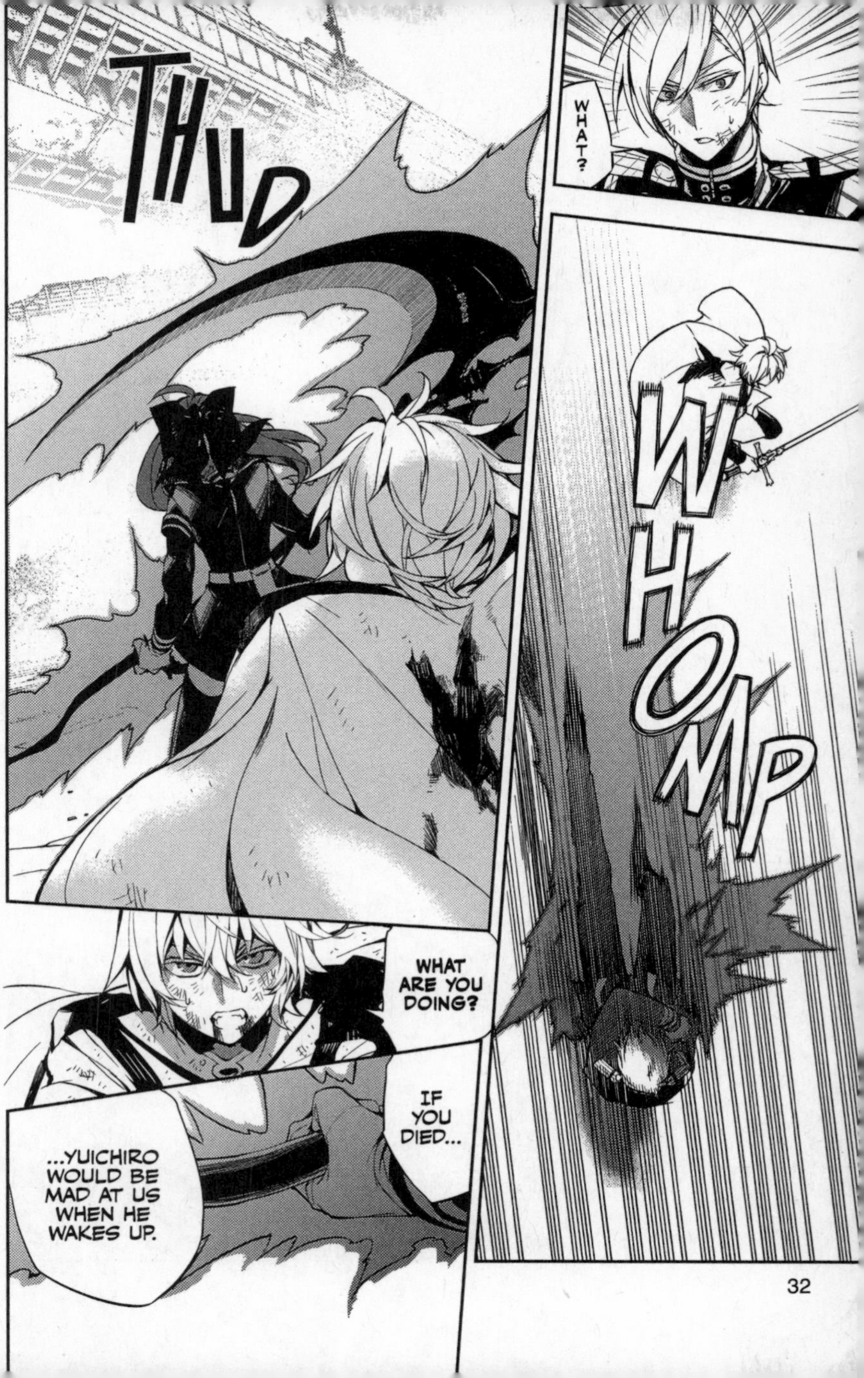
WHAT?
WHOMP
THUD
WHAT ARE YOU DOING?
IF YOU DIED...
...YUICHIRO WOULD BE MAD AT US WHEN HE WAKES UP.

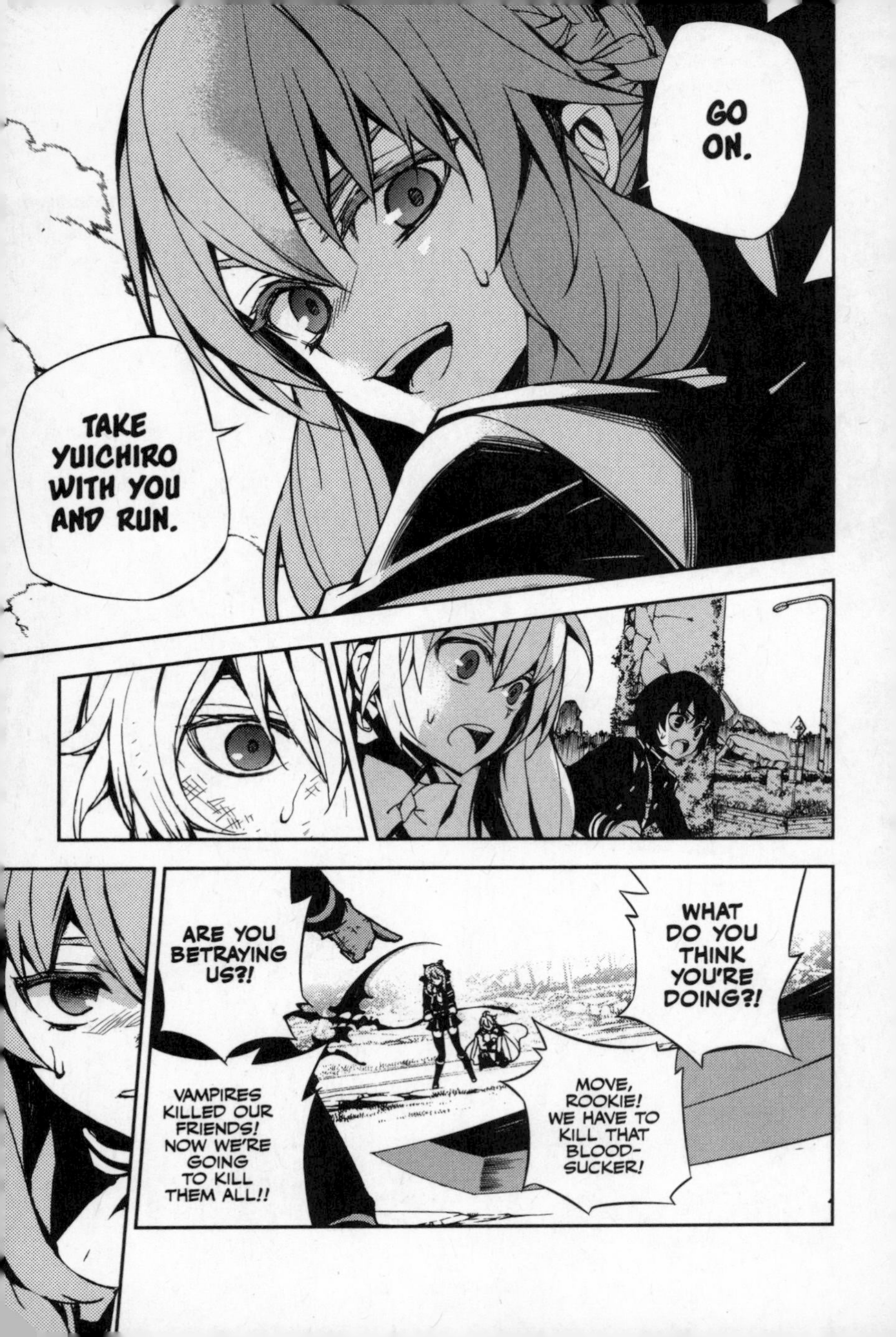
GO ON.
TAKE YUICHIRO WITH YOU AND RUN.
WHAT DO YOU THINK YOU'RE DOING?!
ARE YOU BETRAYING US?!
MOVE, ROOKIE! WE HAVE TO KILL THAT BLOOD-SUCKER!
VAMPIRES KILLED OUR FRIENDS! NOW WE'RE GOING TO KILL THEM ALL!!

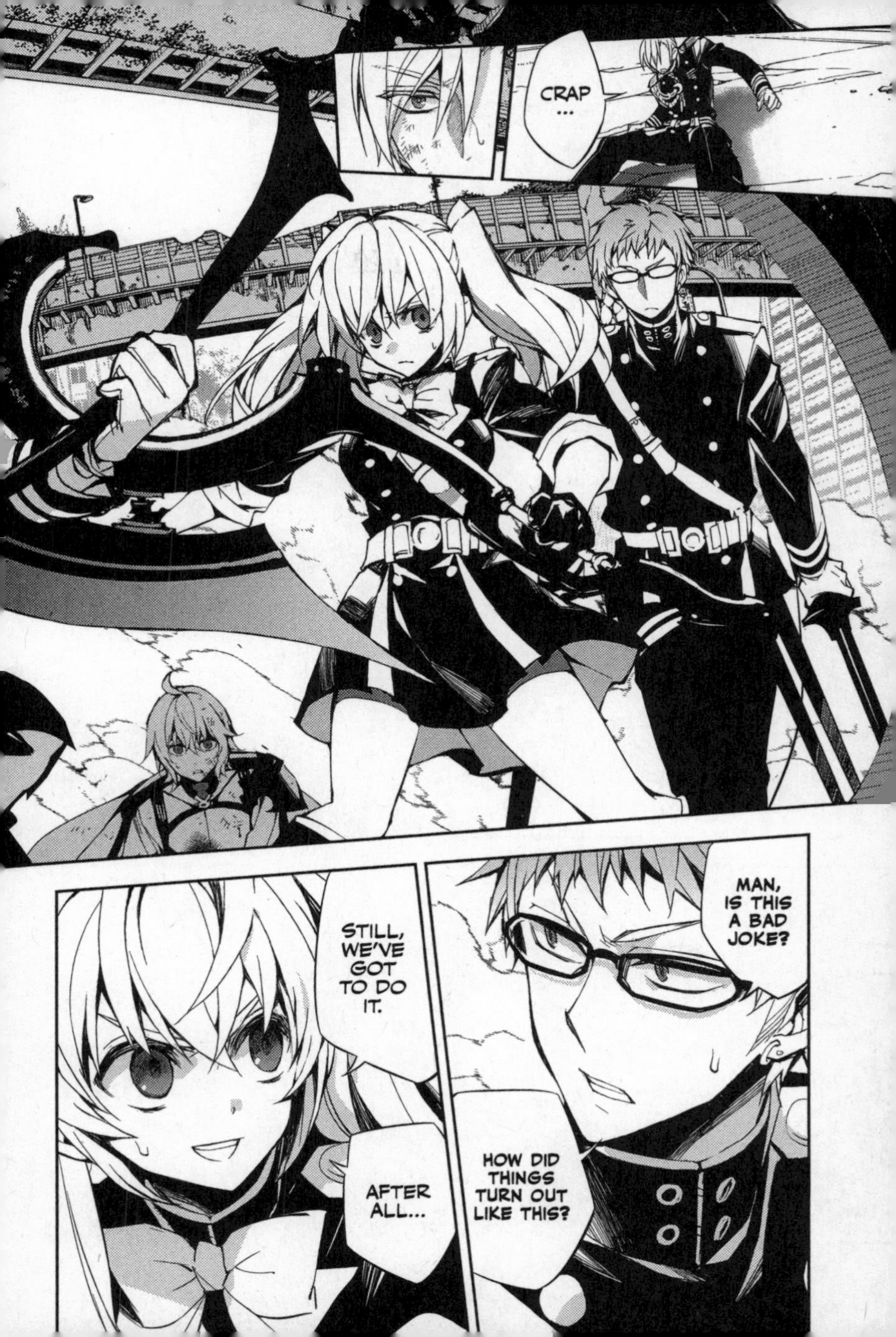
CRAP...
MAN, IS THIS A BAD JOKE?
HOW DID THINGS TURN OUT LIKE THIS?
STILL, WE'VE GOT TO DO IT.
AFTER ALL...

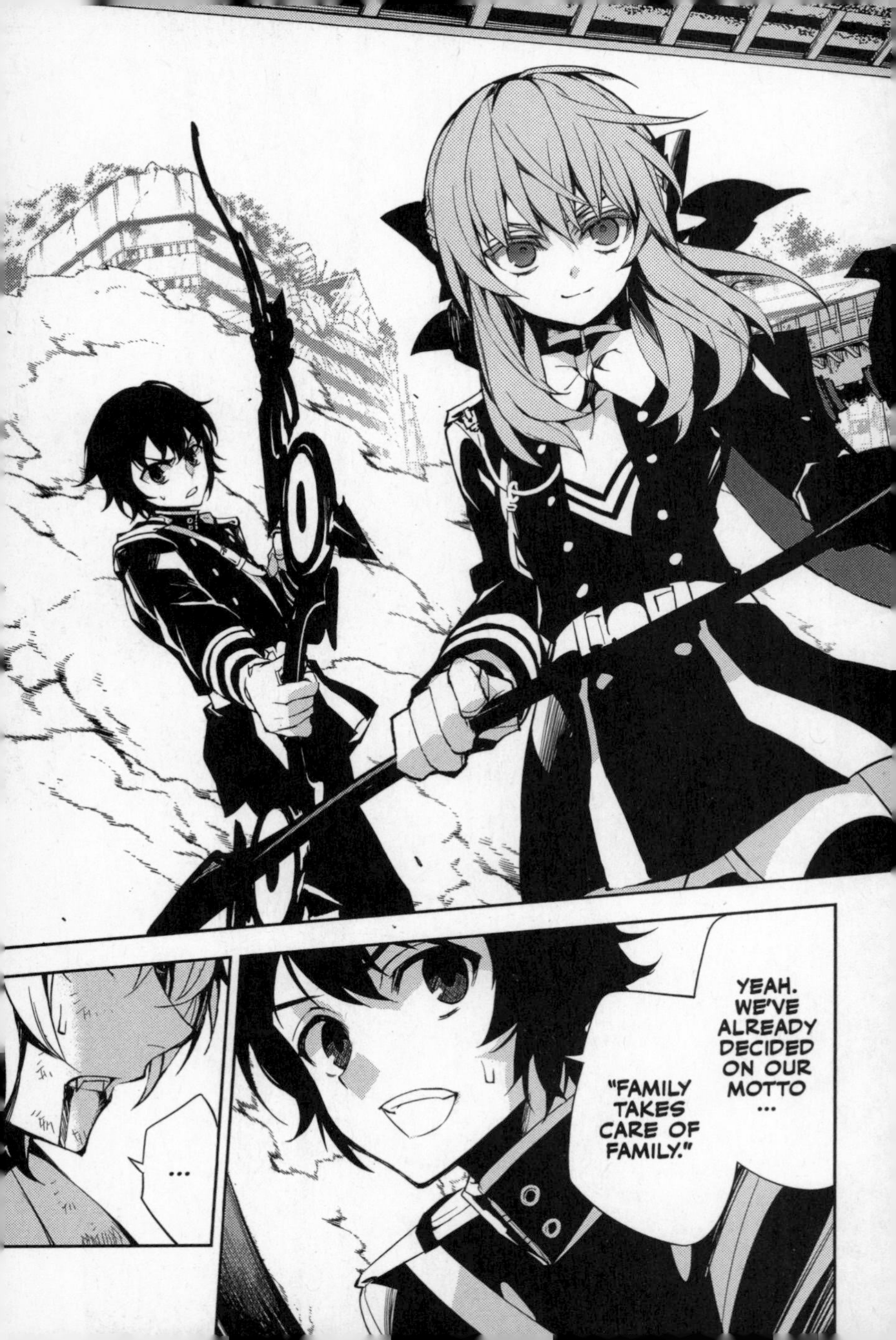
YEAH. WE'VE ALREADY DECIDED ON OUR MOTTO ...
"FAMILY TAKES CARE OF FAMILY."
...

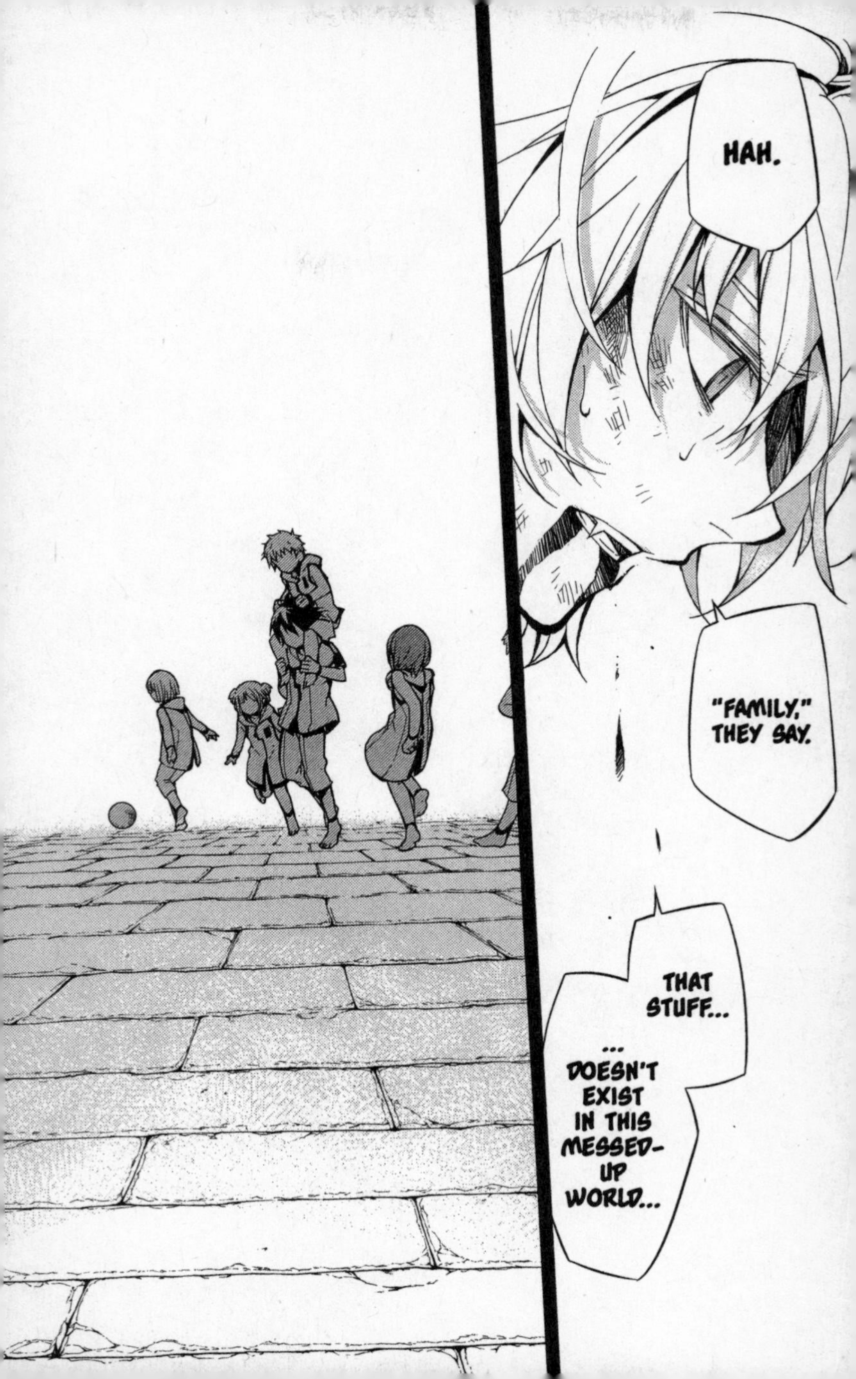
HAH.
"FAMILY," THEY SAY.
THAT STUFF...
...DOESN'T EXIST IN THIS MESSED-UP WORLD...

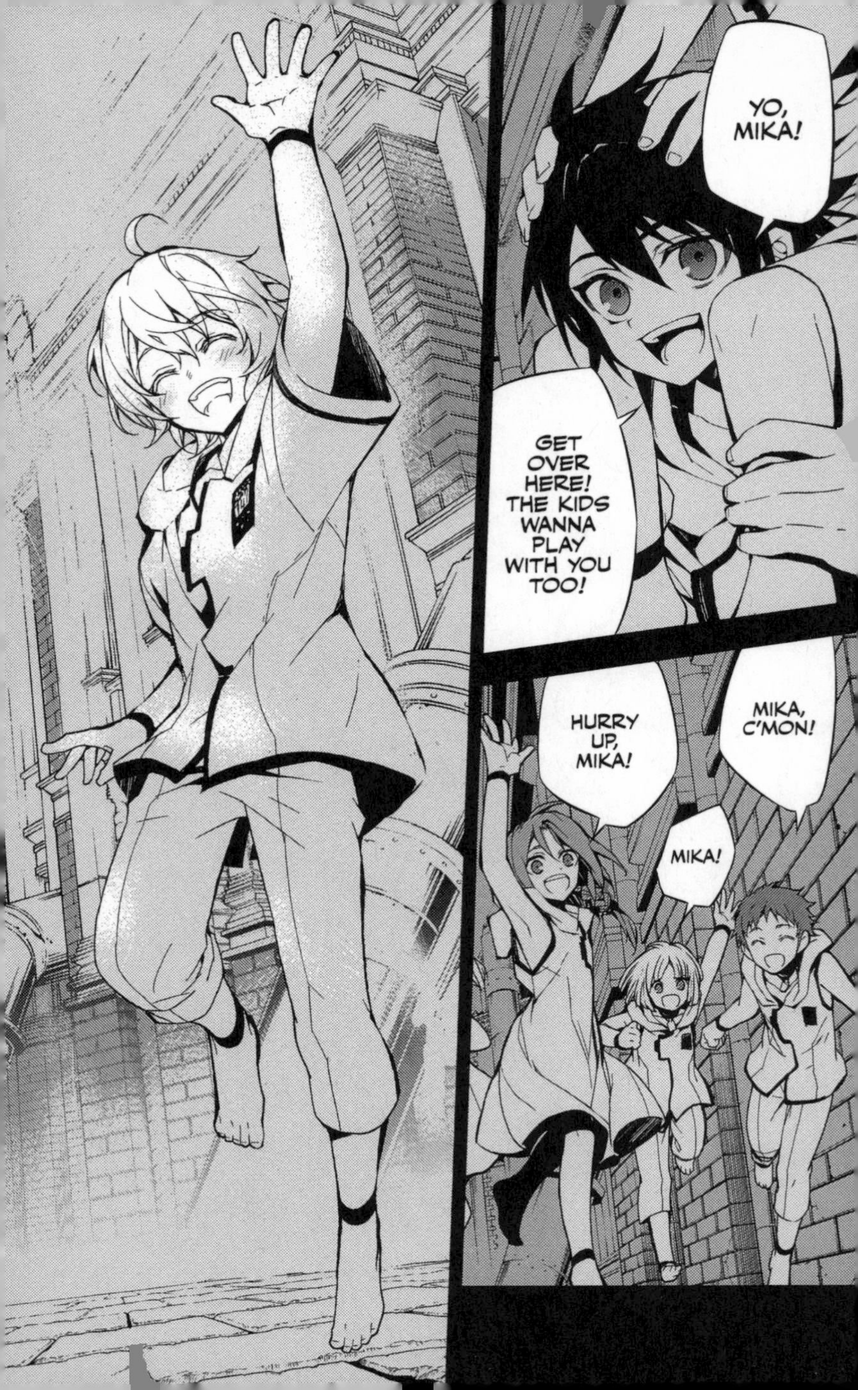
YO, MIKA!
GET OVER HERE! THE KIDS WANNA PLAY WITH YOU TOO!
MIKA, C'MON!
HURRY UP, MIKA!
MIKA!

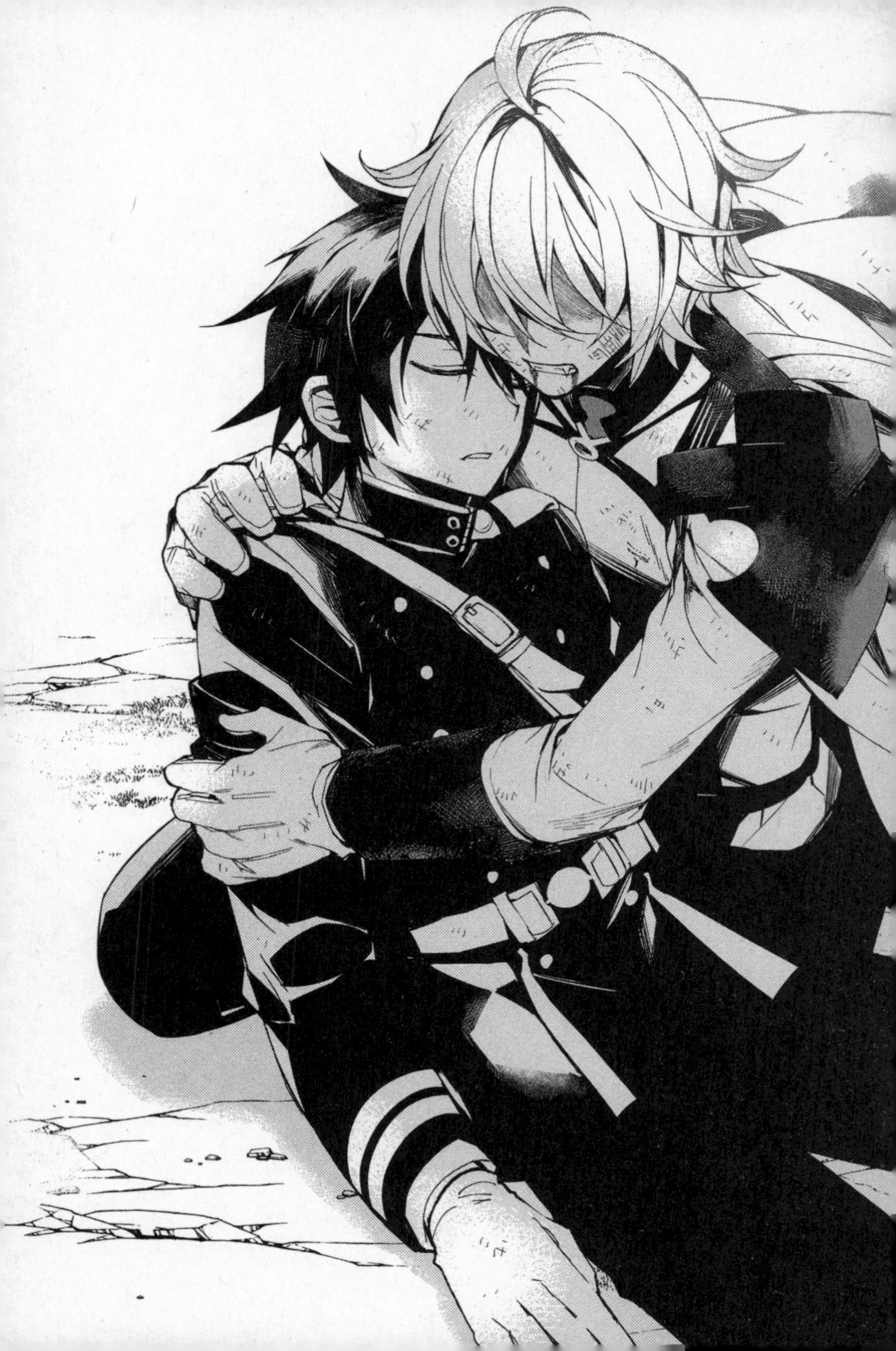

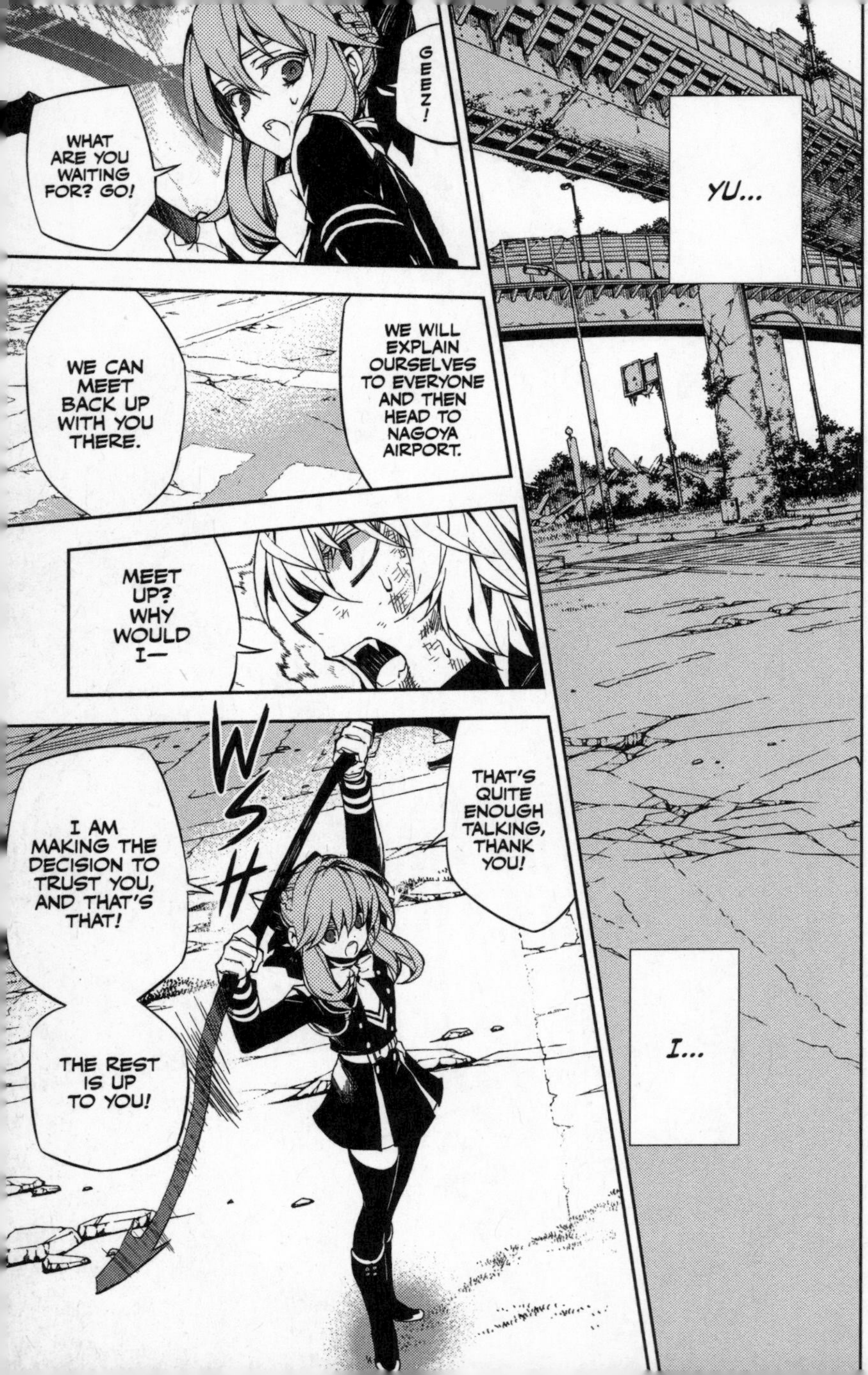
YU...
I...
GEEZ!
WHAT ARE YOU WAITING FOR? GO!
WE WILL EXPLAIN OURSELVES TO EVERYONE AND THEN HEAD TO NAGOYA AIRPORT.
WE CAN MEET BACK UP WITH YOU THERE.
MEET UP? WHY WOULD I—
WSH
THAT'S QUITE ENOUGH TALKING, THANK YOU!
I AM MAKING THE DECISION TO TRUST YOU, AND THAT'S THAT!
THE REST IS UP TO YOU!

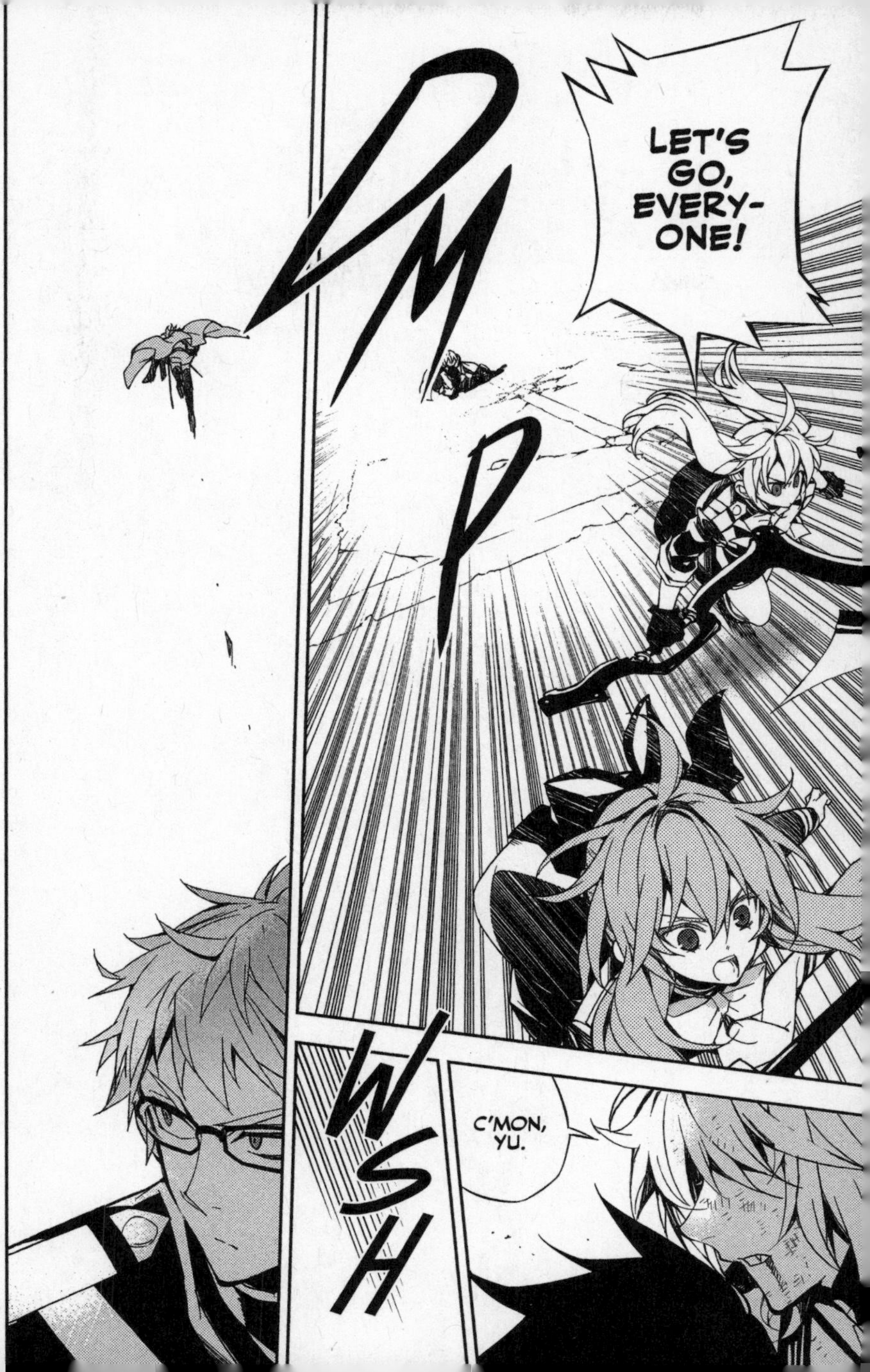
LET'S GO, EVERY-ONE!
DMP
C'MON, YU.
WSH

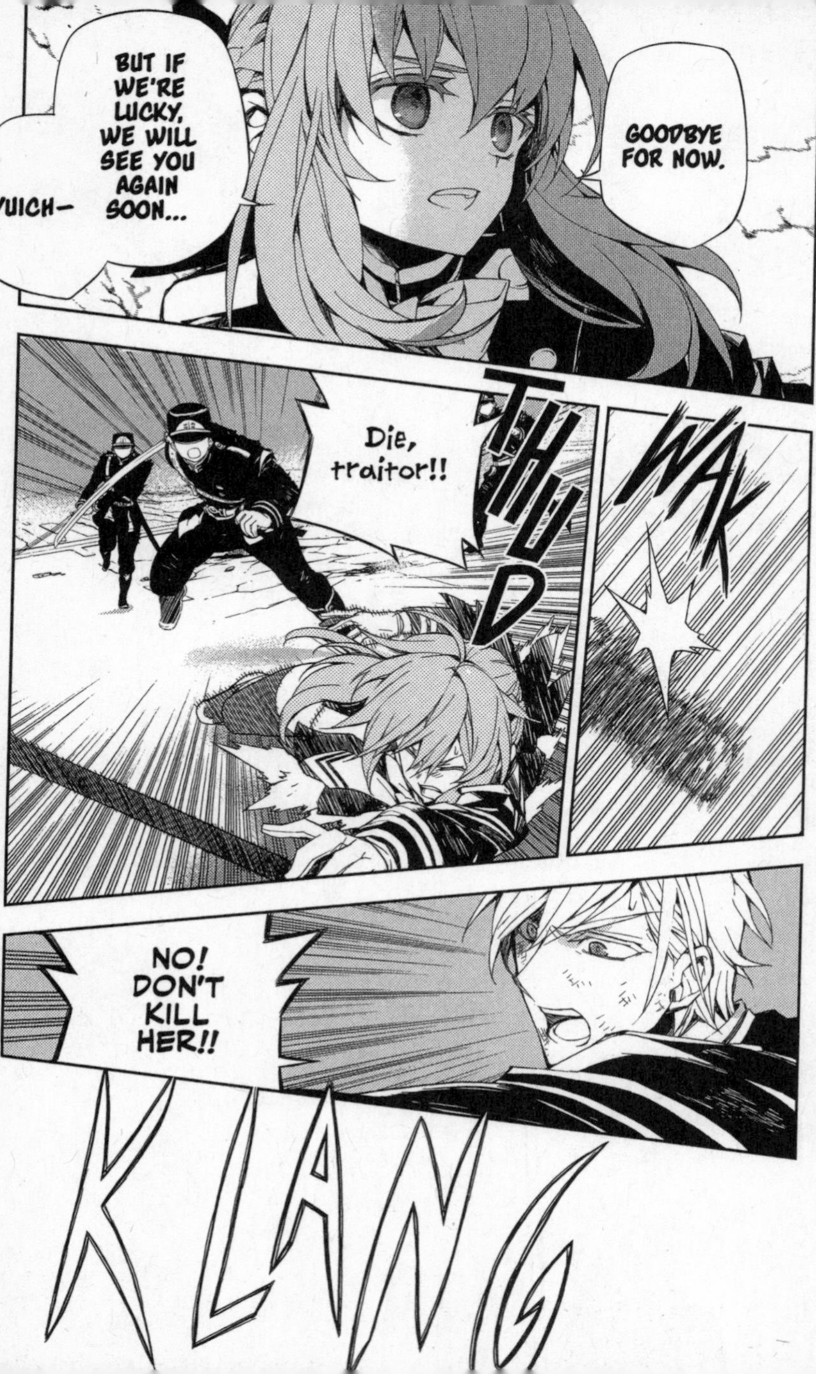
GOODBYE FOR NOW.
BUT IF WE'RE LUCKY, WE WILL SEE YOU AGAIN SOON... YUICH—
WAK
THUD
Die, traitor!!
NO! DON'T KILL HER!!
KLANG

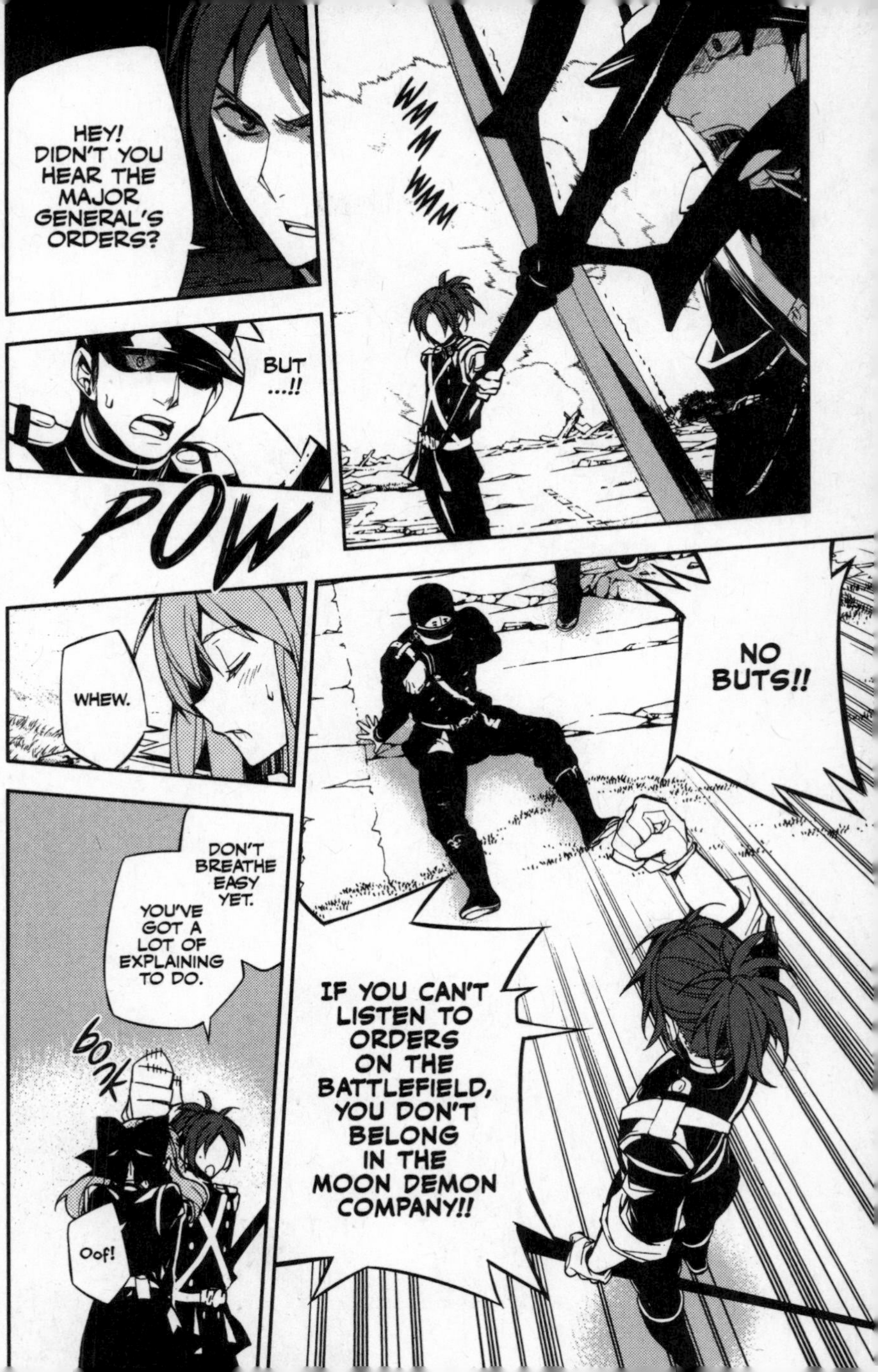
WMM WMM WMM
HEY! DIDN'T YOU HEAR THE MAJOR GENERAL'S ORDERS?
BUT ...!!
POW
NO BUTS!!
IF YOU CAN'T LISTEN TO ORDERS ON THE BATTLEFIELD, YOU DON'T BELONG IN THE MOON DEMON COMPANY!!
WHEW.
DON'T BREATHE EASY YET.
YOU'VE GOT A LOT OF EXPLAINING TO DO.
bonk
Oof!

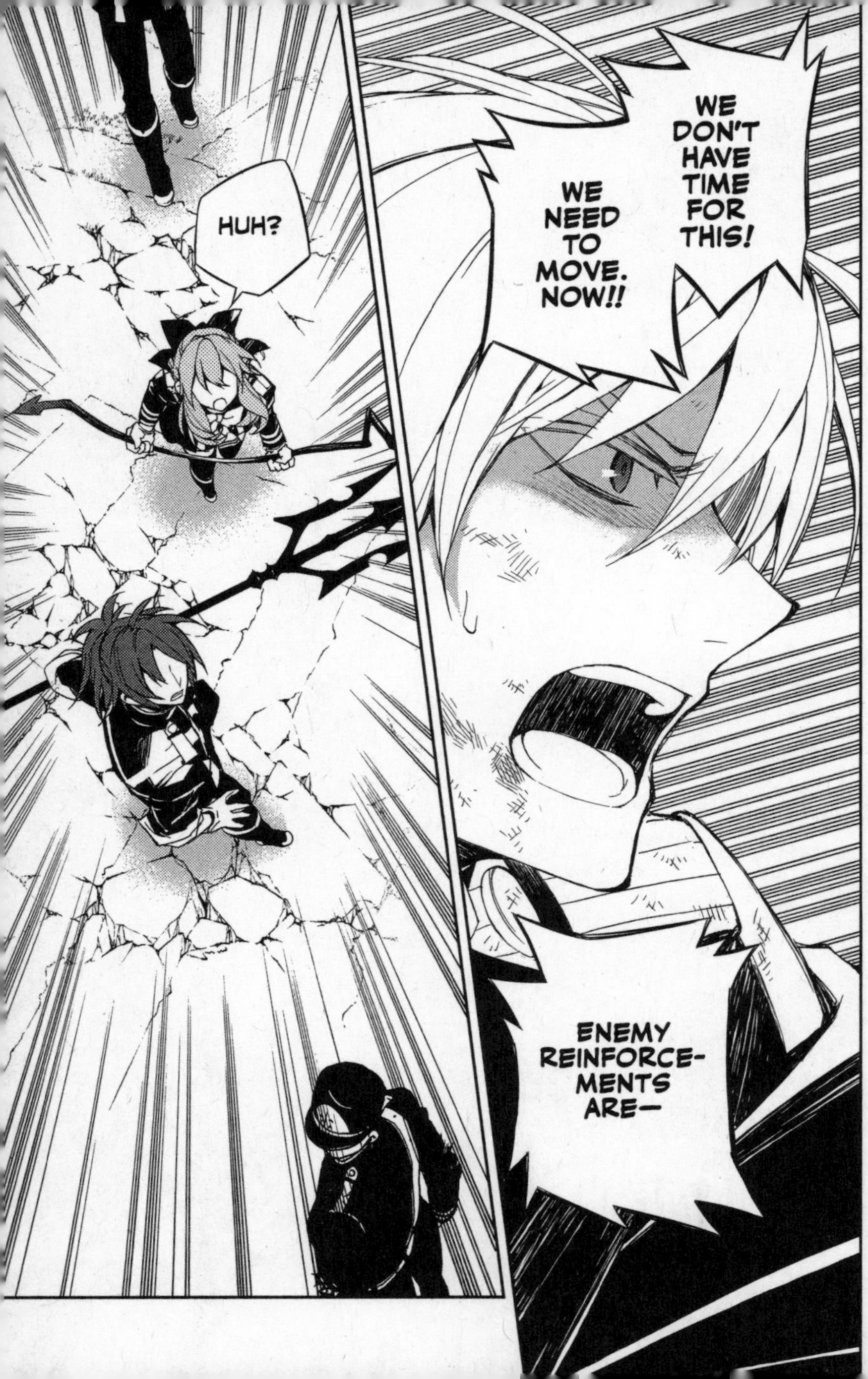
WE DON'T HAVE TIME FOR THIS!
WE NEED TO MOVE. NOW!!
ENEMY REINFORCE-MENTS ARE—
HUH?

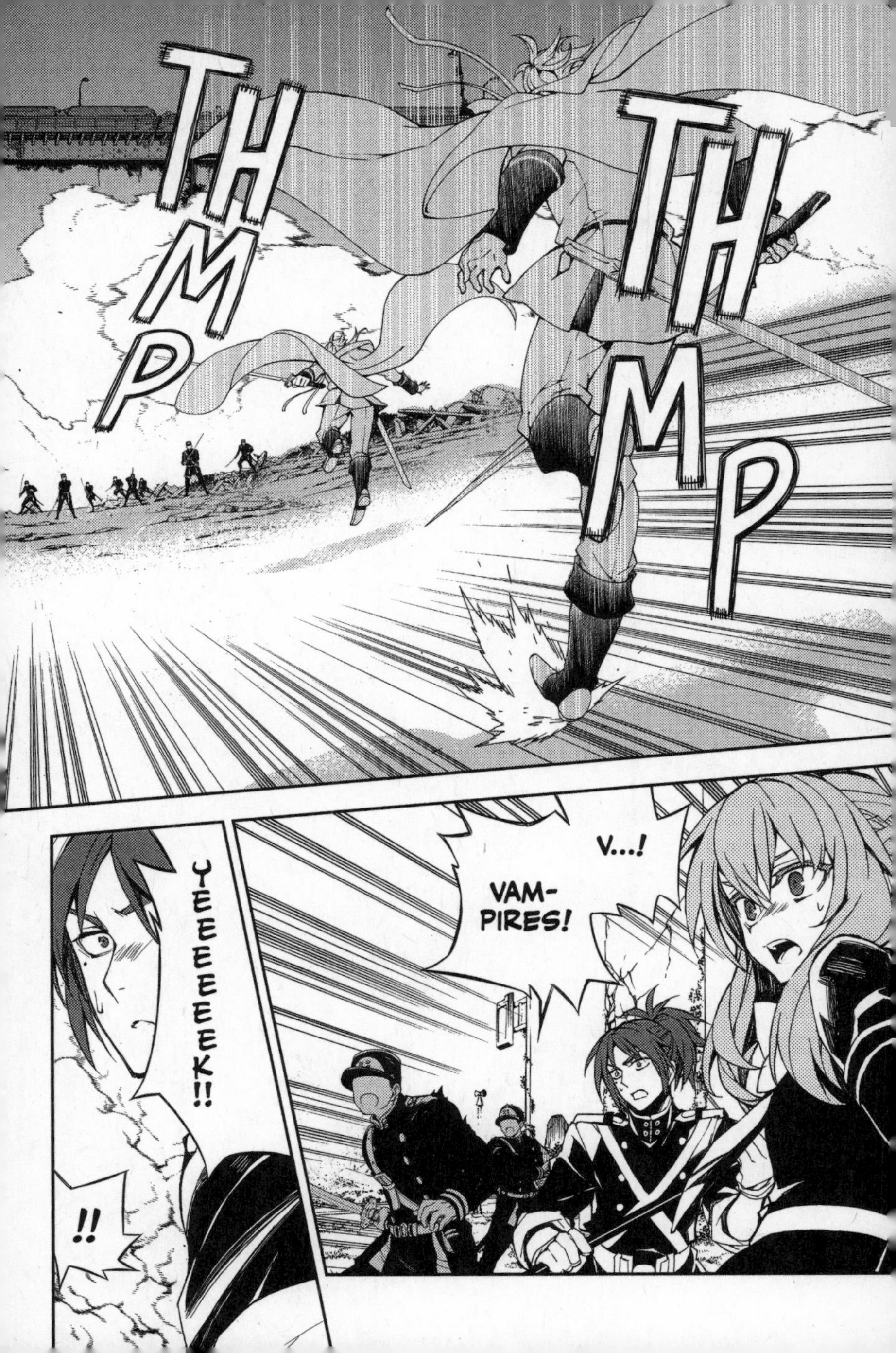
THUMP
THUMP
V...!
VAM-PIRES!
YEEEEEEEK!!
!!

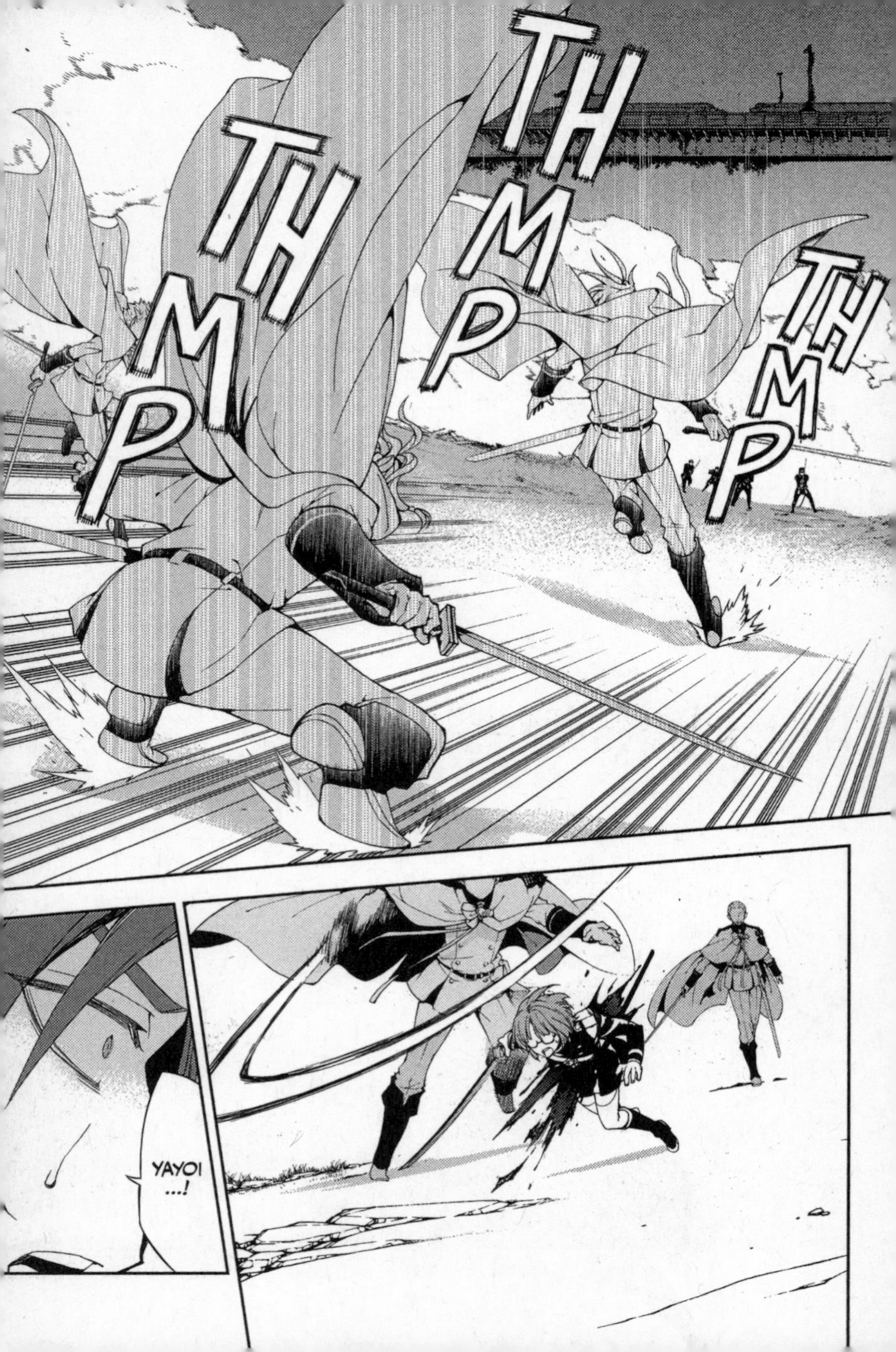
THMP
THMP
THMP
YAYOI ...!

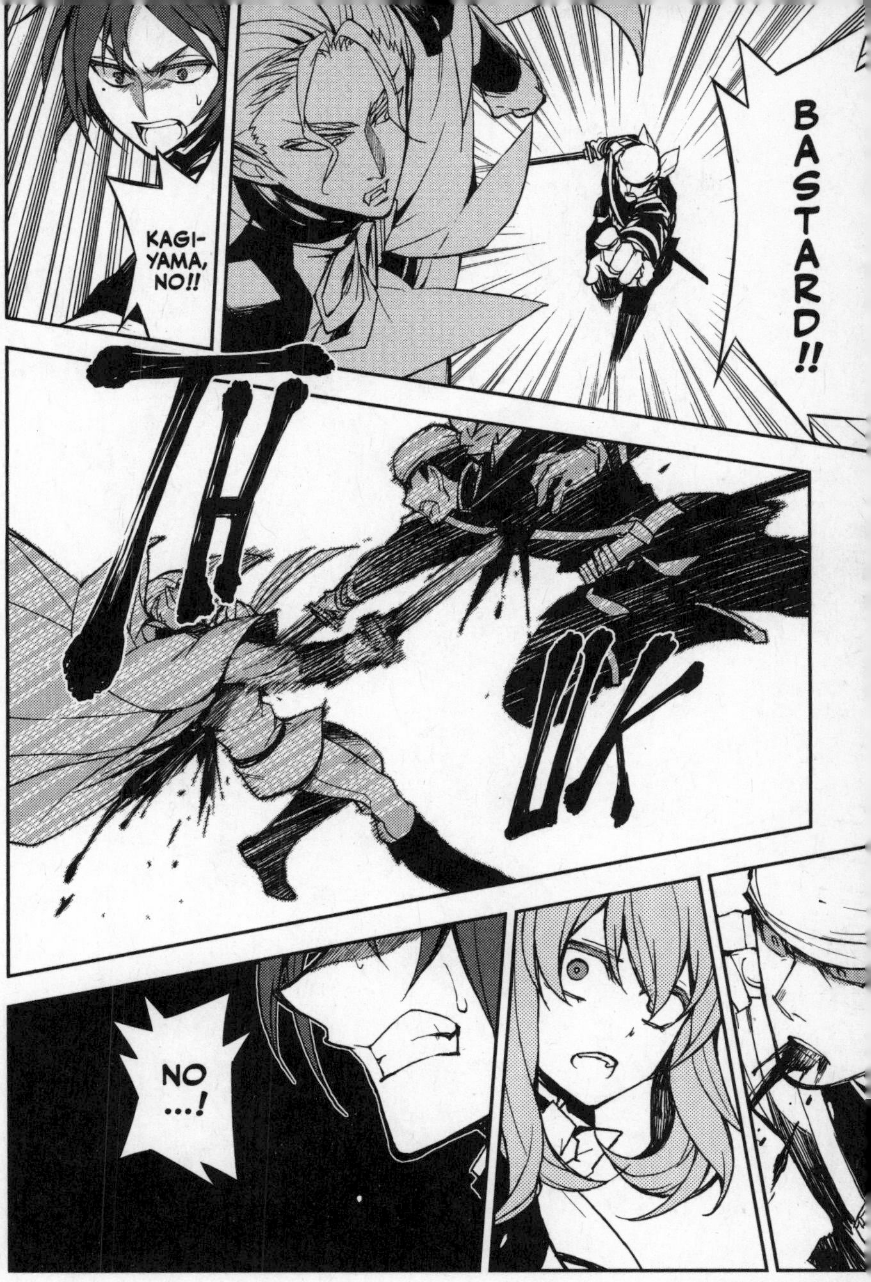
BASTARD!!
KAGI-YAMA, NO!!
THUK
NO ...!

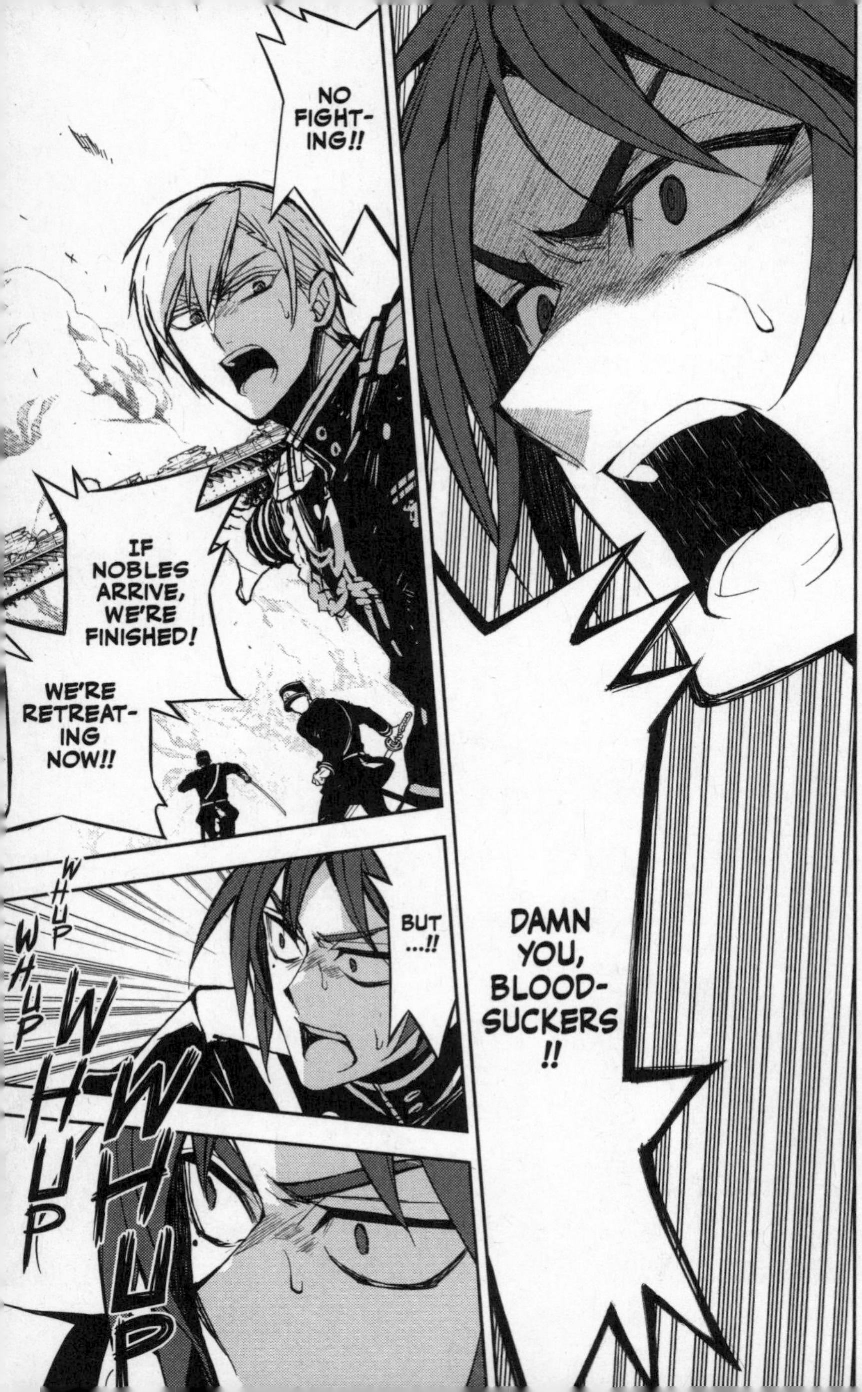
DAMN YOU, BLOODSUCKERS!!
NO FIGHTING!!
IF NOBLES ARRIVE, WE'RE FINISHED!
WE'RE RETREATING NOW!!
BUT...!!
WHUP
WHUP
WHUP
WHUP

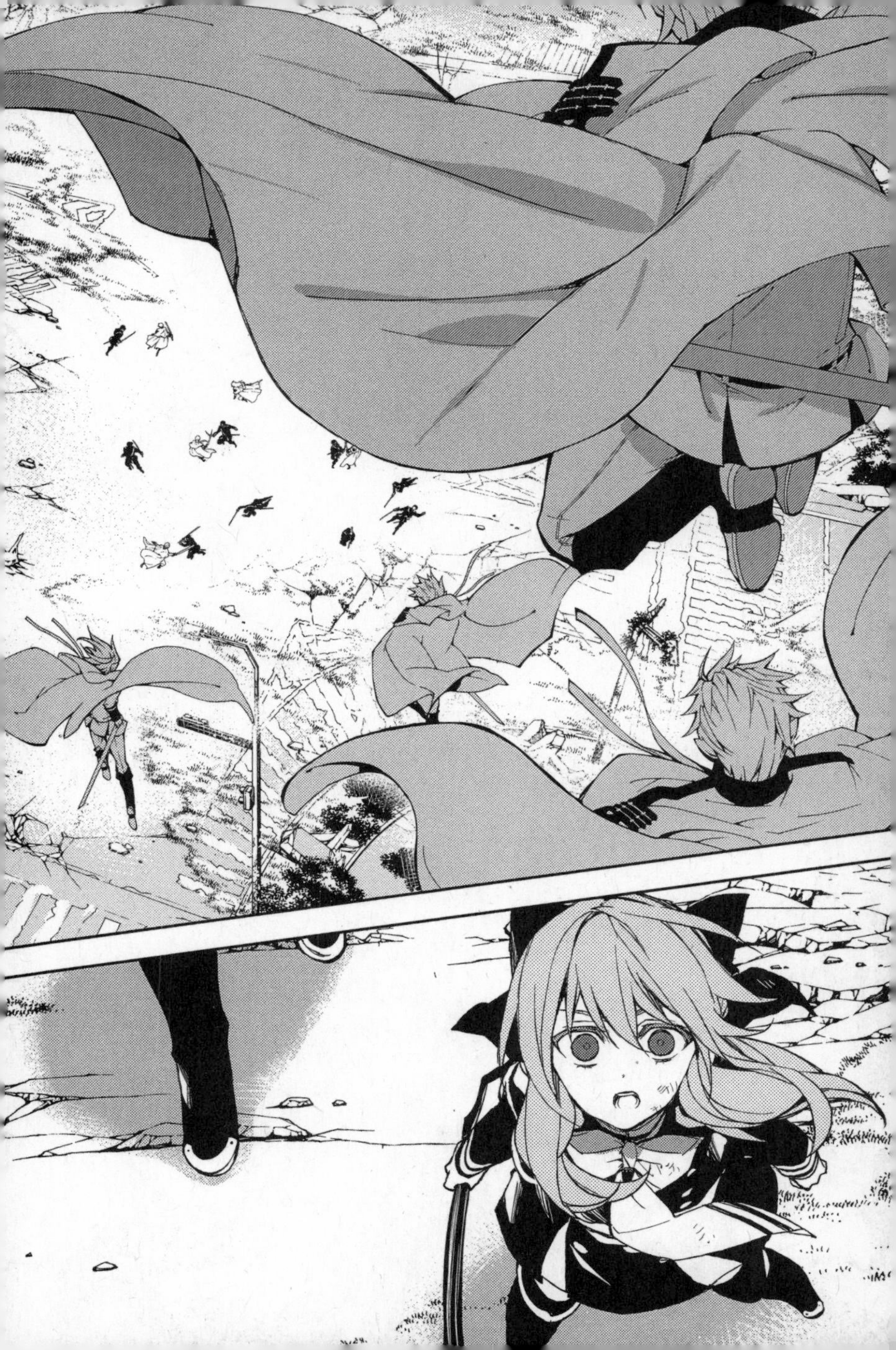

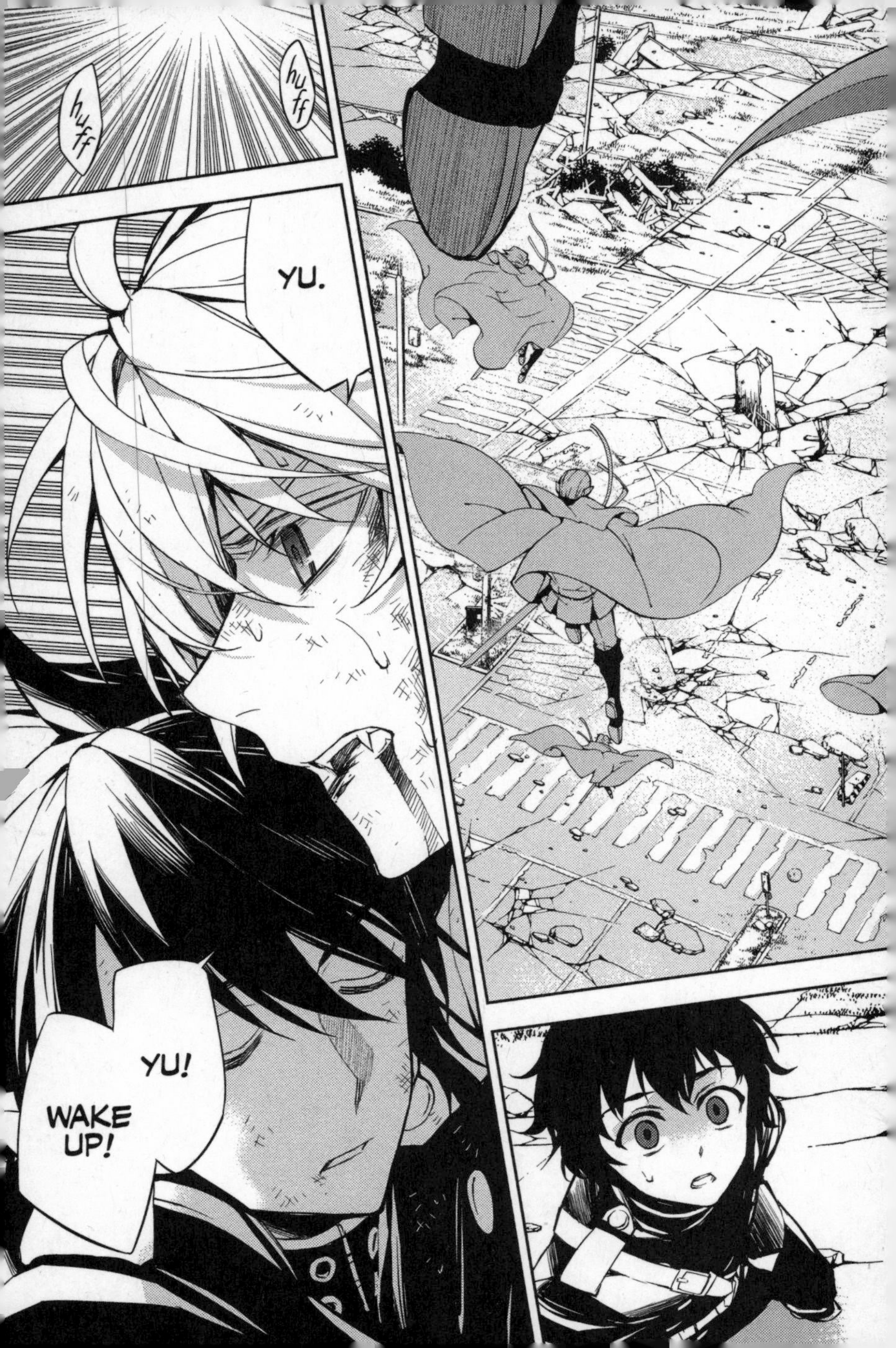
huff
huff
YU.
YU!
WAKE UP!

Seraph of the End

VAMPIRE REIGN

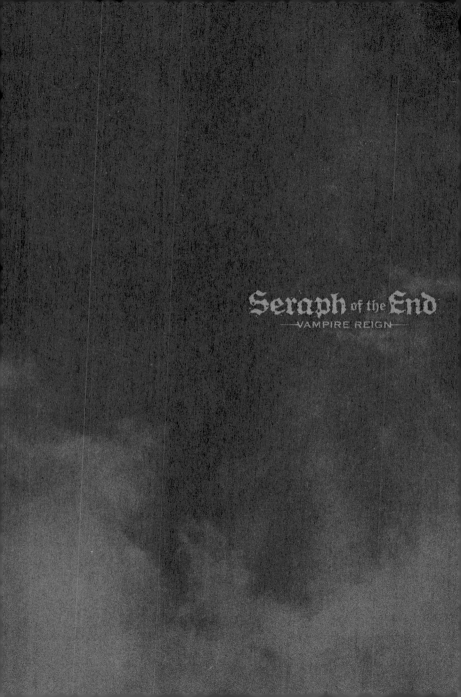

Chapter 36 Yu & Mika

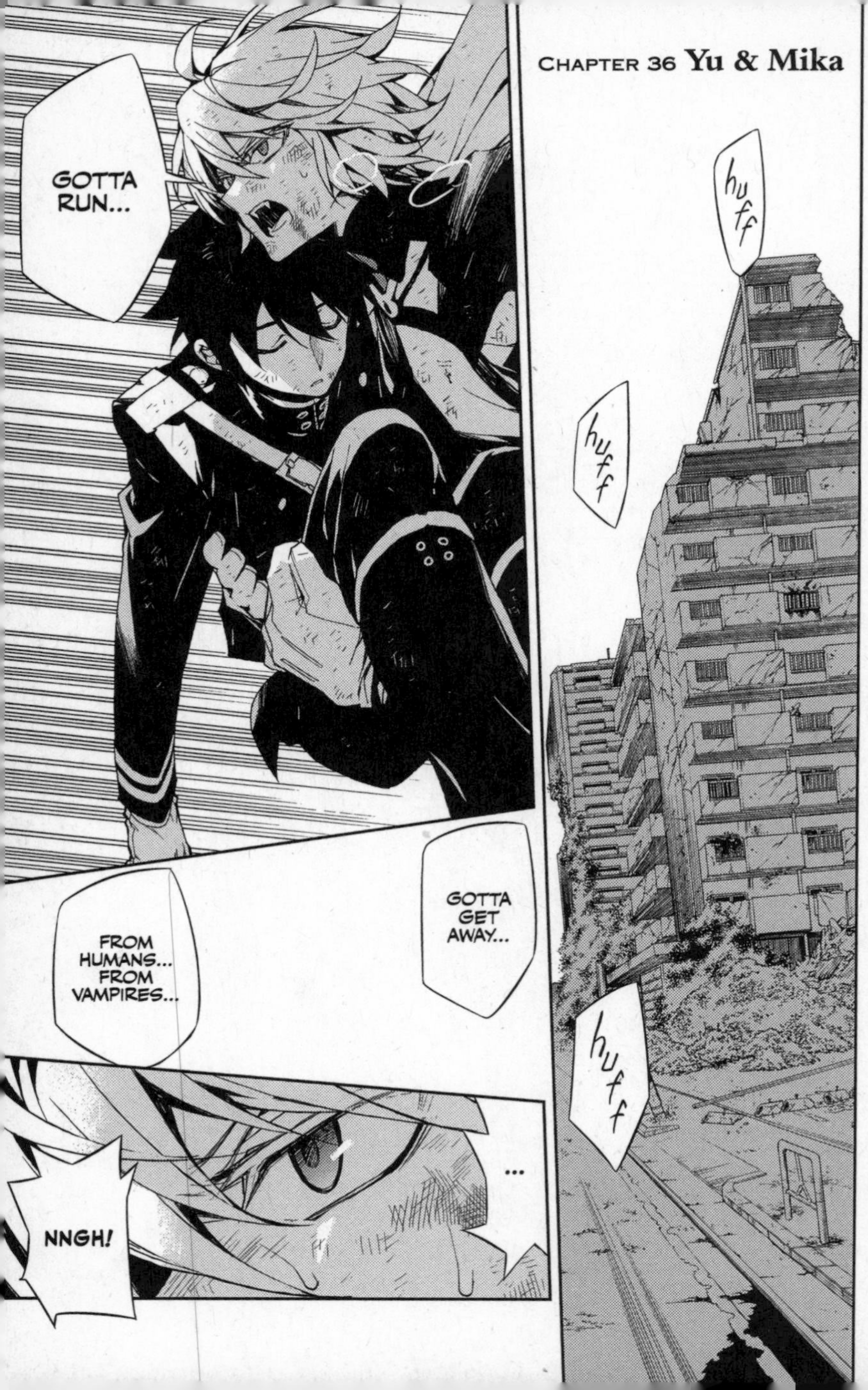
huff
huff
huff
GOTTA RUN...
GOTTA GET AWAY...
FROM HUMANS... FROM VAMPIRES...
...
NNGH!

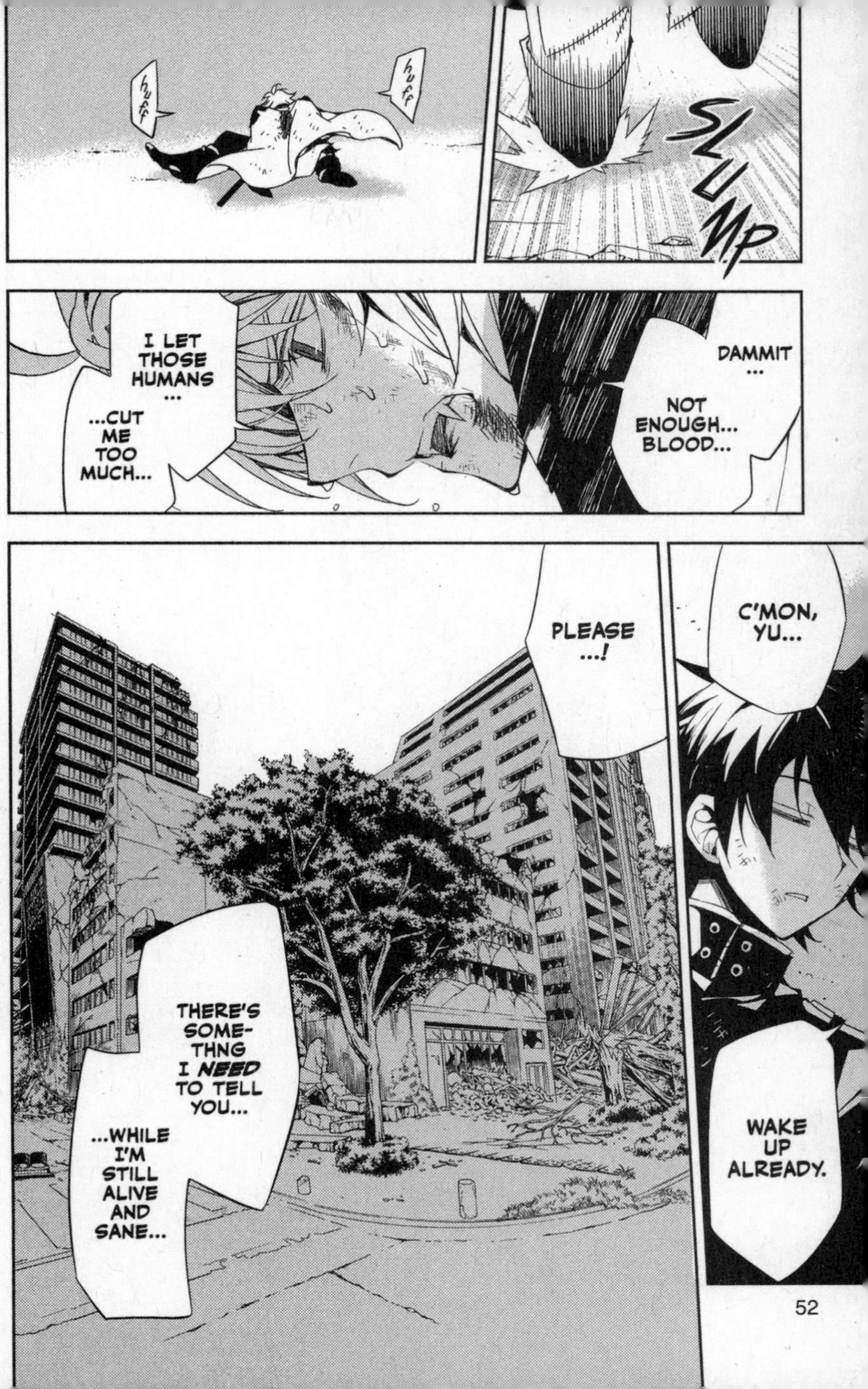
SLUMP
huff
huff
DAMMIT...
NOT ENOUGH... BLOOD...
I LET THOSE HUMANS...
...CUT ME TOO MUCH...
C'MON, YU...
WAKE UP ALREADY.
PLEASE...!
THERE'S SOMETHNG I *NEED* TO TELL YOU...
...WHILE I'M STILL ALIVE AND SANE...

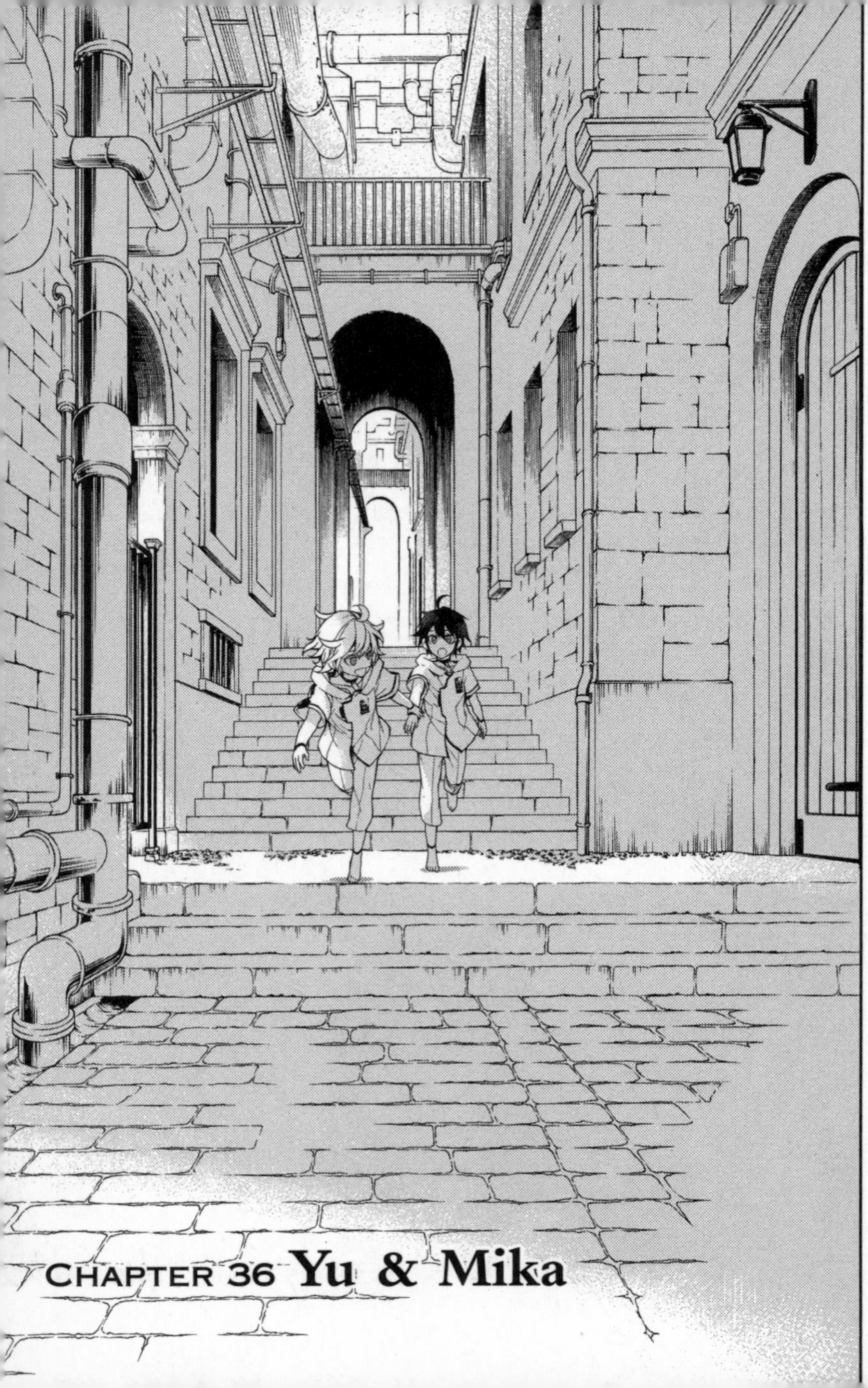

Chapter 36 Yu & Mika

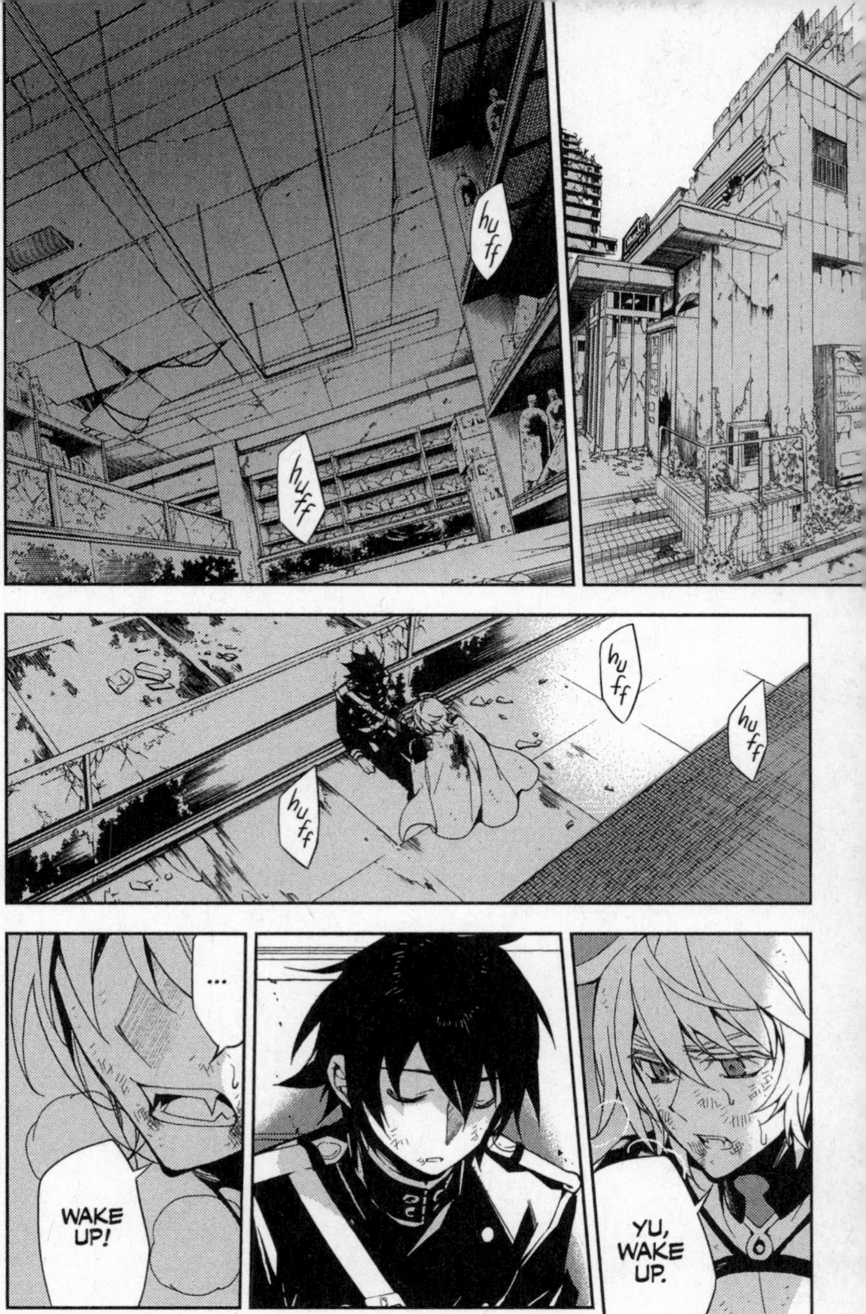
huff
huff
huff
huff
huff
YU, WAKE UP.
...
WAKE UP!

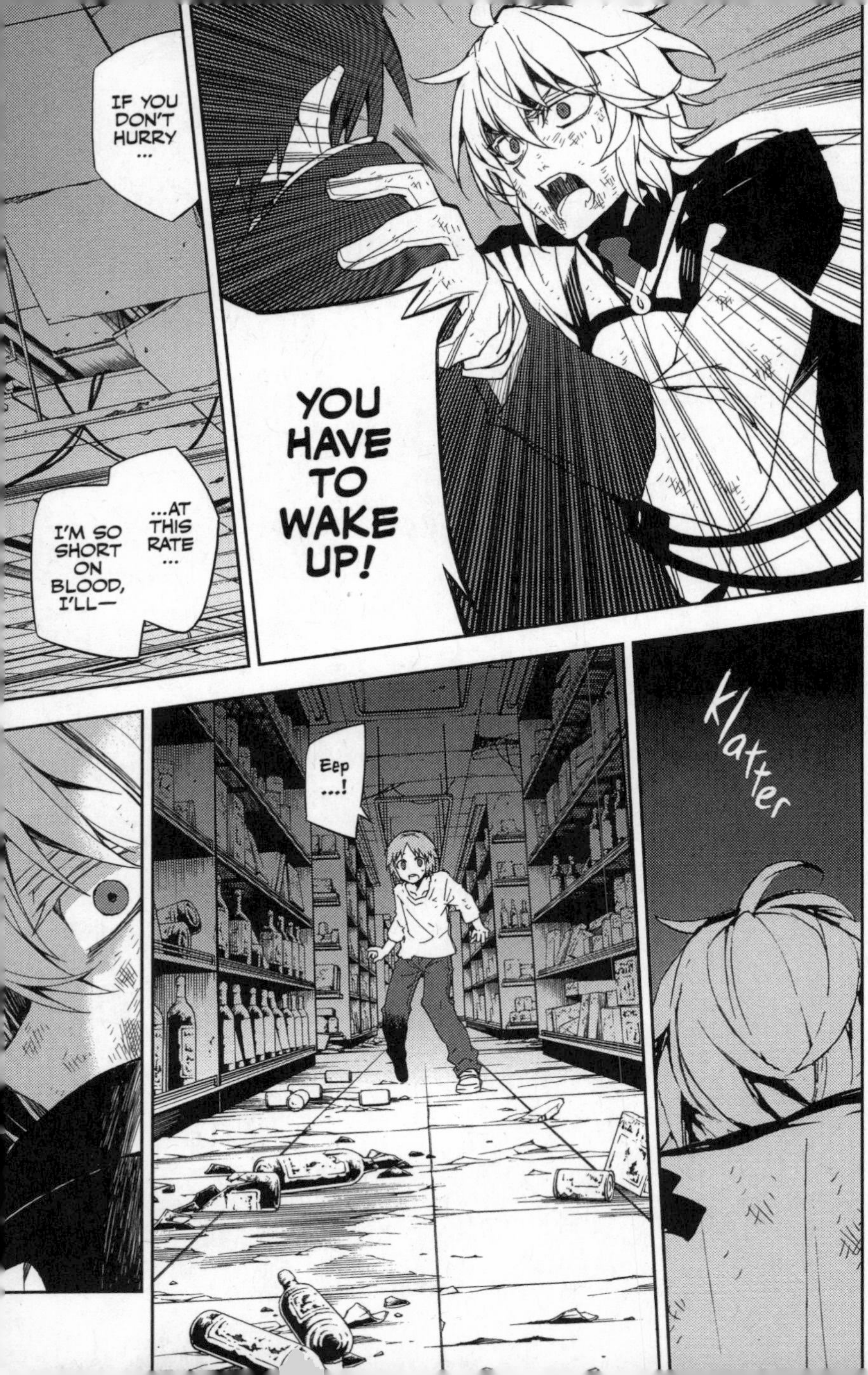
IF YOU DON'T HURRY ...
YOU HAVE TO WAKE UP!
...AT THIS RATE ...
I'M SO SHORT ON BLOOD, I'LL—
Klatter
Eep ...!

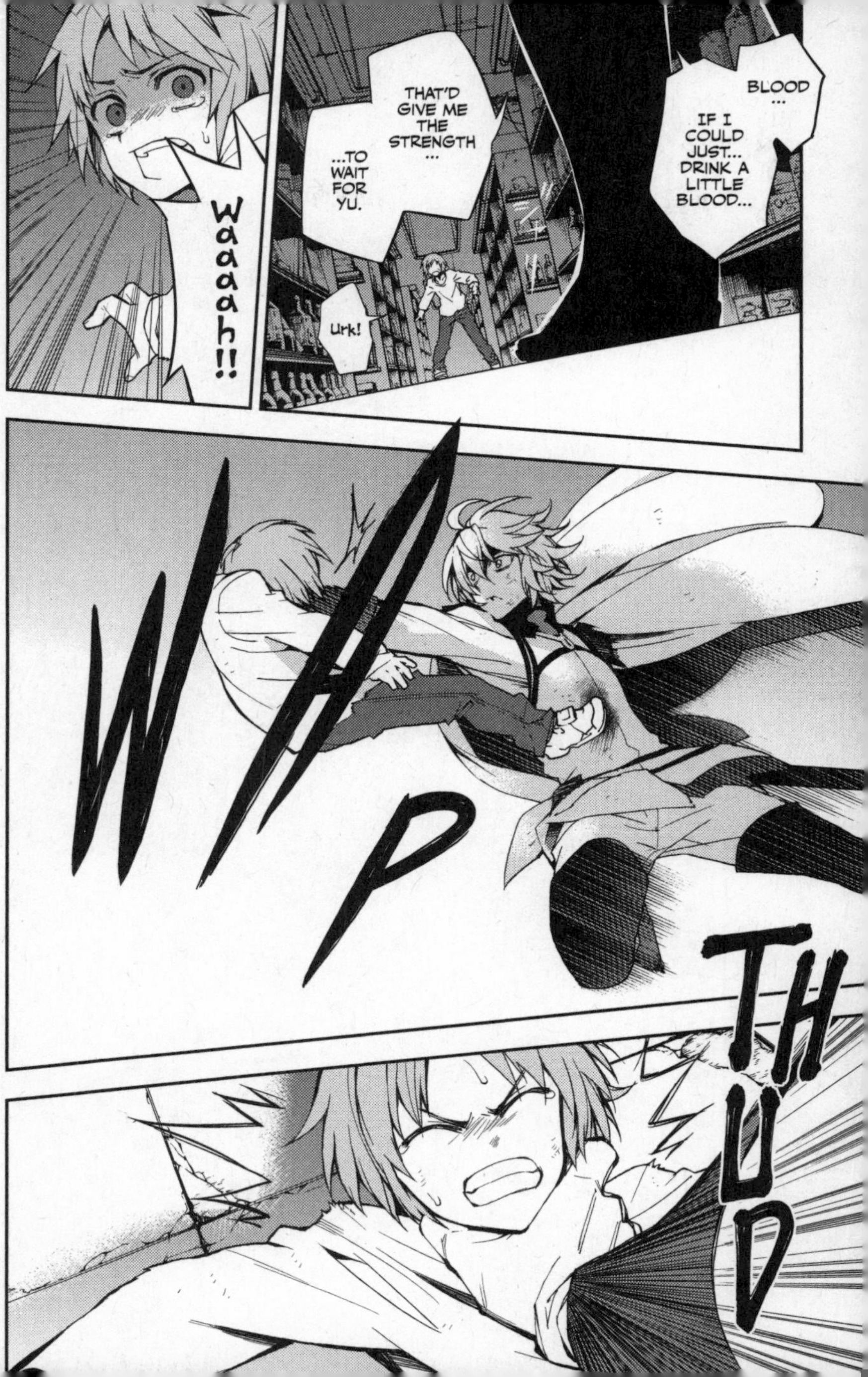
BLOOD ...
IF I COULD JUST... DRINK A LITTLE BLOOD...
THAT'D GIVE ME THE STRENGTH ...
...TO WAIT FOR YU.
Urk!
Waaaaah!!
WHAP
THUD

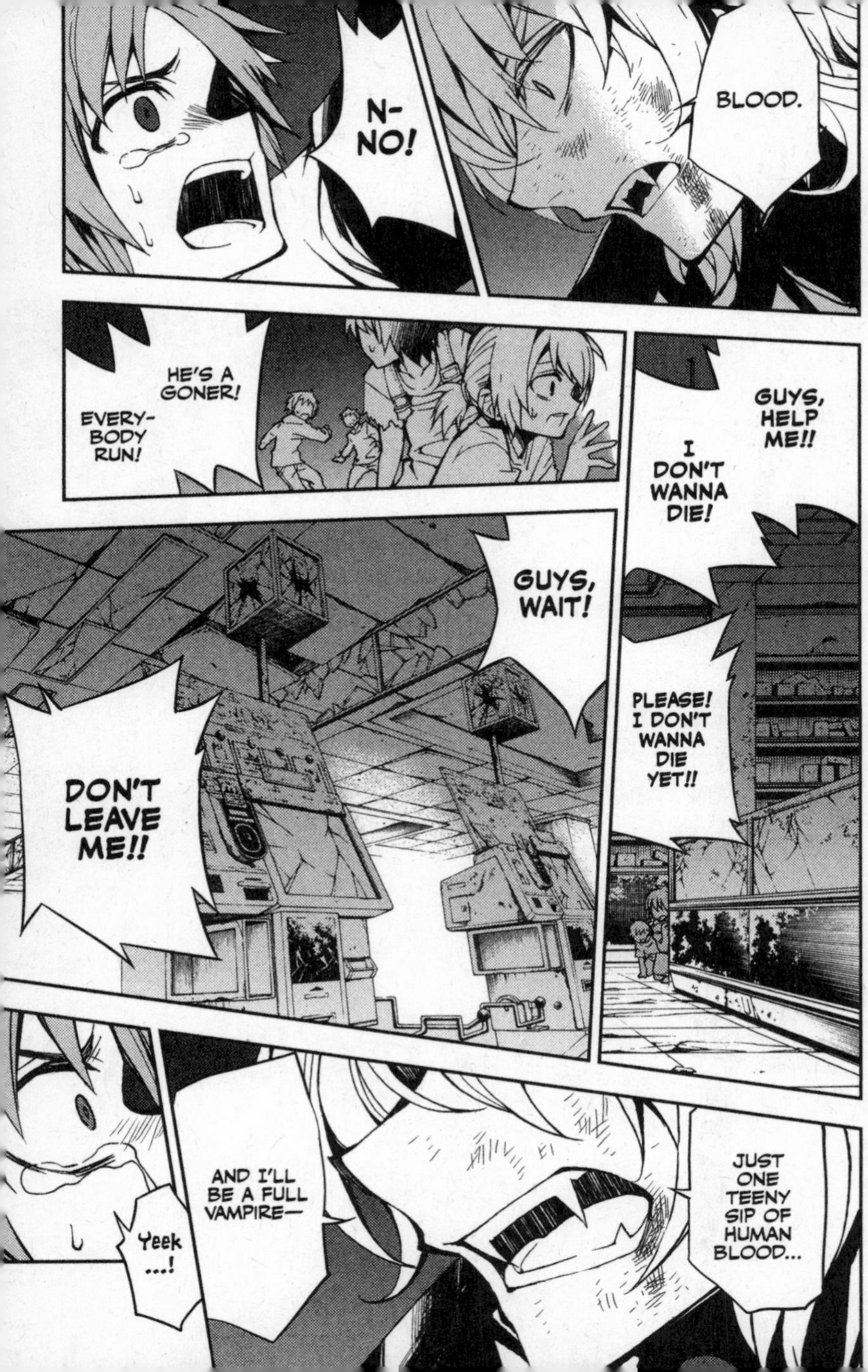
BLOOD.
N- NO!
GUYS, HELP ME!!
I DON'T WANNA DIE!
PLEASE! I DON'T WANNA DIE YET!!
HE'S A GONER!
EVERY-BODY RUN!
GUYS, WAIT!
DON'T LEAVE ME!!
JUST ONE TEENY SIP OF HUMAN BLOOD...
AND I'LL BE A FULL VAMPIRE—
Yeek ...!

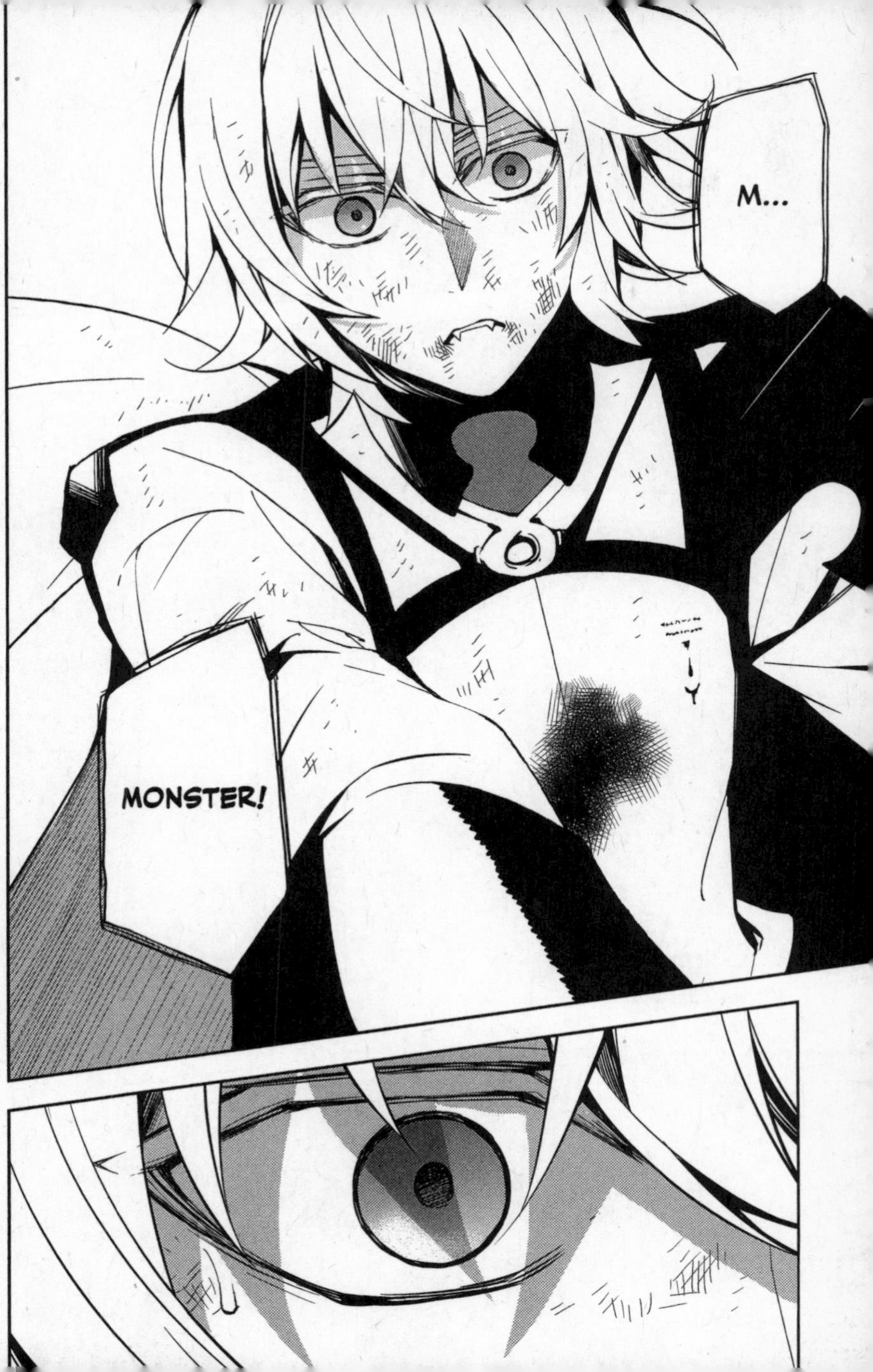
M...
MONSTER!

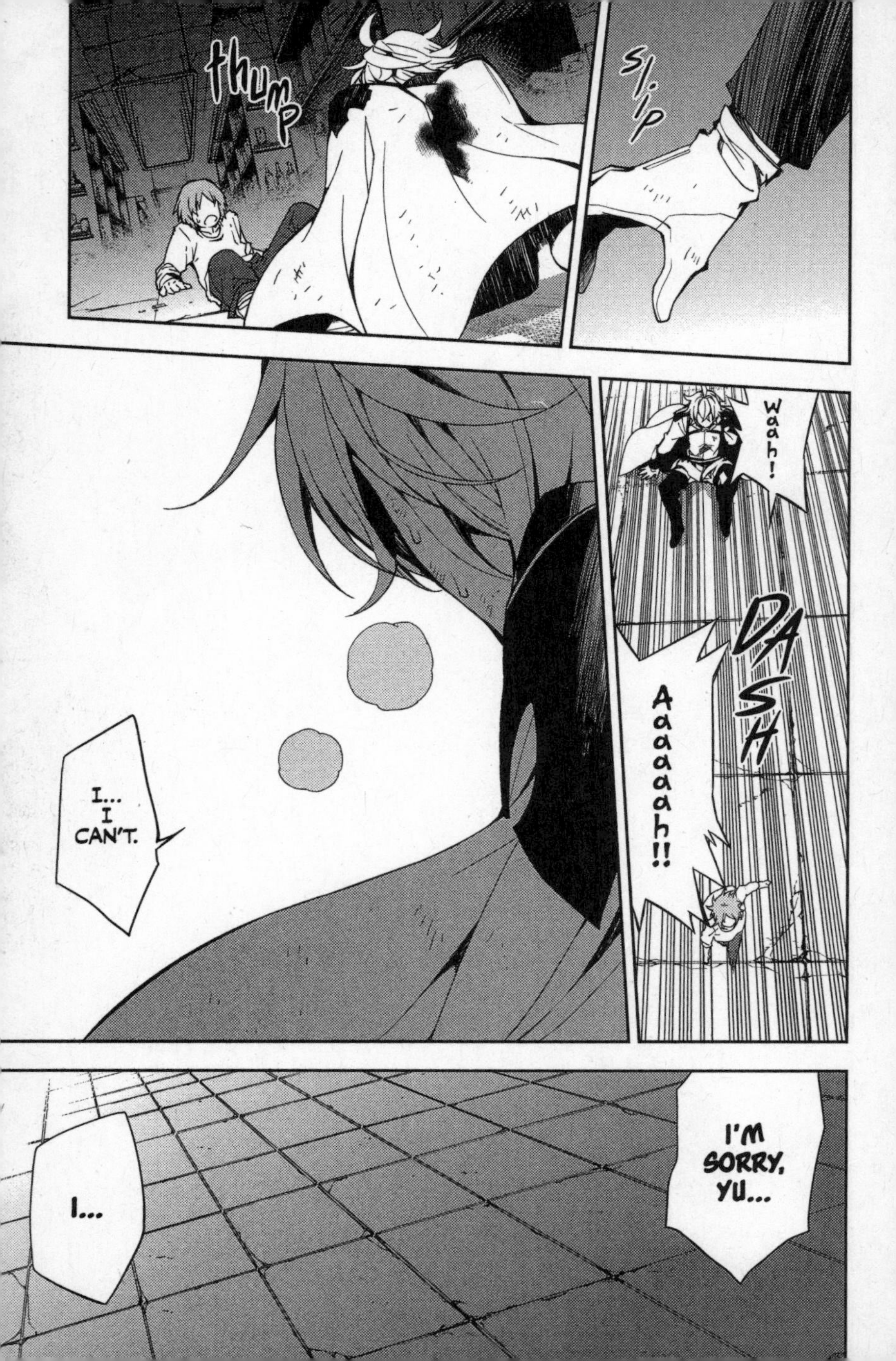
slip
thump
Waah!
DASH
Aaaaaaah!!
I... I CAN'T.
I'M SORRY, YU...
I...

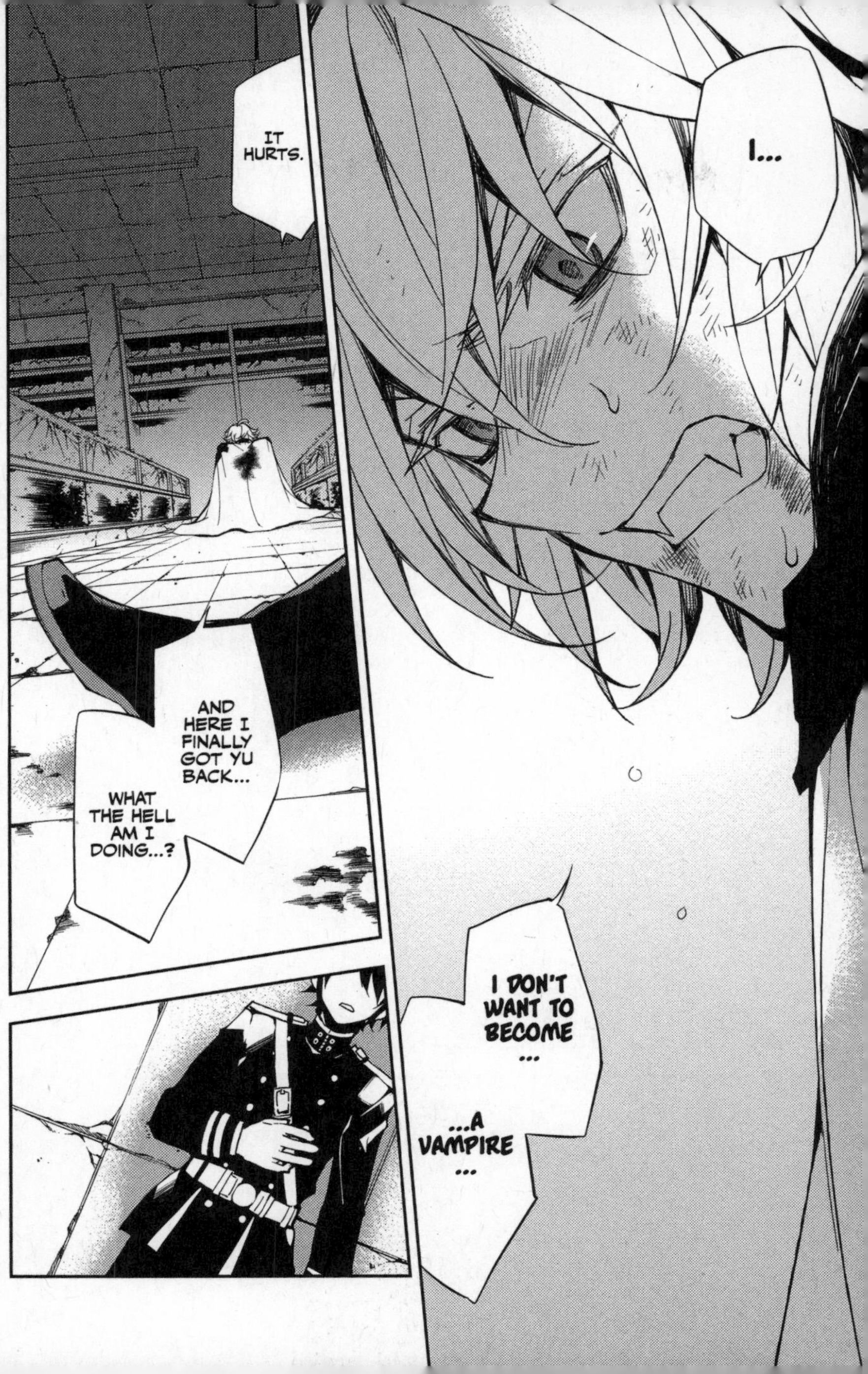
I...
I DON'T WANT TO BECOME ...
...A VAMPIRE ...
IT HURTS.
AND HERE I FINALLY GOT YU BACK...
WHAT THE HELL AM I DOING...?

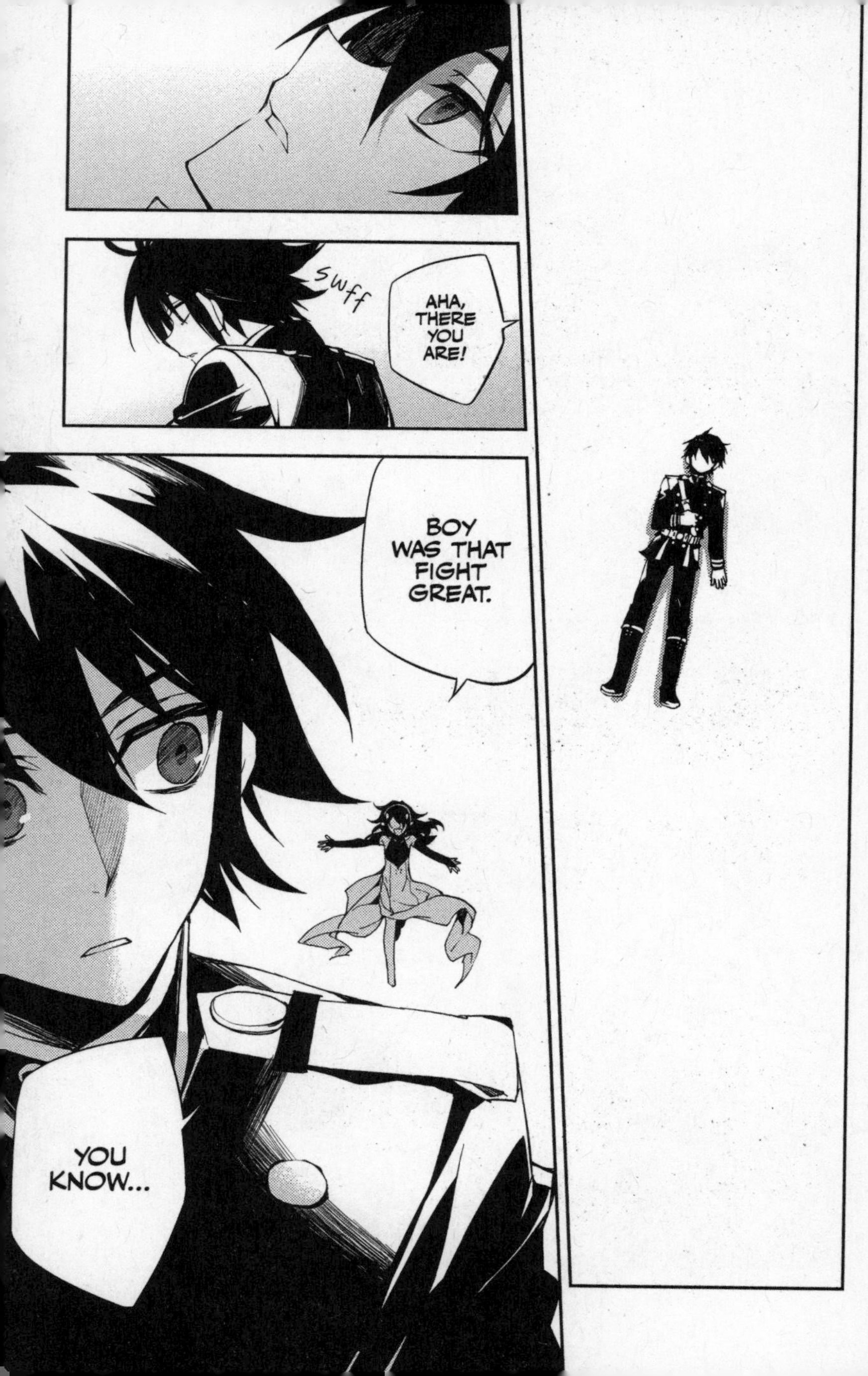
AHA, THERE YOU ARE!
swff
BOY WAS THAT FIGHT GREAT.
YOU KNOW...

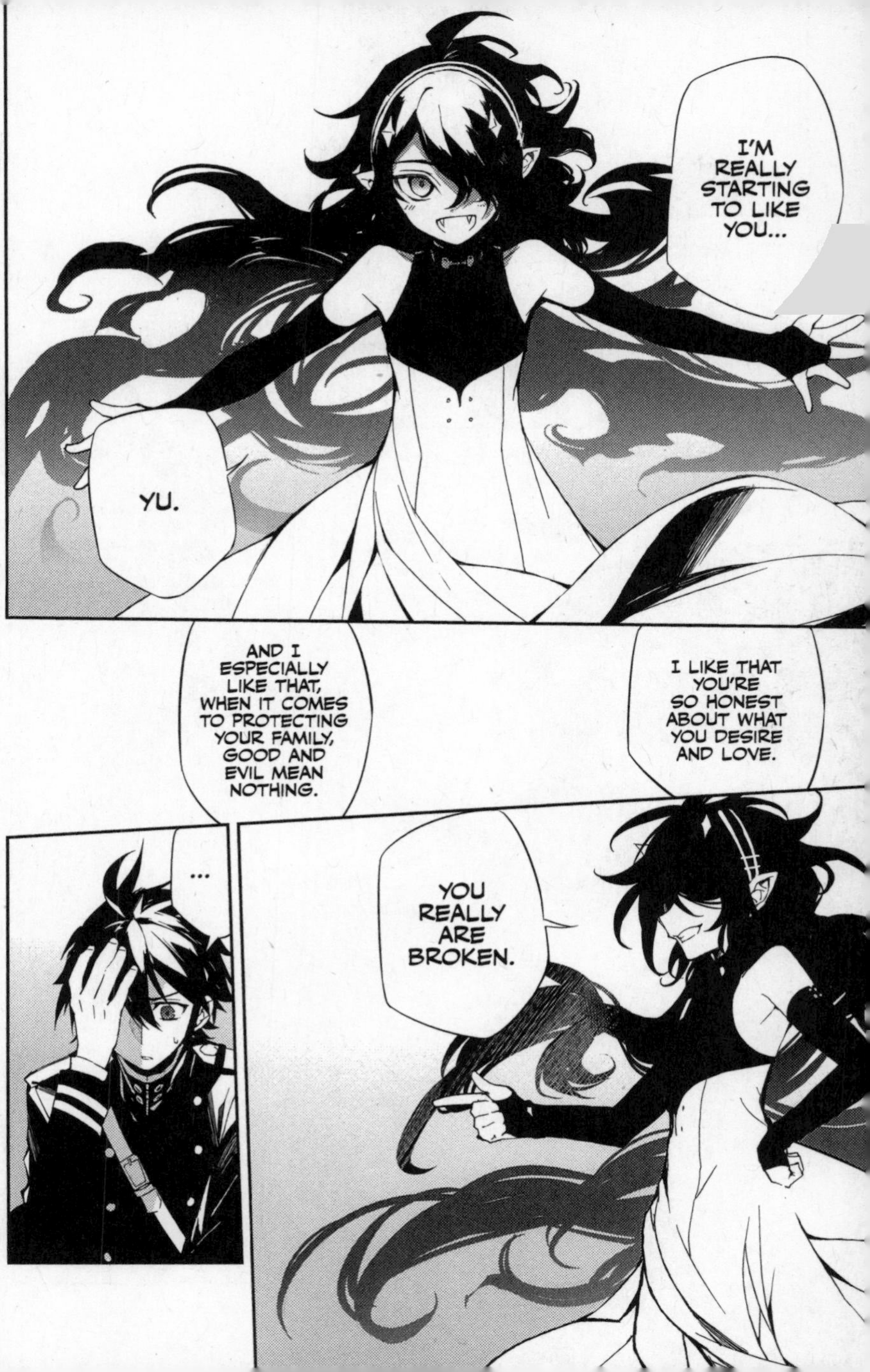
I'M REALLY STARTING TO LIKE YOU...
YU.
I LIKE THAT YOU'RE SO HONEST ABOUT WHAT YOU DESIRE AND LOVE.
AND I ESPECIALLY LIKE THAT, WHEN IT COMES TO PROTECTING YOUR FAMILY, GOOD AND EVIL MEAN NOTHING.
YOU REALLY ARE BROKEN.
...

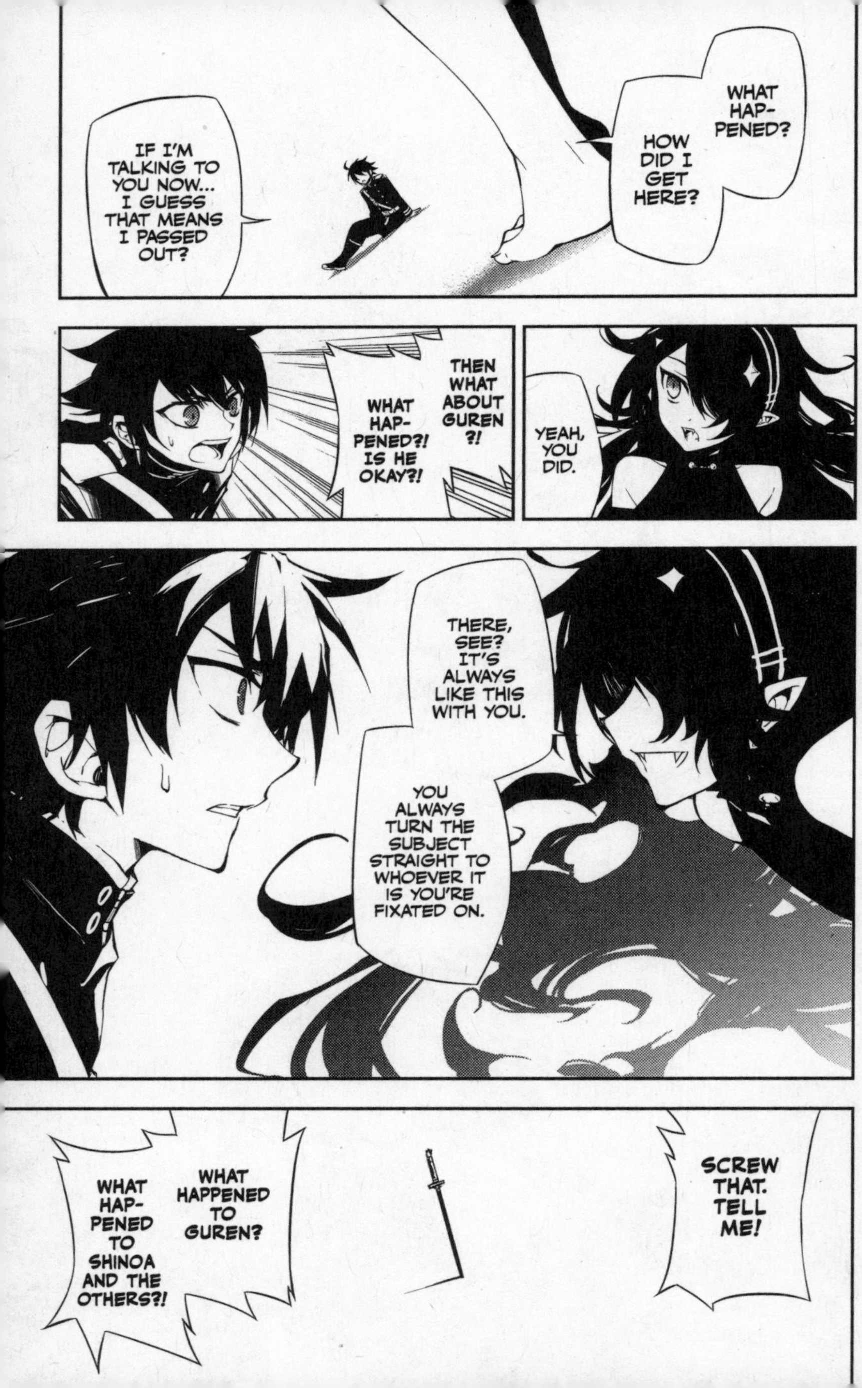
WHAT HAP-PENED?
HOW DID I GET HERE?
IF I'M TALKING TO YOU NOW... I GUESS THAT MEANS I PASSED OUT?
YEAH, YOU DID.
THEN WHAT ABOUT GUREN ?!
WHAT HAP-PENED?! IS HE OKAY?!
THERE, SEE? IT'S ALWAYS LIKE THIS WITH YOU.
YOU ALWAYS TURN THE SUBJECT STRAIGHT TO WHOEVER IT IS YOU'RE FIXATED ON.
SCREW THAT. TELL ME!
WHAT HAPPENED TO GUREN?
WHAT HAP-PENED TO SHINOA AND THE OTHERS?!

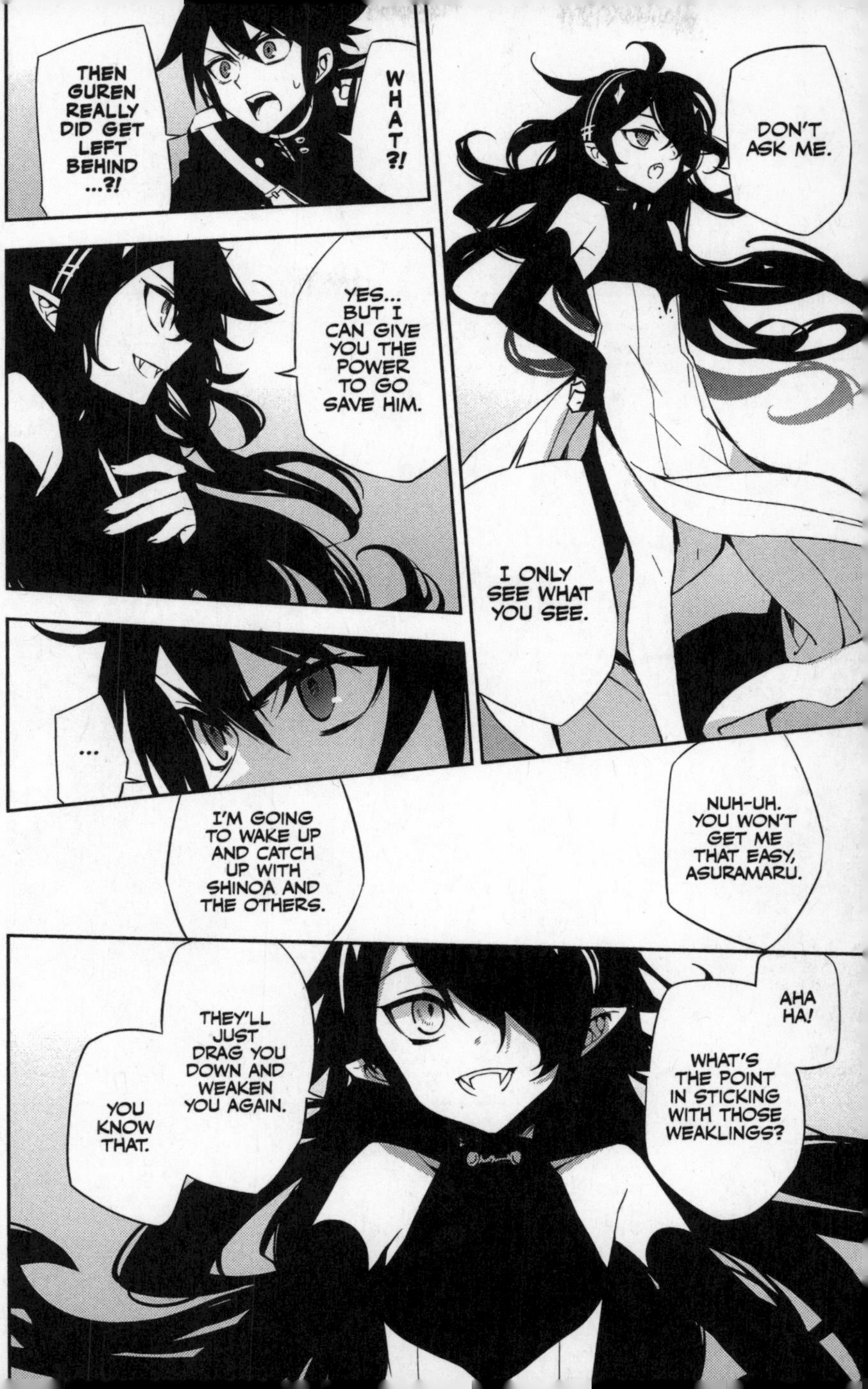
DON'T ASK ME.
I ONLY SEE WHAT YOU SEE.
WHAT?!
THEN GUREN REALLY DID GET LEFT BEHIND ...?!
YES... BUT I CAN GIVE YOU THE POWER TO GO SAVE HIM.
...
NUH-UH. YOU WON'T GET ME THAT EASY, ASURAMARU.
I'M GOING TO WAKE UP AND CATCH UP WITH SHINOA AND THE OTHERS.
AHA HA!
WHAT'S THE POINT IN STICKING WITH THOSE WEAKLINGS?
THEY'LL JUST DRAG YOU DOWN AND WEAKEN YOU AGAIN.
YOU KNOW THAT.

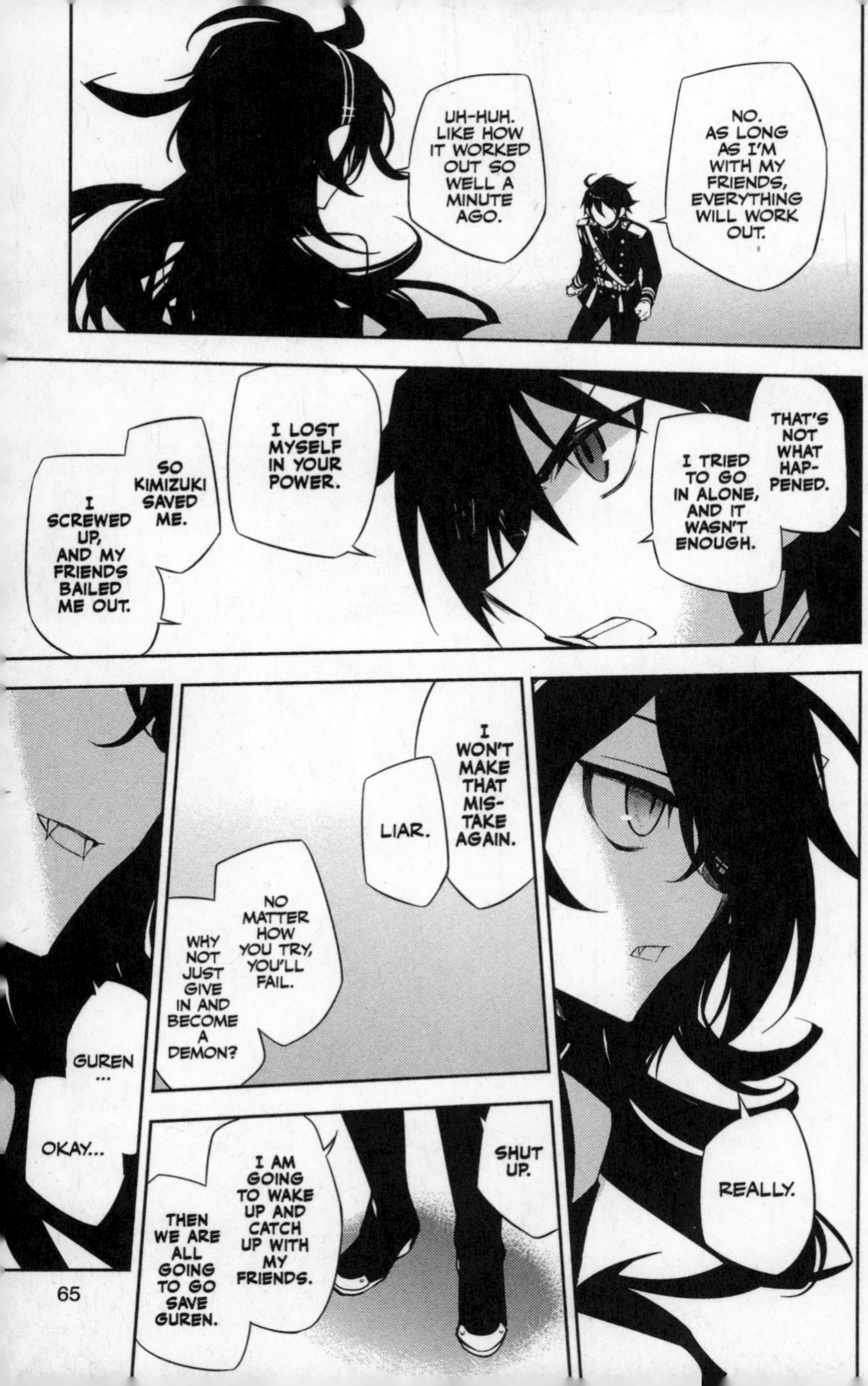
NO. AS LONG AS I'M WITH MY FRIENDS, EVERYTHING WILL WORK OUT.
UH-HUH. LIKE HOW IT WORKED OUT SO WELL A MINUTE AGO.
THAT'S NOT WHAT HAP-PENED.
I TRIED TO GO IN ALONE, AND IT WASN'T ENOUGH.
I LOST MYSELF IN YOUR POWER.
SO KIMIZUKI SAVED ME.
I SCREWED UP, AND MY FRIENDS BAILED ME OUT.
REALLY.
I WON'T MAKE THAT MIS-TAKE AGAIN.
LIAR.
NO MATTER HOW YOU TRY, YOU'LL FAIL.
WHY NOT JUST GIVE IN AND BECOME A DEMON?
SHUT UP.
I AM GOING TO WAKE UP AND CATCH UP WITH MY FRIENDS.
THEN WE ARE ALL GOING TO GO SAVE GUREN.
GUREN...
OKAY...

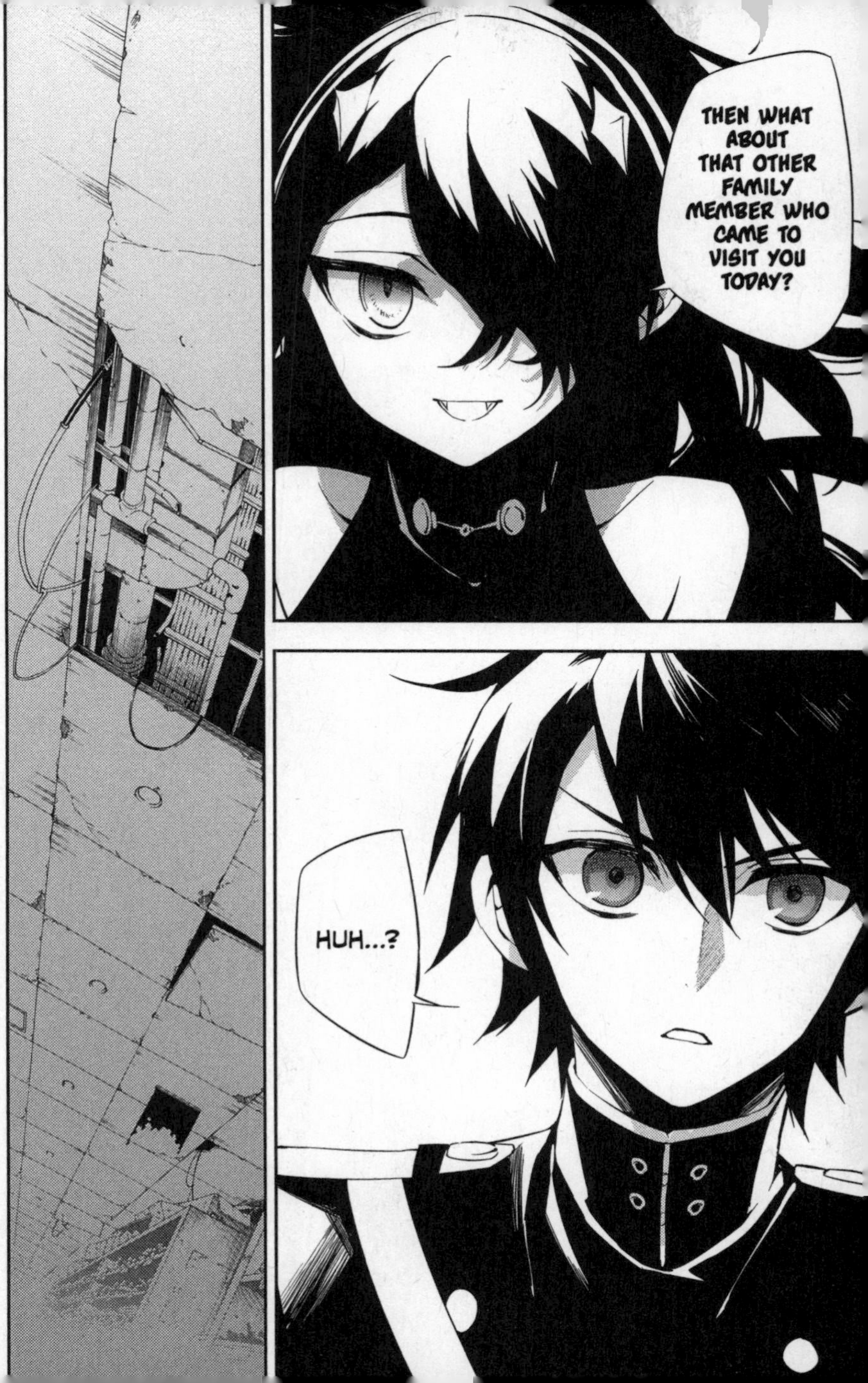
THEN WHAT ABOUT THAT OTHER FAMILY MEMBER WHO CAME TO VISIT YOU TODAY?
HUH...?

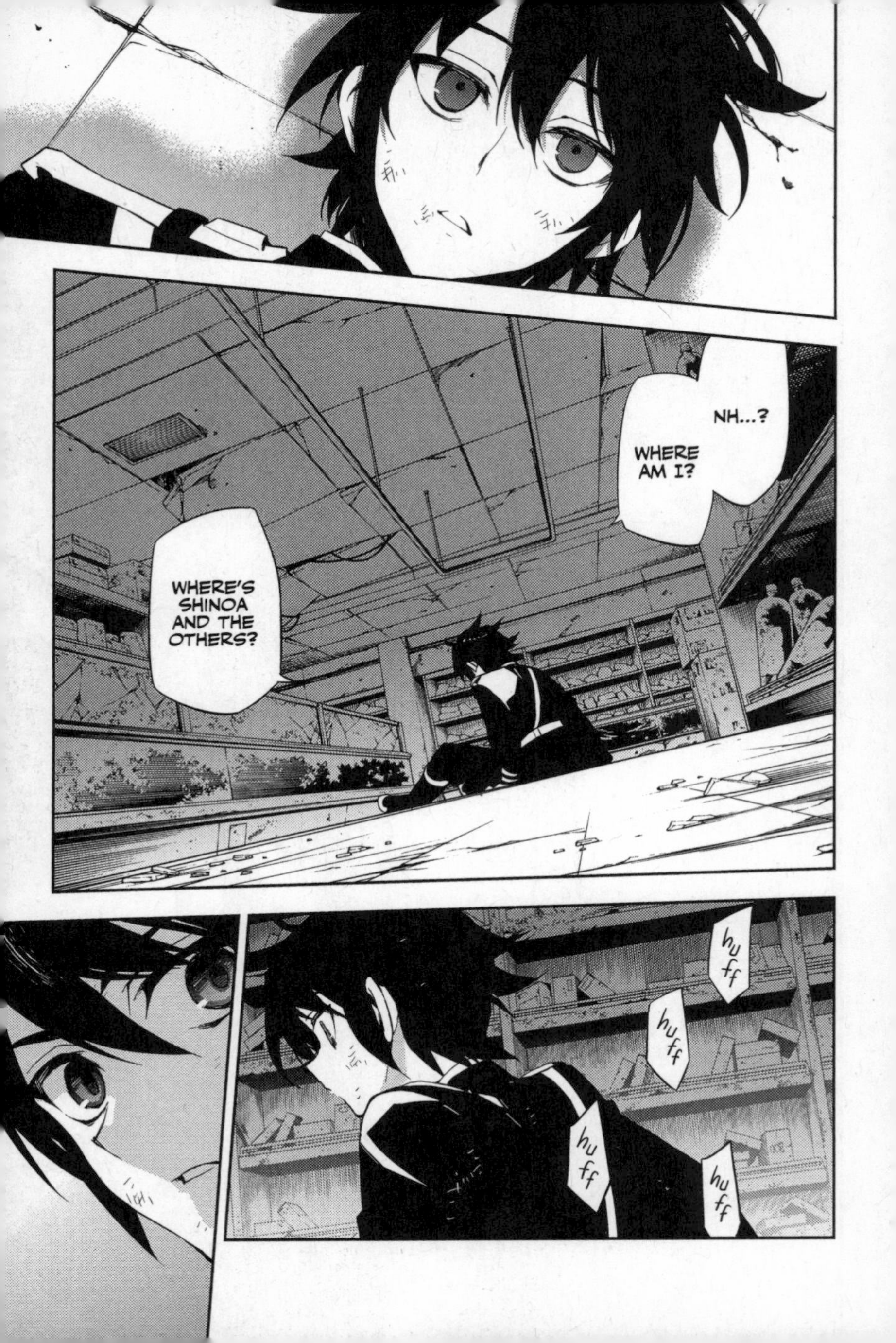
NH...?
WHERE AM I?
WHERE'S SHINOA AND THE OTHERS?
huff
huff
huff
huff

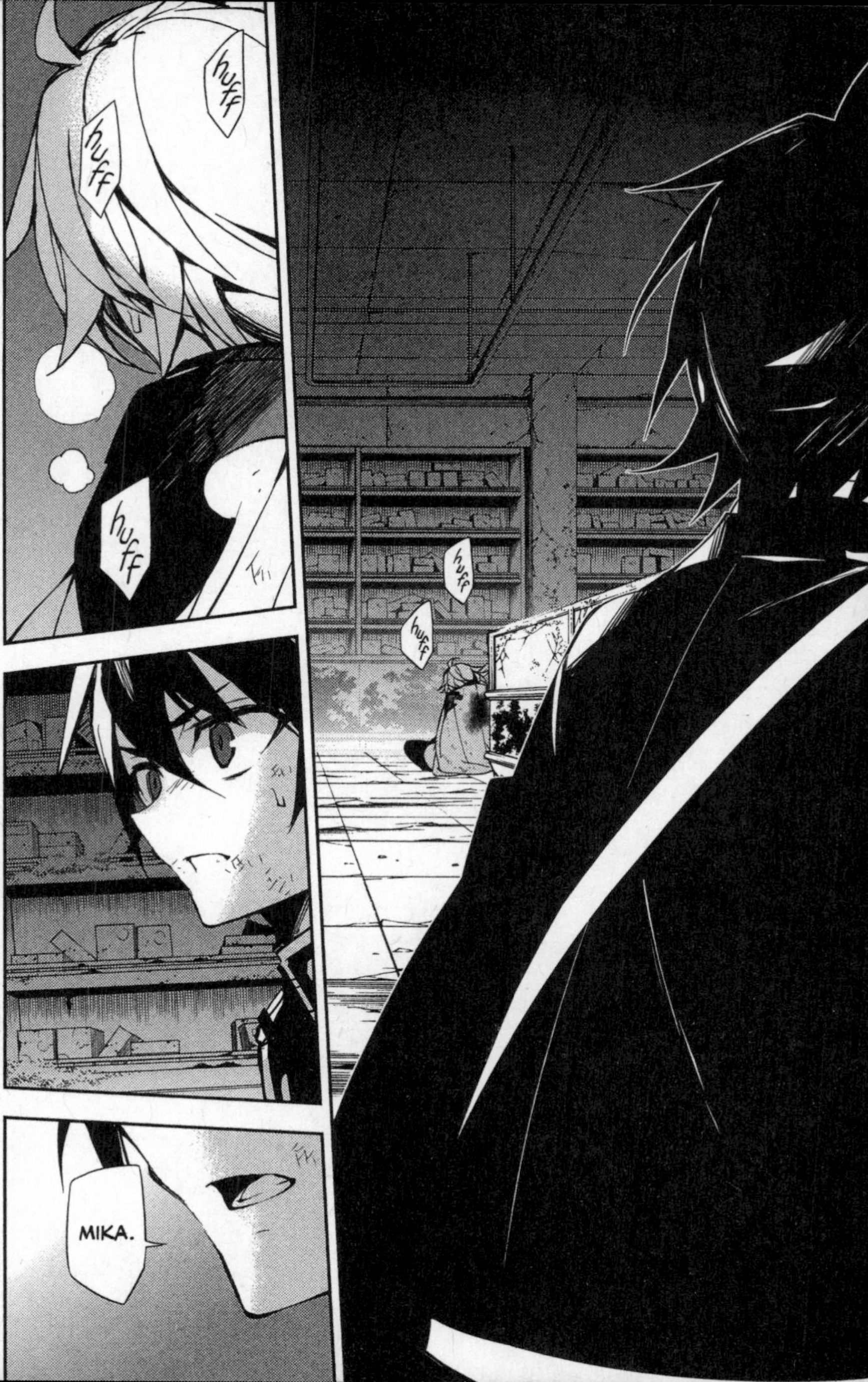
huff
huff
huff
huff
huff
MIKA.

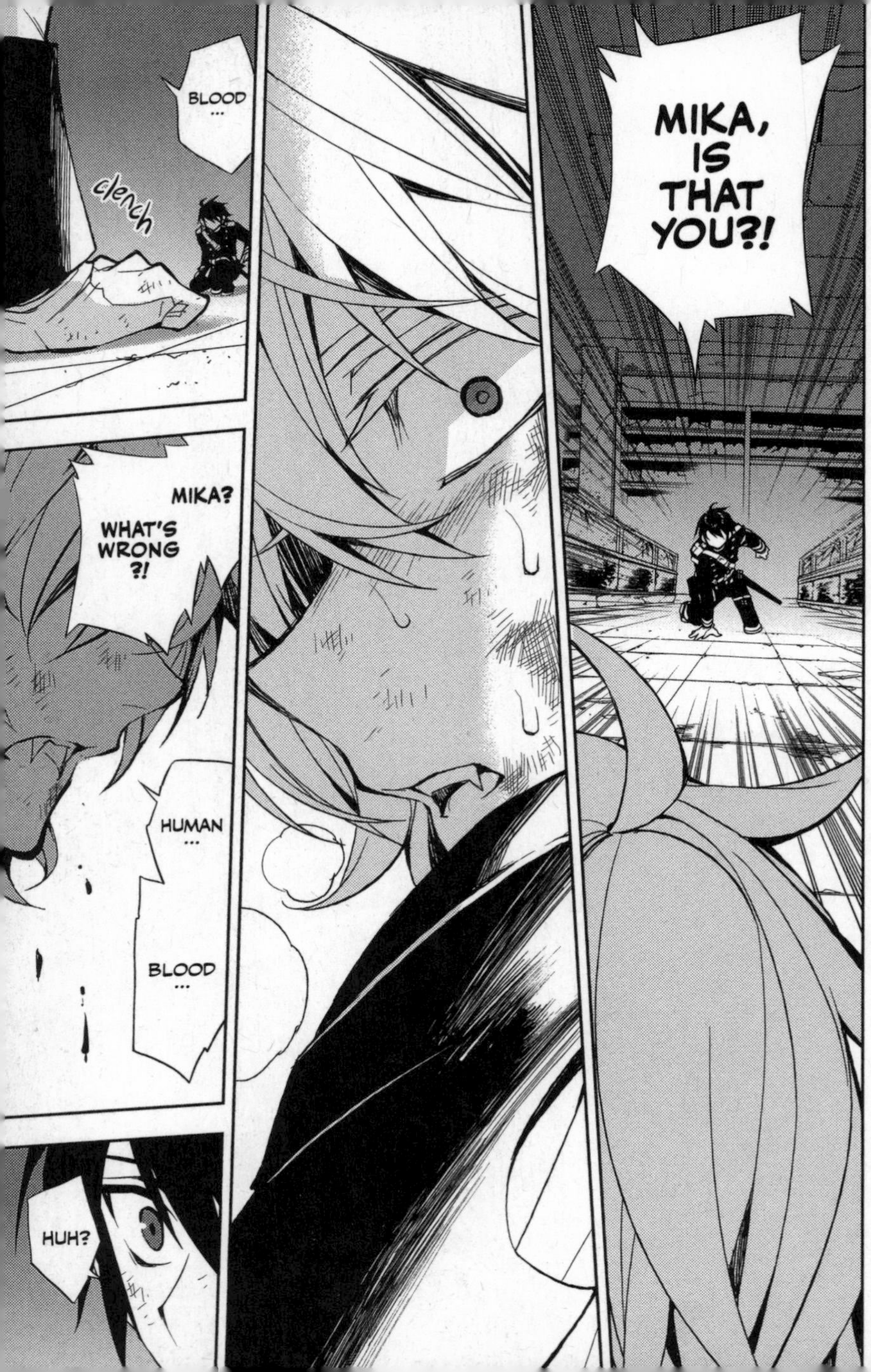
MIKA, IS THAT YOU?!
BLOOD...
clench
MIKA? WHAT'S WRONG?!
HUMAN...
BLOOD...
HUH?

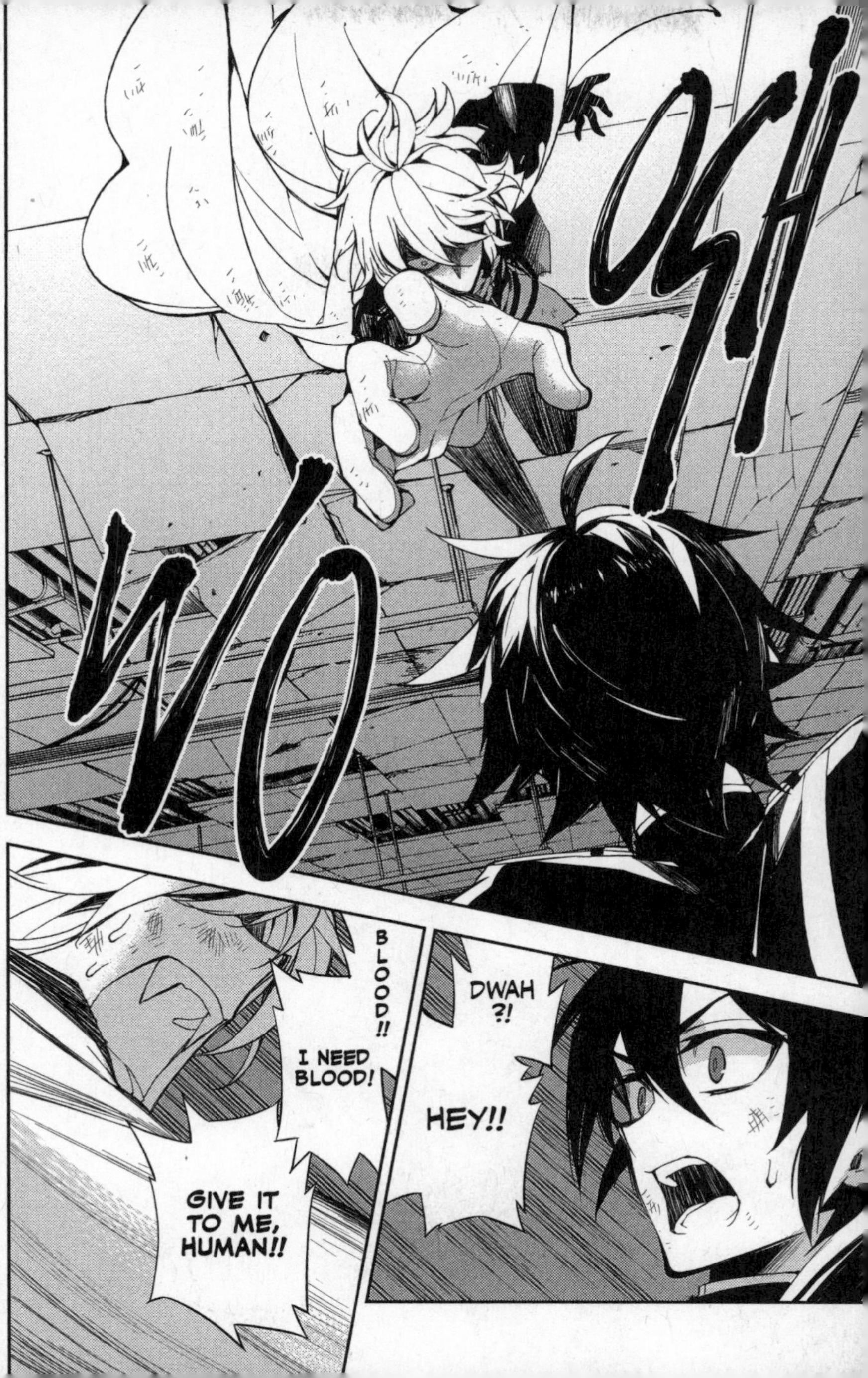
WOOSH
DWAH ?!
HEY!!
BLOOD!!
I NEED BLOOD!
GIVE IT TO ME, HUMAN!!

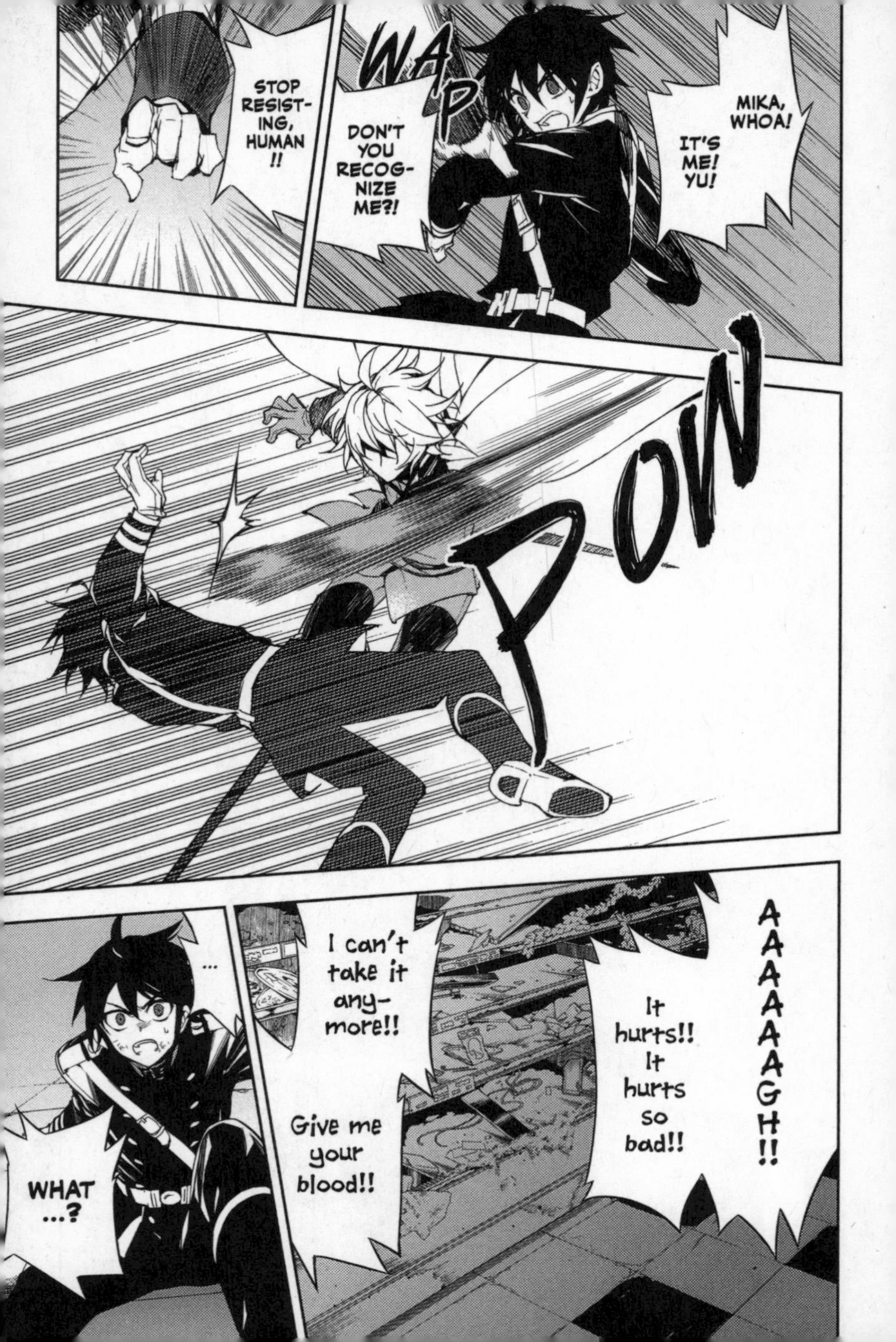
MIKA, WHOA!
IT'S ME! YU!
DON'T YOU RECOGNIZE ME?!
WAP
STOP RESISTING, HUMAN!!
POW
AAAAAAAGH!!
It hurts!! It hurts so bad!!
I can't take it anymore!!
Give me your blood!!
...
WHAT...?

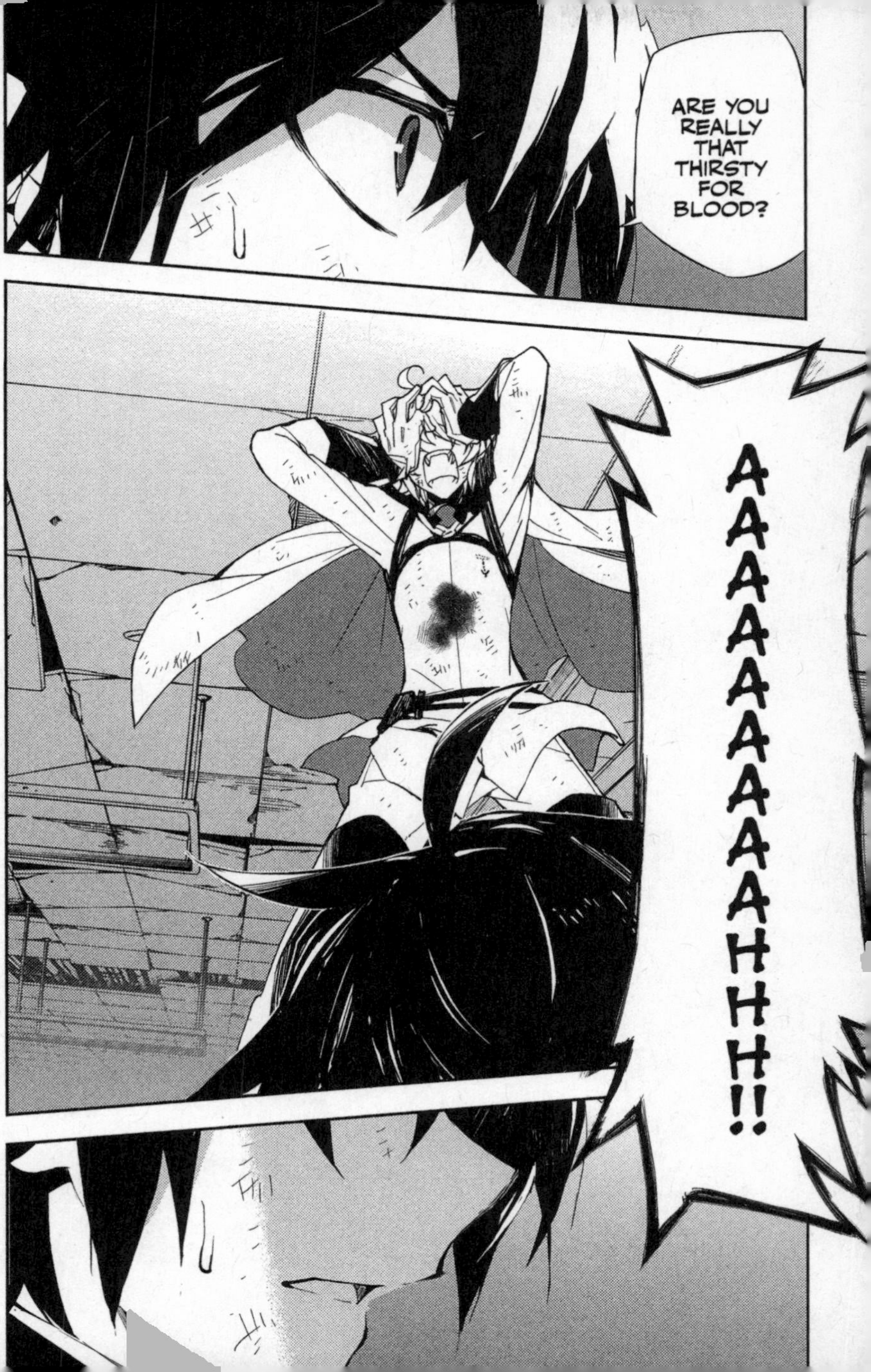
ARE YOU REALLY THAT THIRSTY FOR BLOOD?
AAAAAAAAAAAAHHH!!

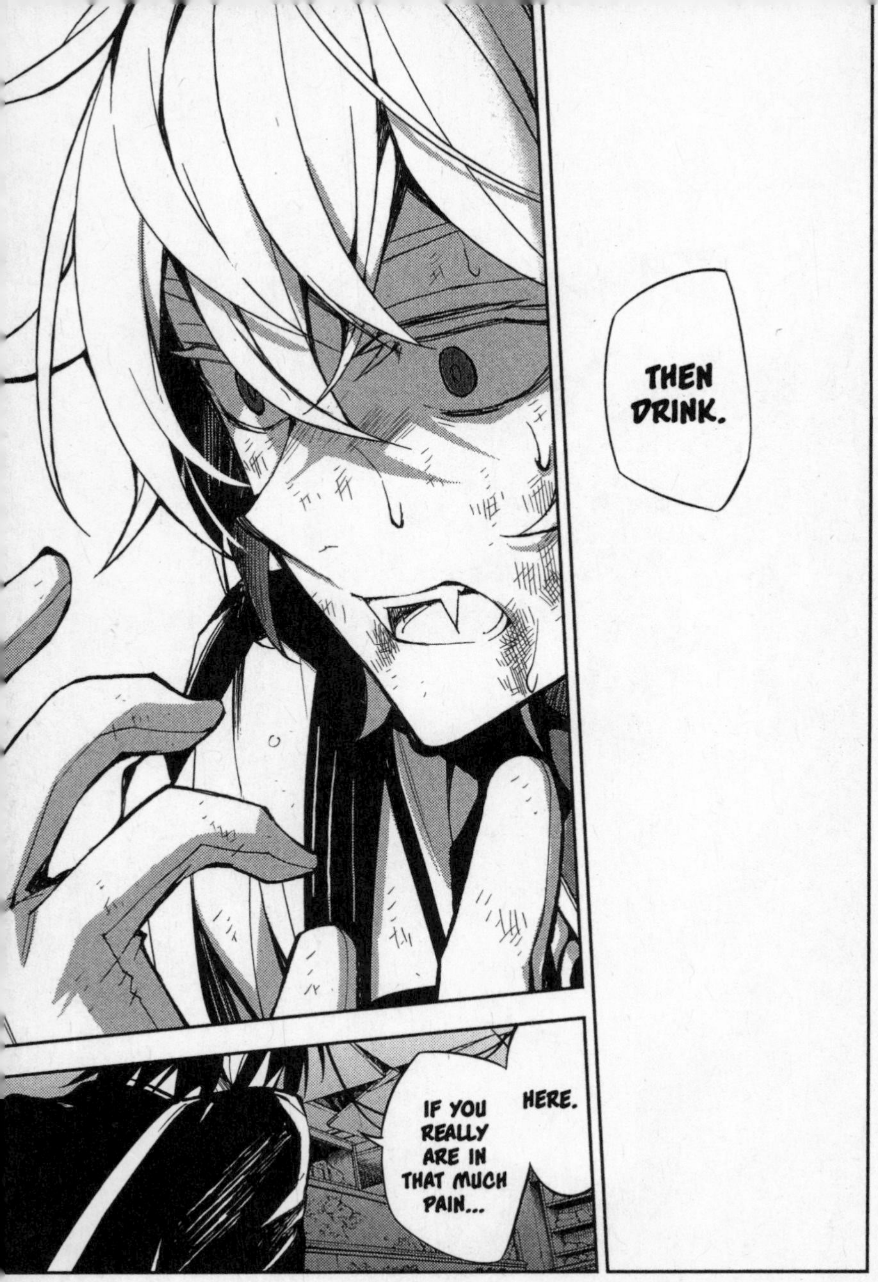
THEN DRINK.
IF YOU REALLY ARE IN THAT MUCH PAIN...
HERE.

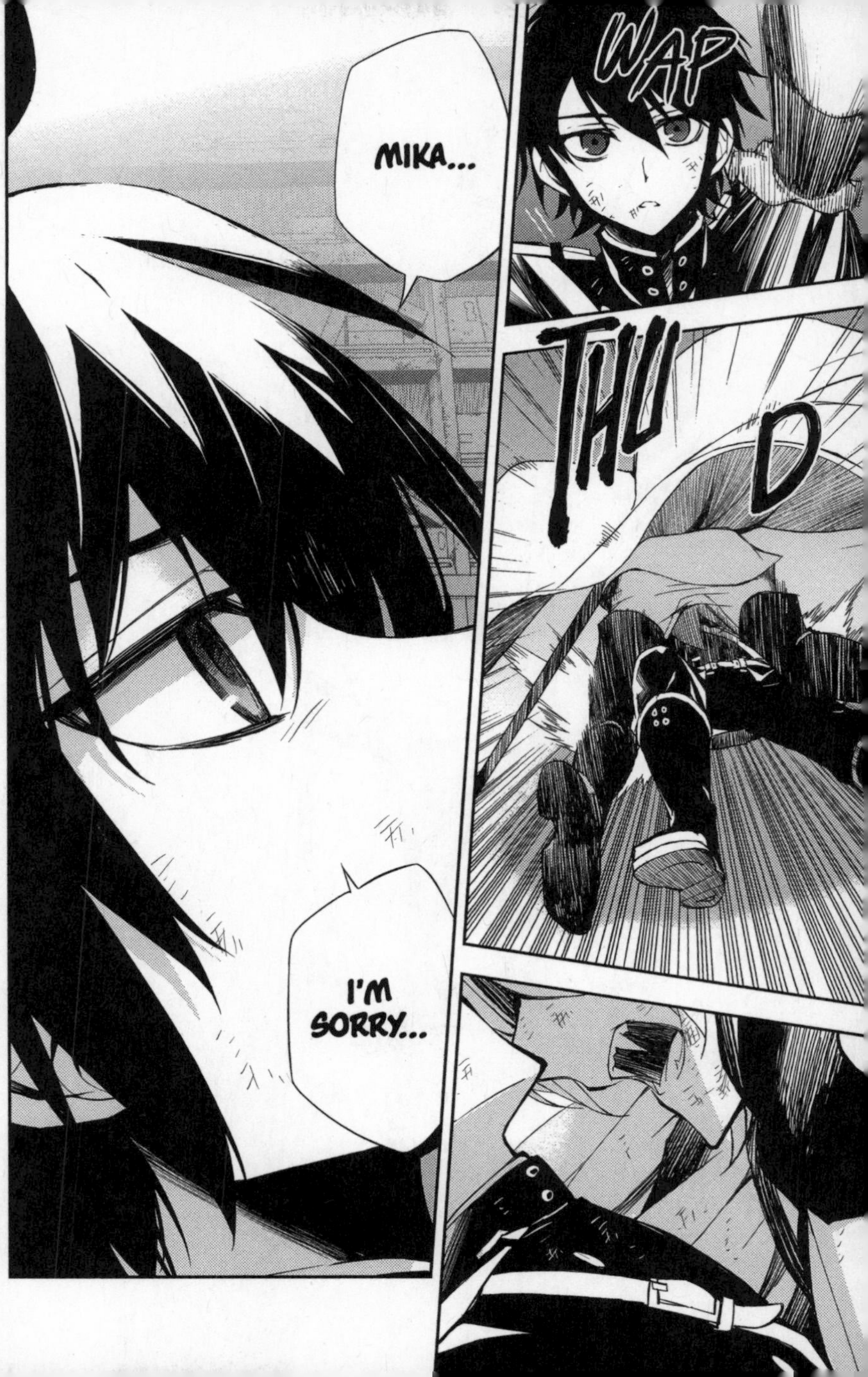
WAP
THUD
MIKA...
I'M SORRY...

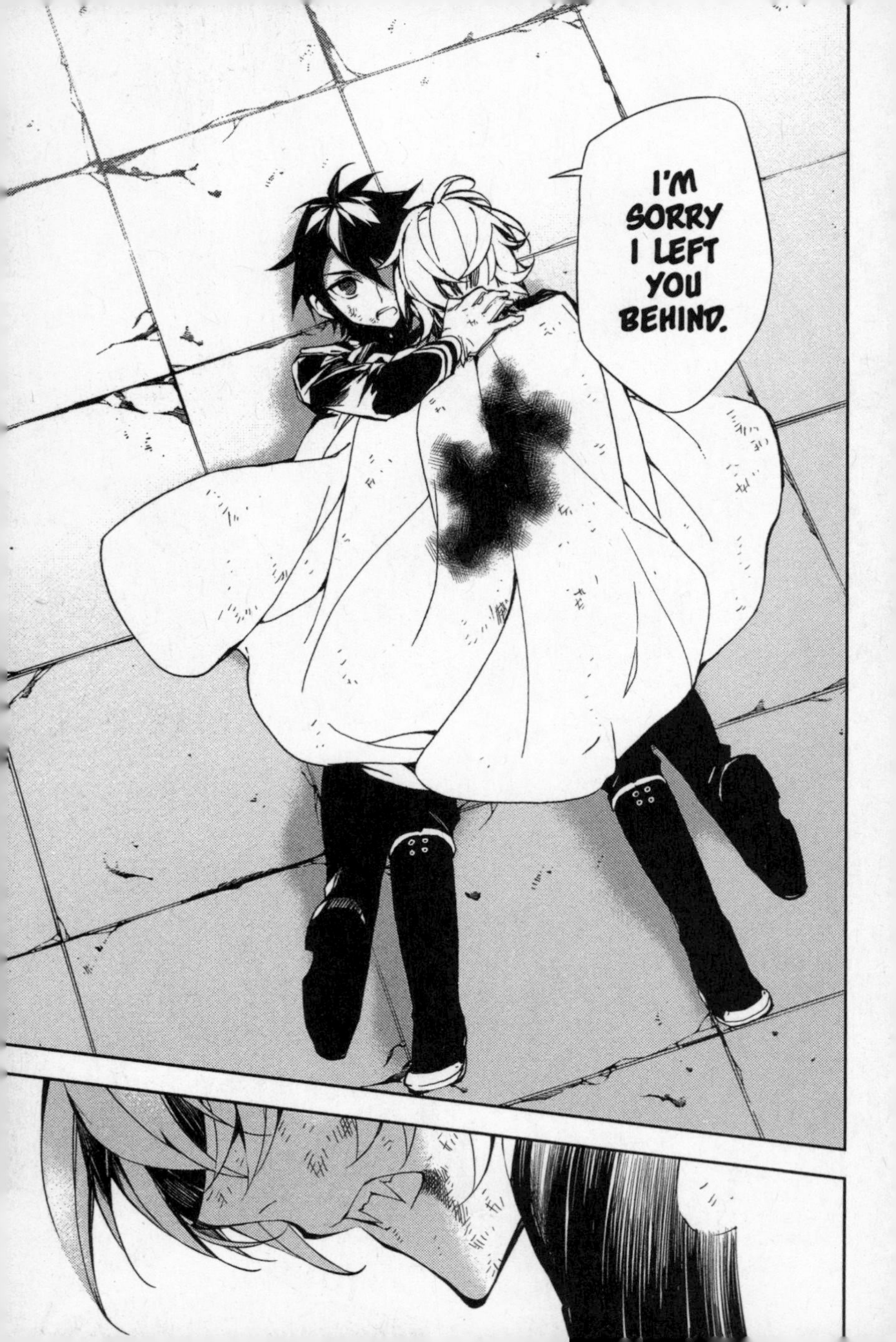
I'M SORRY I LEFT YOU BEHIND.

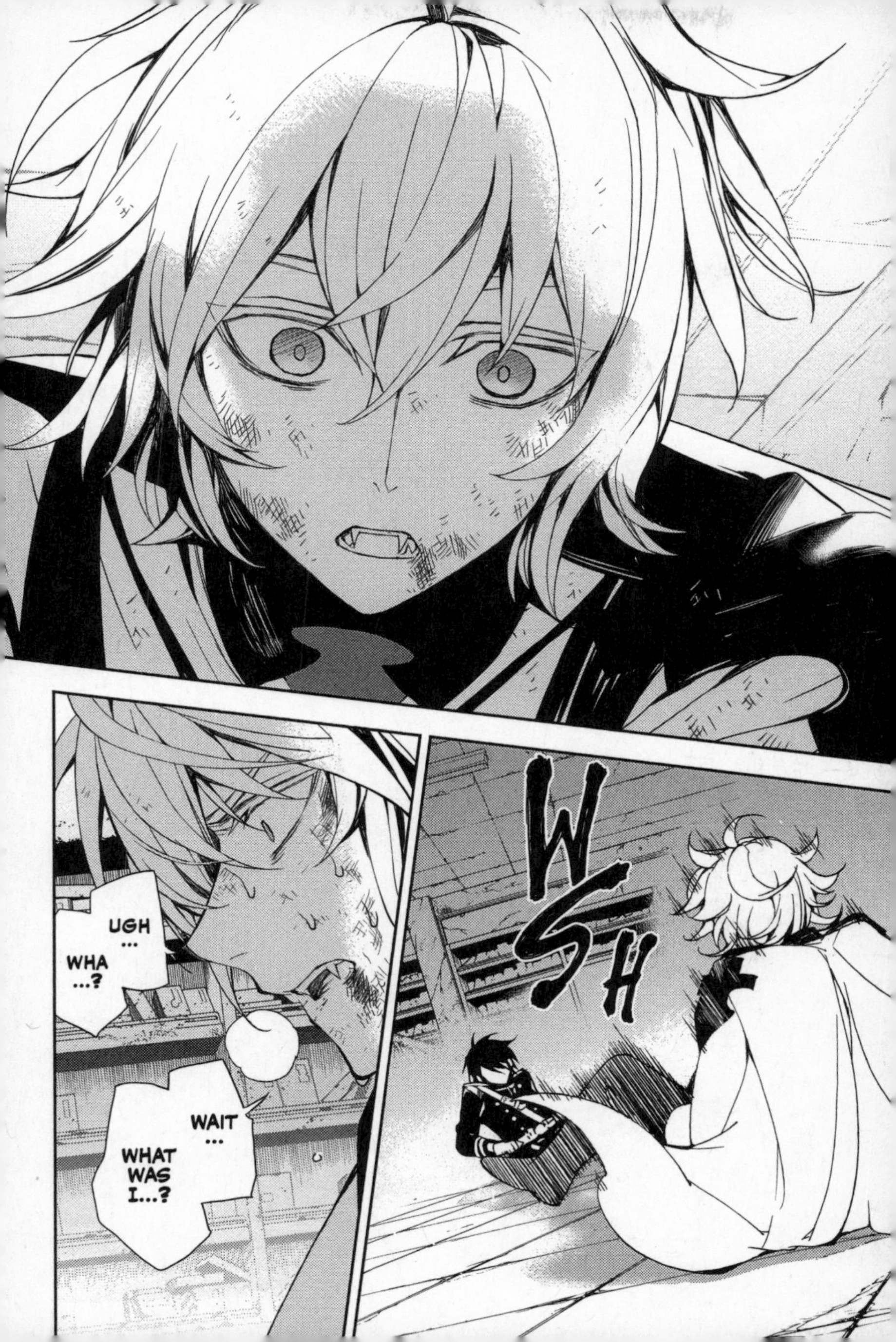
WSH
UGH... WHA...?
WAIT... WHAT WAS I...?

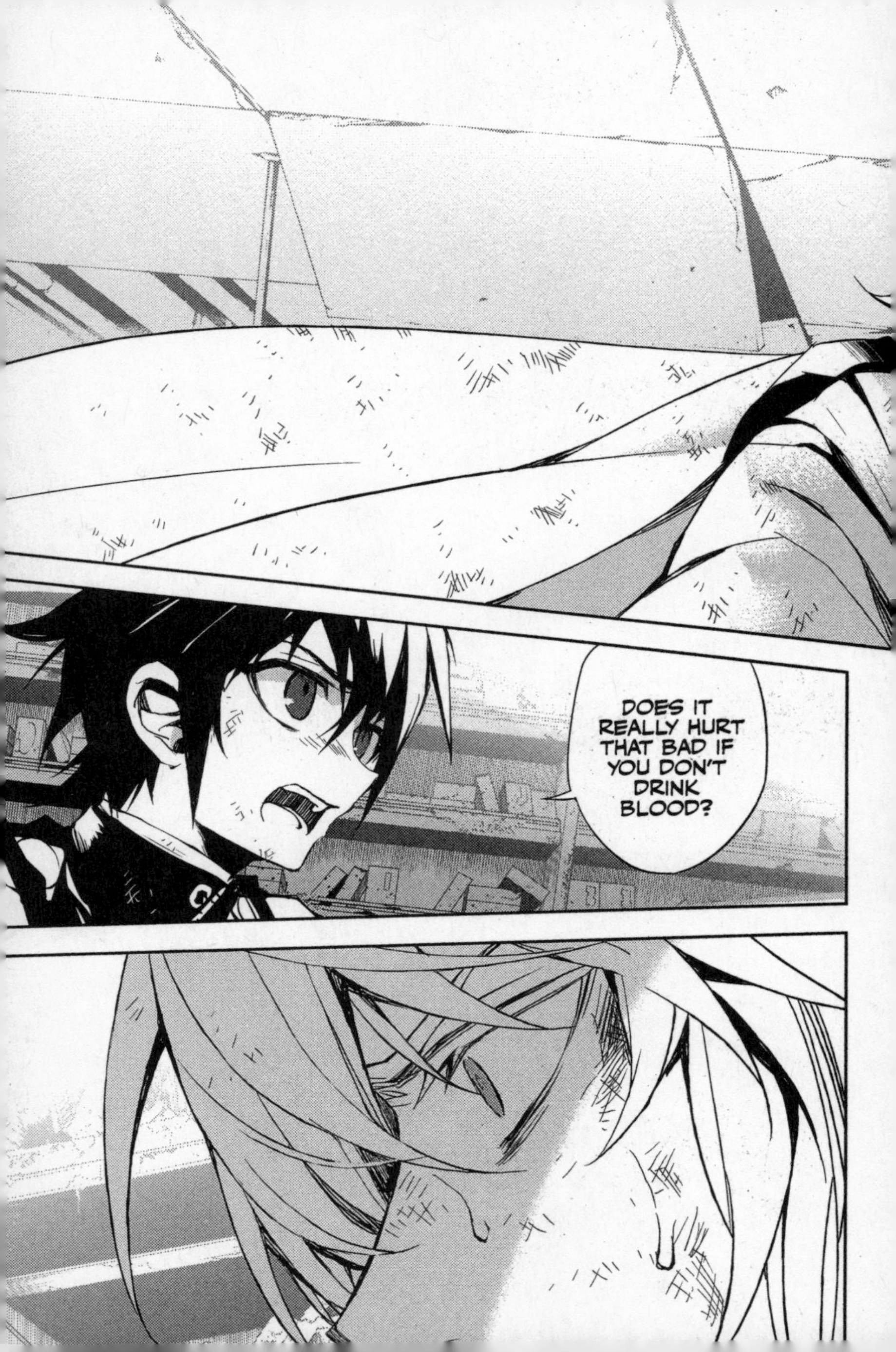
DOES IT REALLY HURT THAT BAD IF YOU DON'T DRINK BLOOD?

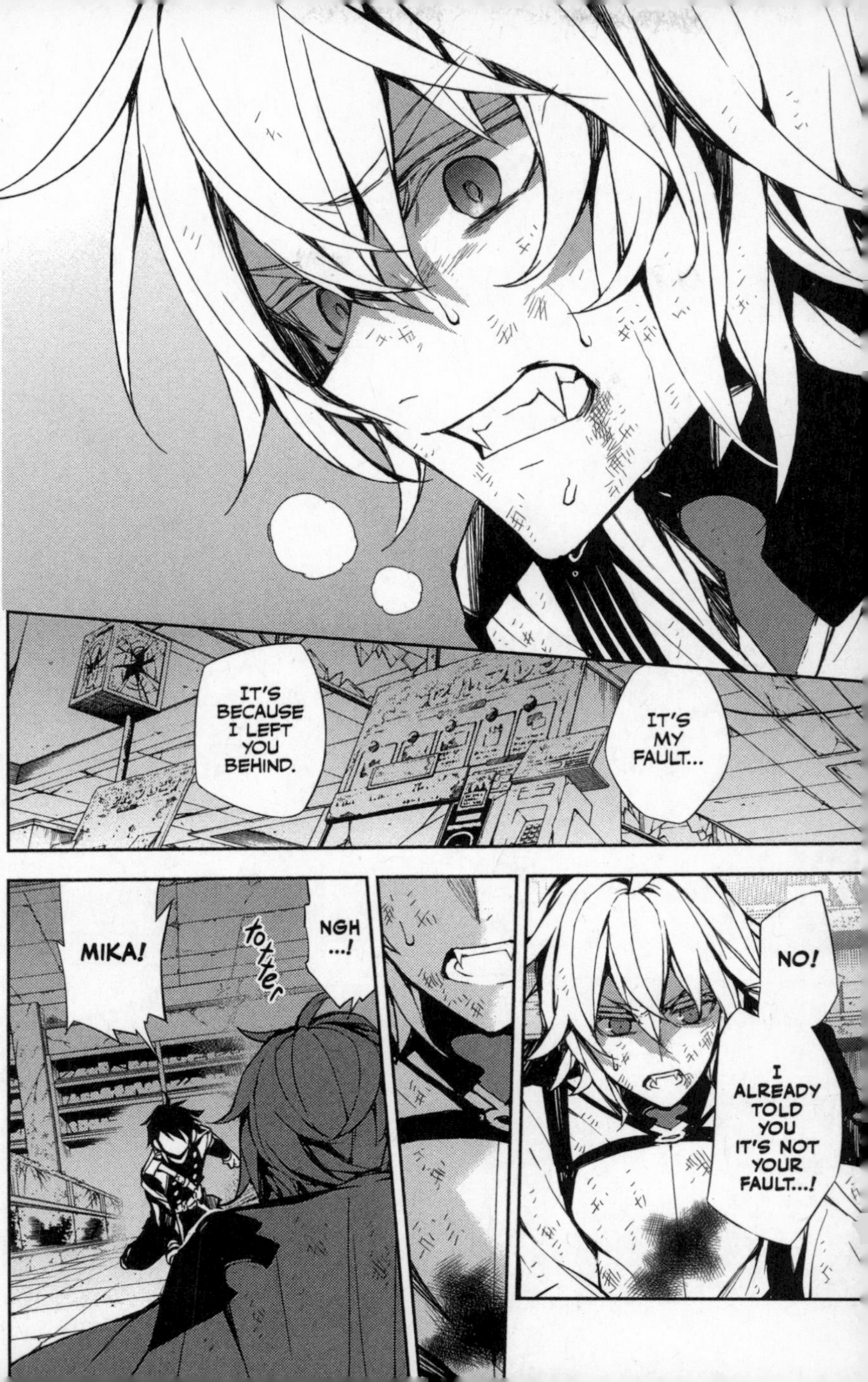
IT'S MY FAULT...
IT'S BECAUSE I LEFT YOU BEHIND.
NO!
I ALREADY TOLD YOU IT'S NOT YOUR FAULT...!
NGH ...!
totter
MIKA!

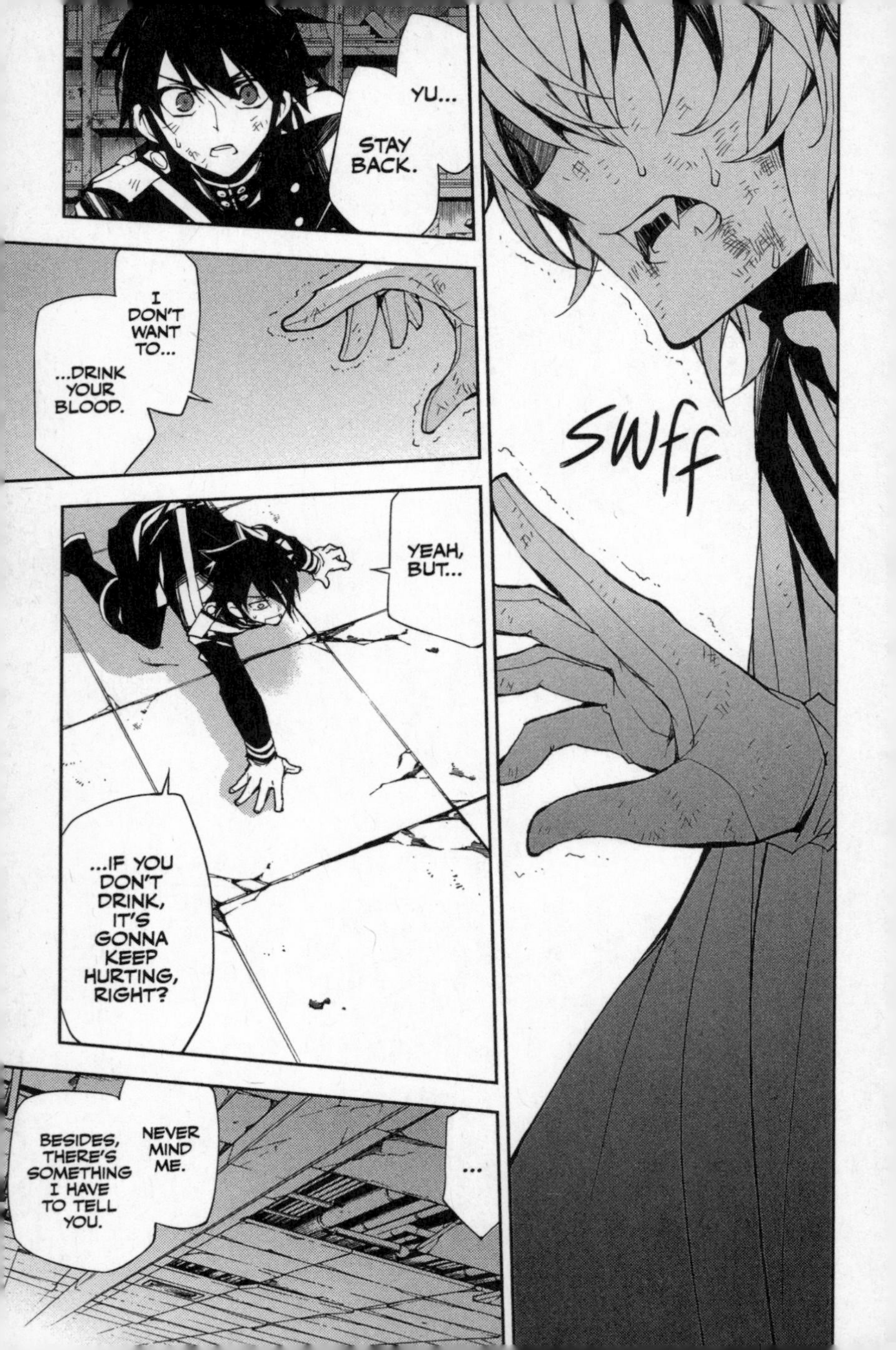
SWFF
YU...
STAY BACK.
I DON'T WANT TO...
...DRINK YOUR BLOOD.
YEAH, BUT...
...IF YOU DON'T DRINK, IT'S GONNA KEEP HURTING, RIGHT?
...
NEVER MIND ME.
BESIDES, THERE'S SOMETHING I HAVE TO TELL YOU.

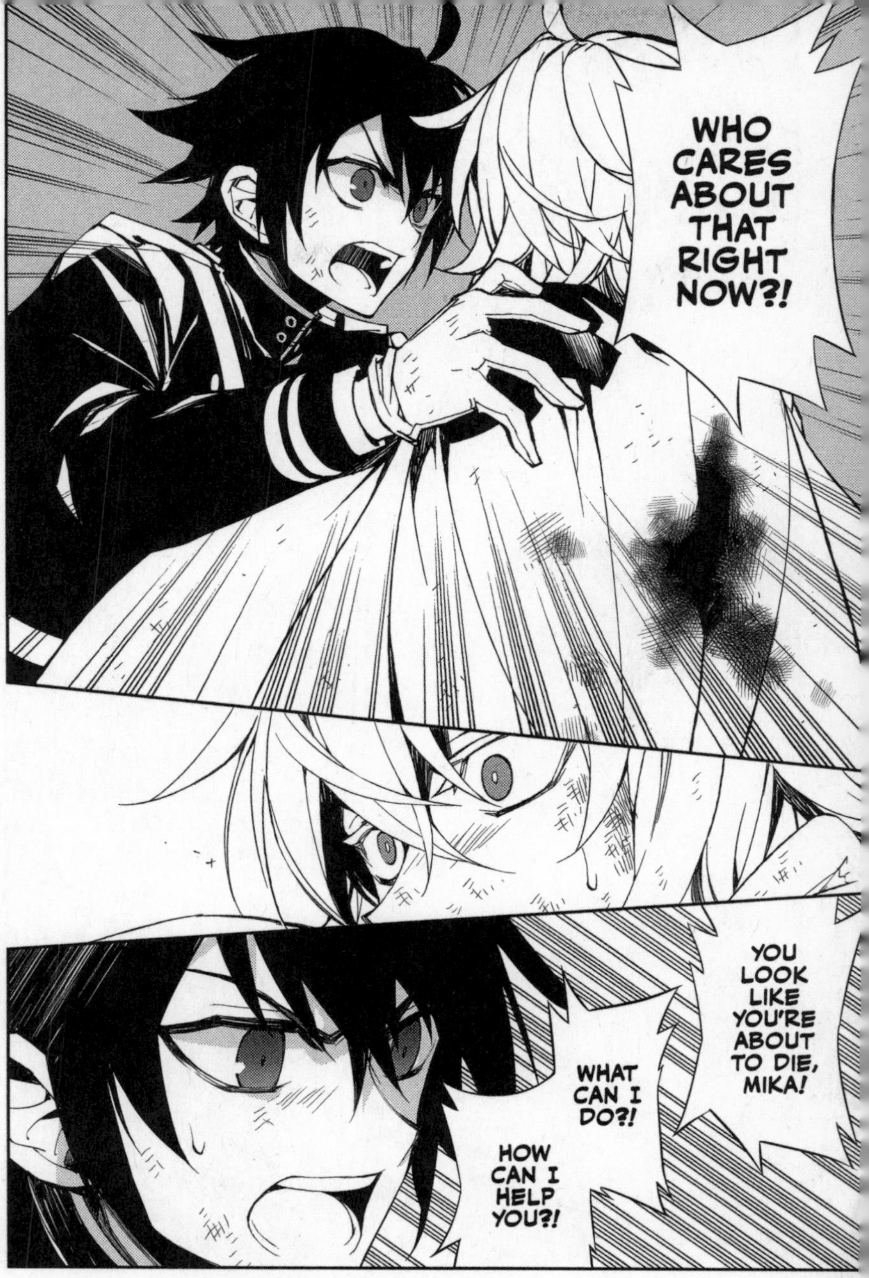
WHO CARES ABOUT THAT RIGHT NOW?!
YOU LOOK LIKE YOU'RE ABOUT TO DIE, MIKA!
WHAT CAN I DO?!
HOW CAN I HELP YOU?!

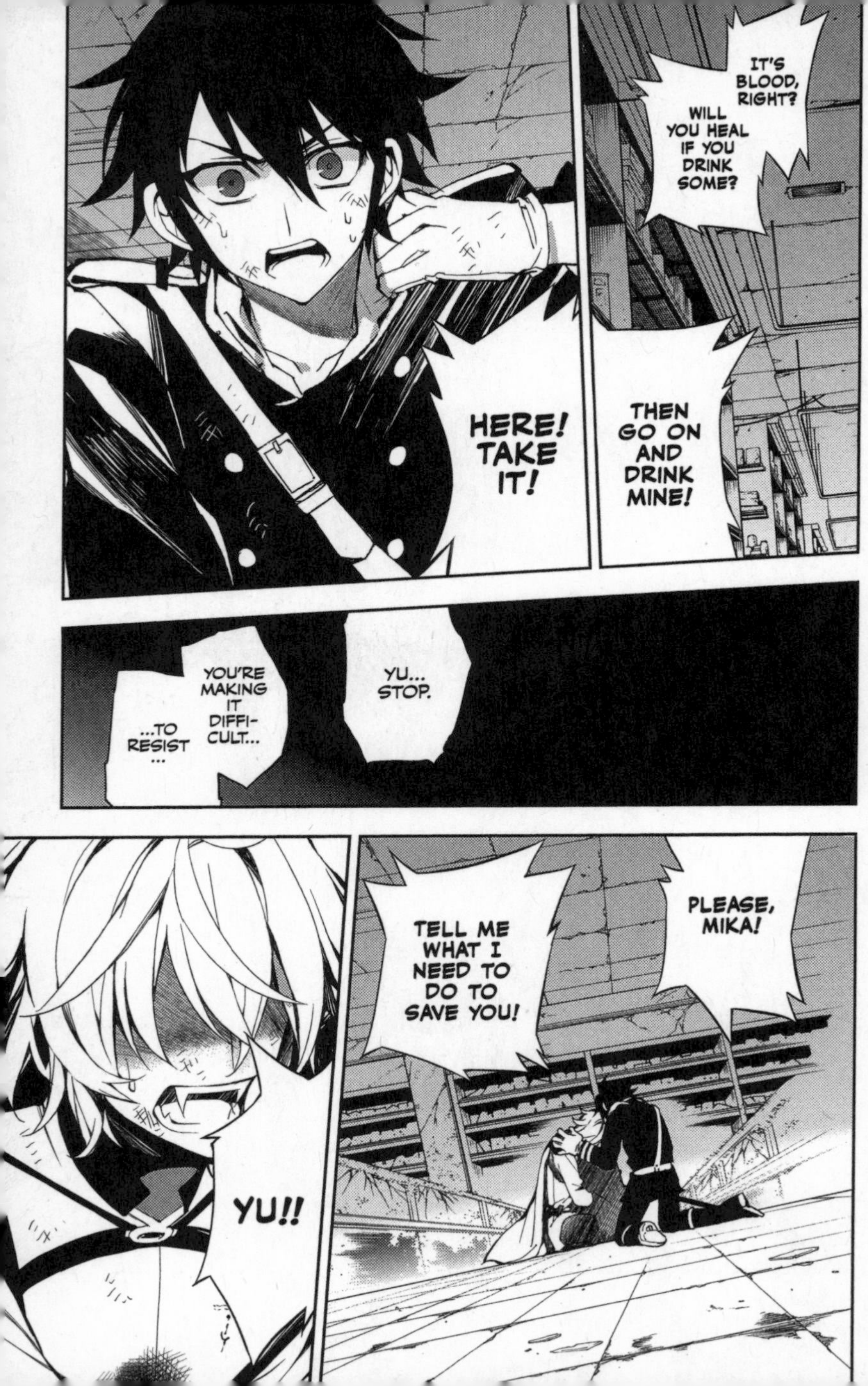
IT'S BLOOD, RIGHT?
WILL YOU HEAL IF YOU DRINK SOME?
THEN GO ON AND DRINK MINE!
HERE! TAKE IT!
YU... STOP.
YOU'RE MAKING IT DIFFI-CULT...
...TO RESIST...
PLEASE, MIKA!
TELL ME WHAT I NEED TO DO TO SAVE YOU!
YU!!

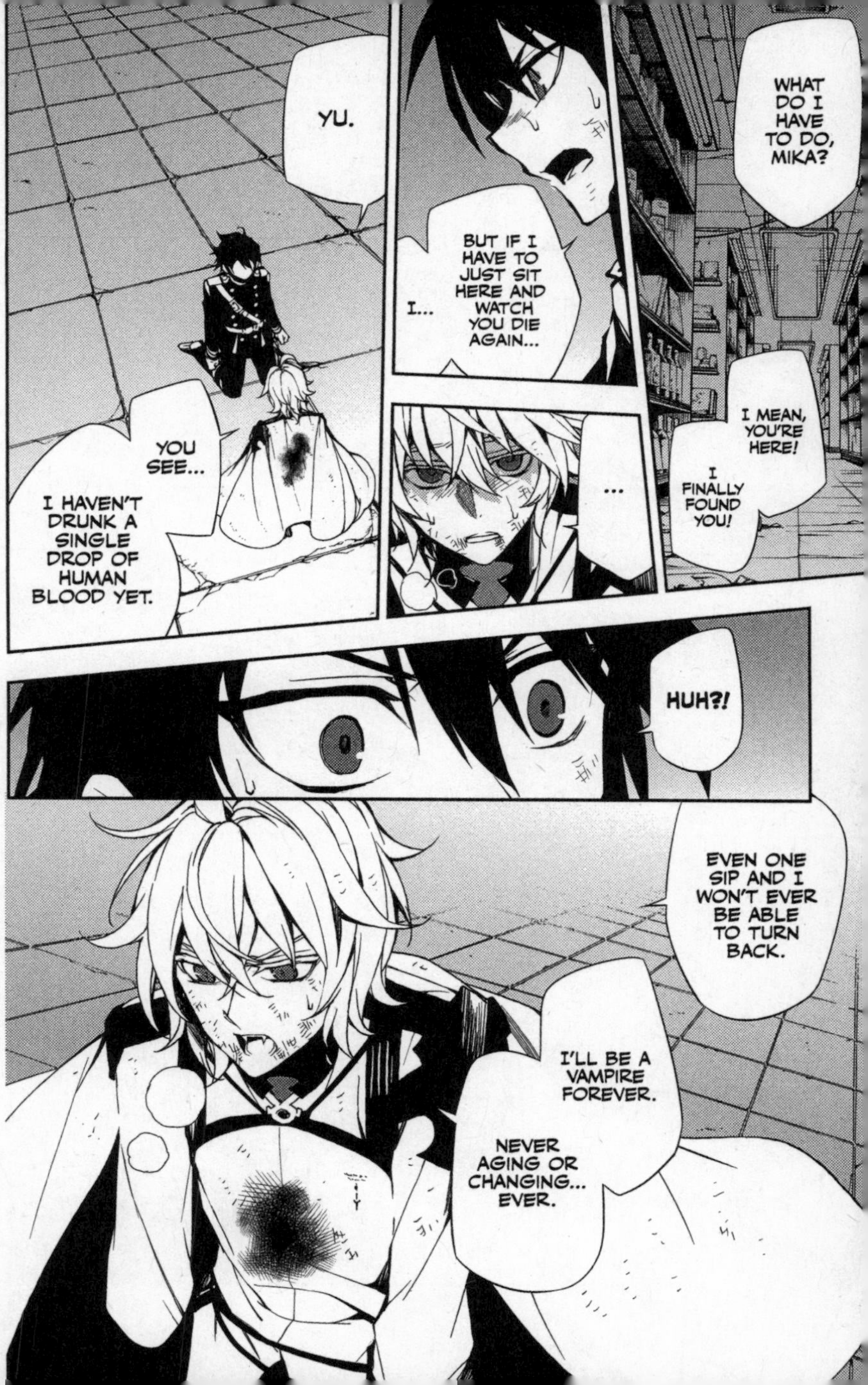
WHAT DO I HAVE TO DO, MIKA?
I MEAN, YOU'RE HERE!
I FINALLY FOUND YOU!
BUT IF I HAVE TO JUST SIT HERE AND WATCH YOU DIE AGAIN...
I...
...
YU.
YOU SEE...
I HAVEN'T DRUNK A SINGLE DROP OF HUMAN BLOOD YET.
HUH?!
EVEN ONE SIP AND I WON'T EVER BE ABLE TO TURN BACK.
I'LL BE A VAMPIRE FOREVER.
NEVER AGING OR CHANGING... EVER.

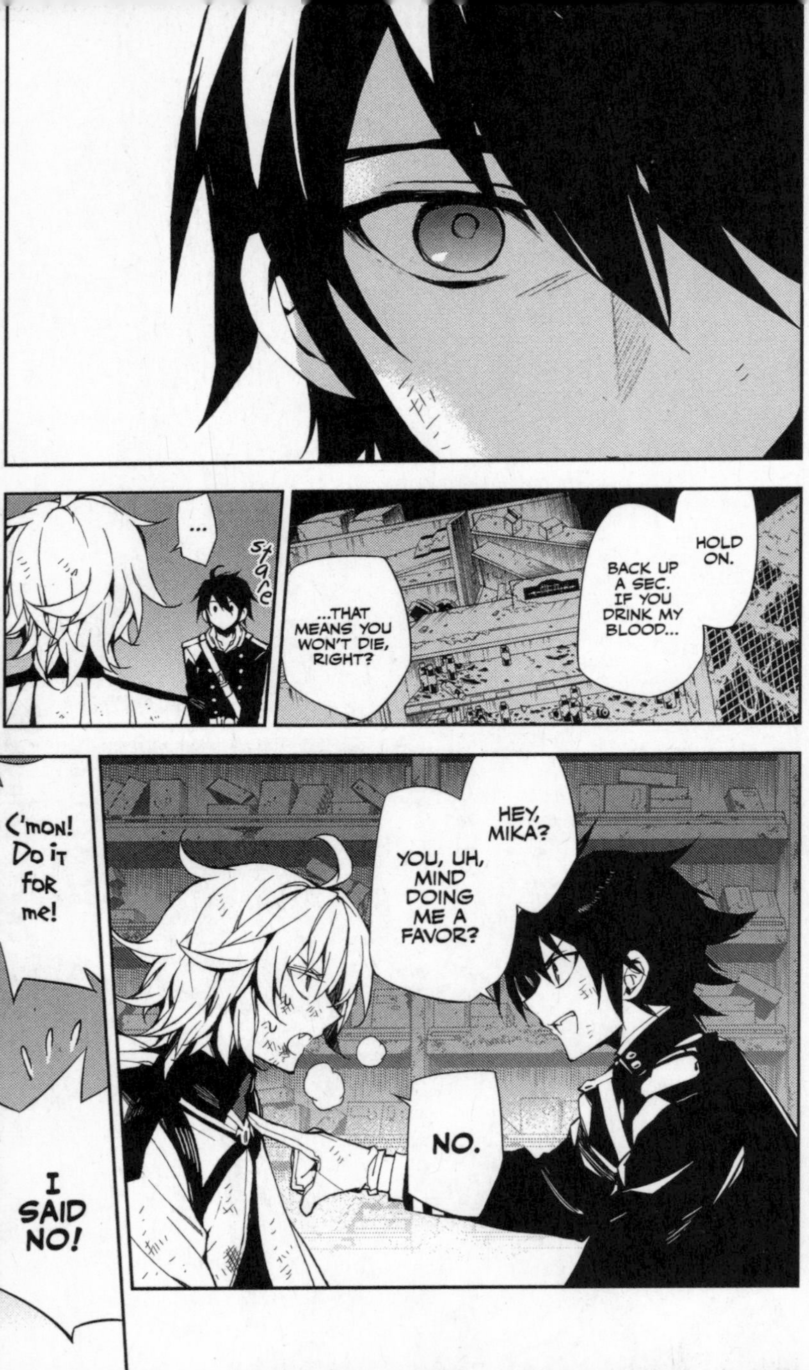
HOLD ON.
BACK UP A SEC. IF YOU DRINK MY BLOOD...
...THAT MEANS YOU WON'T DIE, RIGHT?
...
stare
HEY, MIKA?
YOU, UH, MIND DOING ME A FAVOR?
NO.
C'mon! Do it for me!
I SAID NO!

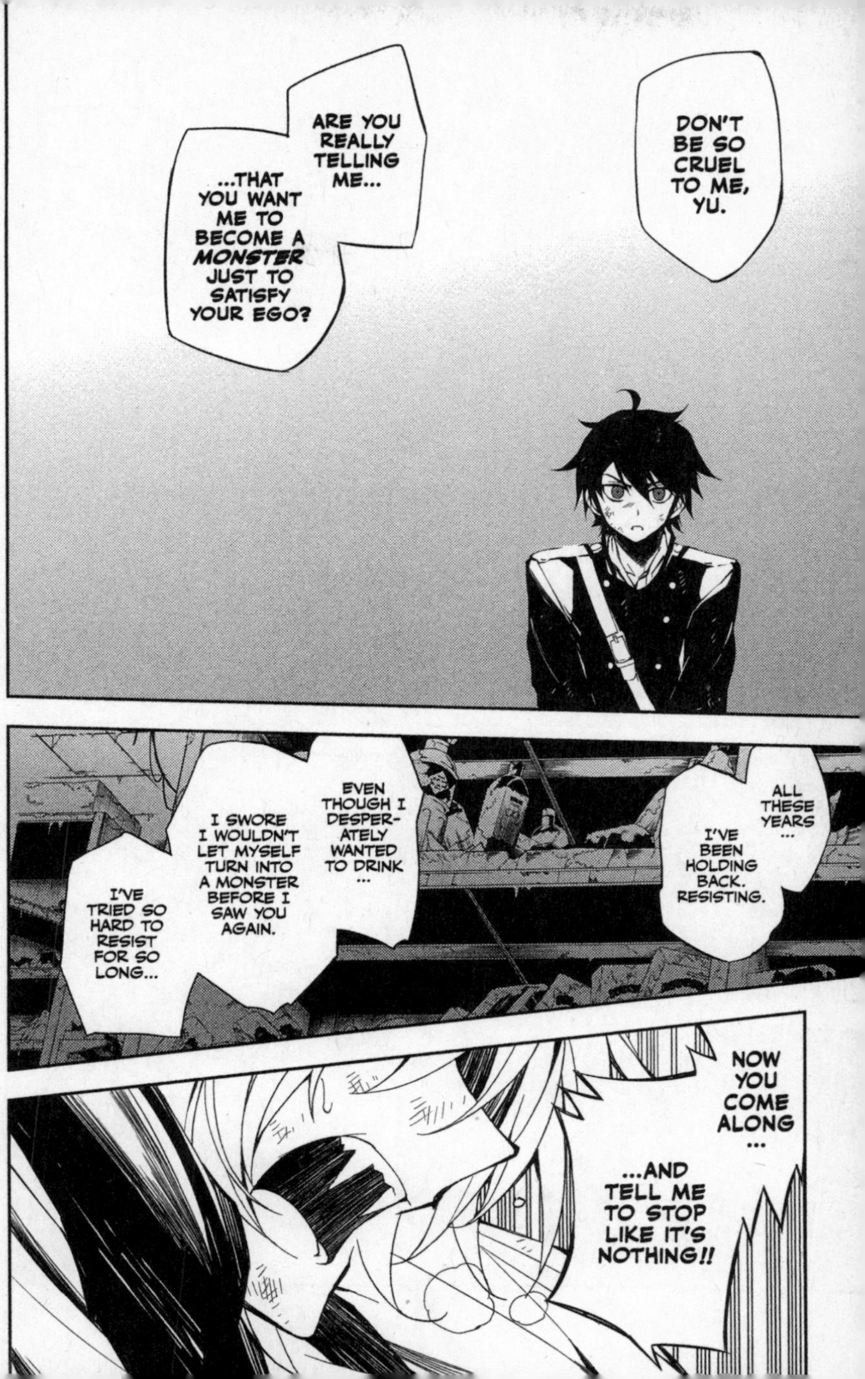
DON'T BE SO CRUEL TO ME, YU.
ARE YOU REALLY TELLING ME...
...THAT YOU WANT ME TO BECOME A *MONSTER* JUST TO SATISFY YOUR EGO?
ALL THESE YEARS...
I'VE BEEN HOLDING BACK. RESISTING.
EVEN THOUGH I DESPER-ATELY WANTED TO DRINK...
I SWORE I WOULDN'T LET MYSELF TURN INTO A MONSTER BEFORE I SAW YOU AGAIN.
I'VE TRIED SO HARD TO RESIST FOR SO LONG...
NOW YOU COME ALONG...
...AND TELL ME TO STOP LIKE IT'S NOTHING!!

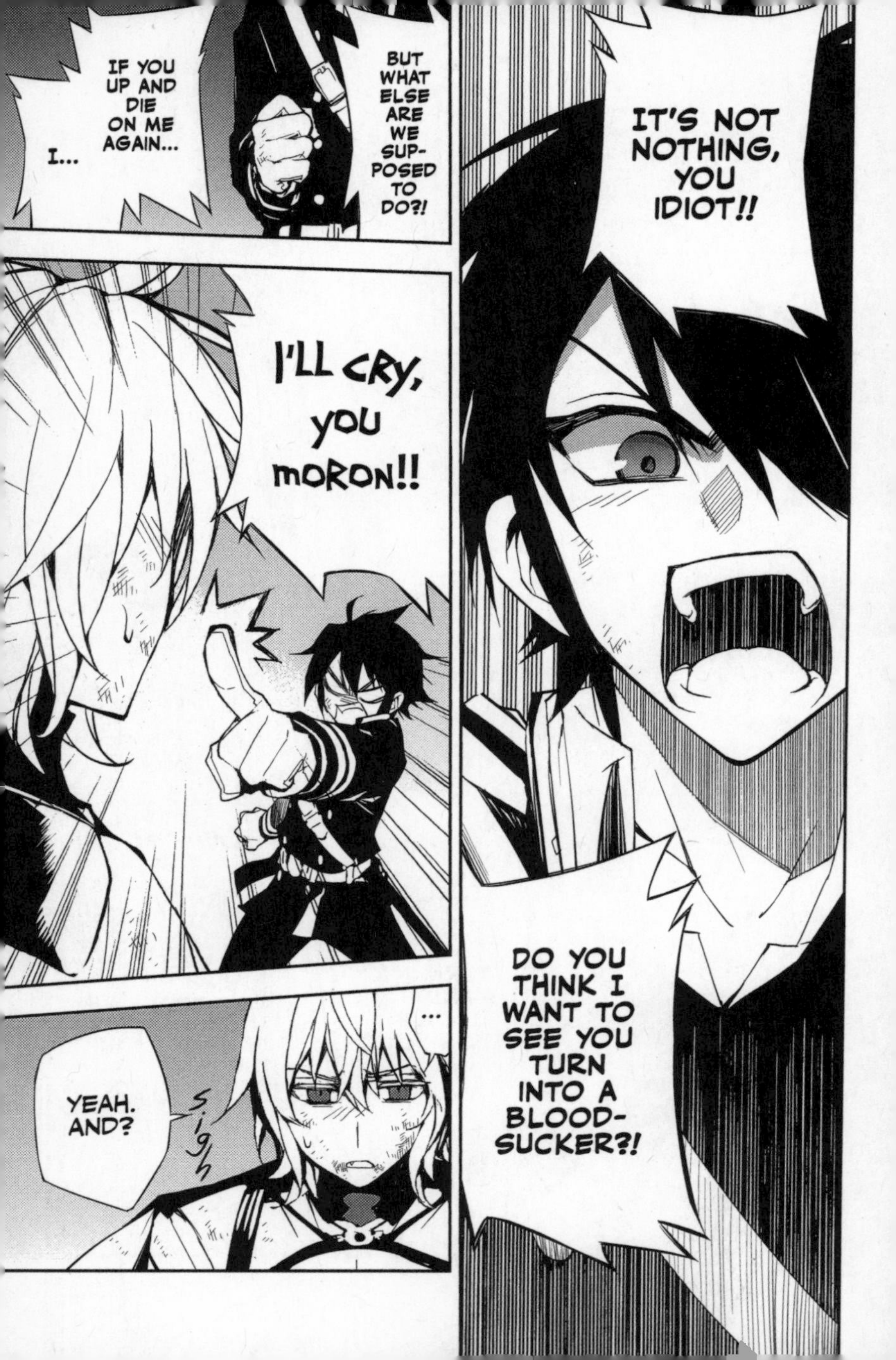
IT'S NOT NOTHING, YOU IDIOT!!
DO YOU THINK I WANT TO SEE YOU TURN INTO A BLOOD-SUCKER?!
BUT WHAT ELSE ARE WE SUP-POSED TO DO?!
IF YOU UP AND DIE ON ME AGAIN... I...
I'LL CRY, YOU MORON!!
...
sigh
YEAH. AND?

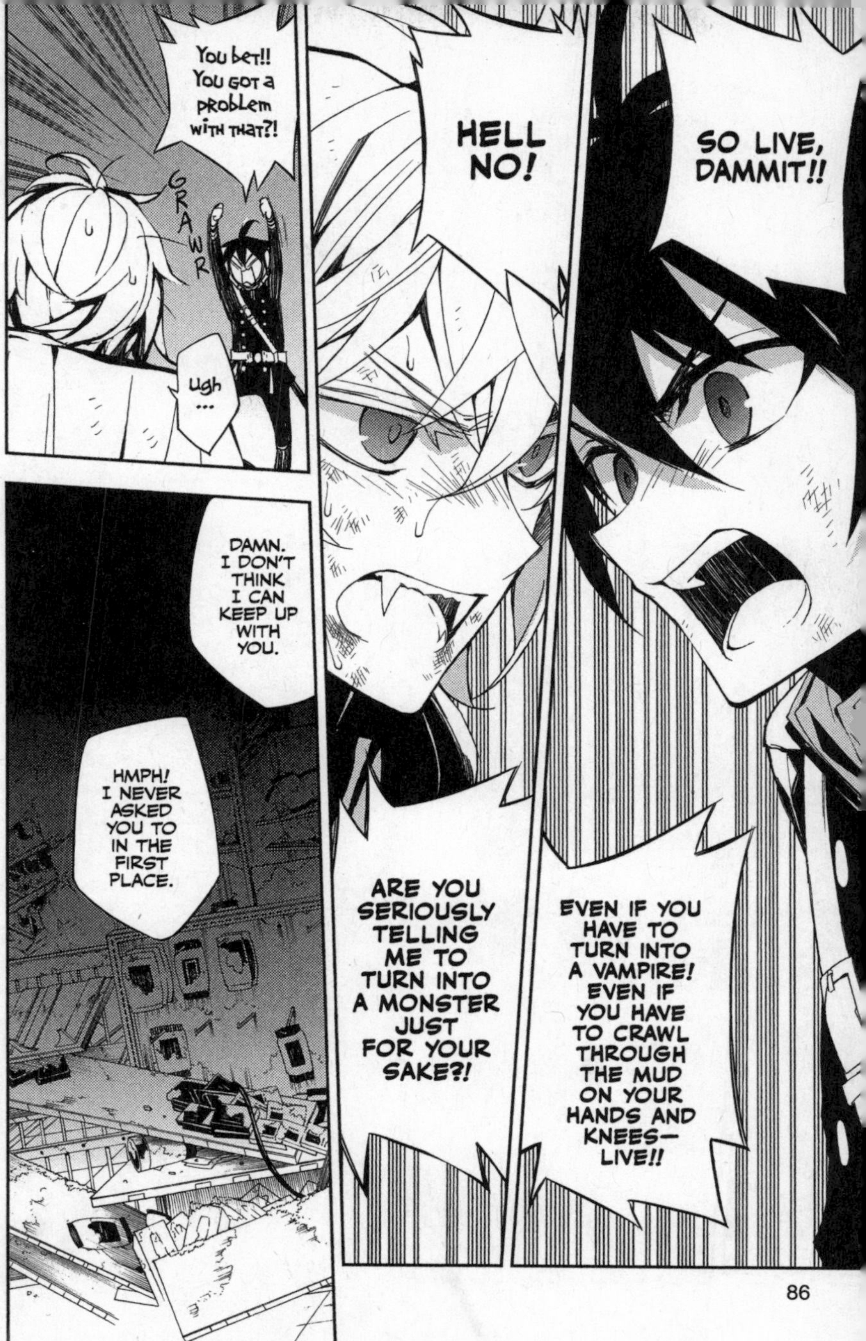
SO LIVE, DAMMIT!!
EVEN IF YOU HAVE TO TURN INTO A VAMPIRE! EVEN IF YOU HAVE TO CRAWL THROUGH THE MUD ON YOUR HANDS AND KNEES—LIVE!!
HELL NO!
ARE YOU SERIOUSLY TELLING ME TO TURN INTO A MONSTER JUST FOR YOUR SAKE?!
You bet!! You got a problem with that?!
GRAWR
Ugh...
DAMN. I DON'T THINK I CAN KEEP UP WITH YOU.
HMPH! I NEVER ASKED YOU TO IN THE FIRST PLACE.

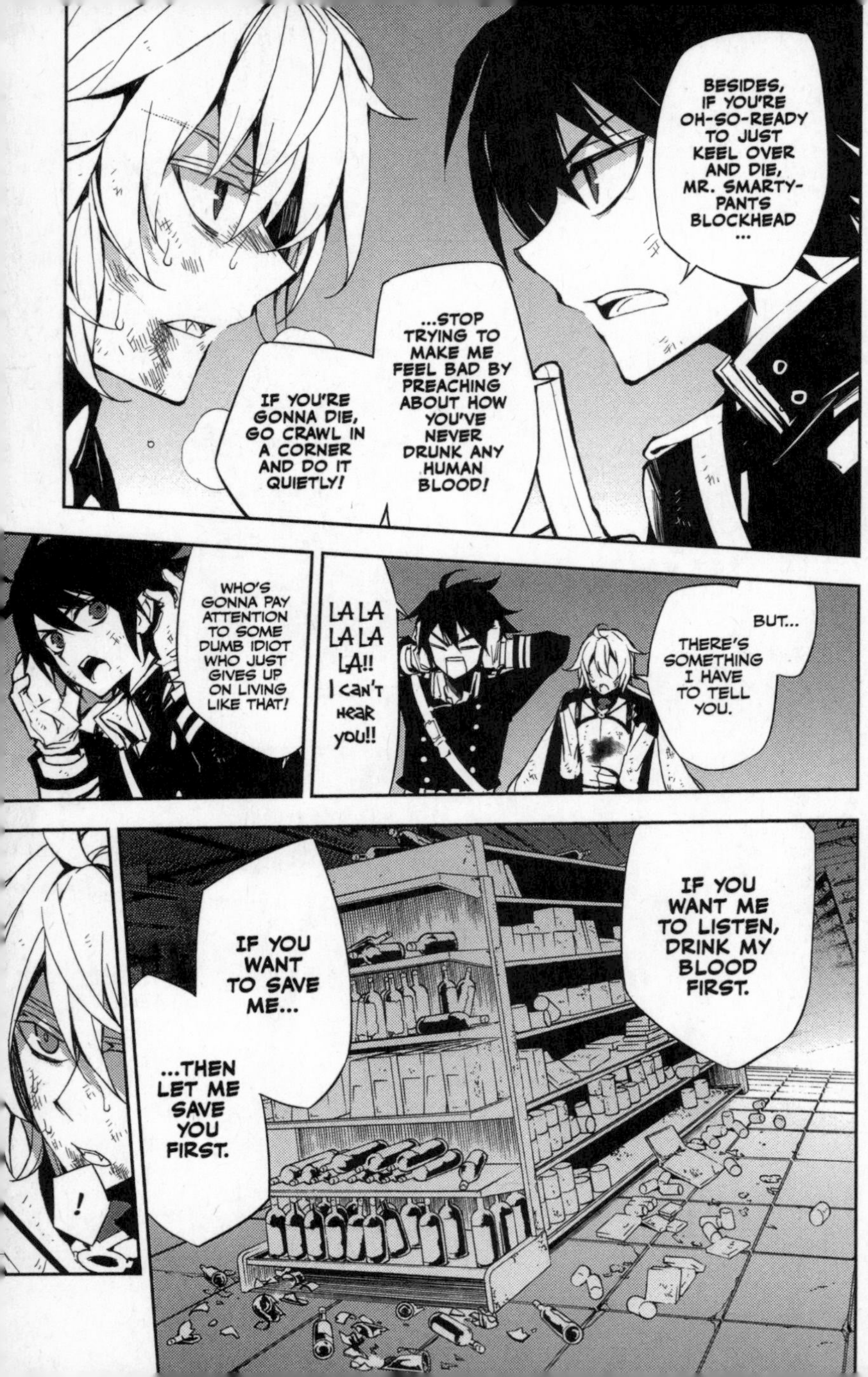
BESIDES, IF YOU'RE OH-SO-READY TO JUST KEEL OVER AND DIE, MR. SMARTY-PANTS BLOCKHEAD ...
...STOP TRYING TO MAKE ME FEEL BAD BY PREACHING ABOUT HOW YOU'VE NEVER DRUNK ANY HUMAN BLOOD!
IF YOU'RE GONNA DIE, GO CRAWL IN A CORNER AND DO IT QUIETLY!
BUT... THERE'S SOMETHING I HAVE TO TELL YOU.
LA LA LA LA LA!! I can't hear you!!
WHO'S GONNA PAY ATTENTION TO SOME DUMB IDIOT WHO JUST GIVES UP ON LIVING LIKE THAT!
IF YOU WANT ME TO LISTEN, DRINK MY BLOOD FIRST.
IF YOU WANT TO SAVE ME...
...THEN LET ME SAVE YOU FIRST.
!

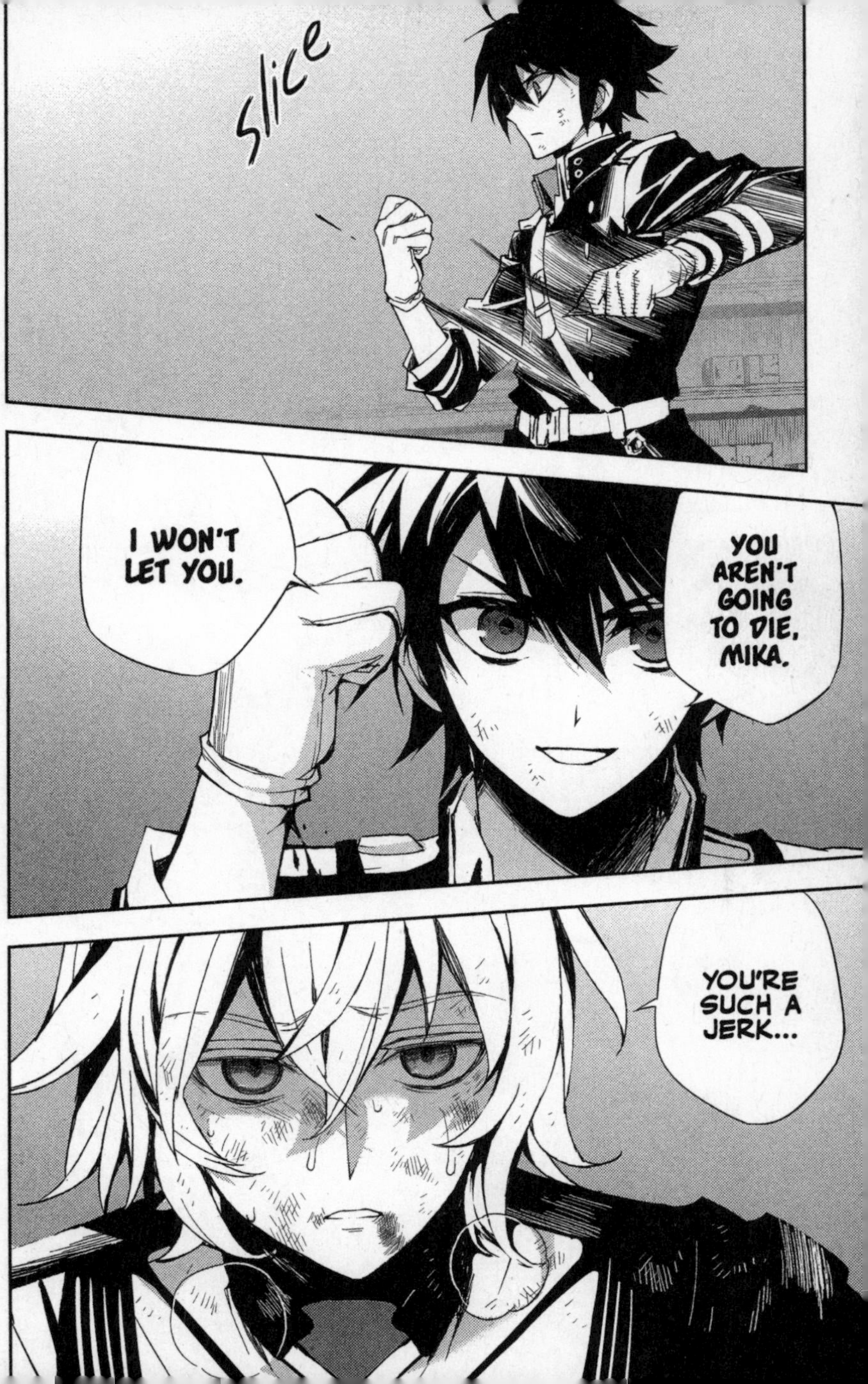
slice
YOU AREN'T GOING TO DIE, MIKA.
I WON'T LET YOU.
YOU'RE SUCH A JERK...

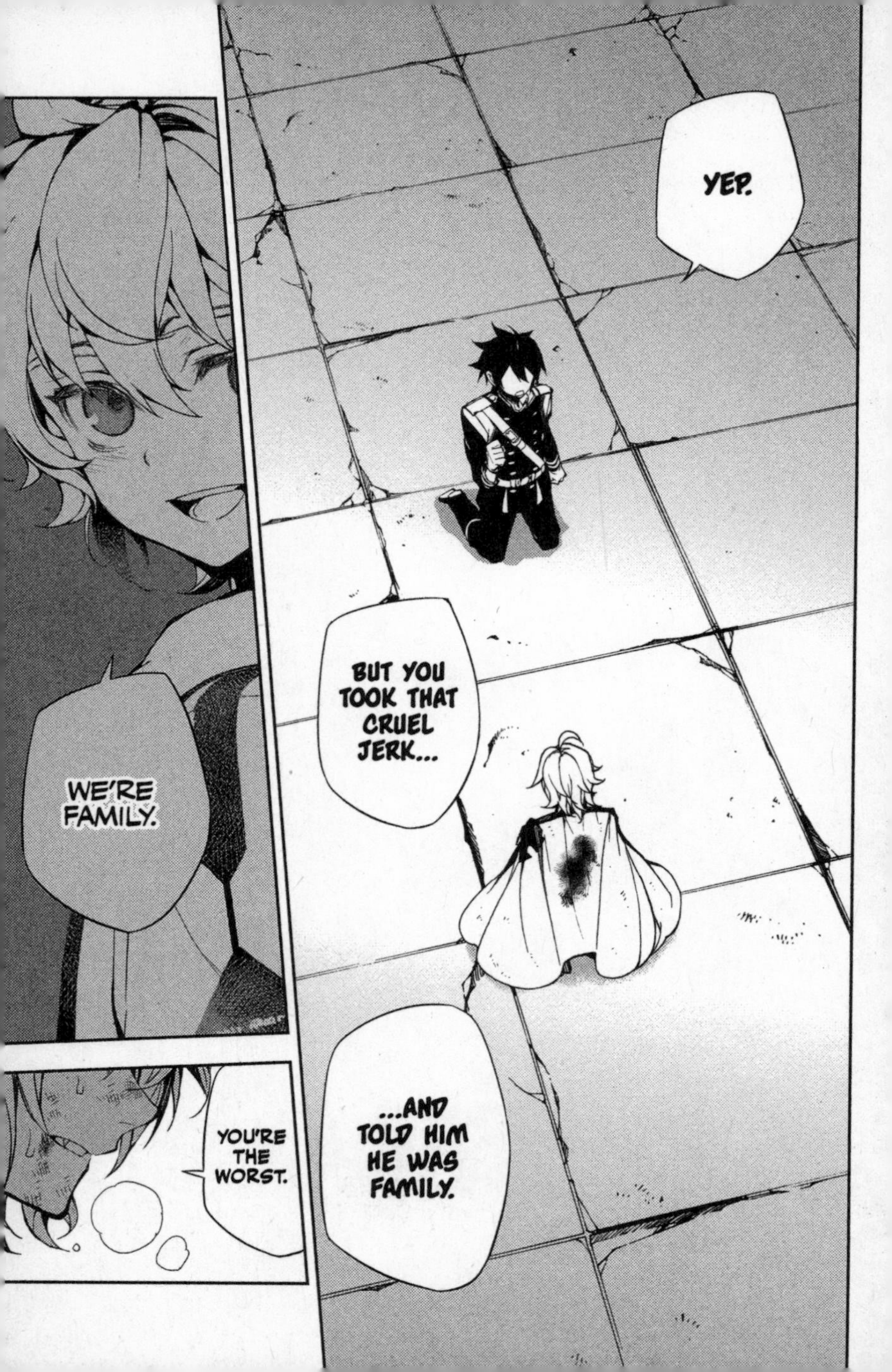
YEP.
BUT YOU TOOK THAT CRUEL JERK...
...AND TOLD HIM HE WAS FAMILY.
WE'RE FAMILY.
YOU'RE THE WORST.

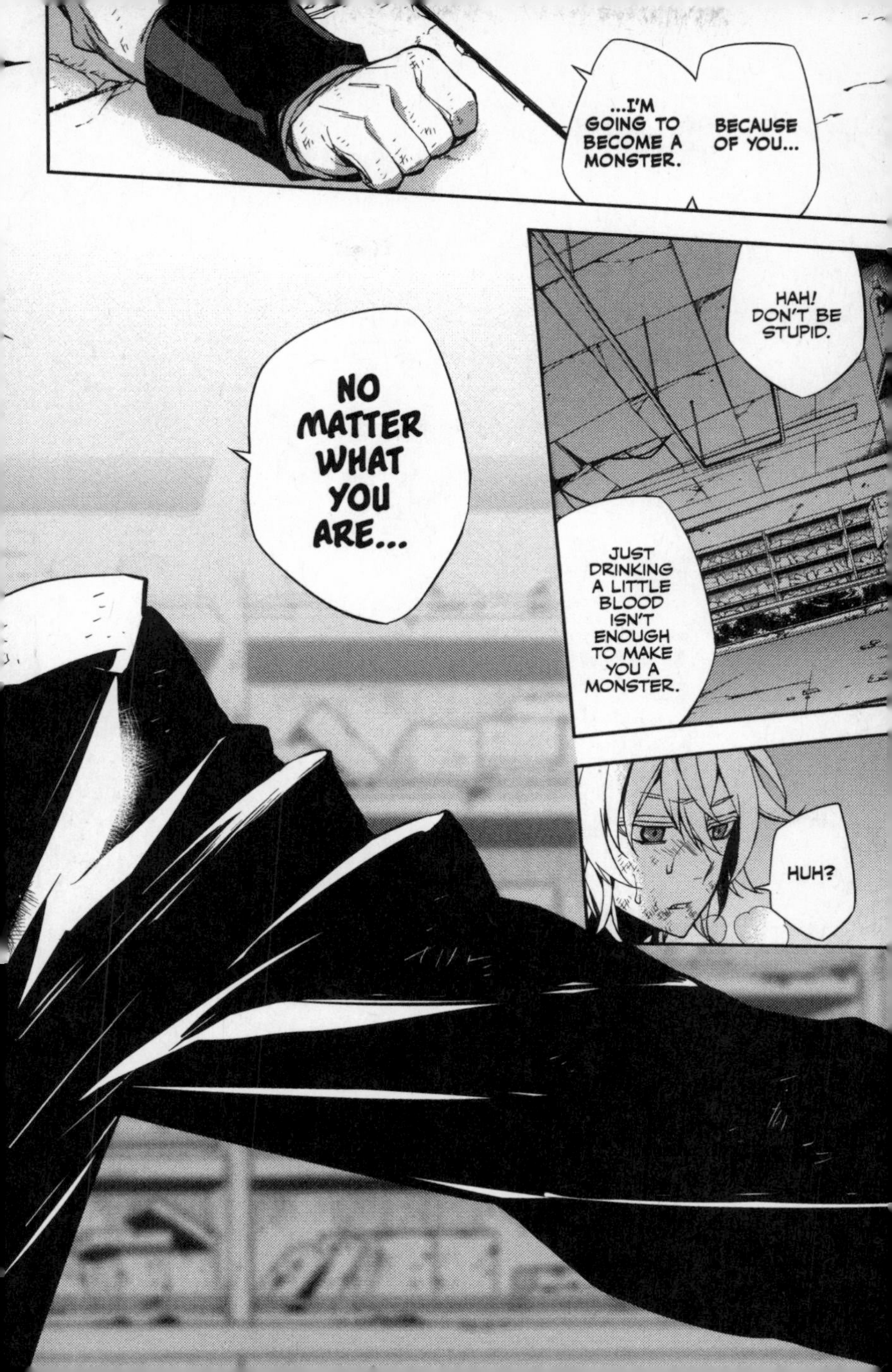
BECAUSE OF YOU...
...I'M GOING TO BECOME A MONSTER.
HAH! DON'T BE STUPID.
JUST DRINKING A LITTLE BLOOD ISN'T ENOUGH TO MAKE YOU A MONSTER.
HUH?
NO MATTER WHAT YOU ARE...

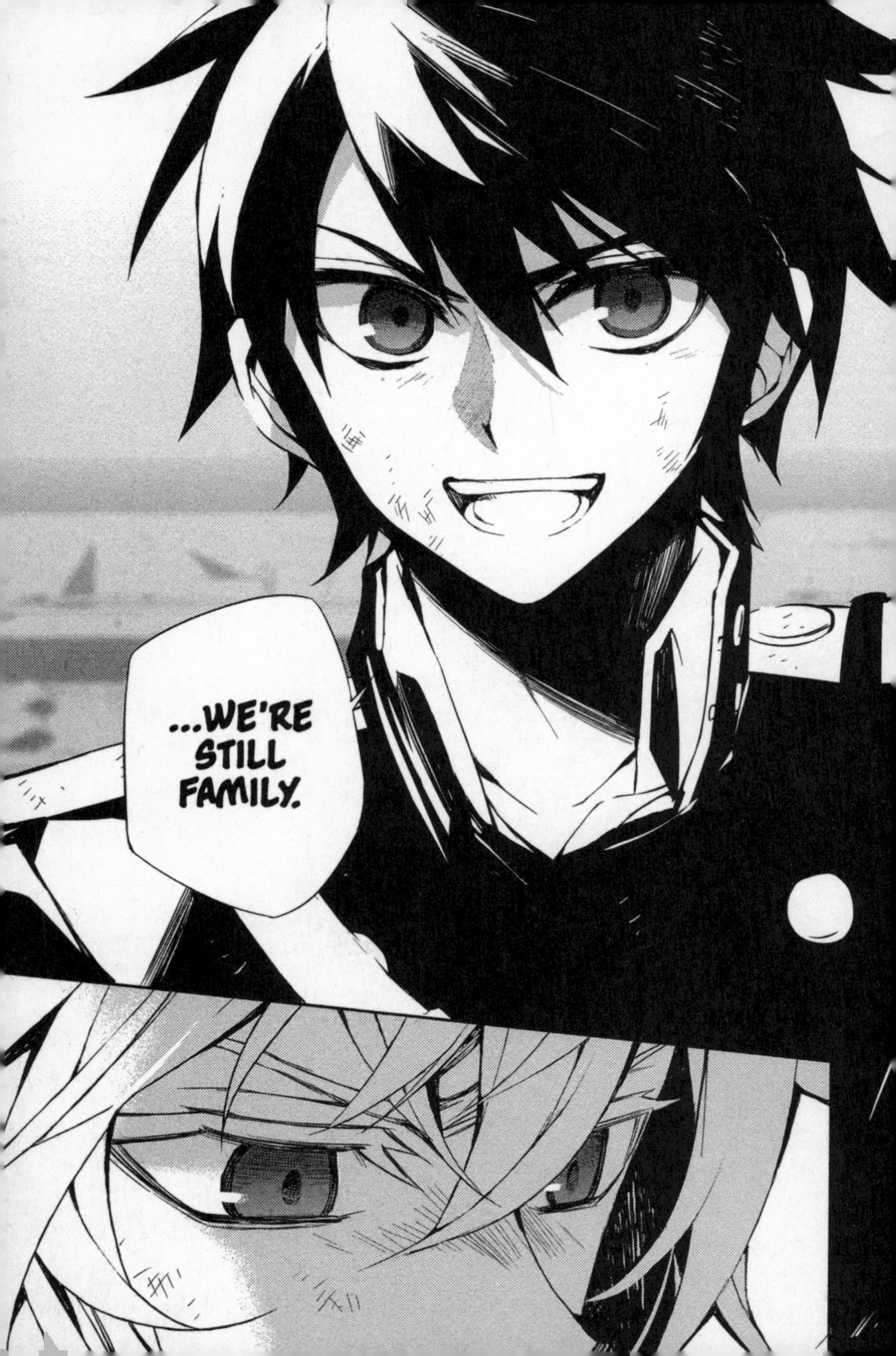
...WE'RE STILL FAMILY.

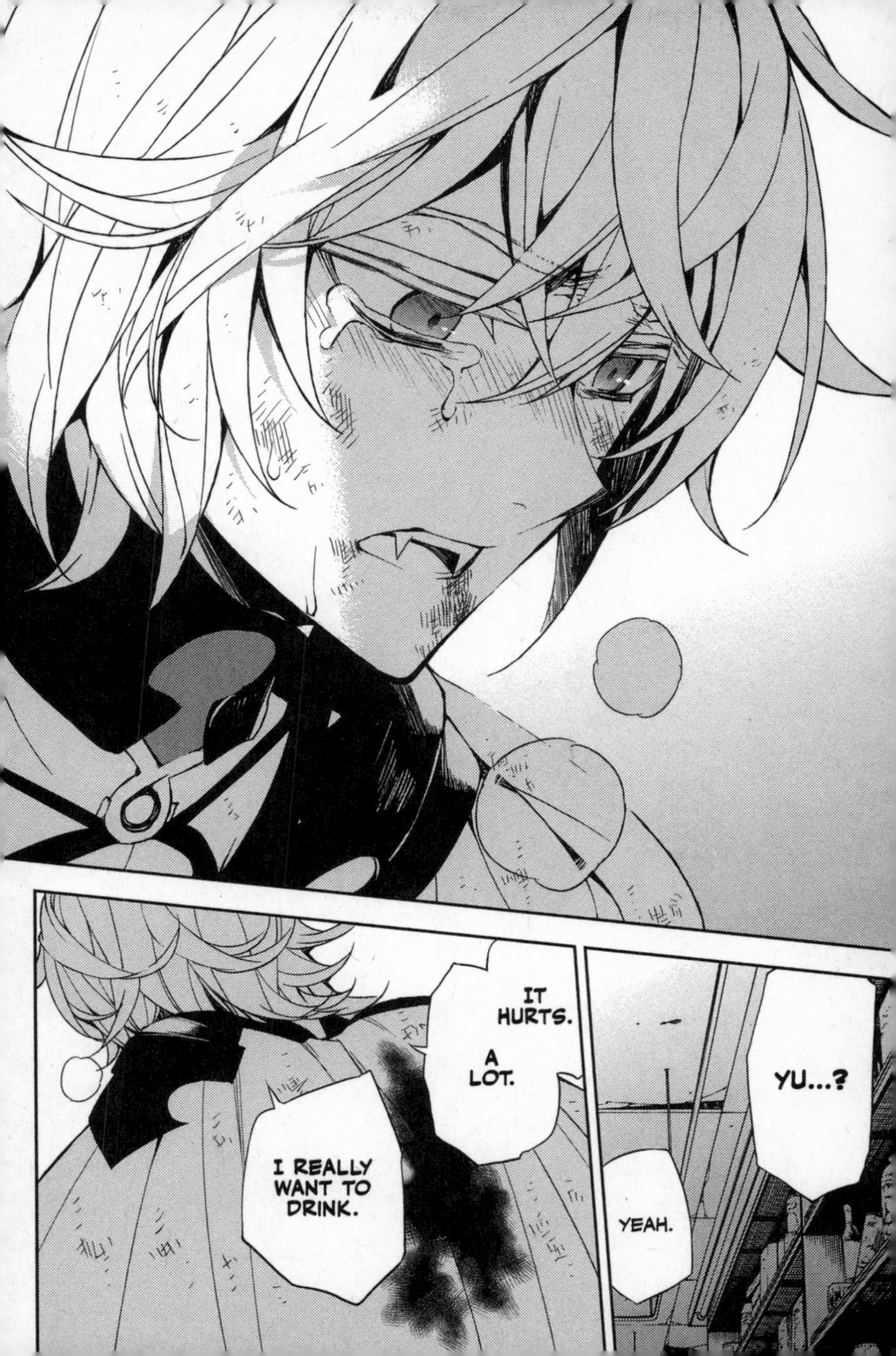
YU...?
YEAH.
IT HURTS.
A LOT.
I REALLY WANT TO DRINK.

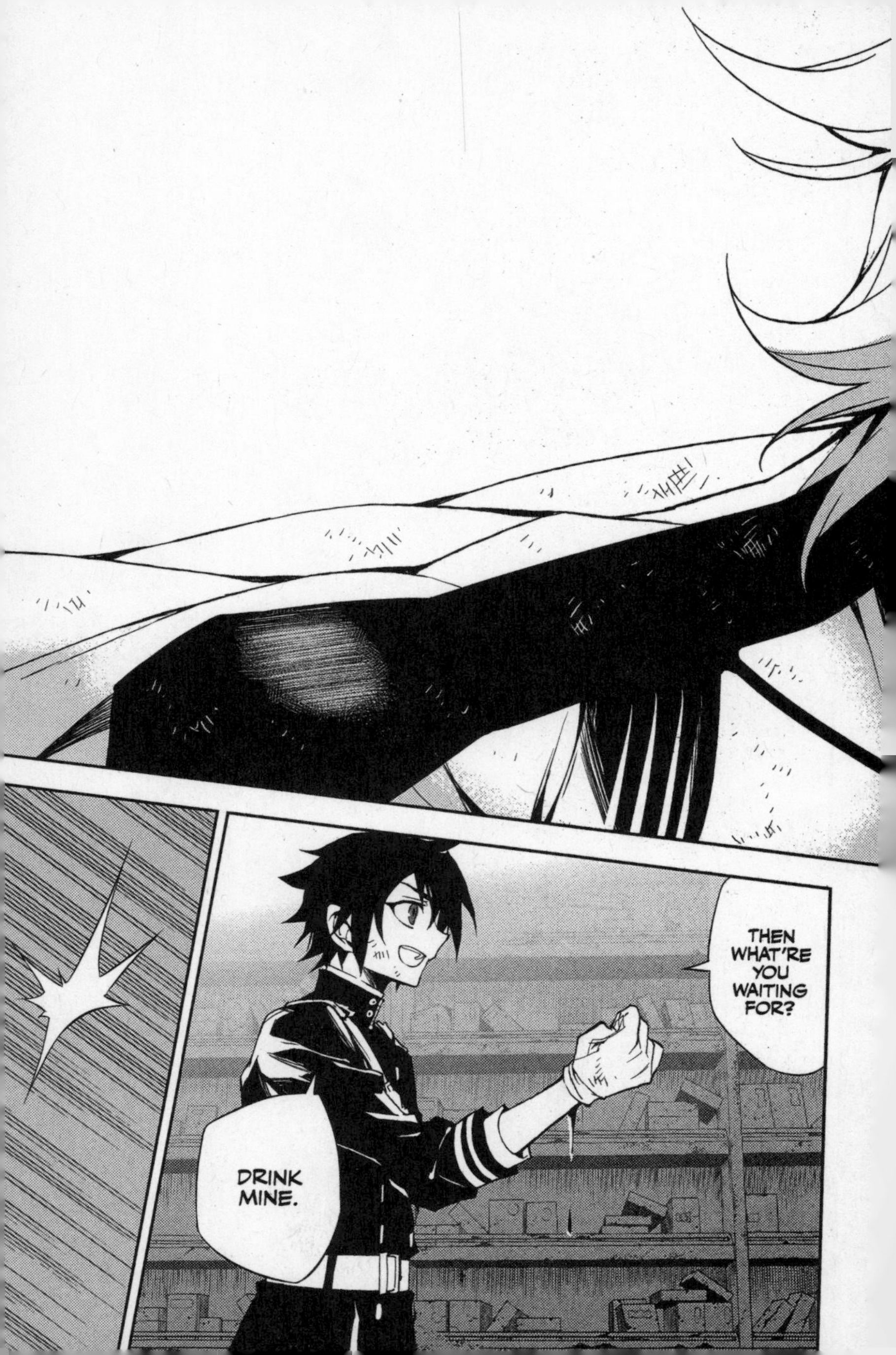
THEN WHAT'RE YOU WAITING FOR?
DRINK MINE.

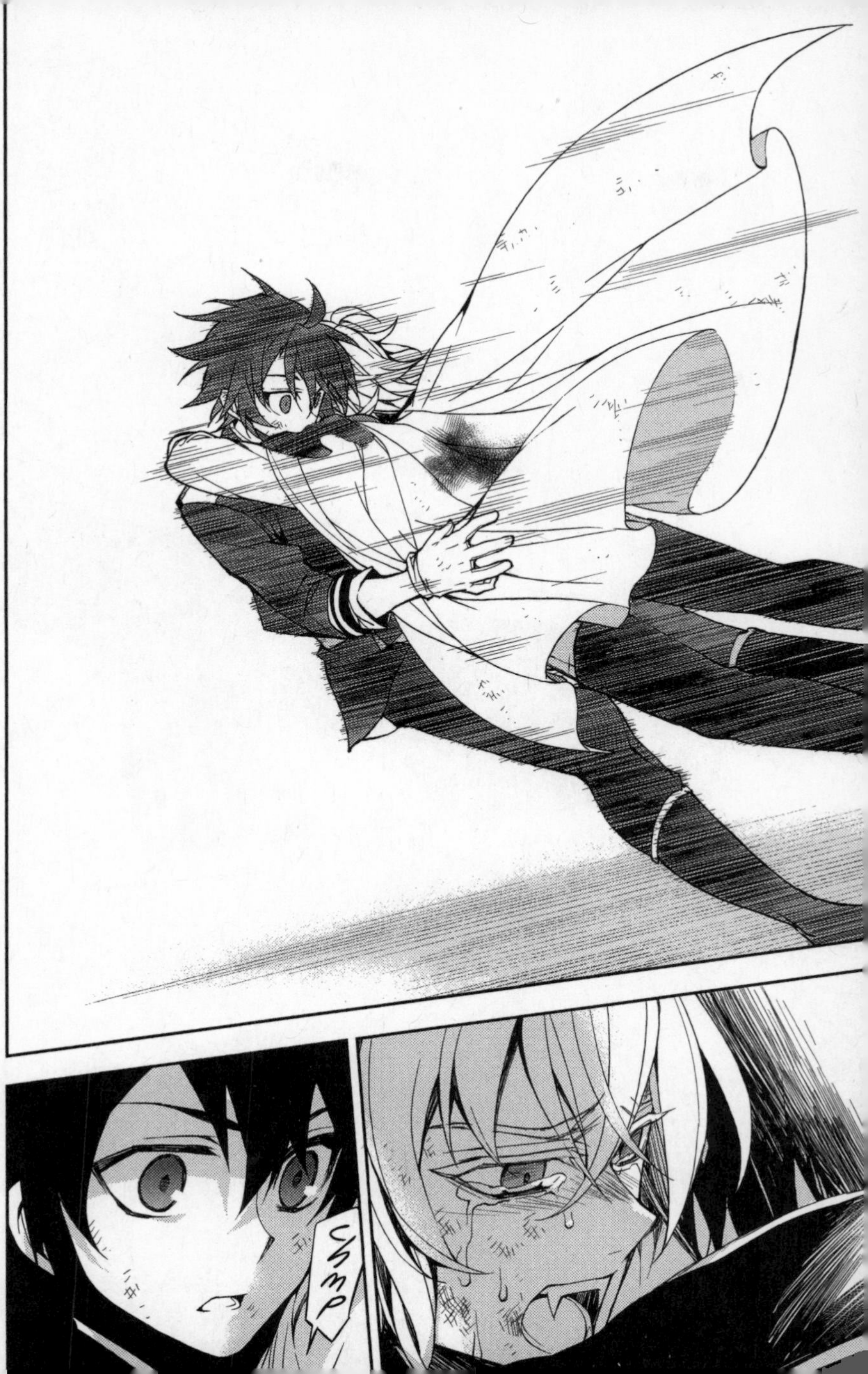

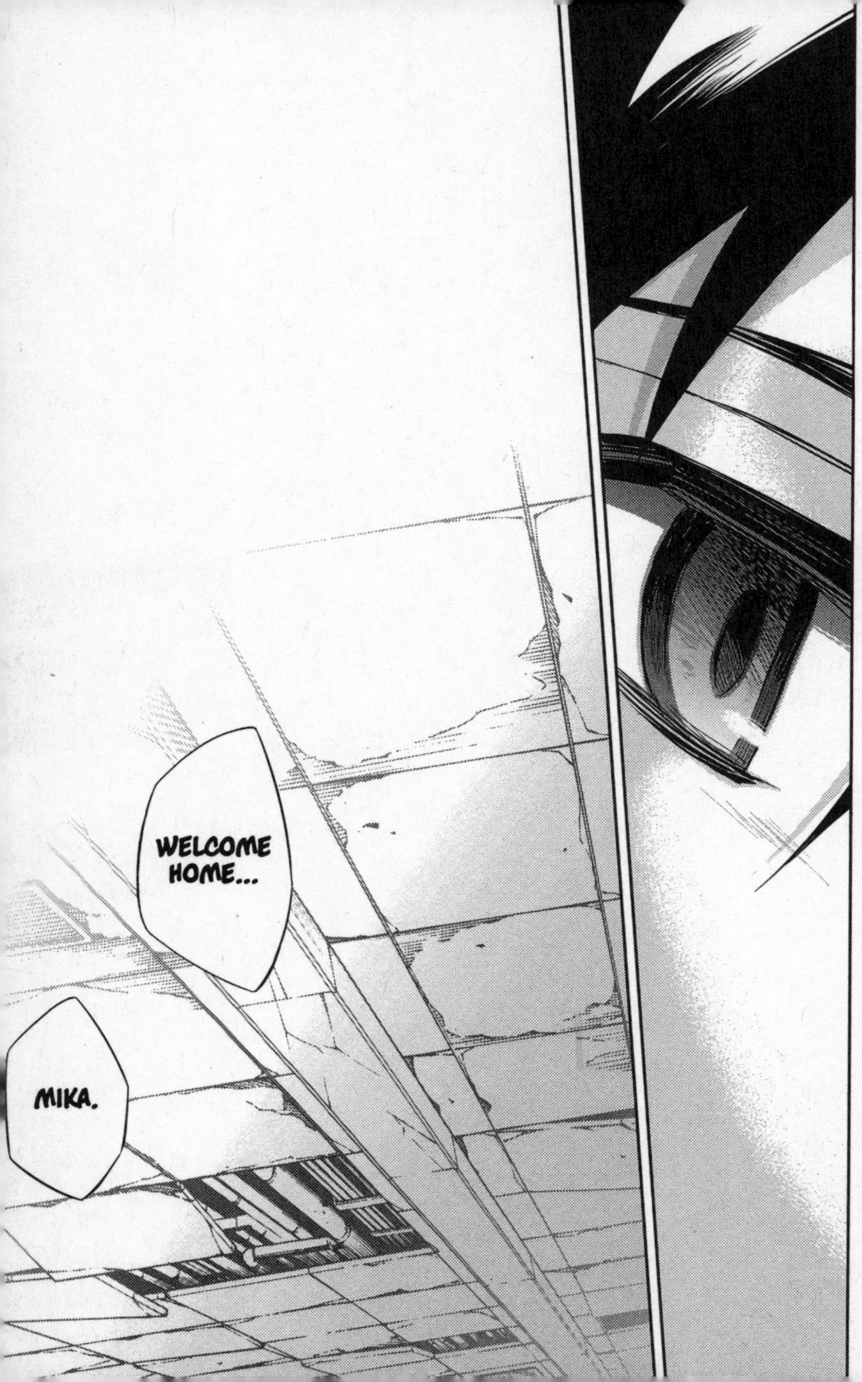
WELCOME HOME...
MIKA.

Seraph of the End
VAMPIRE REIGN

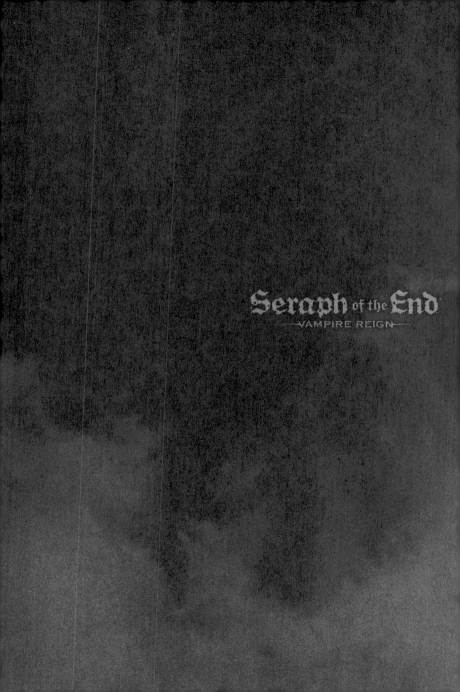

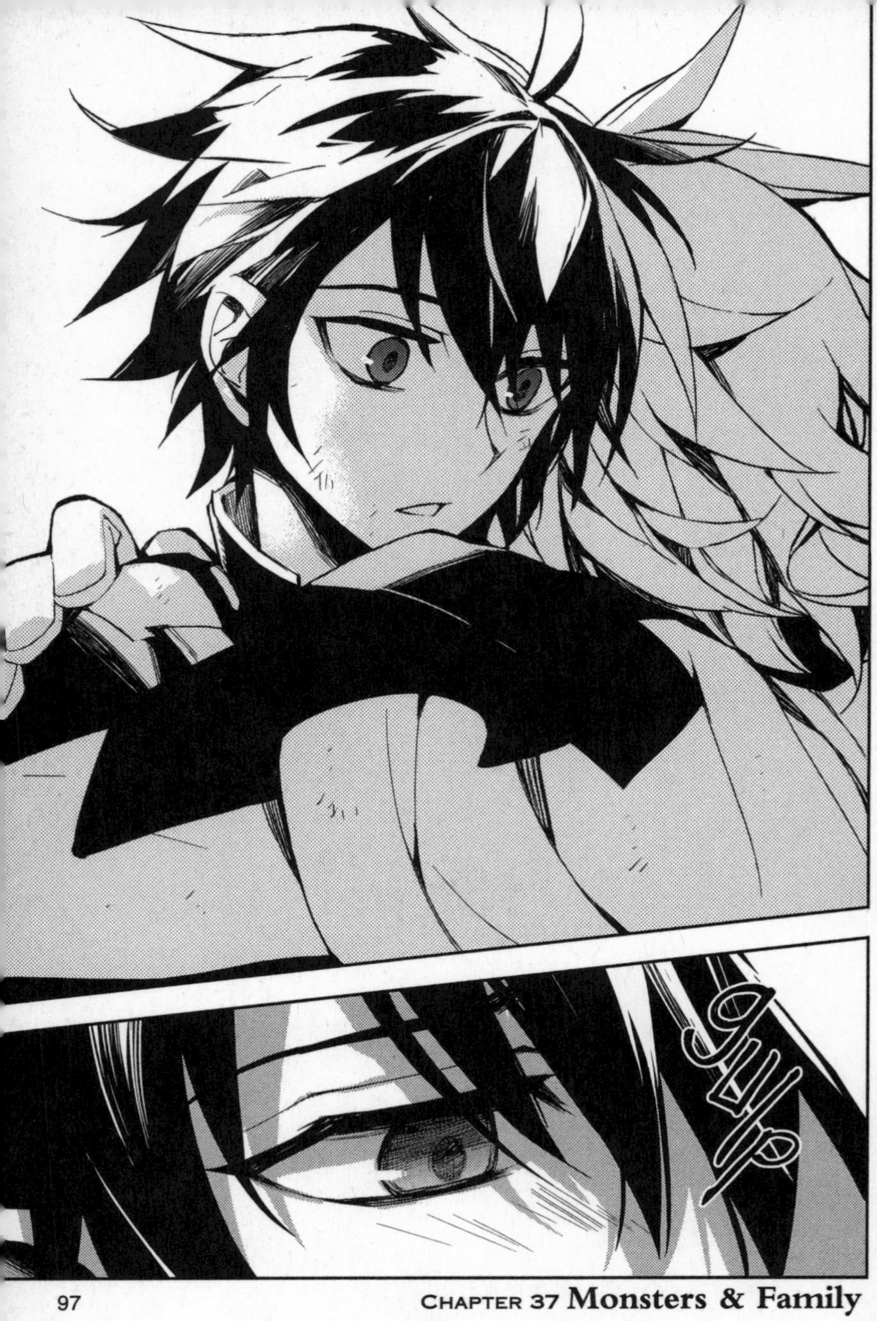
gulp

CHAPTER 37 Monsters & Family

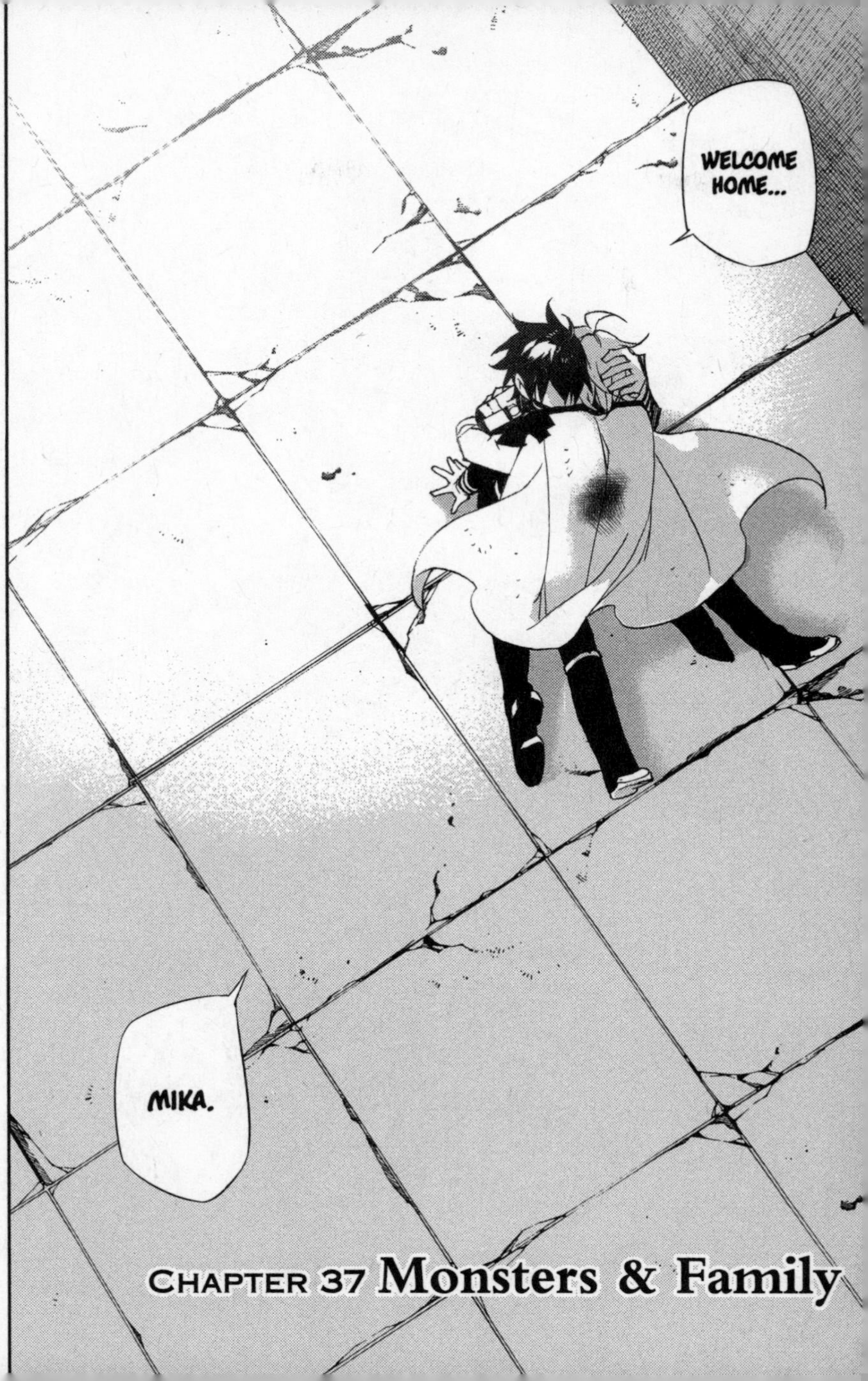
WELCOME HOME...
MIKA.

CHAPTER 37 Monsters & Family

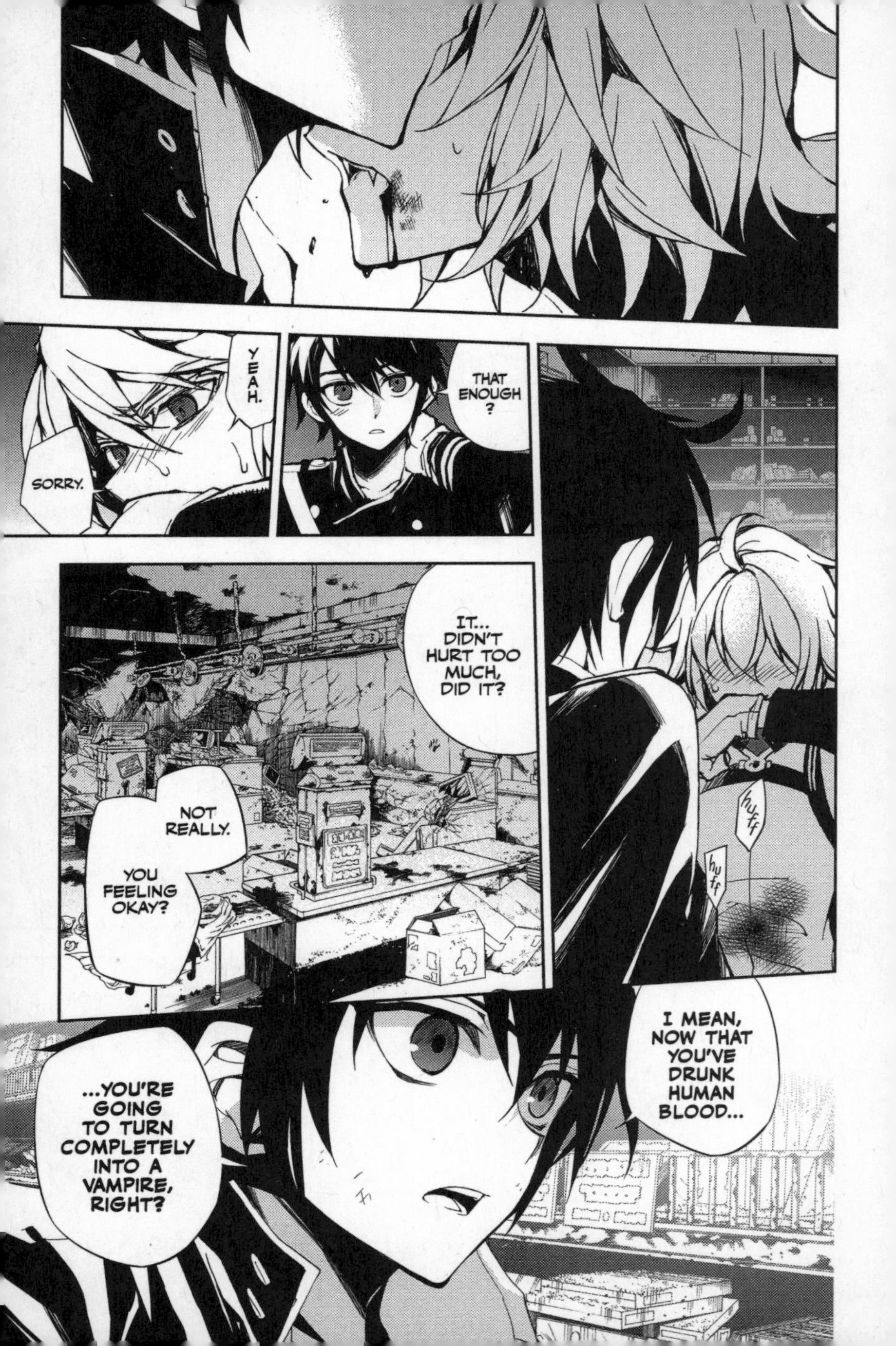
huff
huff
THAT ENOUGH?
YEAH.
SORRY.
IT... DIDN'T HURT TOO MUCH, DID IT?
NOT REALLY.
YOU FEELING OKAY?
I MEAN, NOW THAT YOU'VE DRUNK HUMAN BLOOD...
...YOU'RE GOING TO TURN COMPLETELY INTO A VAMPIRE, RIGHT?

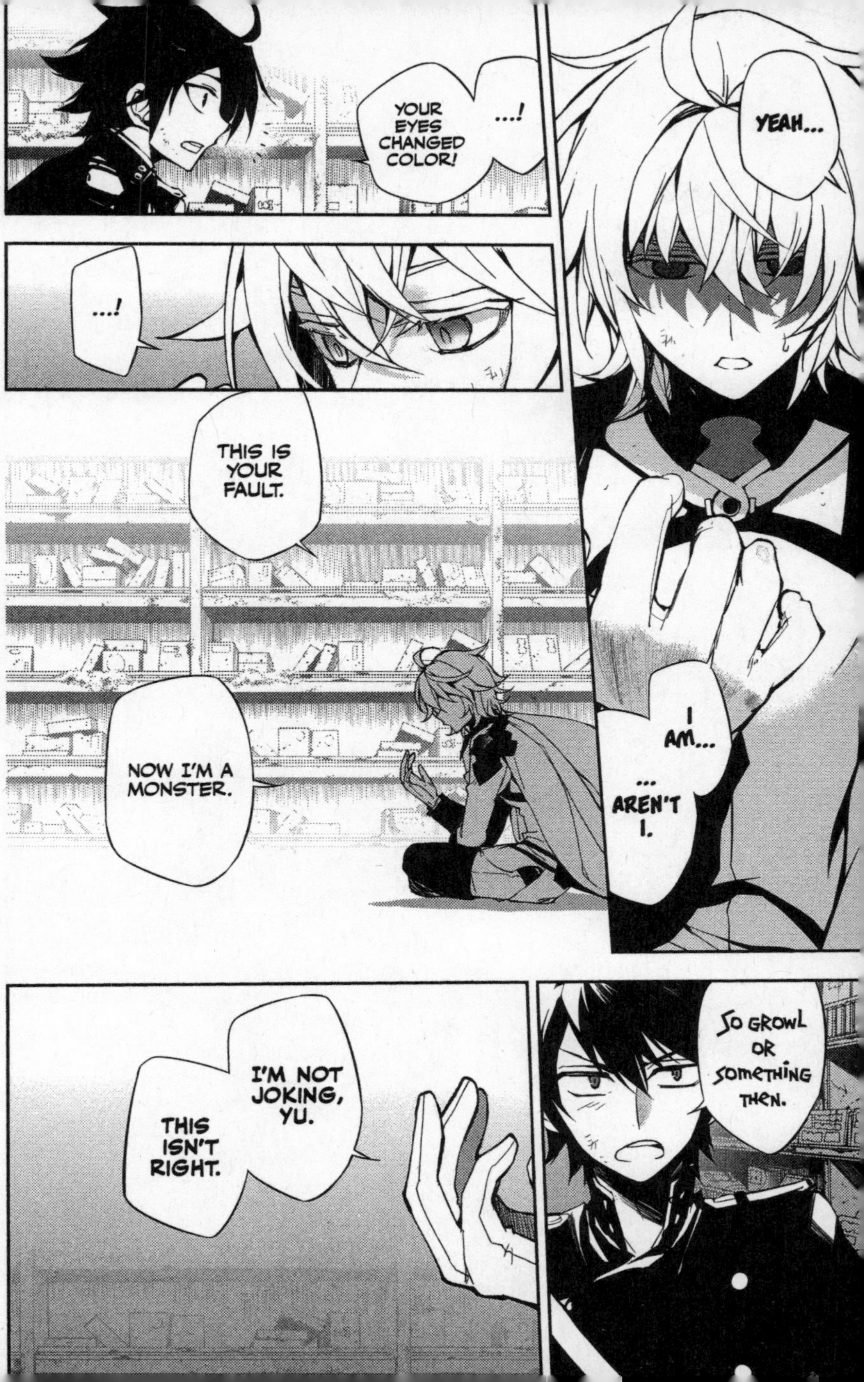
YEAH...
I AM...
... AREN'T I.
...!
YOUR EYES CHANGED COLOR!
...!
THIS IS YOUR FAULT.
NOW I'M A MONSTER.
SO GROWL OR SOMETHING THEN.
I'M NOT JOKING, YU.
THIS ISN'T RIGHT.

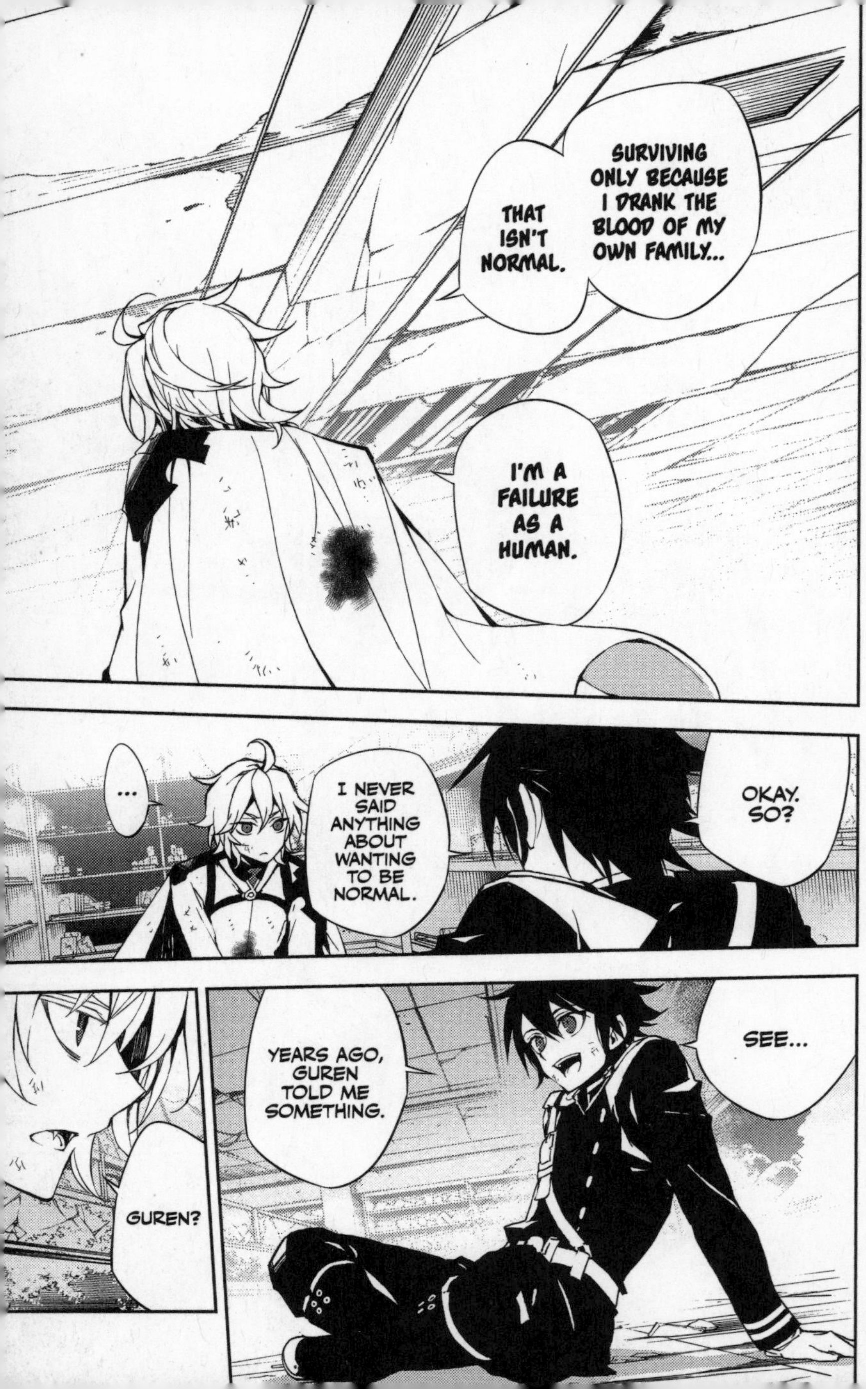
SURVIVING ONLY BECAUSE I DRANK THE BLOOD OF MY OWN FAMILY...
THAT ISN'T NORMAL.
I'M A FAILURE AS A HUMAN.
OKAY. SO?
I NEVER SAID ANYTHING ABOUT WANTING TO BE NORMAL.
...
SEE...
YEARS AGO, GUREN TOLD ME SOMETHING.
GUREN?

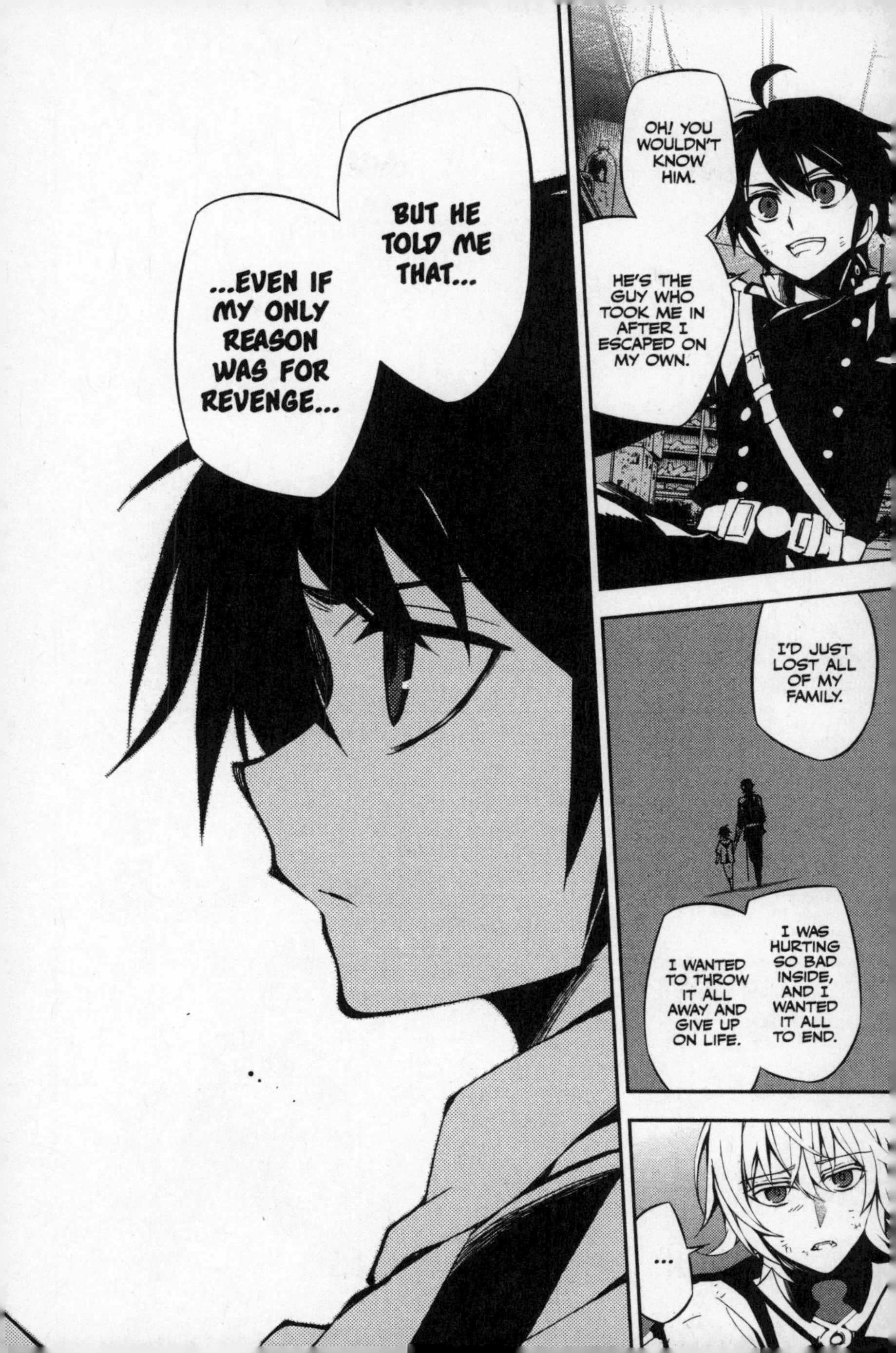
OH! YOU WOULDN'T KNOW HIM.
HE'S THE GUY WHO TOOK ME IN AFTER I ESCAPED ON MY OWN.
I'D JUST LOST ALL OF MY FAMILY.
I WAS HURTING SO BAD INSIDE, AND I WANTED IT ALL TO END.
I WANTED TO THROW IT ALL AWAY AND GIVE UP ON LIFE.
...
BUT HE TOLD ME THAT...
...EVEN IF MY ONLY REASON WAS FOR REVENGE...

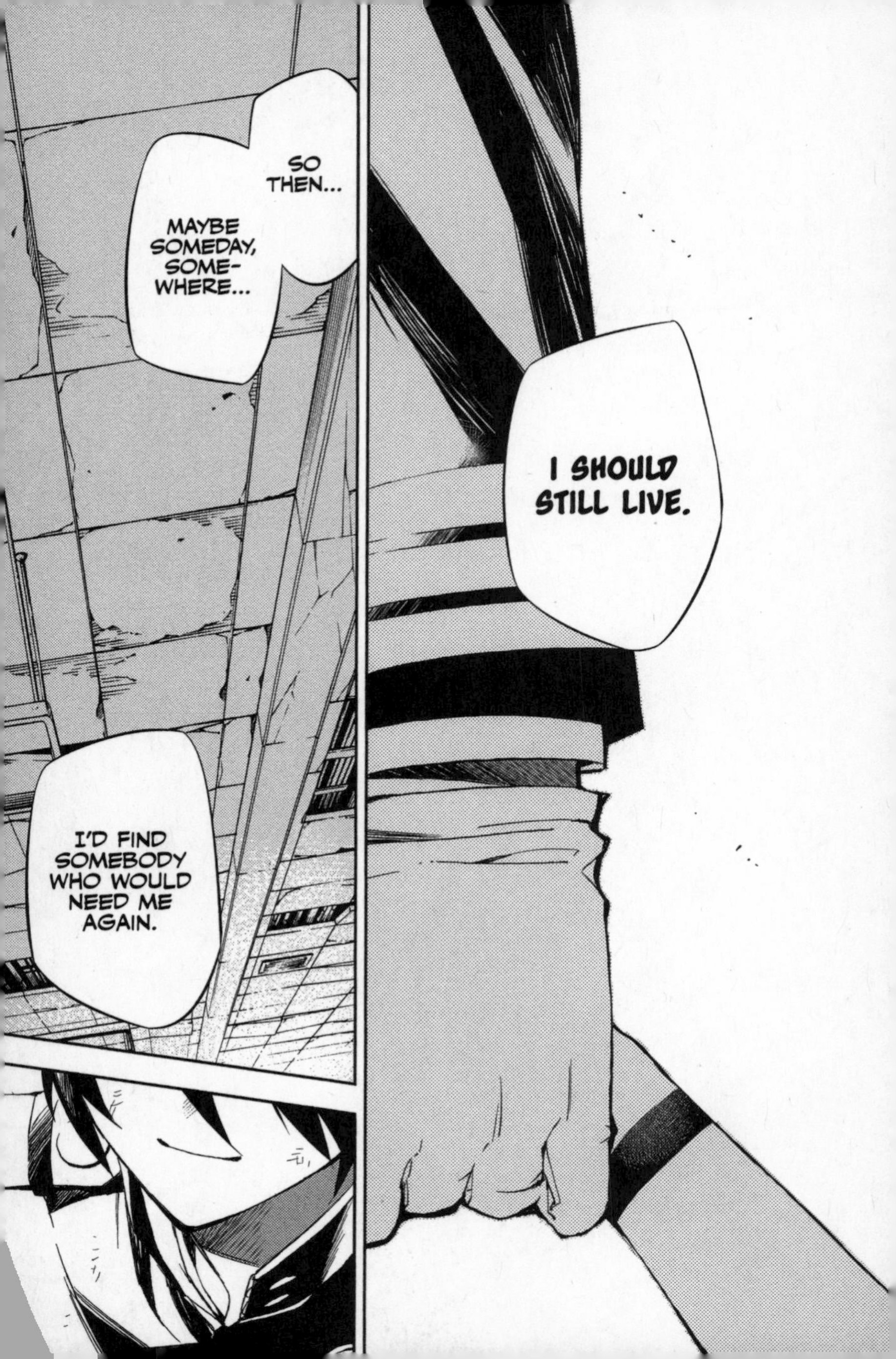
I SHOULD STILL LIVE.
SO THEN...
MAYBE SOMEDAY, SOME-WHERE...
I'D FIND SOMEBODY WHO WOULD NEED ME AGAIN.

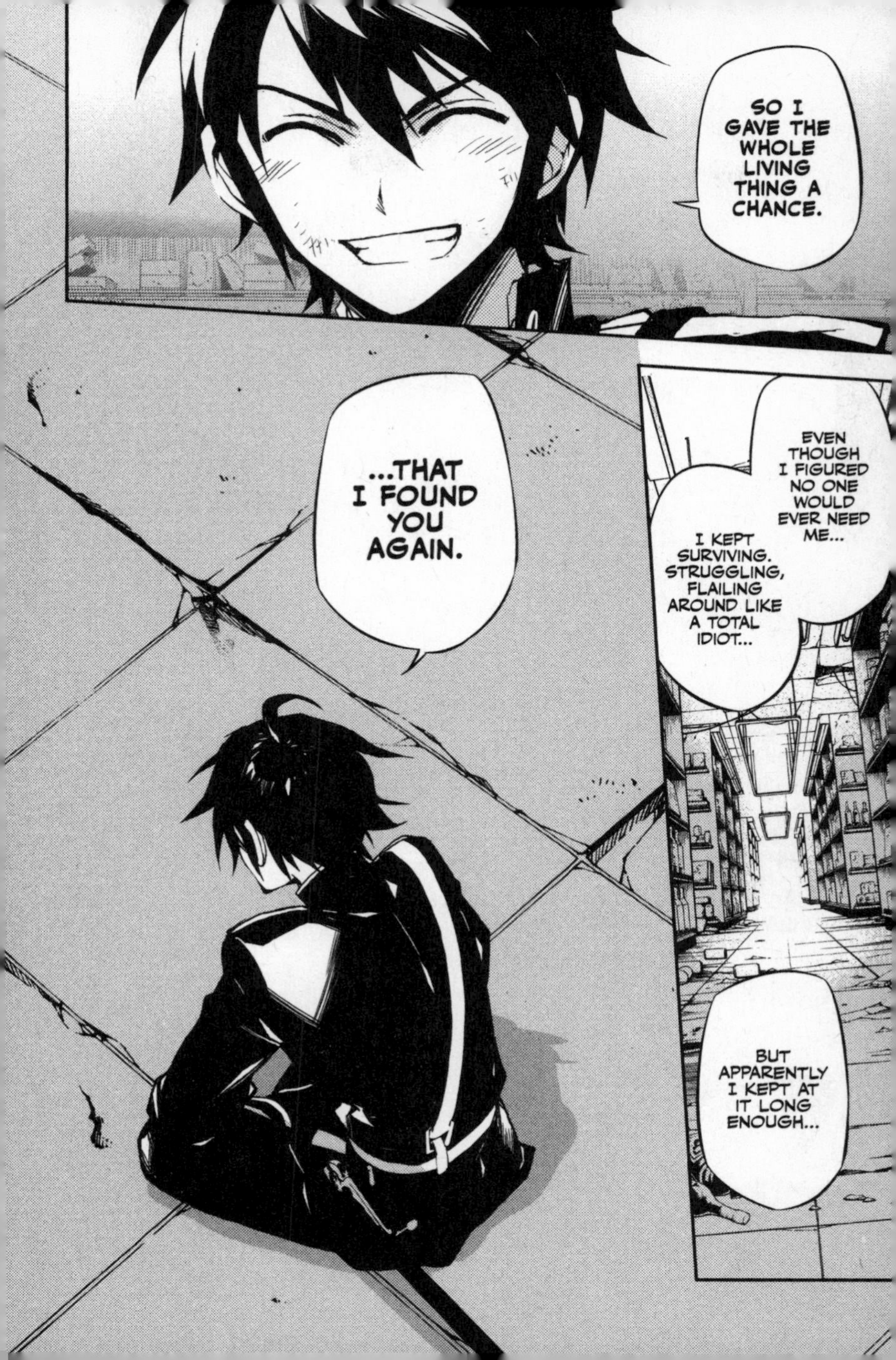
SO I GAVE THE WHOLE LIVING THING A CHANCE.
EVEN THOUGH I FIGURED NO ONE WOULD EVER NEED ME...
I KEPT SURVIVING. STRUGGLING, FLAILING AROUND LIKE A TOTAL IDIOT...
BUT APPARENTLY I KEPT AT IT LONG ENOUGH...
...THAT I FOUND YOU AGAIN.

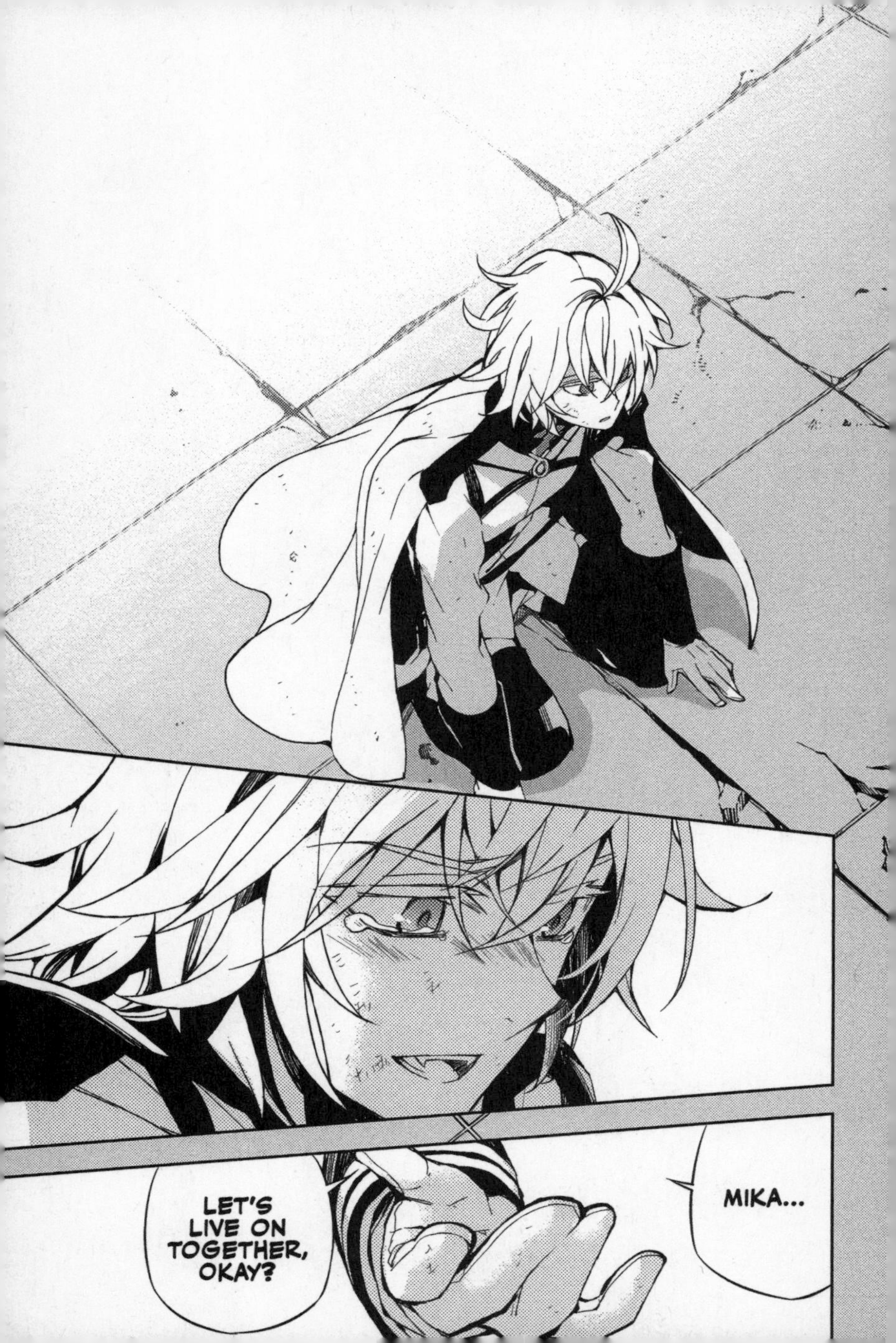
MIKA...
LET'S LIVE ON TOGETHER, OKAY?

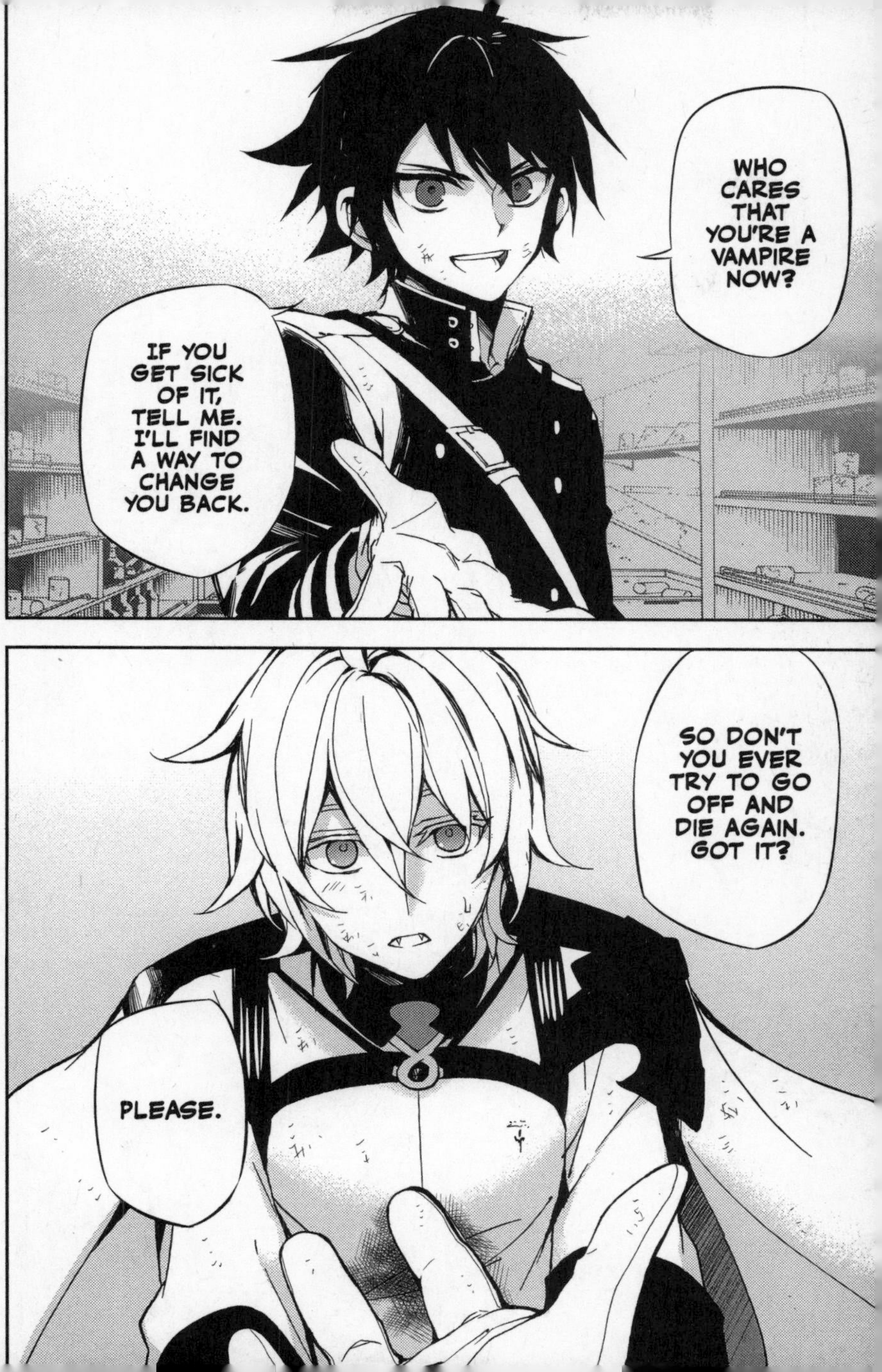
WHO CARES THAT YOU'RE A VAMPIRE NOW?
IF YOU GET SICK OF IT, TELL ME. I'LL FIND A WAY TO CHANGE YOU BACK.
SO DON'T YOU EVER TRY TO GO OFF AND DIE AGAIN. GOT IT?
PLEASE.

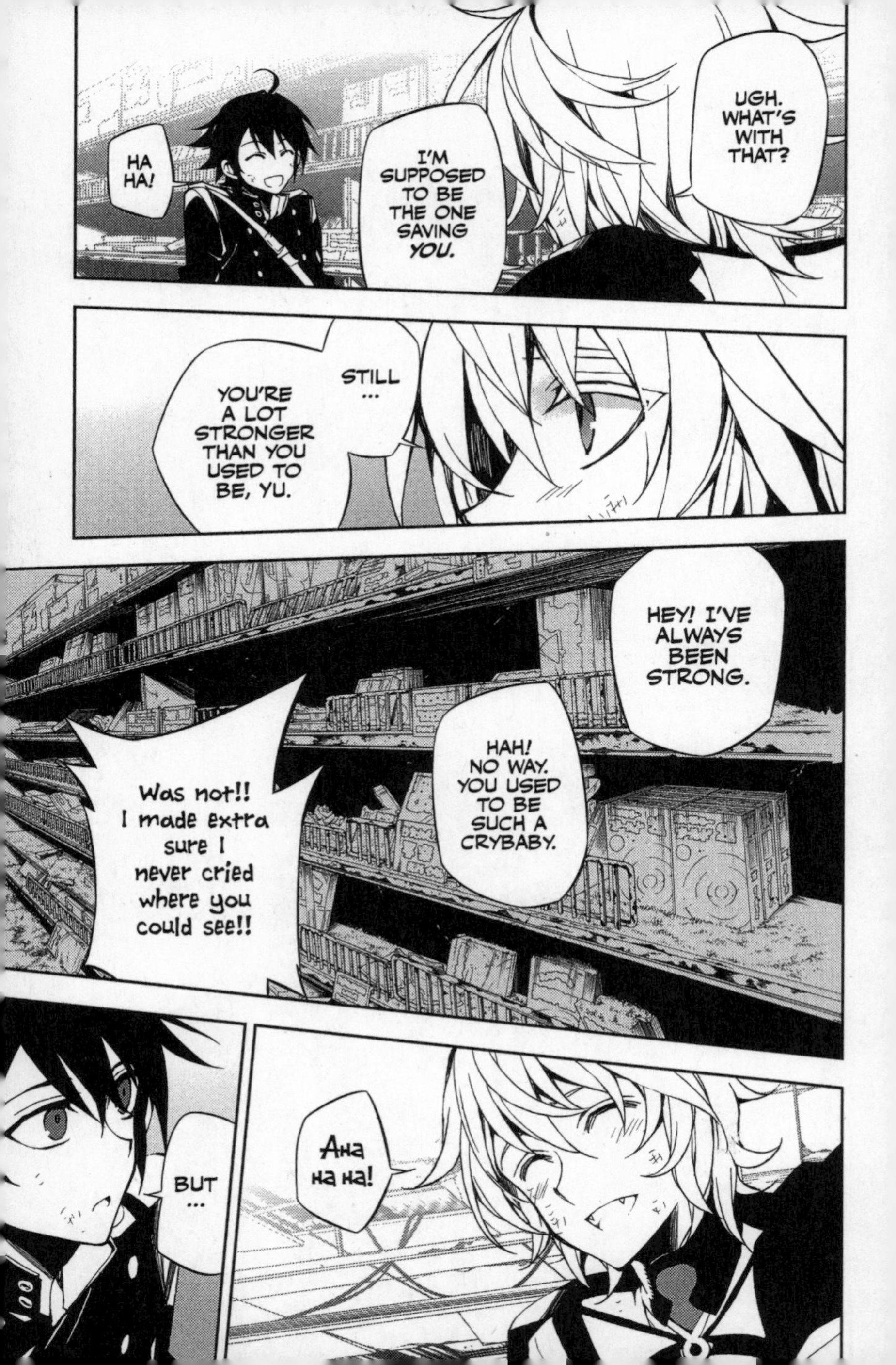
UGH. WHAT'S WITH THAT?
I'M SUPPOSED TO BE THE ONE SAVING *YOU*.
HA HA!
STILL ...
YOU'RE A LOT STRONGER THAN YOU USED TO BE, YU.
HEY! I'VE ALWAYS BEEN STRONG.
HAH! NO WAY. YOU USED TO BE SUCH A CRYBABY.
Was not!! I made extra sure I never cried where you could see!!
Aha ha ha!
BUT ...

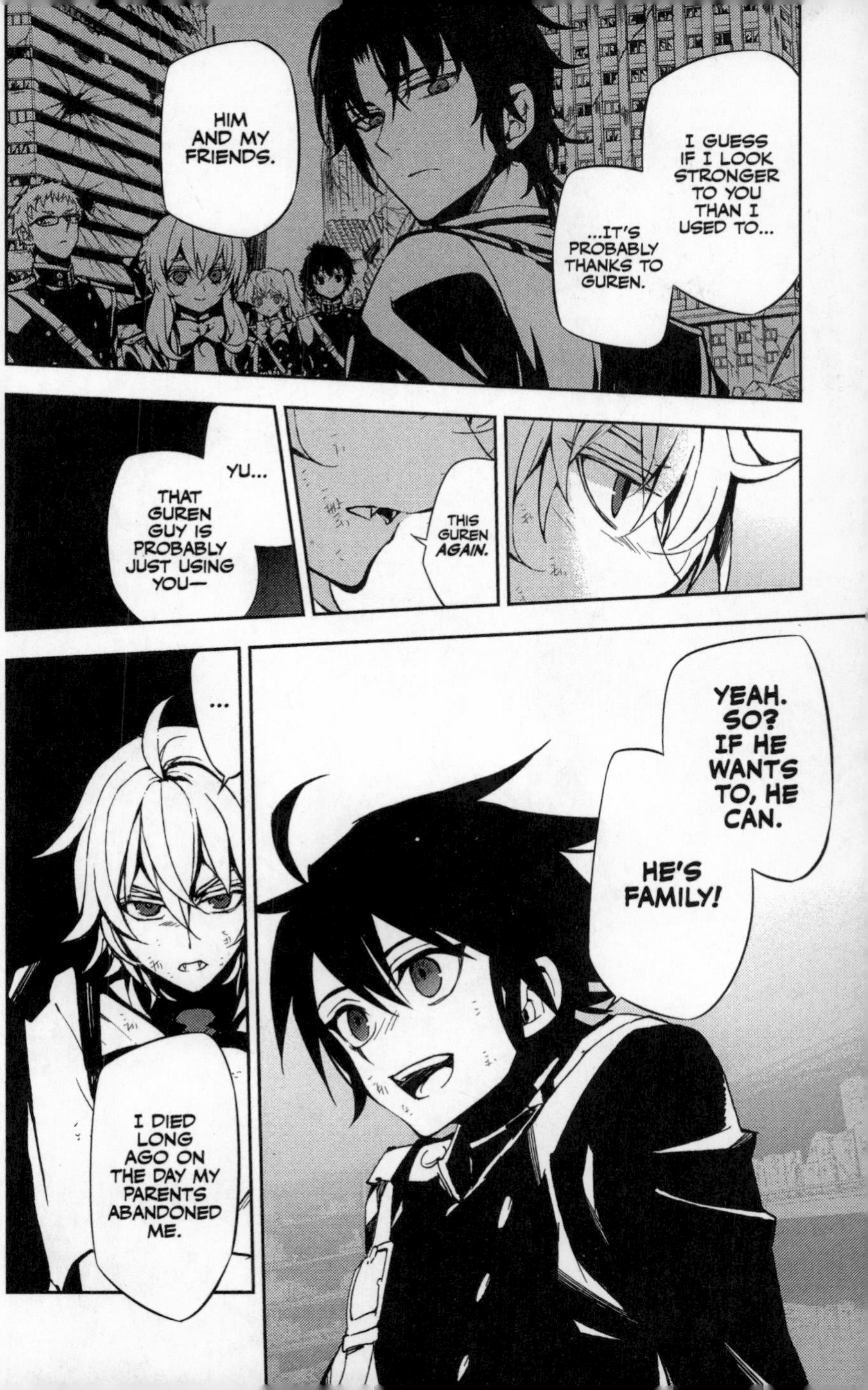
I GUESS IF I LOOK STRONGER TO YOU THAN I USED TO...
...IT'S PROBABLY THANKS TO GUREN.
HIM AND MY FRIENDS.
THIS GUREN *AGAIN.*
YU...
THAT GUREN GUY IS PROBABLY JUST USING YOU—
YEAH. SO? IF HE WANTS TO, HE CAN.
HE'S FAMILY!
...
I DIED LONG AGO ON THE DAY MY PARENTS ABANDONED ME.

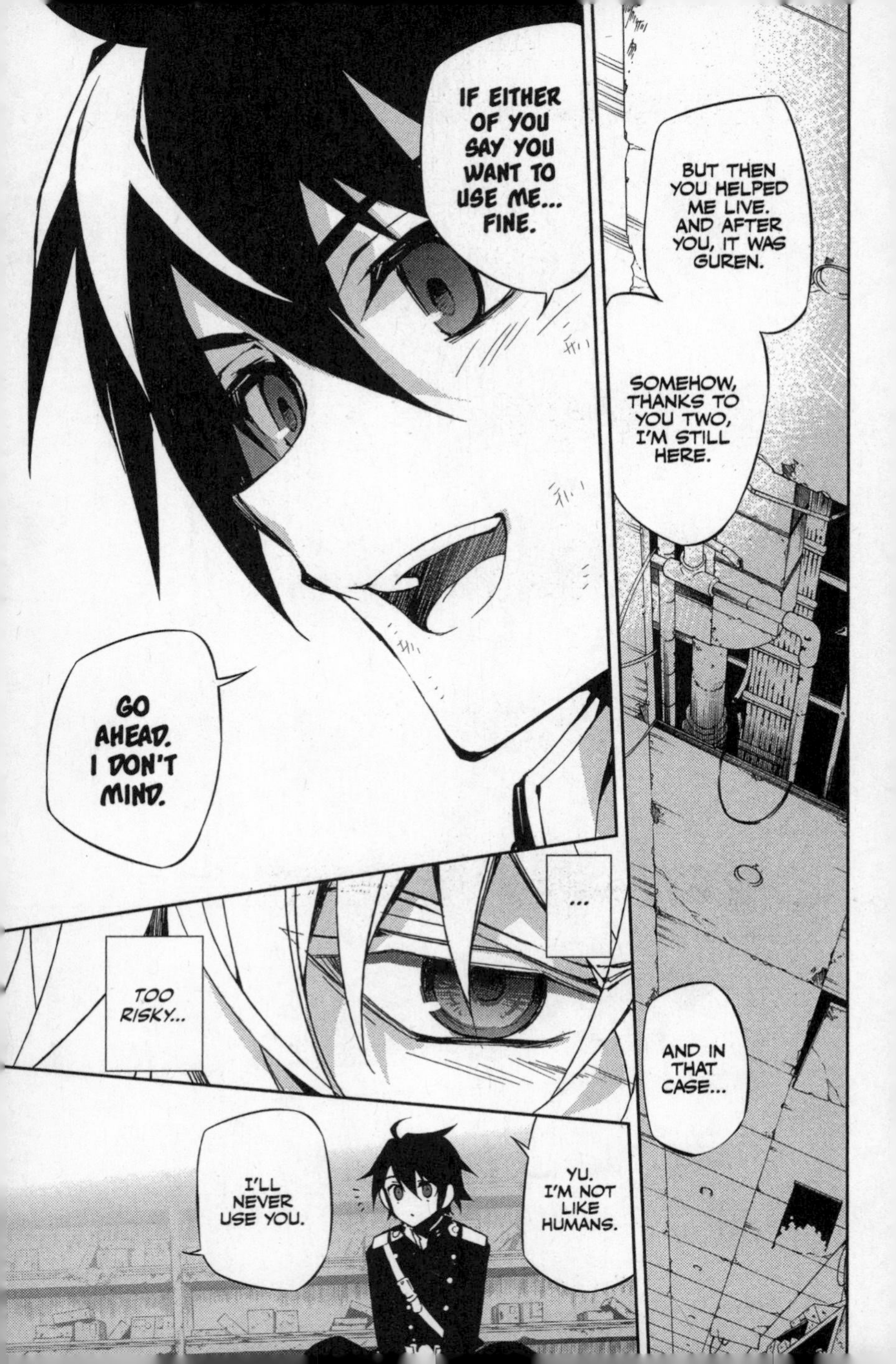
BUT THEN YOU HELPED ME LIVE. AND AFTER YOU, IT WAS GUREN.
SOMEHOW, THANKS TO YOU TWO, I'M STILL HERE.
AND IN THAT CASE...
IF EITHER OF YOU SAY YOU WANT TO USE ME... FINE.
GO AHEAD. I DON'T MIND.
...
TOO RISKY...
YU. I'M NOT LIKE HUMANS.
I'LL NEVER USE YOU.

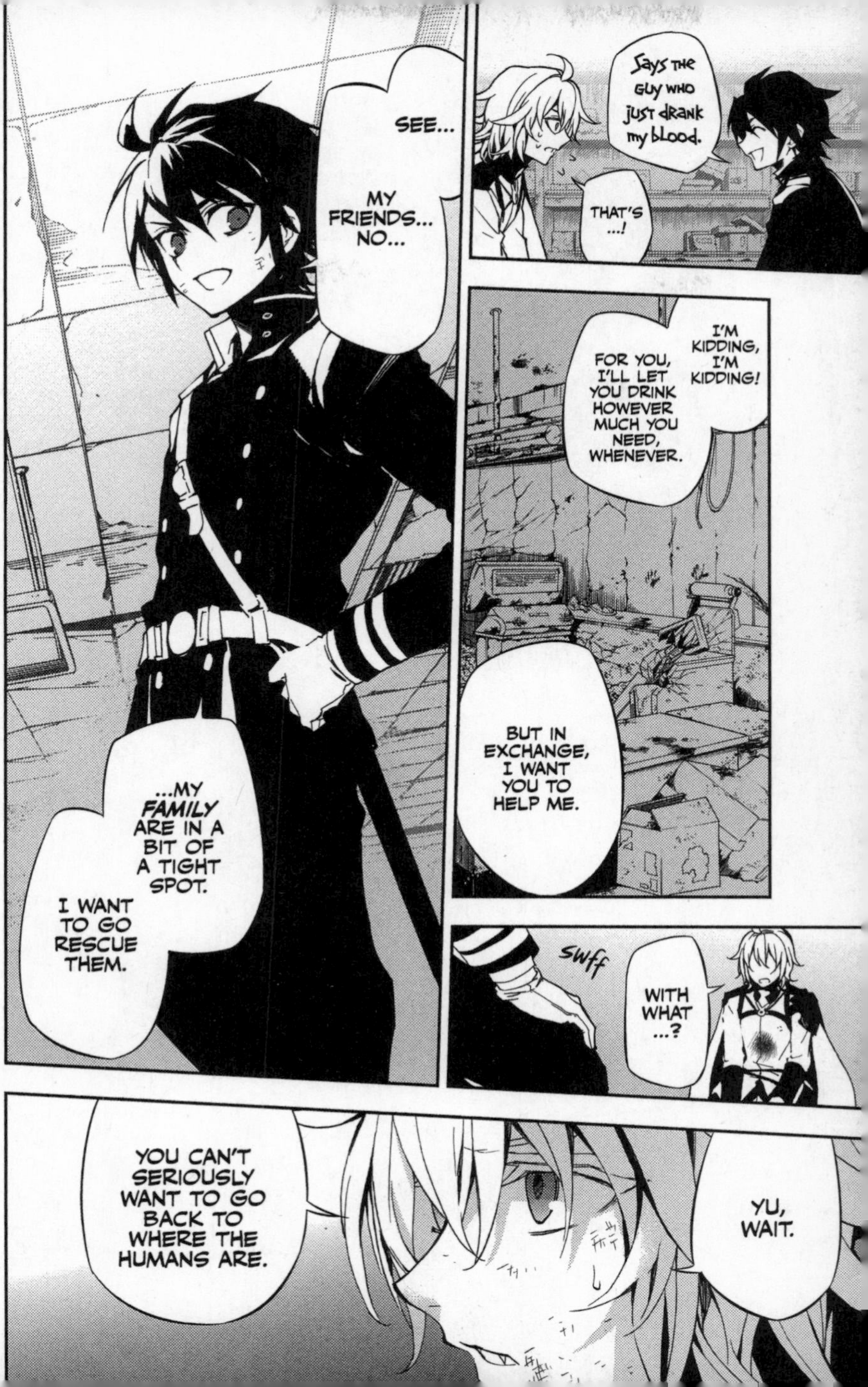
Says the guy who just drank my blood.
THAT'S ...!
I'M KIDDING, I'M KIDDING!
FOR YOU, I'LL LET YOU DRINK HOWEVER MUCH YOU NEED, WHENEVER.
BUT IN EXCHANGE, I WANT YOU TO HELP ME.
SWFF
WITH WHAT ...?
SEE...
MY FRIENDS... NO...
...MY *FAMILY* ARE IN A BIT OF A TIGHT SPOT.
I WANT TO GO RESCUE THEM.
YU, WAIT.
YOU CAN'T SERIOUSLY WANT TO GO BACK TO WHERE THE HUMANS ARE.

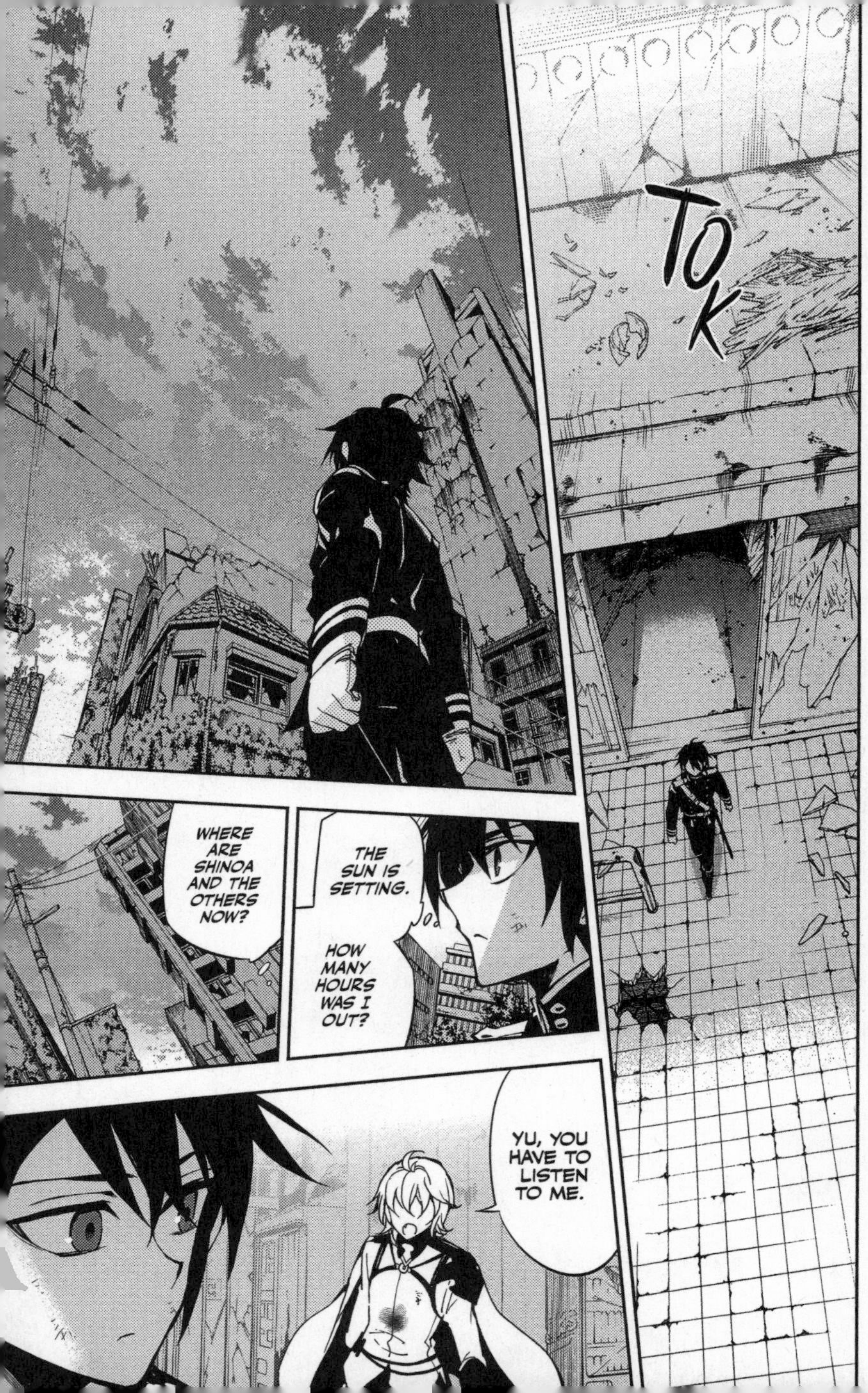

TOK
THE SUN IS SETTING.
HOW MANY HOURS WAS I OUT?
WHERE ARE SHINOA AND THE OTHERS NOW?
YU, YOU HAVE TO LISTEN TO ME.

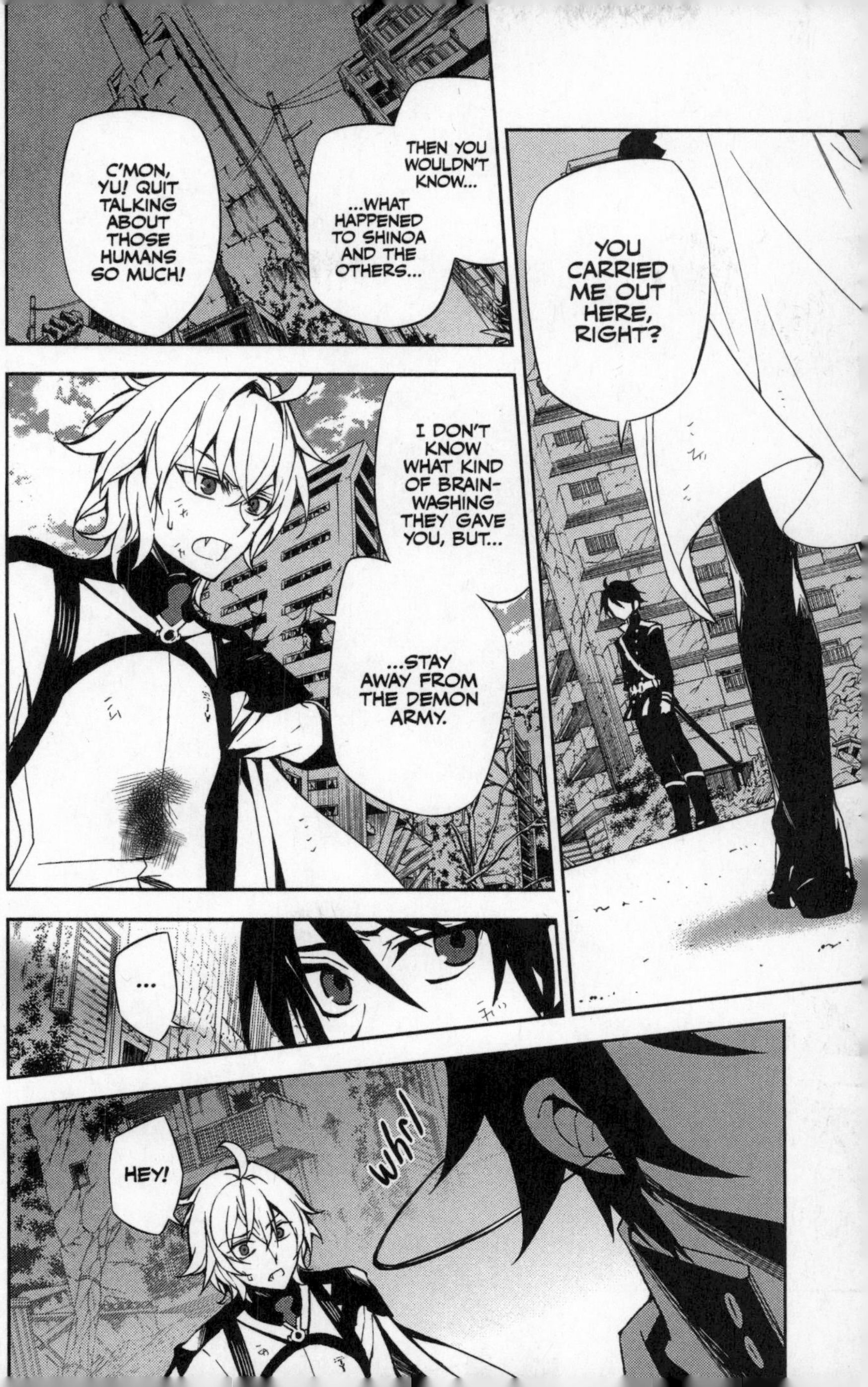
YOU CARRIED ME OUT HERE, RIGHT?
THEN YOU WOULDN'T KNOW...
...WHAT HAPPENED TO SHINOA AND THE OTHERS...
C'MON, YU! QUIT TALKING ABOUT THOSE HUMANS SO MUCH!
I DON'T KNOW WHAT KIND OF BRAIN-WASHING THEY GAVE YOU, BUT...
...STAY AWAY FROM THE DEMON ARMY.
...
whrl
HEY!

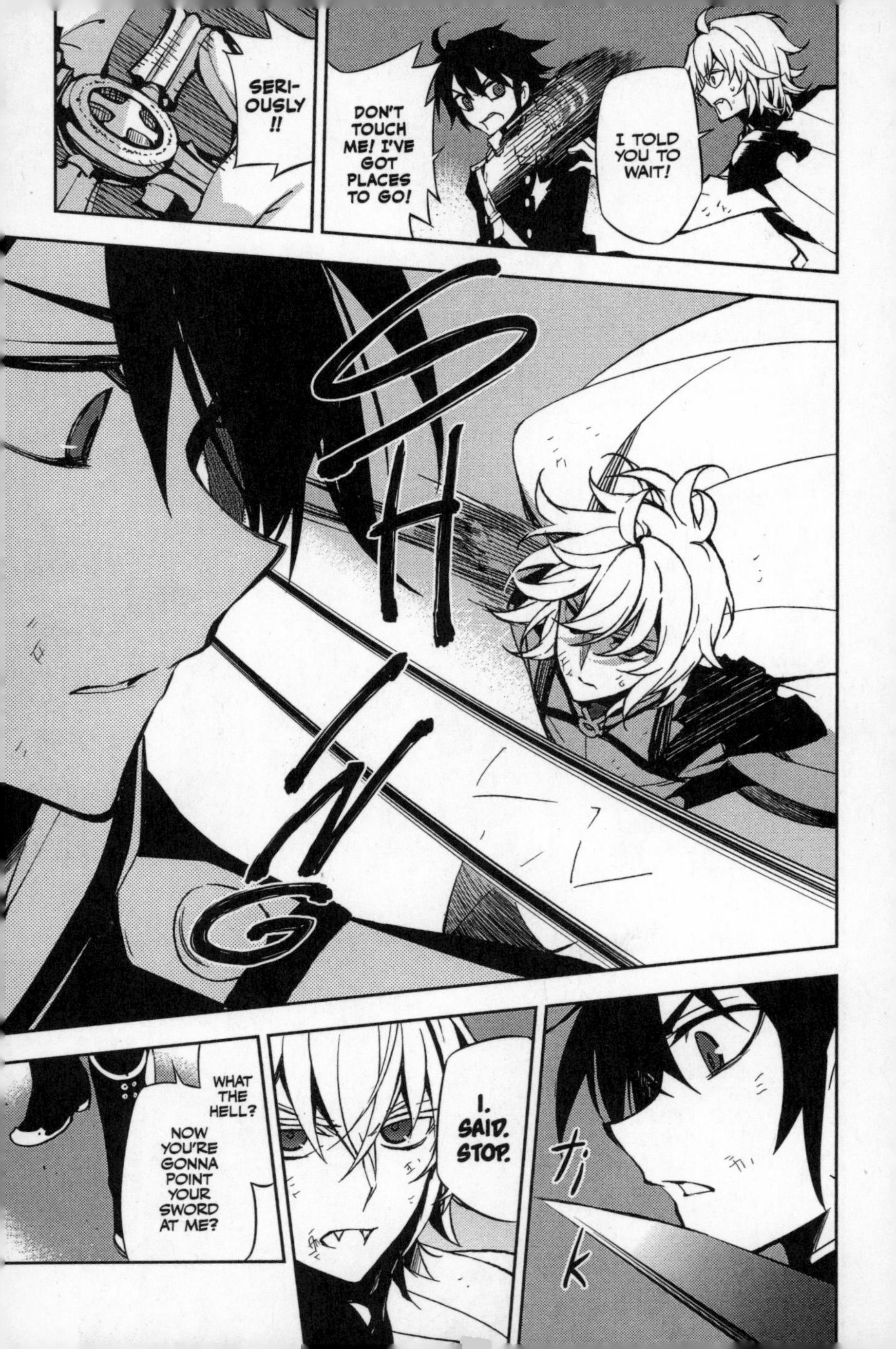
I TOLD YOU TO WAIT!
DON'T TOUCH ME! I'VE GOT PLACES TO GO!
SERI-OUSLY !!
SHING
tik
I. SAID. STOP.
WHAT THE HELL?
NOW YOU'RE GONNA POINT YOUR SWORD AT ME?

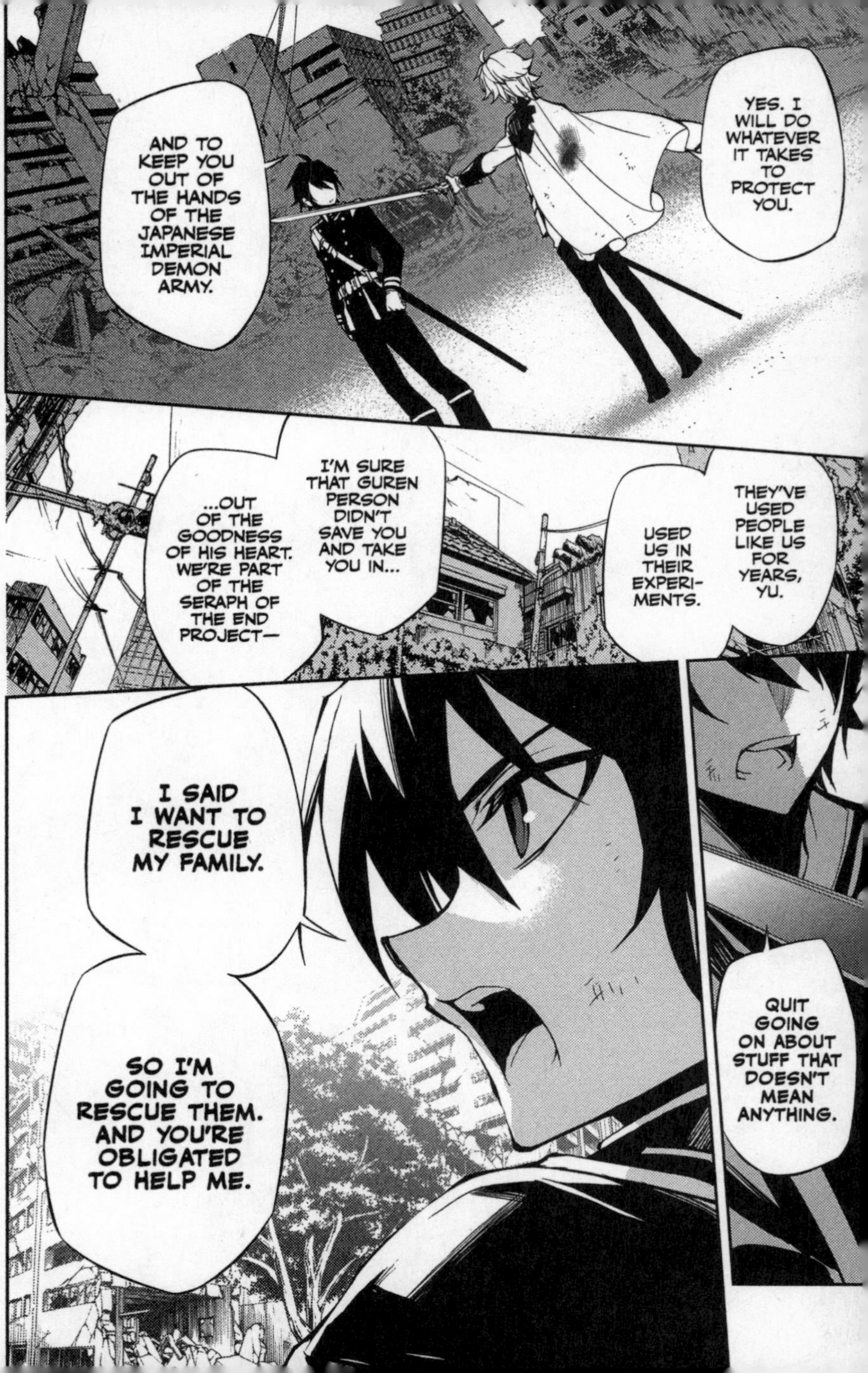
YES. I WILL DO WHATEVER IT TAKES TO PROTECT YOU.
AND TO KEEP YOU OUT OF THE HANDS OF THE JAPANESE IMPERIAL DEMON ARMY.
THEY'VE USED PEOPLE LIKE US FOR YEARS, YU.
USED US IN THEIR EXPERIMENTS.
I'M SURE THAT GUREN PERSON DIDN'T SAVE YOU AND TAKE YOU IN...
...OUT OF THE GOODNESS OF HIS HEART. WE'RE PART OF THE SERAPH OF THE END PROJECT—
QUIT GOING ON ABOUT STUFF THAT DOESN'T MEAN ANYTHING.
I SAID I WANT TO RESCUE MY FAMILY.
SO I'M GOING TO RESCUE THEM. AND YOU'RE OBLIGATED TO HELP ME.

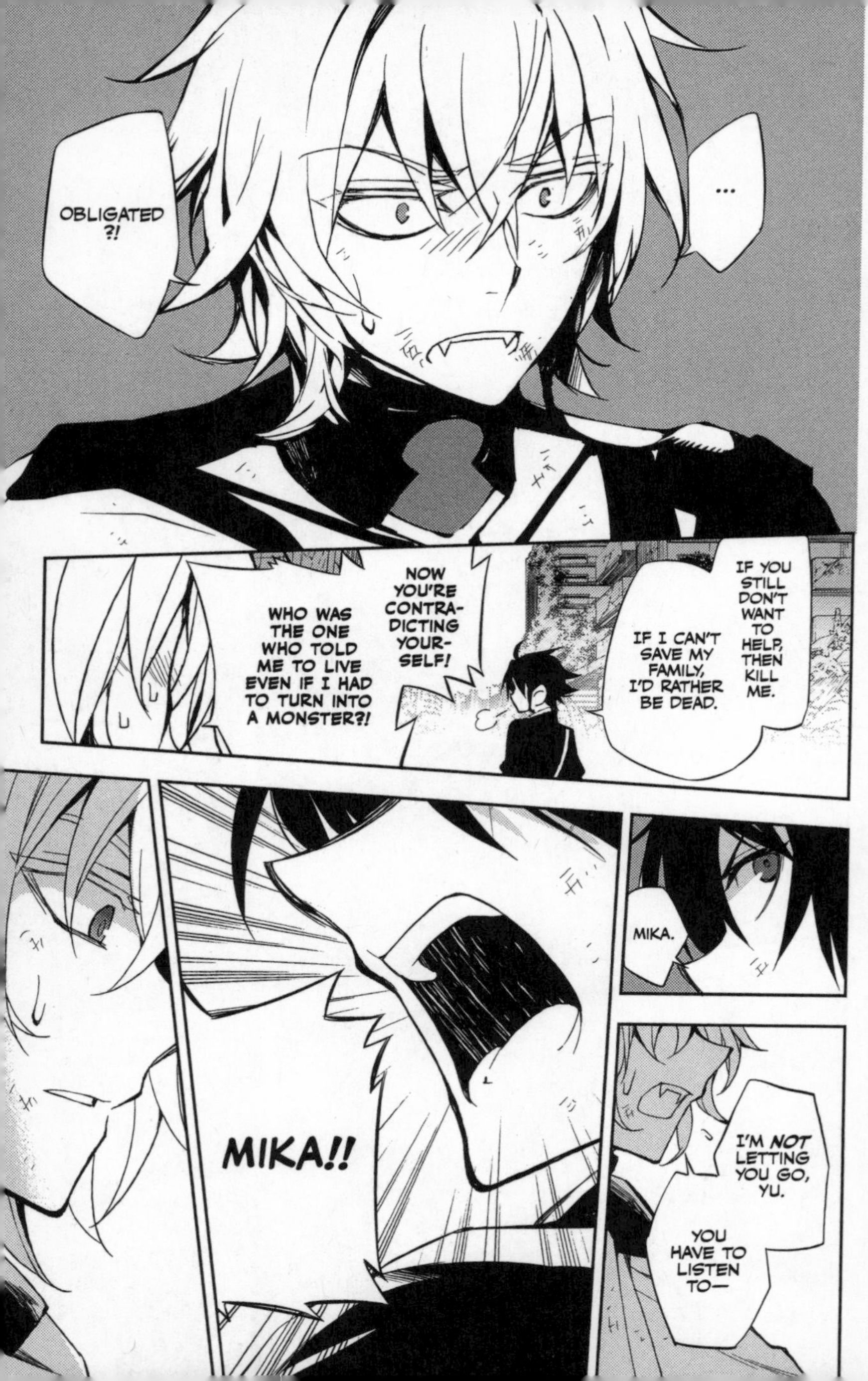

...
OBLIGATED?!
IF YOU STILL DON'T WANT TO HELP, THEN KILL ME.
IF I CAN'T SAVE MY FAMILY, I'D RATHER BE DEAD.
NOW YOU'RE CONTRA-DICTING YOUR-SELF!
WHO WAS THE ONE WHO TOLD ME TO LIVE EVEN IF I HAD TO TURN INTO A MONSTER?!
MIKA.
I'M NOT LETTING YOU GO, YU.
YOU HAVE TO LISTEN TO—
MIKA!!

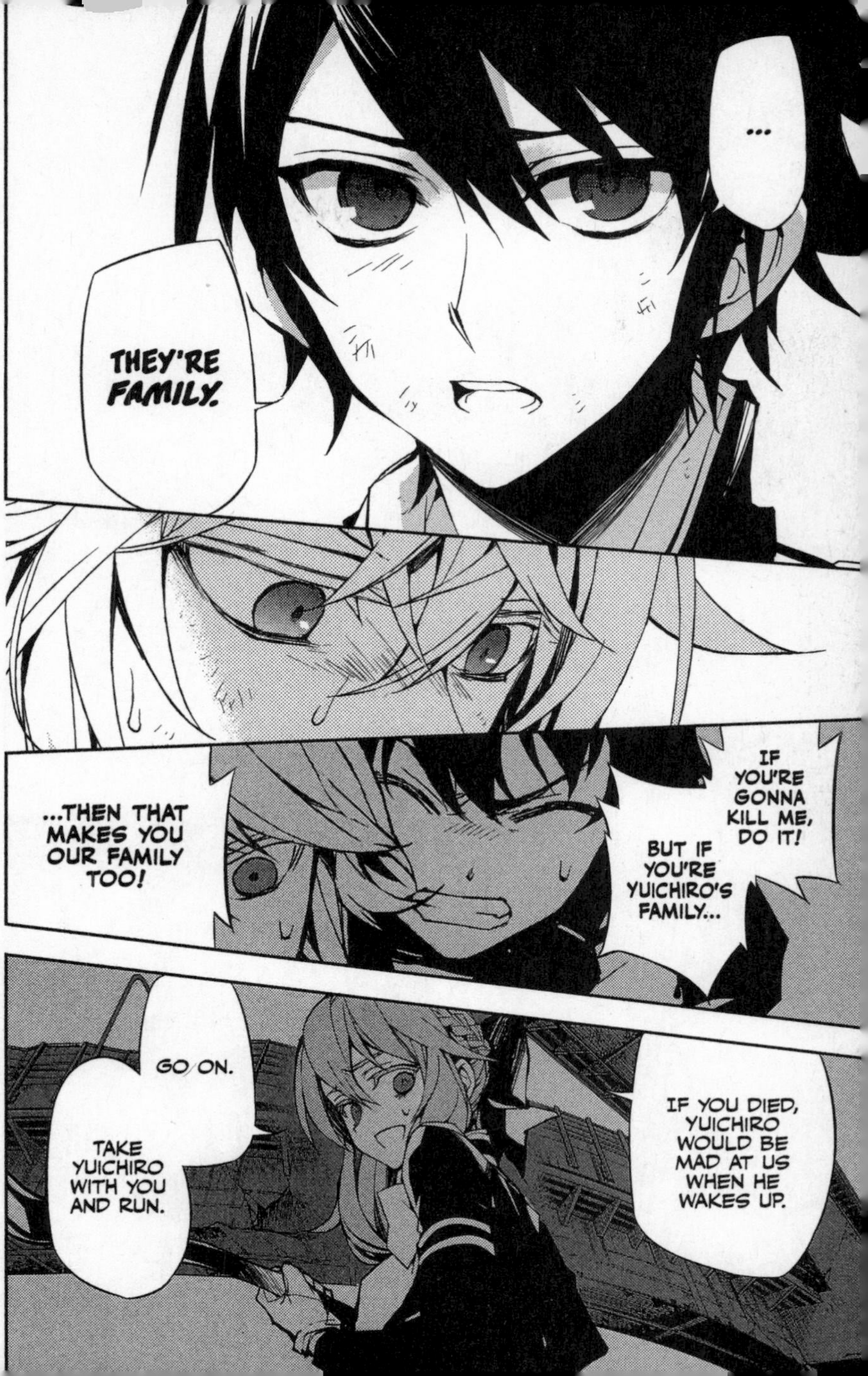
...
THEY'RE FAMILY.
IF YOU'RE GONNA KILL ME, DO IT!
BUT IF YOU'RE YUICHIRO'S FAMILY...
...THEN THAT MAKES YOU OUR FAMILY TOO!
IF YOU DIED, YUICHIRO WOULD BE MAD AT US WHEN HE WAKES UP.
GO ON.
TAKE YUICHIRO WITH YOU AND RUN.

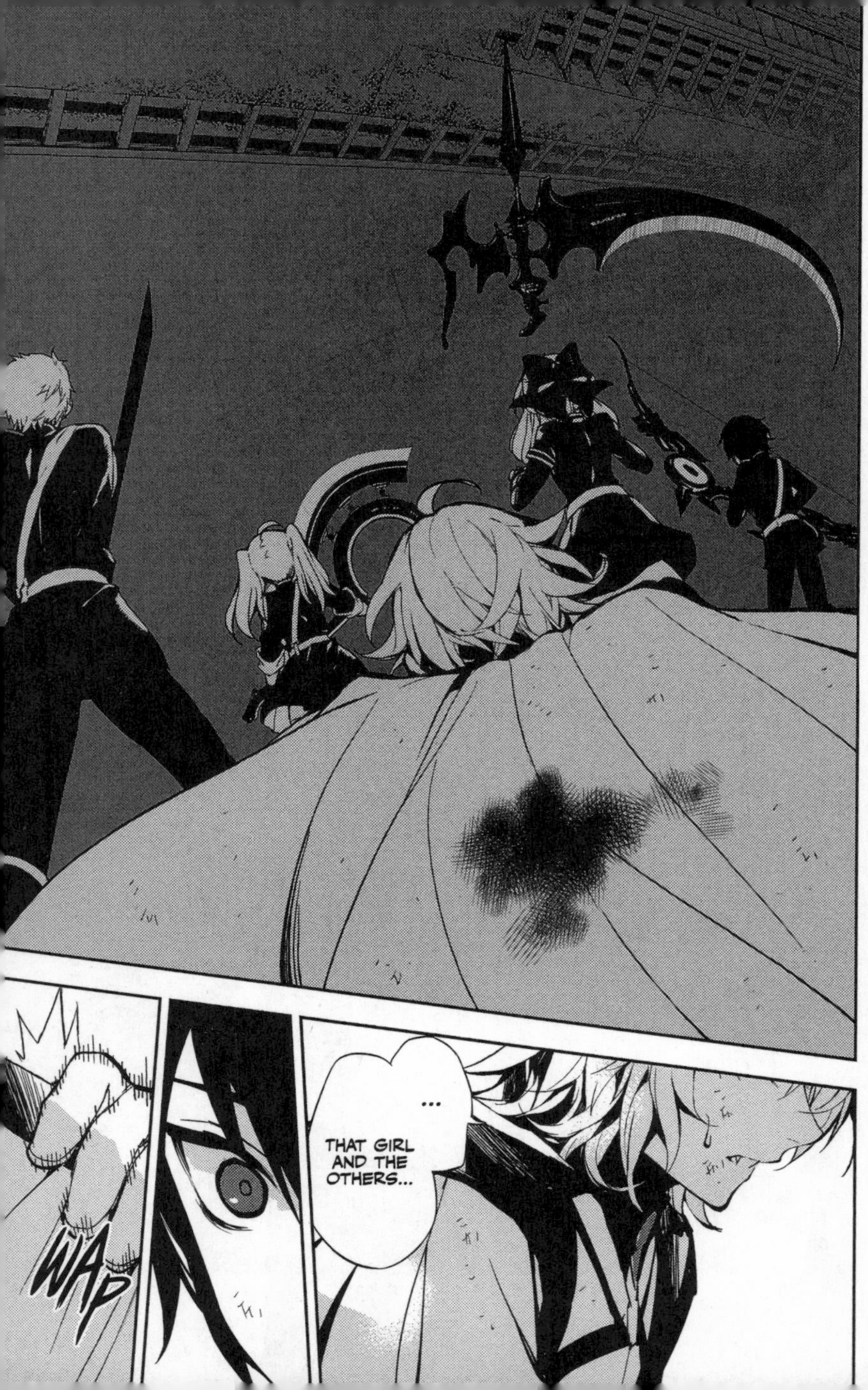
...
THAT GIRL AND THE OTHERS...
WAP

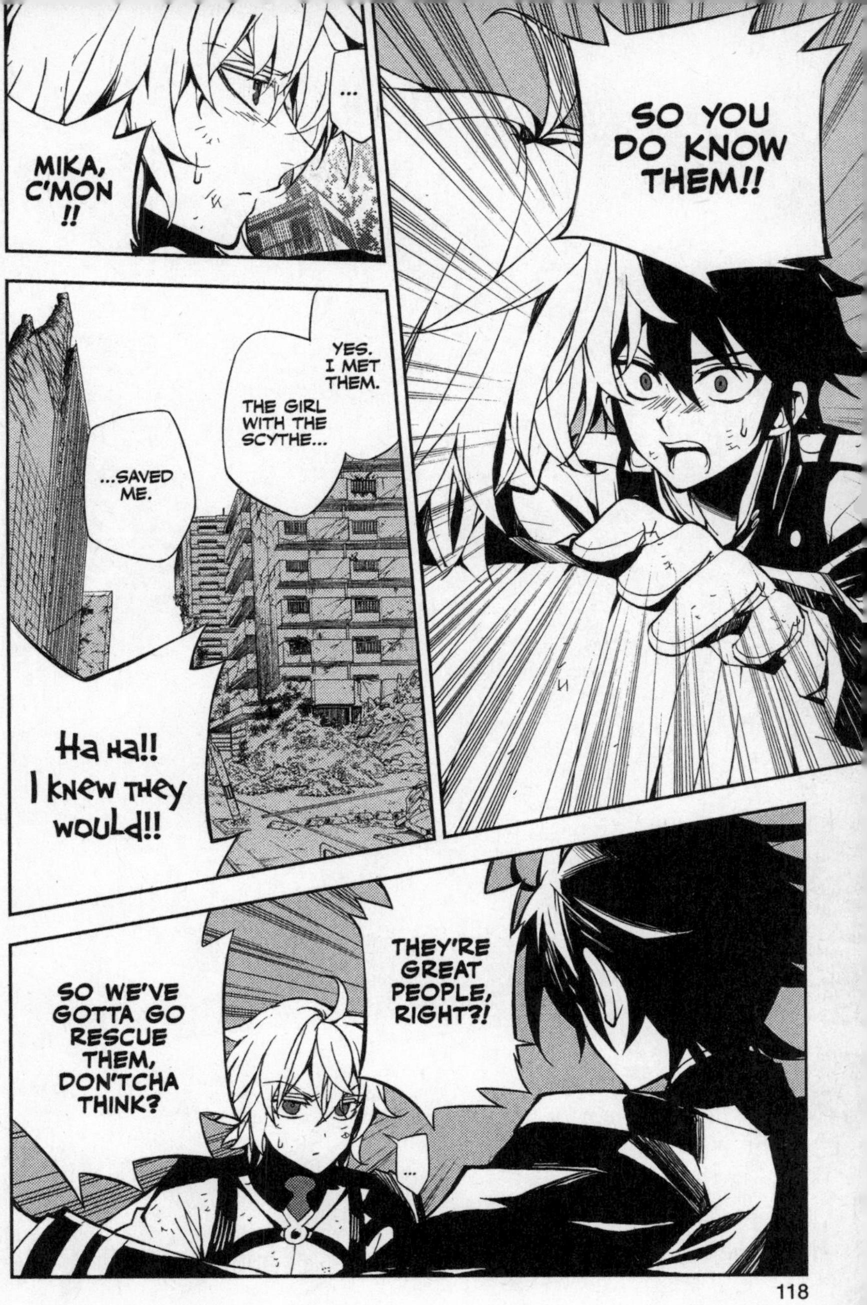
SO YOU DO KNOW THEM!!
...
MIKA, C'MON !!
YES. I MET THEM.
THE GIRL WITH THE SCYTHE...
...SAVED ME.
Ha ha!! I knew they would!!
THEY'RE GREAT PEOPLE, RIGHT?!
SO WE'VE GOTTA GO RESCUE THEM, DON'TCHA THINK?
...

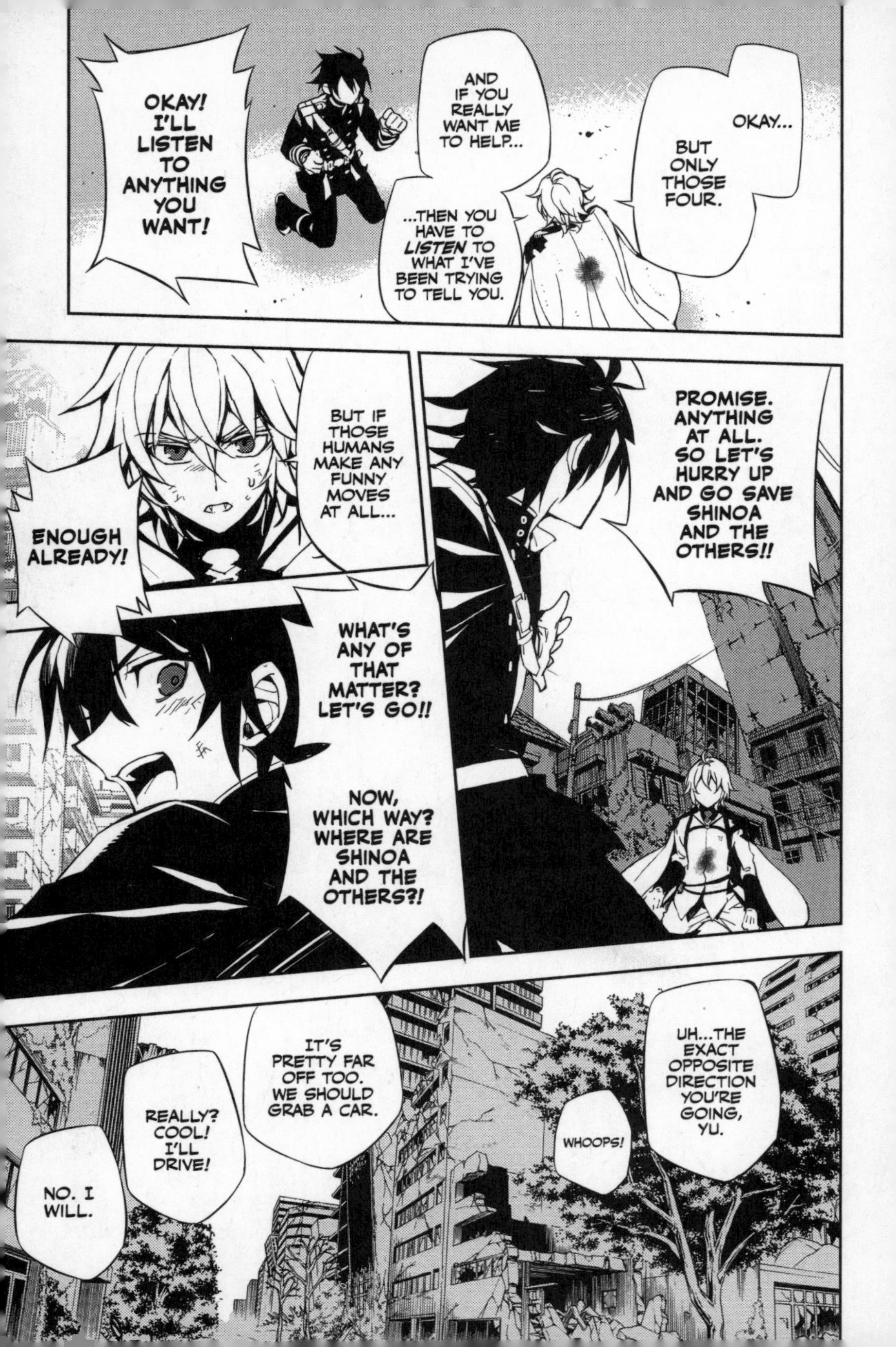
OKAY...
BUT ONLY THOSE FOUR.
AND IF YOU REALLY WANT ME TO HELP...
...THEN YOU HAVE TO *LISTEN* TO WHAT I'VE BEEN TRYING TO TELL YOU.
OKAY! I'LL LISTEN TO ANYTHING YOU WANT!
PROMISE. ANYTHING AT ALL. SO LET'S HURRY UP AND GO SAVE SHINOA AND THE OTHERS!!
BUT IF THOSE HUMANS MAKE ANY FUNNY MOVES AT ALL...
ENOUGH ALREADY!
WHAT'S ANY OF THAT MATTER? LET'S GO!!
NOW, WHICH WAY? WHERE ARE SHINOA AND THE OTHERS?!
UH...THE EXACT OPPOSITE DIRECTION YOU'RE GOING, YU.
WHOOPS!
IT'S PRETTY FAR OFF TOO. WE SHOULD GRAB A CAR.
REALLY? COOL! I'LL DRIVE!
NO. I WILL.

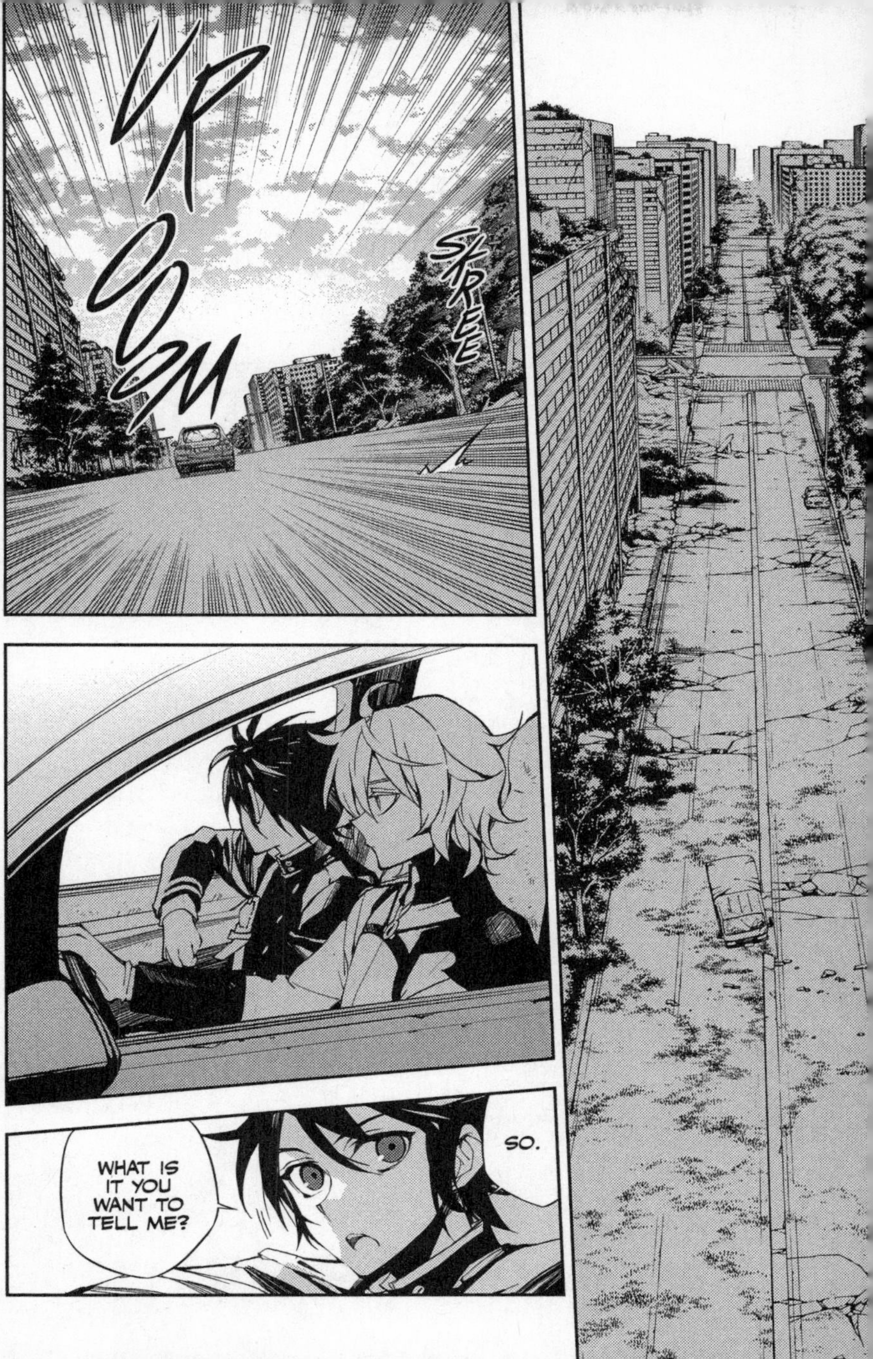
VROOOM
SKREE
SO.
WHAT IS IT YOU WANT TO TELL ME?

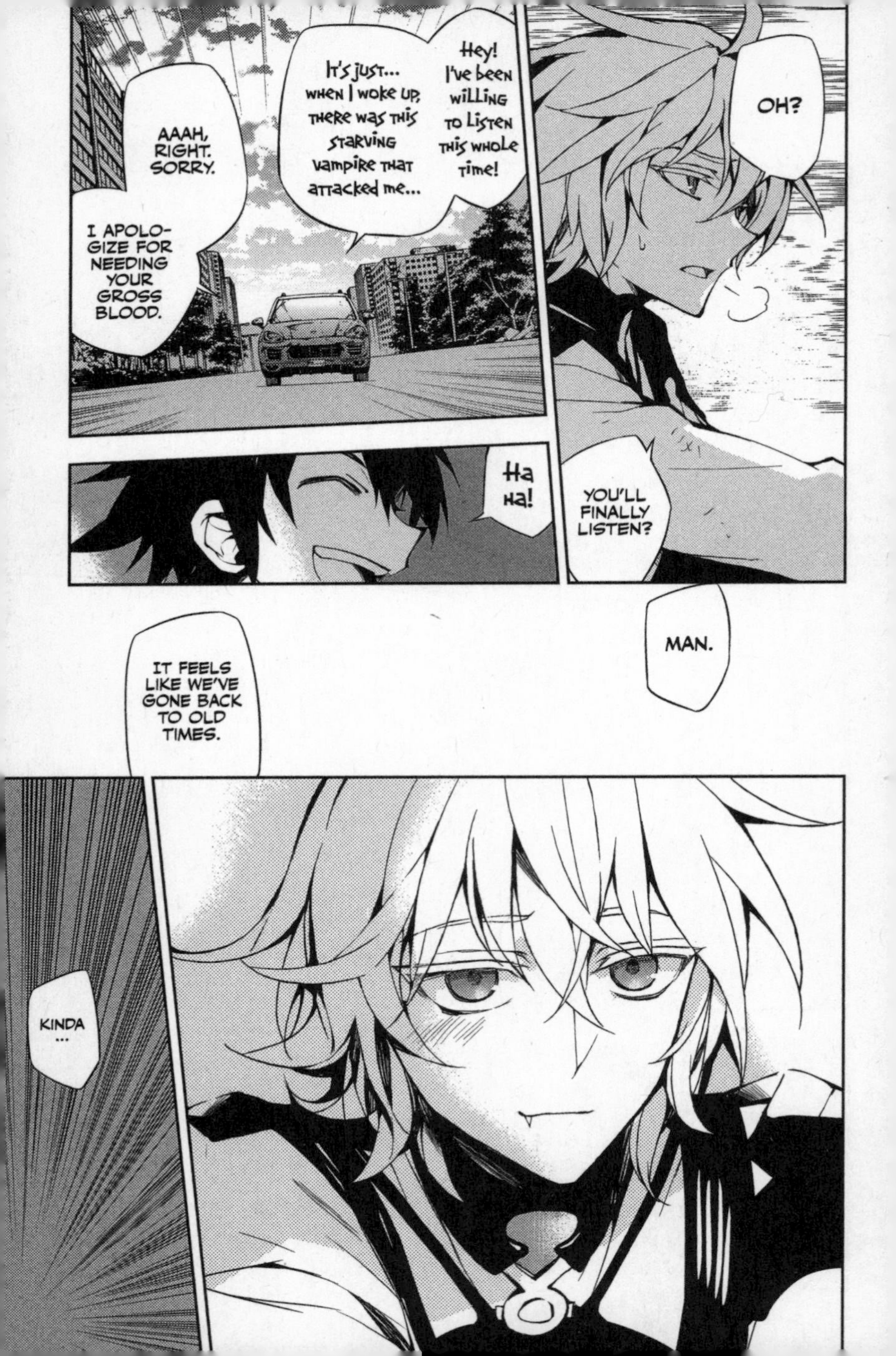
OH?
YOU'LL FINALLY LISTEN?
Hey! I've been willing to listen this whole time!
It's just... when I woke up, there was this starving vampire that attacked me...
AAAH, RIGHT. SORRY.
I APOLO-GIZE FOR NEEDING YOUR GROSS BLOOD.
Ha ha!
MAN.
IT FEELS LIKE WE'VE GONE BACK TO OLD TIMES.
KINDA ...

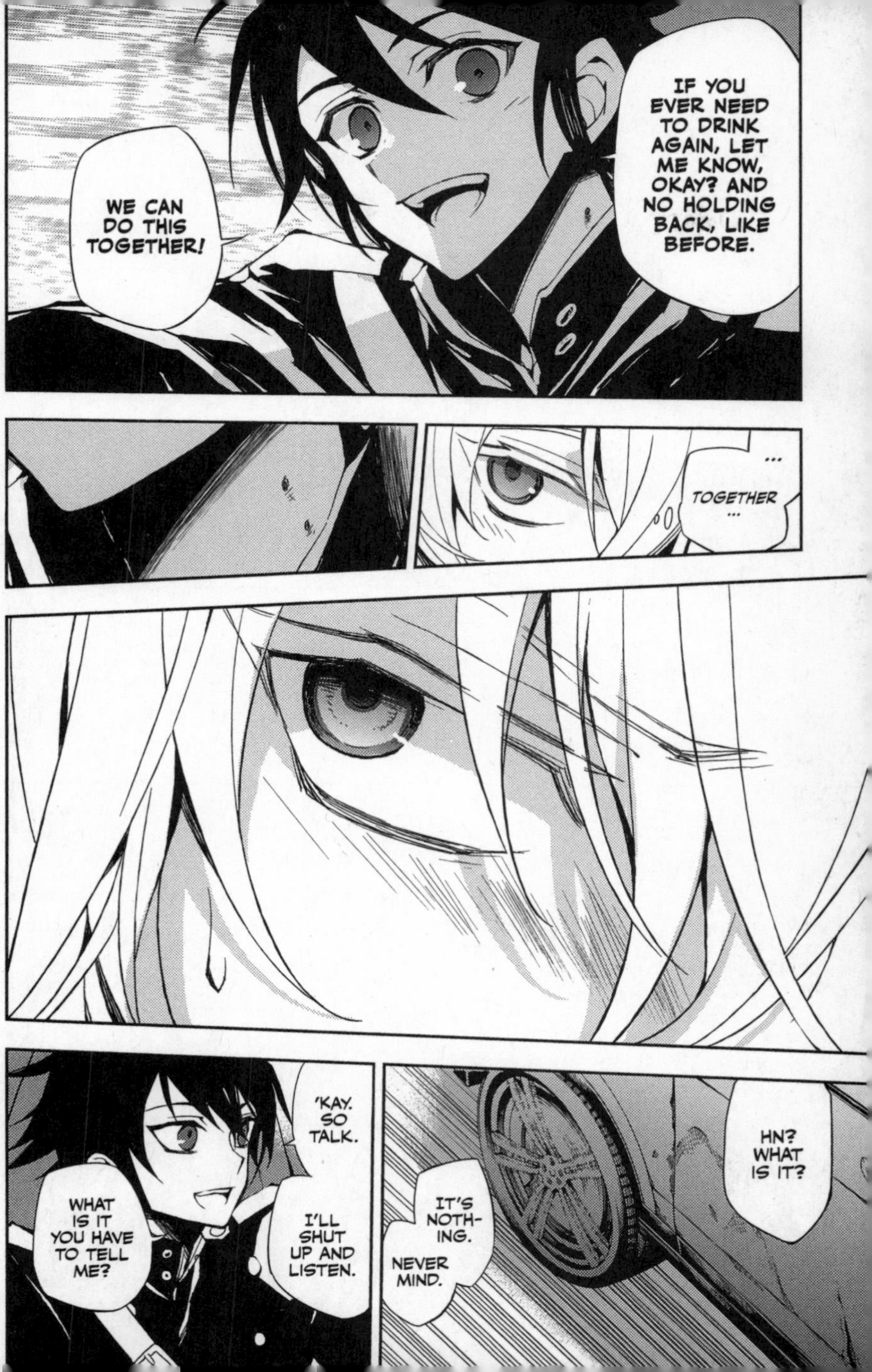
IF YOU EVER NEED TO DRINK AGAIN, LET ME KNOW, OKAY? AND NO HOLDING BACK, LIKE BEFORE.
WE CAN DO THIS TOGETHER!
... TOGETHER ...
HN? WHAT IS IT?
IT'S NOTHING-ING.
NEVER MIND.
'KAY. SO TALK.
I'LL SHUT UP AND LISTEN.
WHAT IS IT YOU HAVE TO TELL ME?

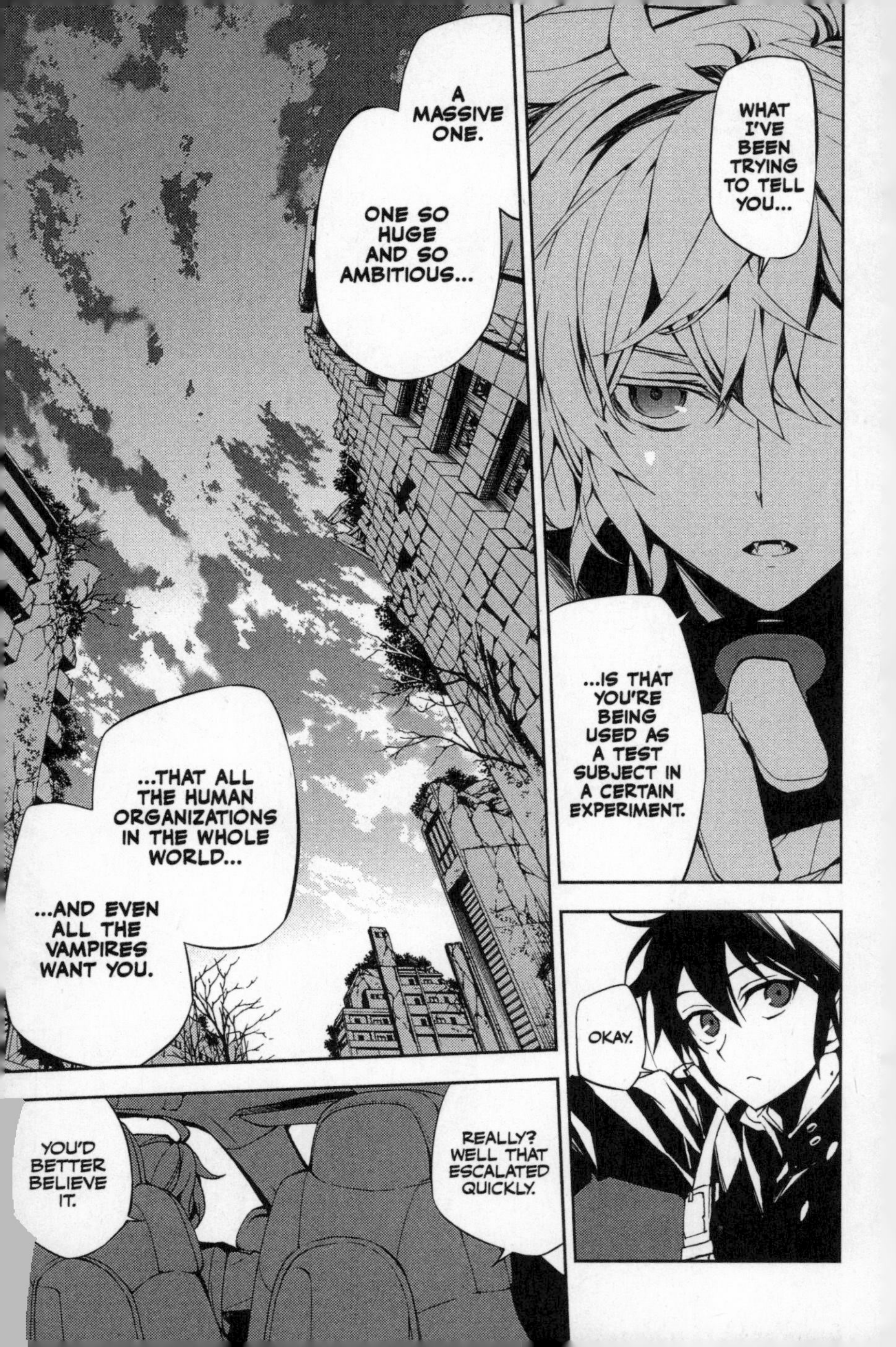
WHAT I'VE BEEN TRYING TO TELL YOU...
...IS THAT YOU'RE BEING USED AS A TEST SUBJECT IN A CERTAIN EXPERIMENT.
A MASSIVE ONE.
ONE SO HUGE AND SO AMBITIOUS...
...THAT ALL THE HUMAN ORGANIZATIONS IN THE WHOLE WORLD...
...AND EVEN ALL THE VAMPIRES WANT YOU.
OKAY.
REALLY? WELL THAT ESCALATED QUICKLY.
YOU'D BETTER BELIEVE IT.

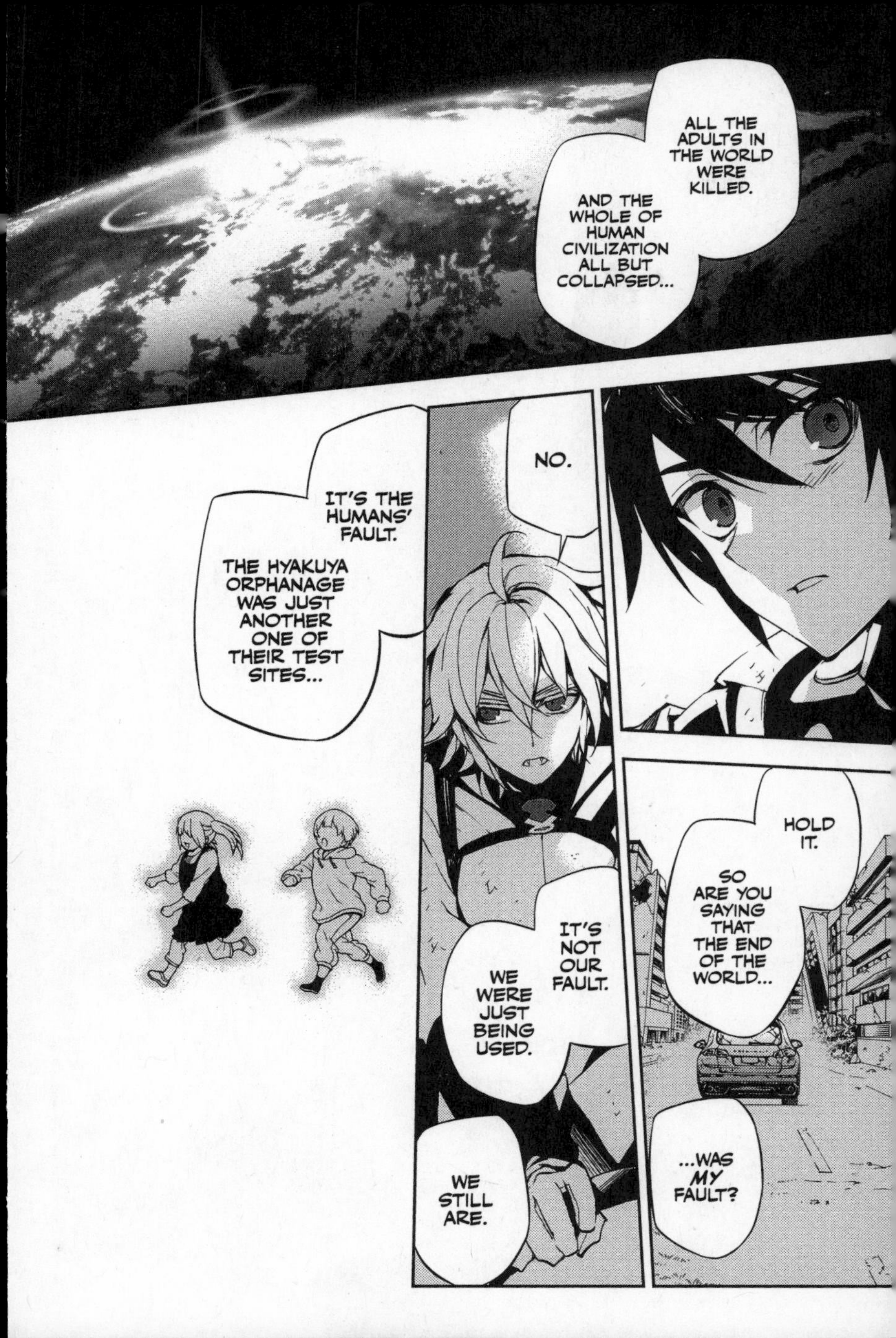
ALL THE ADULTS IN THE WORLD WERE KILLED.
AND THE WHOLE OF HUMAN CIVILIZATION ALL BUT COLLAPSED...
HOLD IT.
SO ARE YOU SAYING THAT THE END OF THE WORLD...
...WAS *MY* FAULT?
NO.
IT'S THE HUMANS' FAULT.
THE HYAKUYA ORPHANAGE WAS JUST ANOTHER ONE OF THEIR TEST SITES...
IT'S NOT OUR FAULT.
WE WERE JUST BEING USED.
WE STILL ARE.

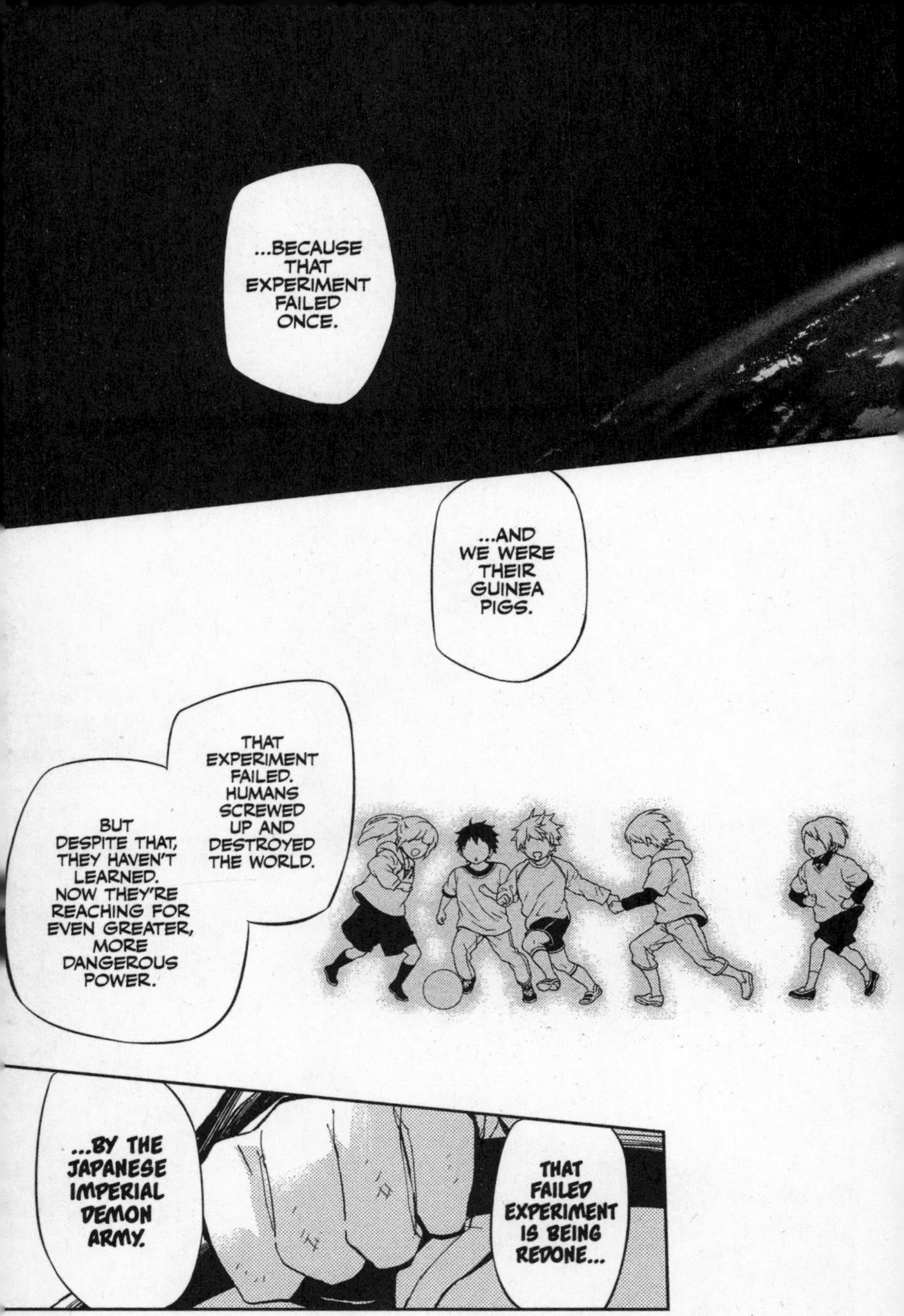
...BECAUSE THAT EXPERIMENT FAILED ONCE.
...AND WE WERE THEIR GUINEA PIGS.
THAT EXPERIMENT FAILED. HUMANS SCREWED UP AND DESTROYED THE WORLD.
BUT DESPITE THAT, THEY HAVEN'T LEARNED. NOW THEY'RE REACHING FOR EVEN GREATER, MORE DANGEROUS POWER.
THAT FAILED EXPERIMENT IS BEING REDONE...
...BY THE JAPANESE IMPERIAL DEMON ARMY.

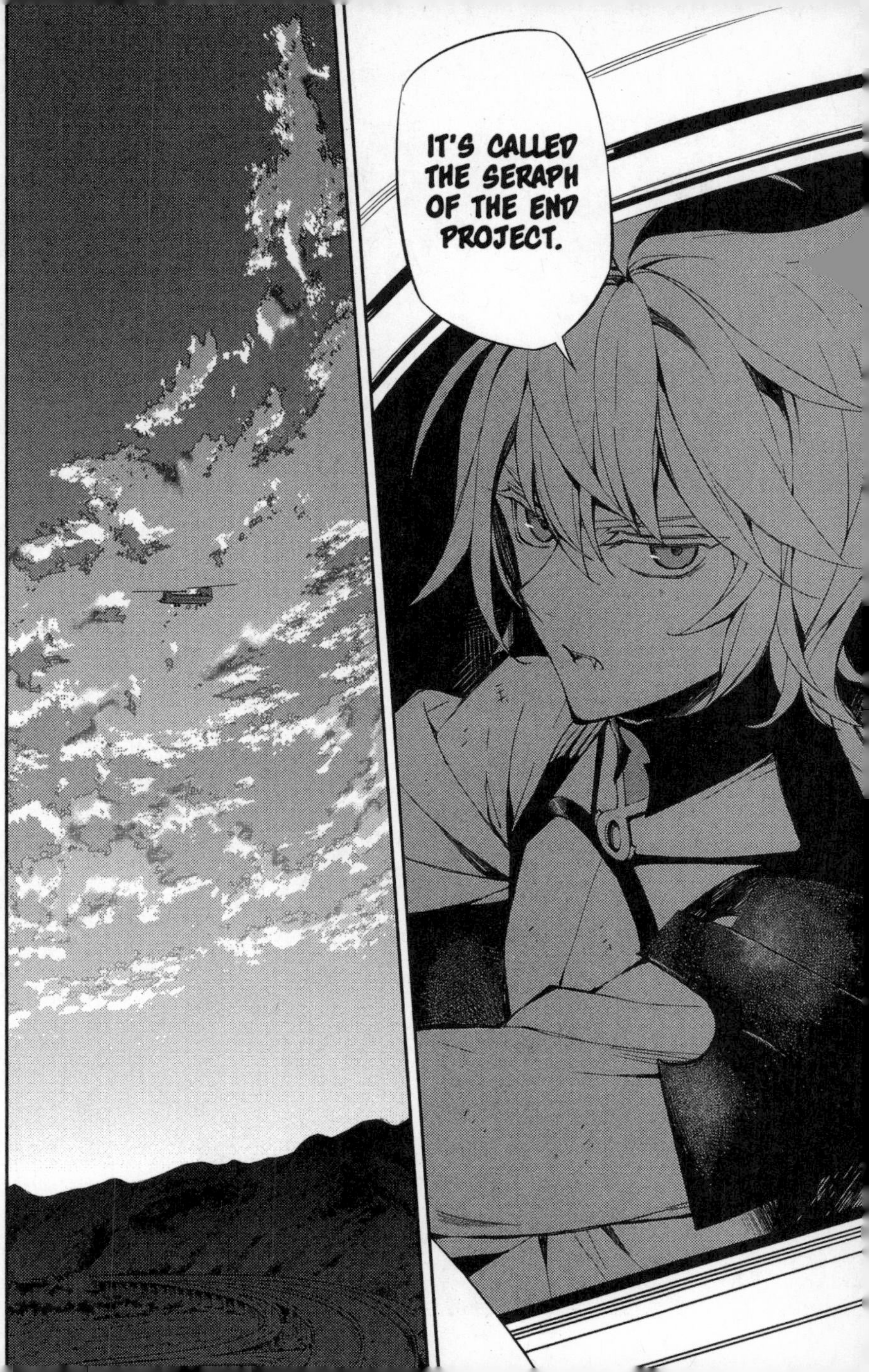
IT'S CALLED THE SERAPH OF THE END PROJECT.

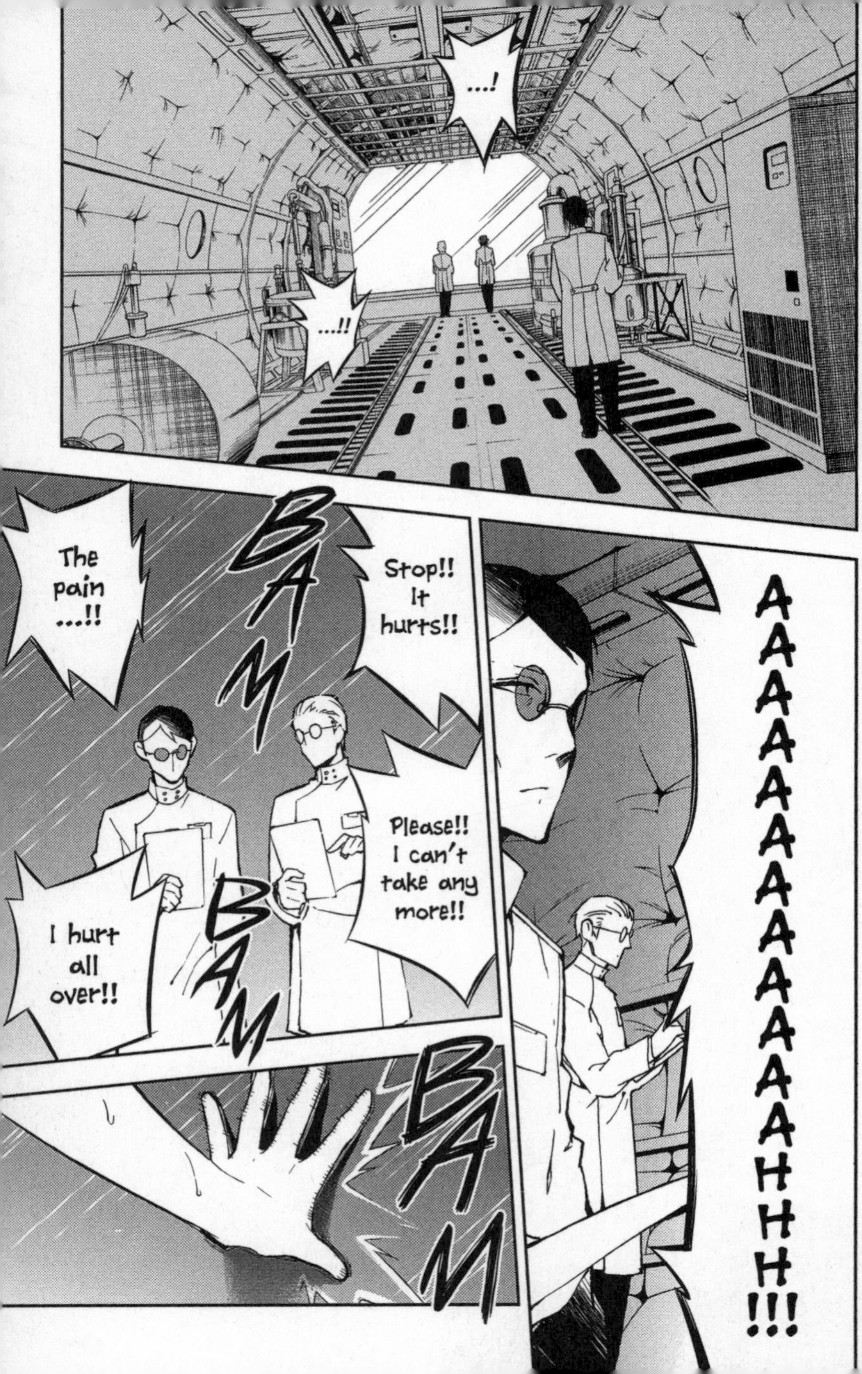
...!
...!!
AAAAAAAAAAAAAAAHHH!!!
Stop!! It hurts!!
BAM
The pain ...!!
Please!! I can't take any more!!
BAM
I hurt all over!!
BAM

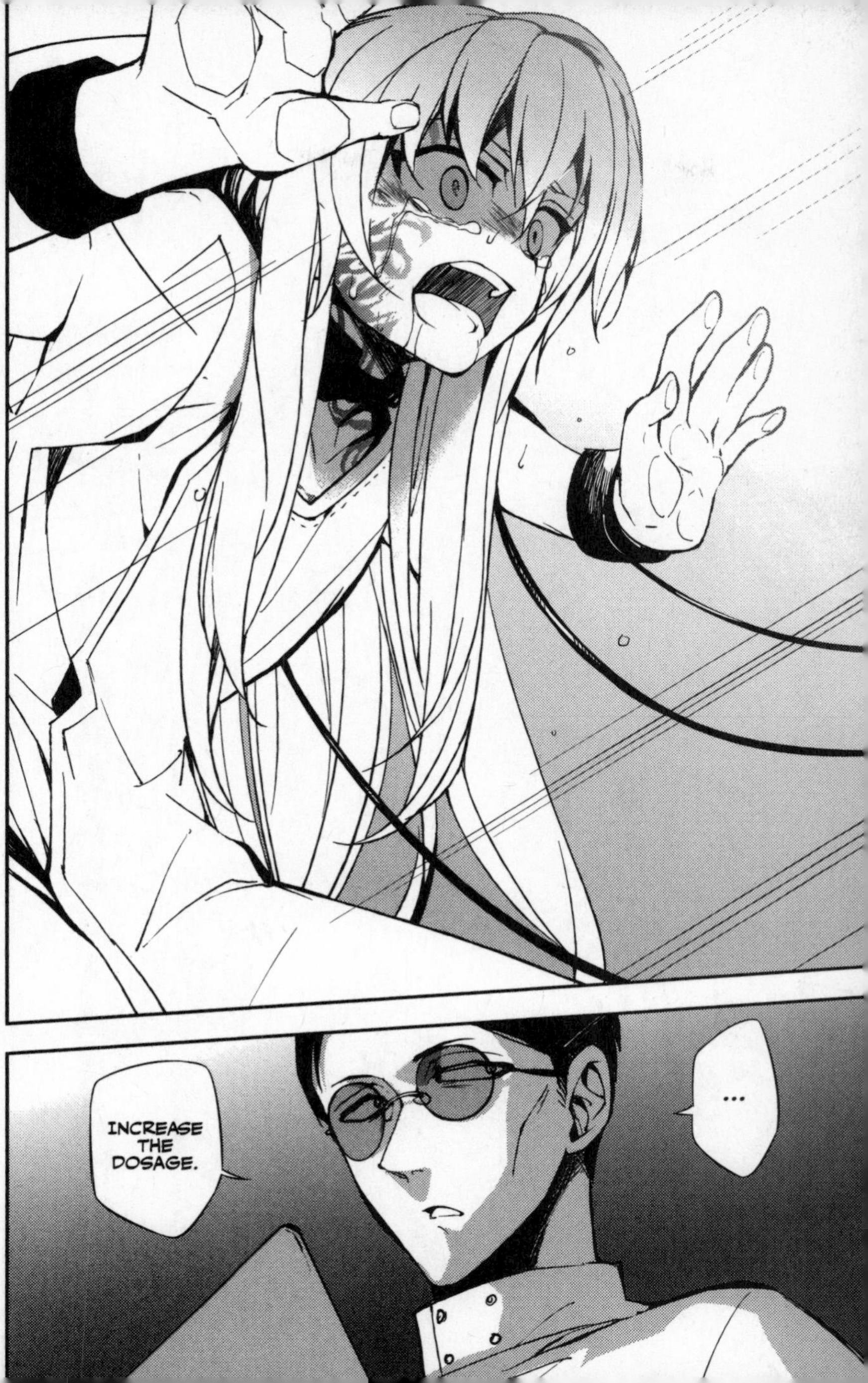
...
INCREASE THE DOSAGE.

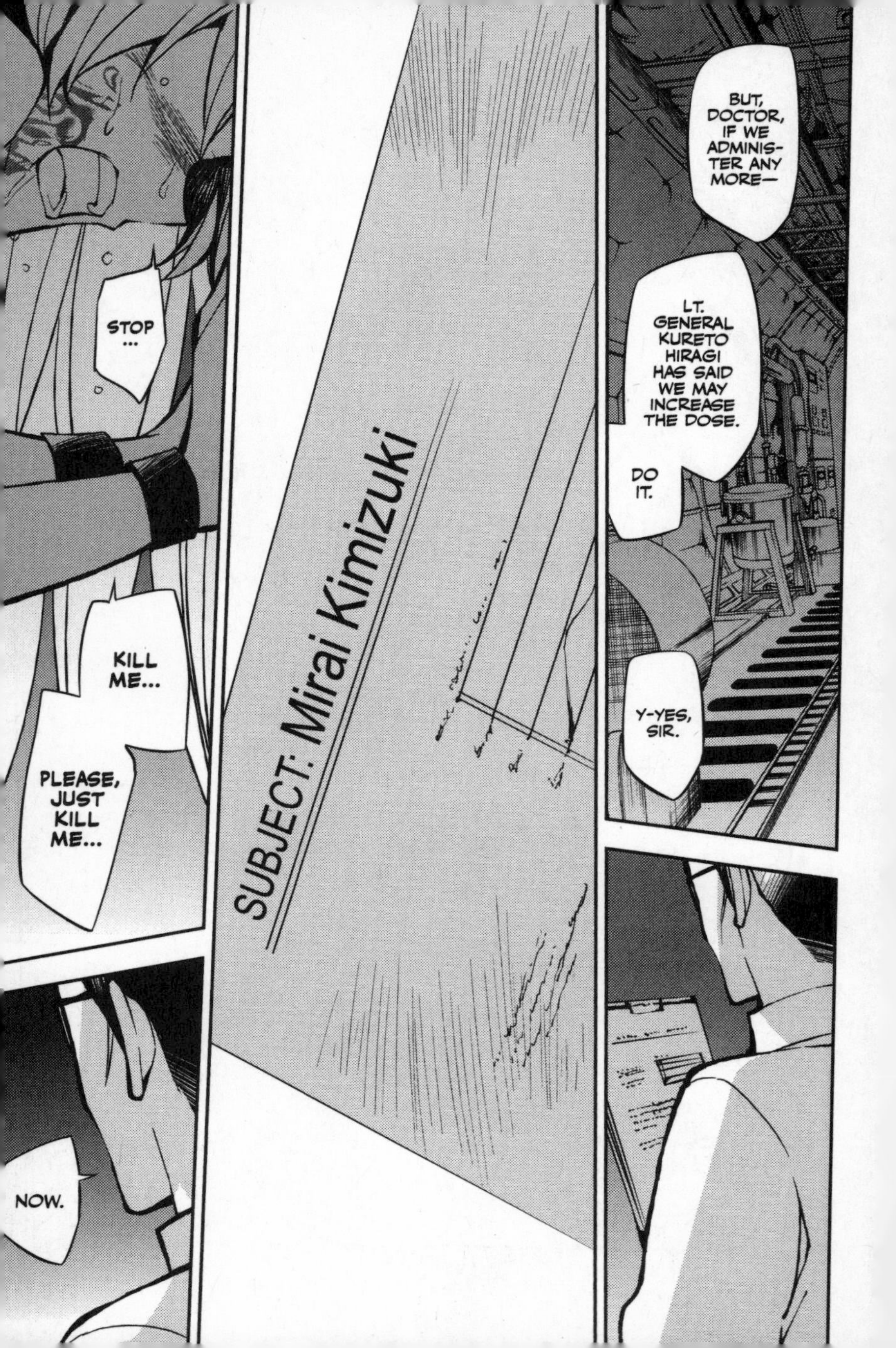
BUT, DOCTOR, IF WE ADMINISTER ANY MORE—
LT. GENERAL KURETO HIRAGI HAS SAID WE MAY INCREASE THE DOSE.
DO IT.
Y-YES, SIR.
SUBJECT: Mirai Kimizuki
STOP ...
KILL ME...
PLEASE, JUST KILL ME...
NOW.

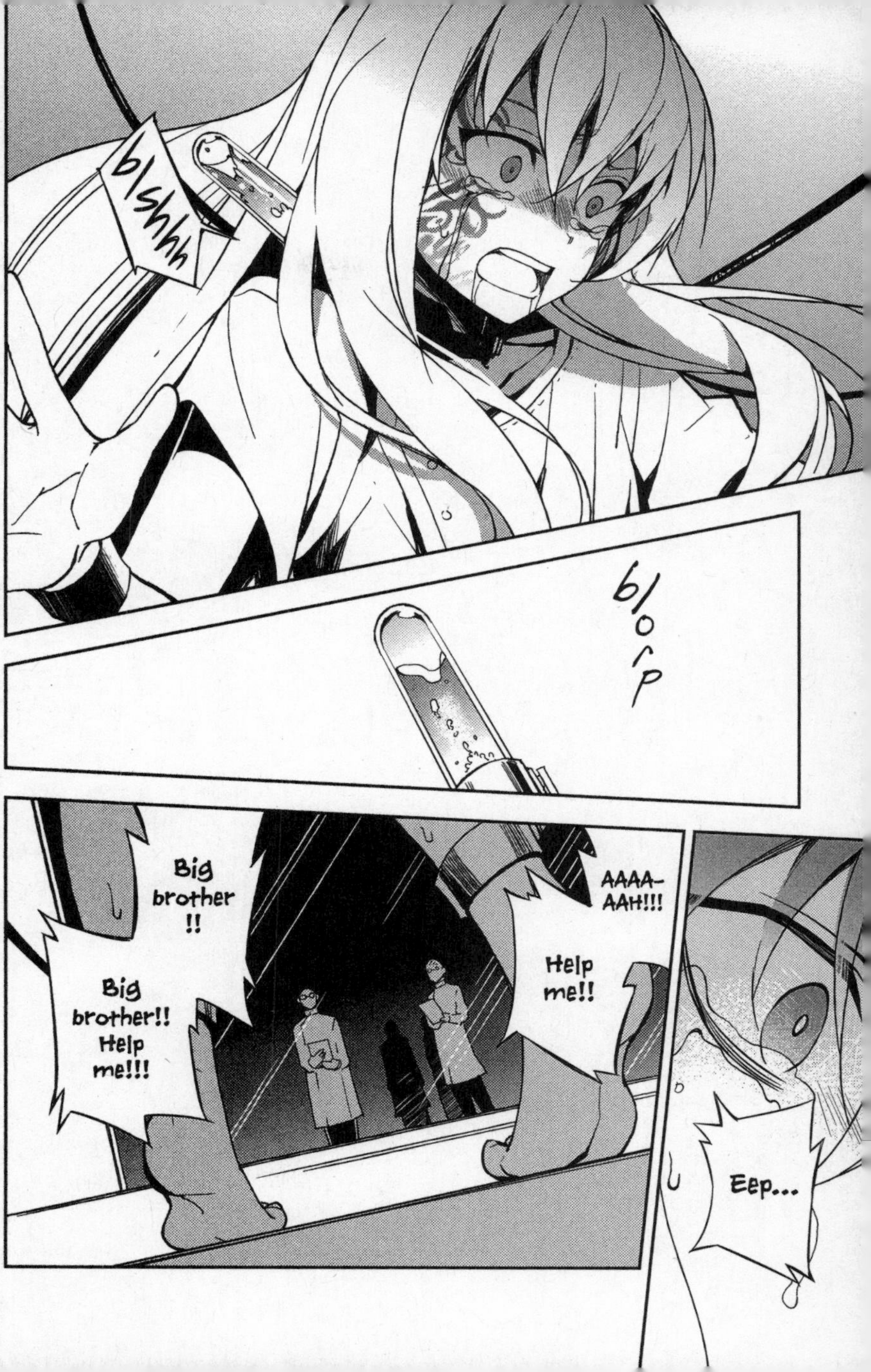
blshhh
blorp
Eep...
AAAA-AAH!!!
Big brother !!
Help me!!
Big brother!! Help me!!!

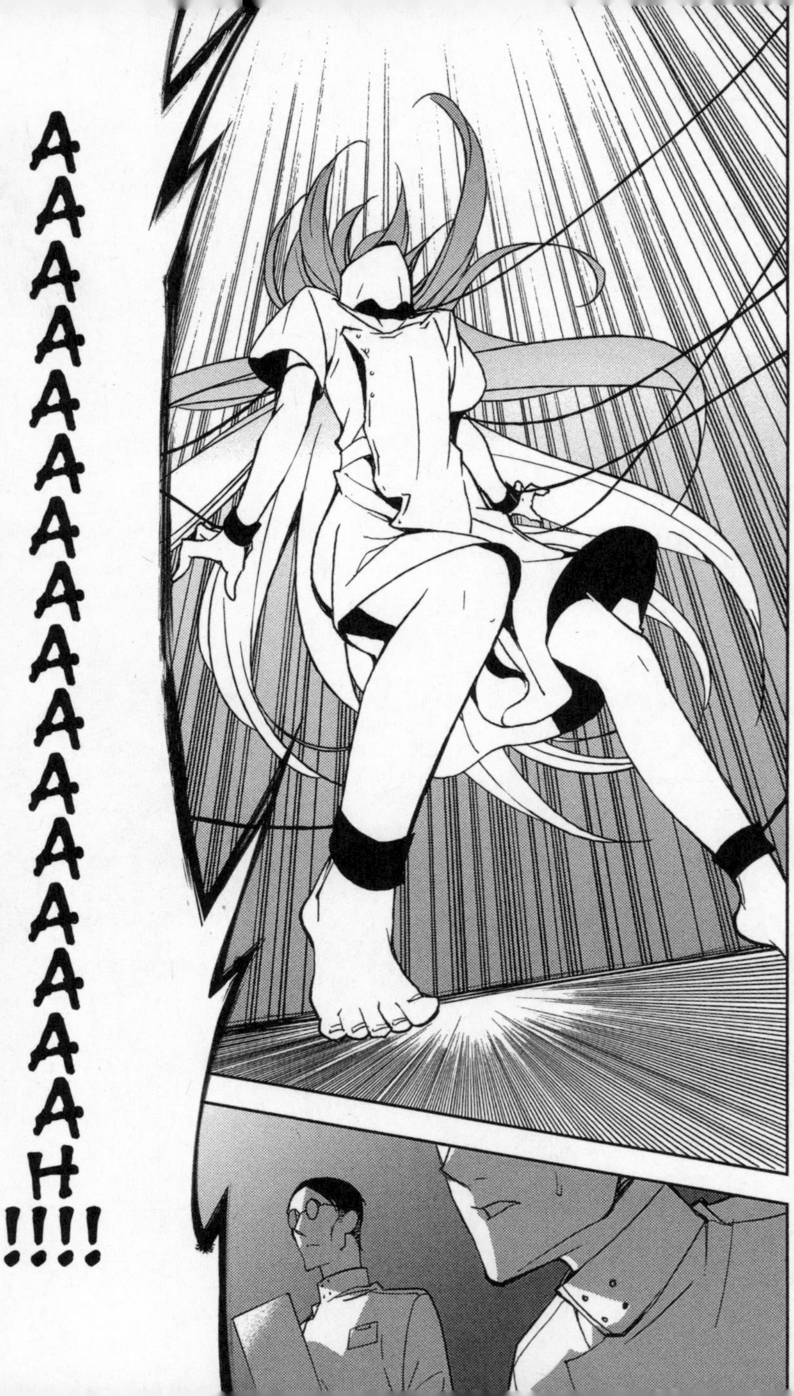
AAAAAAAAAAAAAAAAAAAAH!!!!

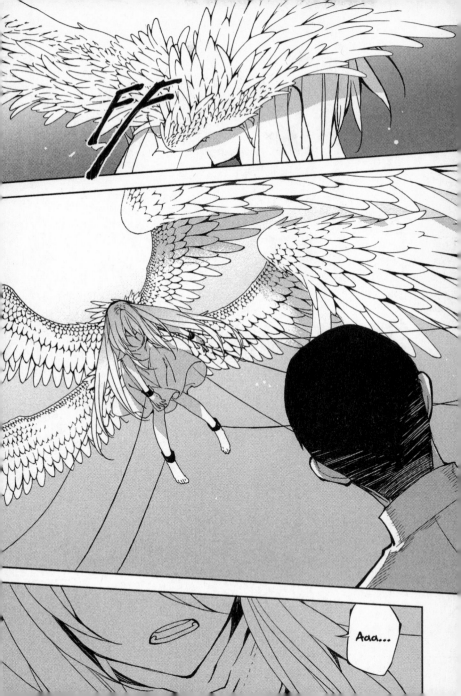

FF

Aaa...

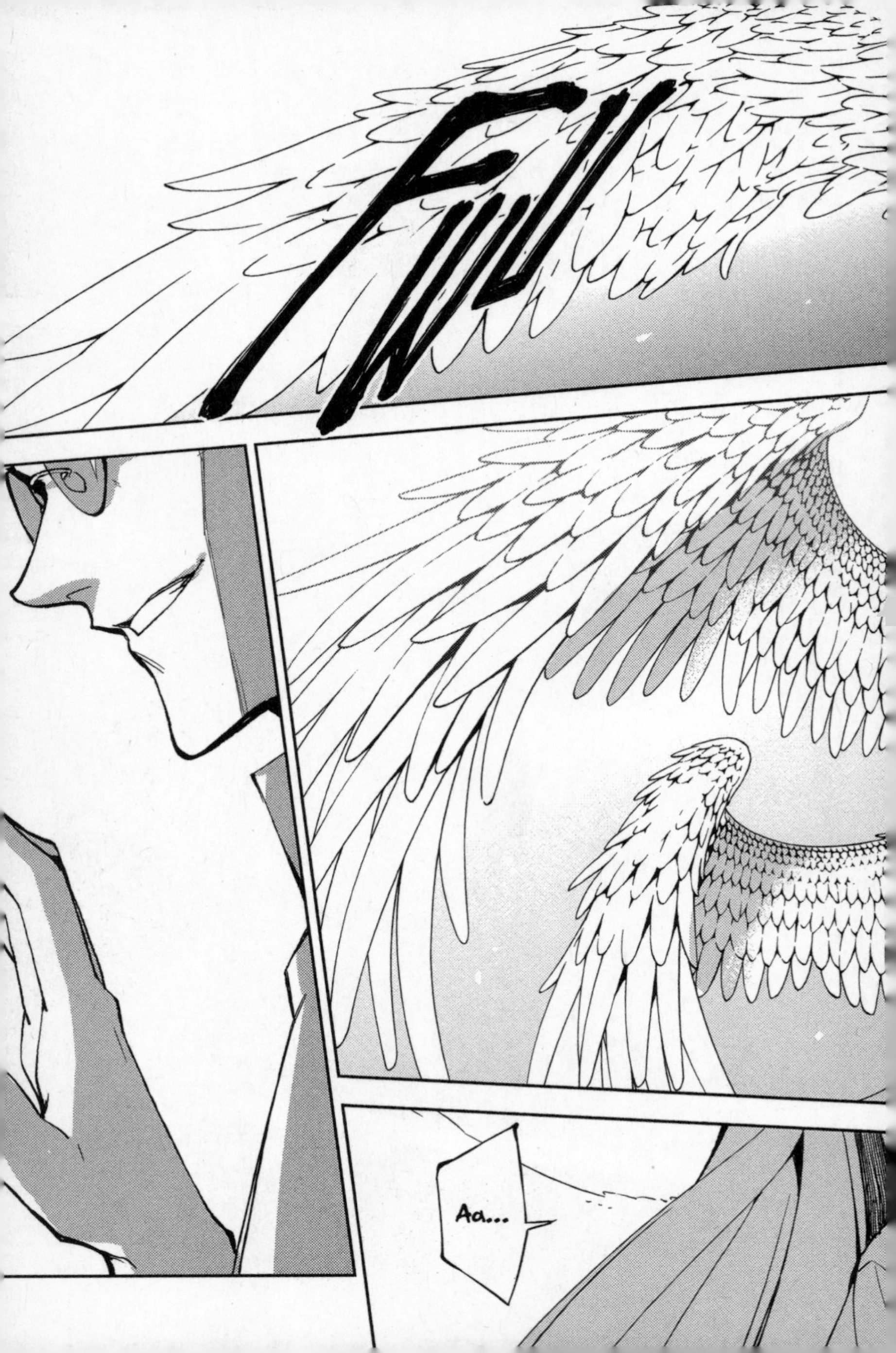
Aa...

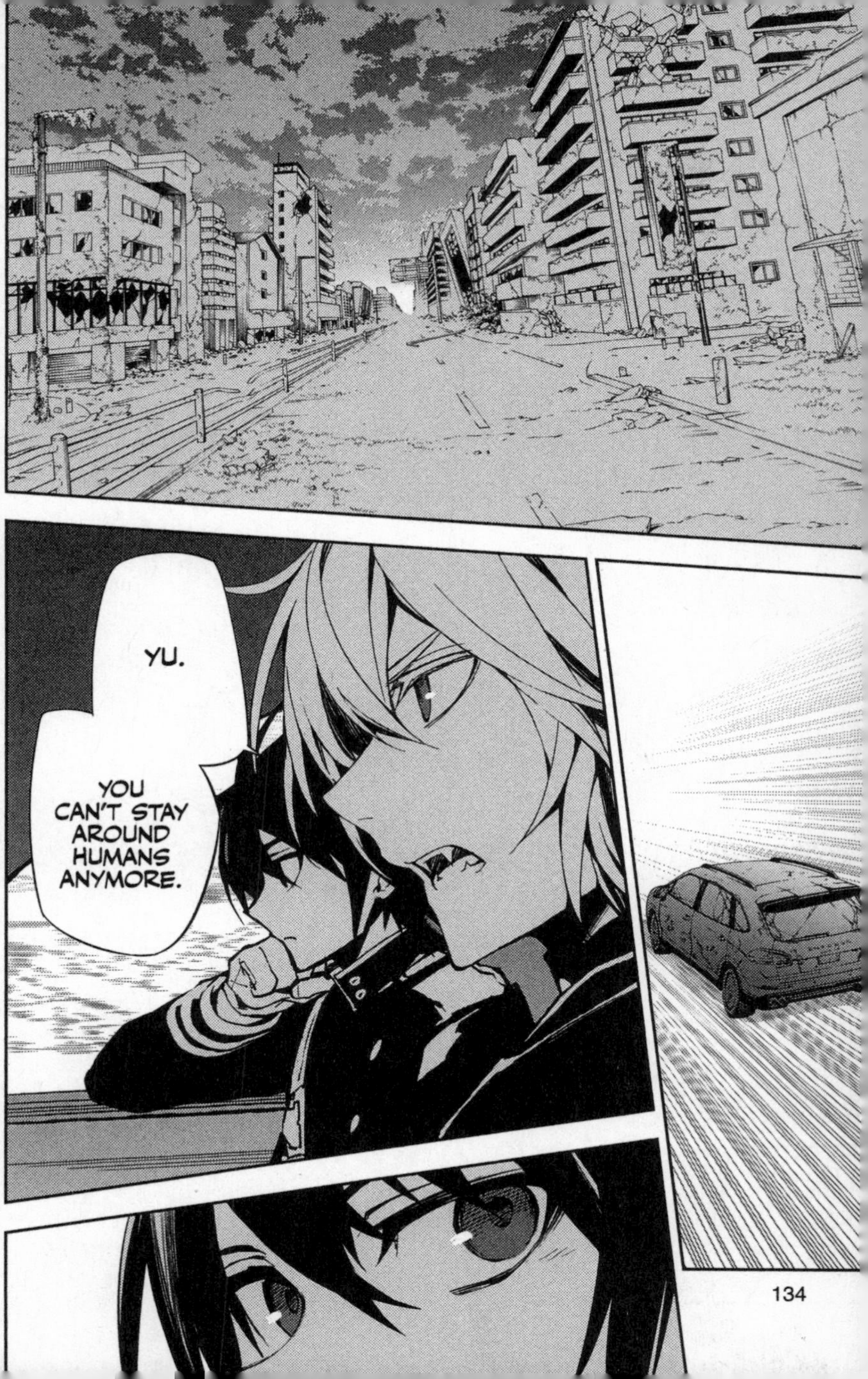
YU.
YOU CAN'T STAY AROUND HUMANS ANYMORE.

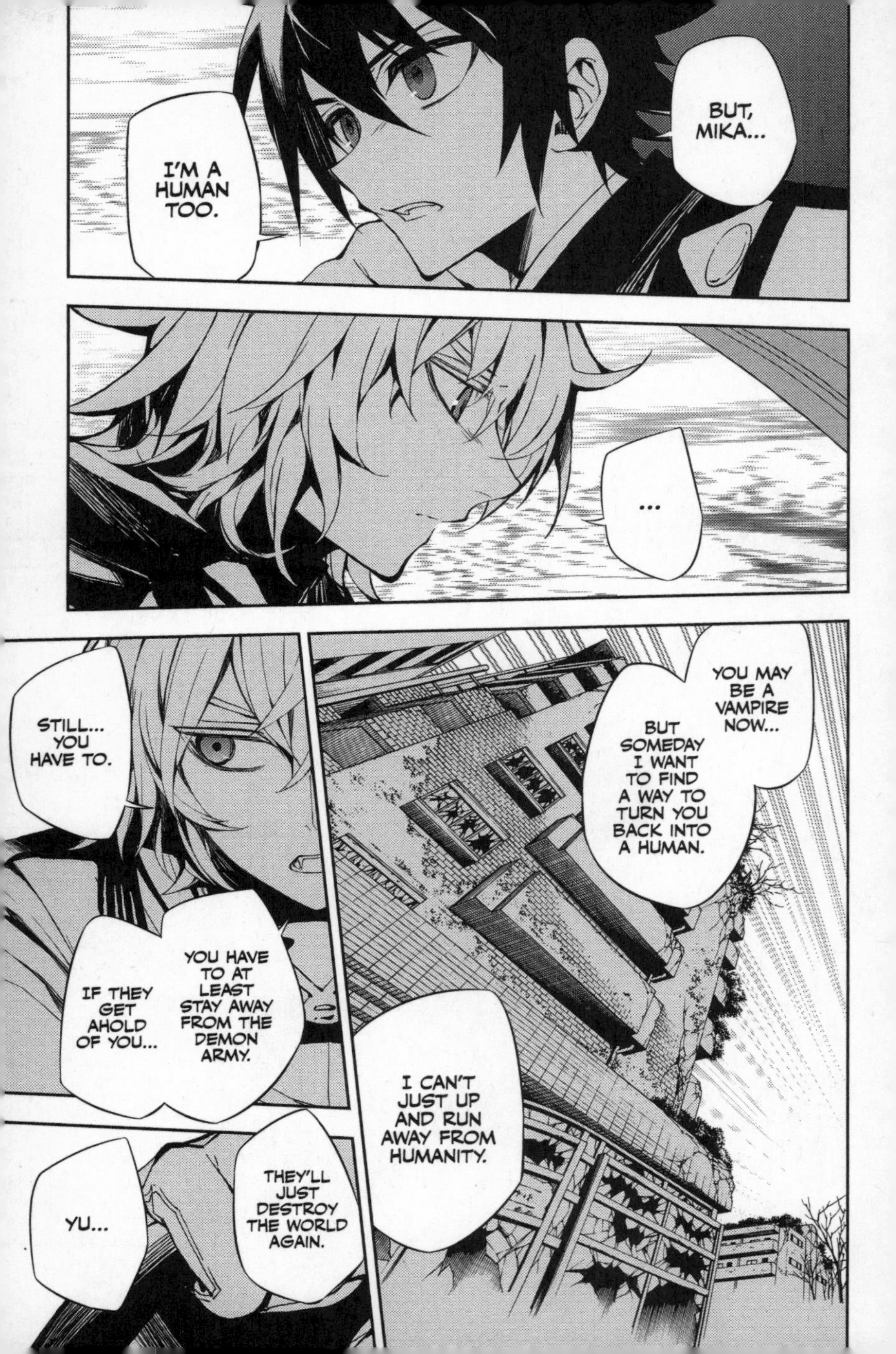
BUT, MIKA...
I'M A HUMAN TOO.
...
YOU MAY BE A VAMPIRE NOW...
BUT SOMEDAY I WANT TO FIND A WAY TO TURN YOU BACK INTO A HUMAN.
I CAN'T JUST UP AND RUN AWAY FROM HUMANITY.
STILL... YOU HAVE TO.
YOU HAVE TO AT LEAST STAY AWAY FROM THE DEMON ARMY.
IF THEY GET AHOLD OF YOU...
THEY'LL JUST DESTROY THE WORLD AGAIN.
YU...

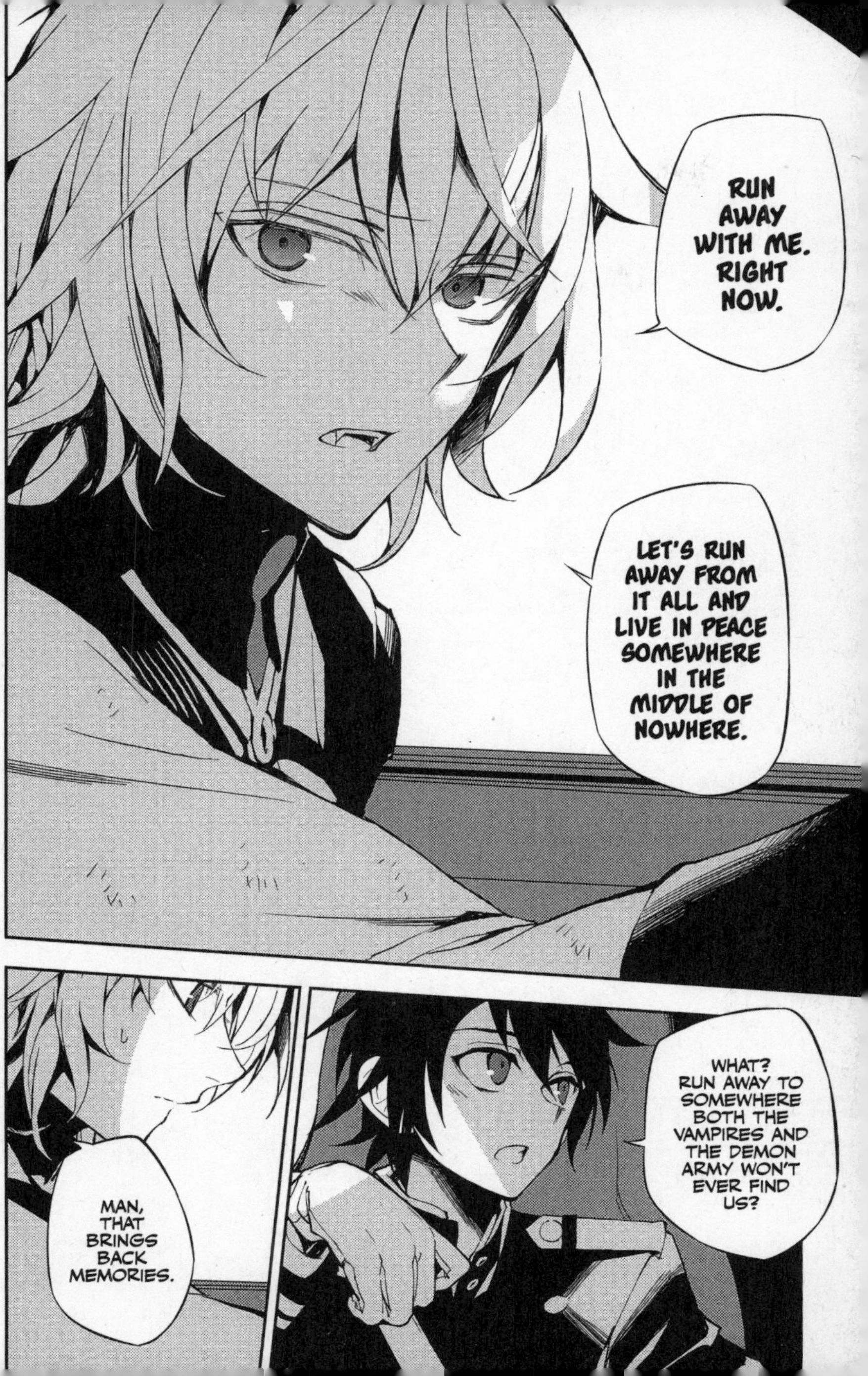
RUN AWAY WITH ME. RIGHT NOW.
LET'S RUN AWAY FROM IT ALL AND LIVE IN PEACE SOMEWHERE IN THE MIDDLE OF NOWHERE.
WHAT? RUN AWAY TO SOMEWHERE BOTH THE VAMPIRES AND THE DEMON ARMY WON'T EVER FIND US?
MAN, THAT BRINGS BACK MEMORIES.

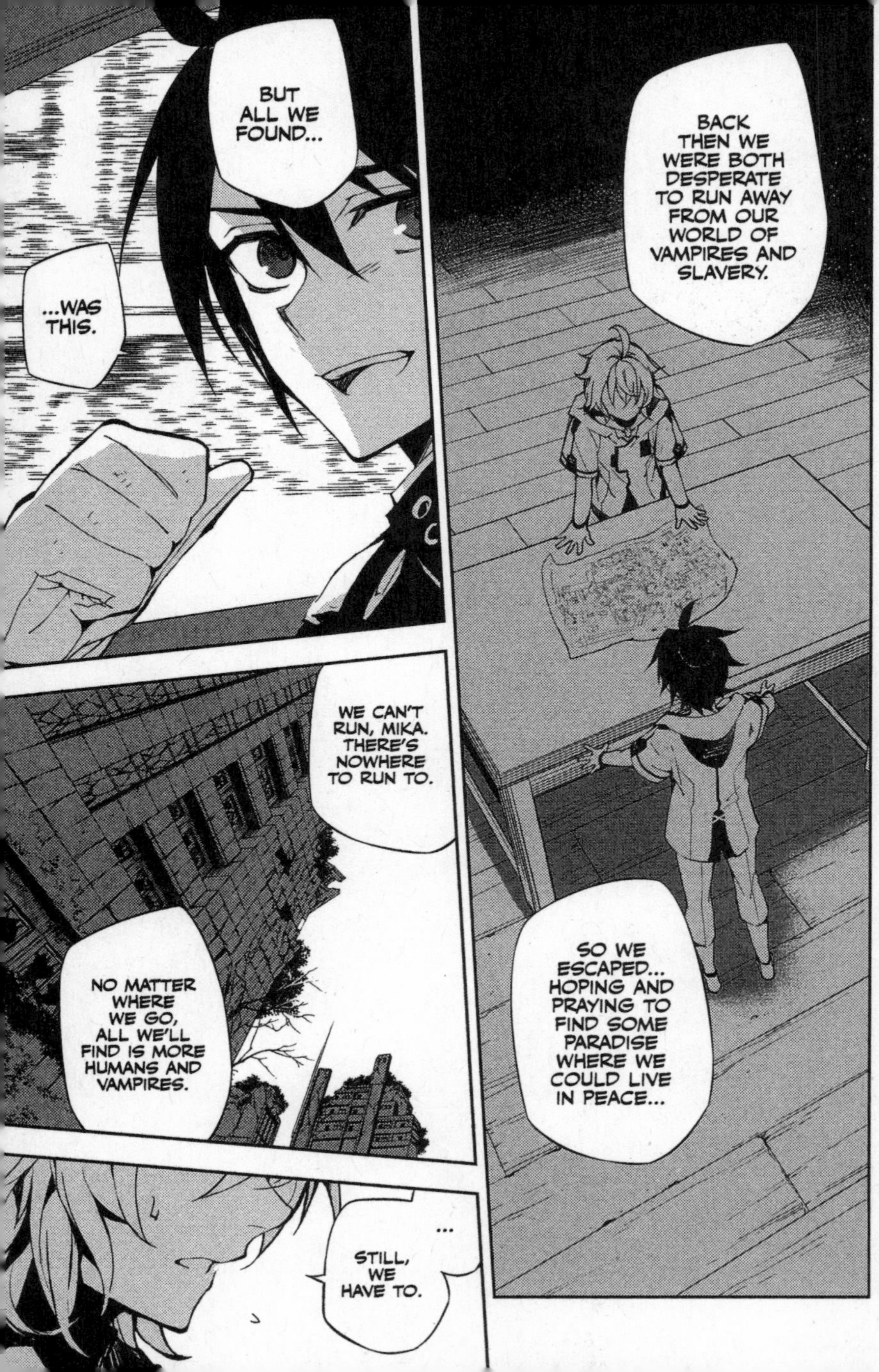
BACK THEN WE WERE BOTH DESPERATE TO RUN AWAY FROM OUR WORLD OF VAMPIRES AND SLAVERY.
SO WE ESCAPED... HOPING AND PRAYING TO FIND SOME PARADISE WHERE WE COULD LIVE IN PEACE...
BUT ALL WE FOUND...
...WAS THIS.
WE CAN'T RUN, MIKA. THERE'S NOWHERE TO RUN TO.
NO MATTER WHERE WE GO, ALL WE'LL FIND IS MORE HUMANS AND VAMPIRES.
...
STILL, WE HAVE TO.

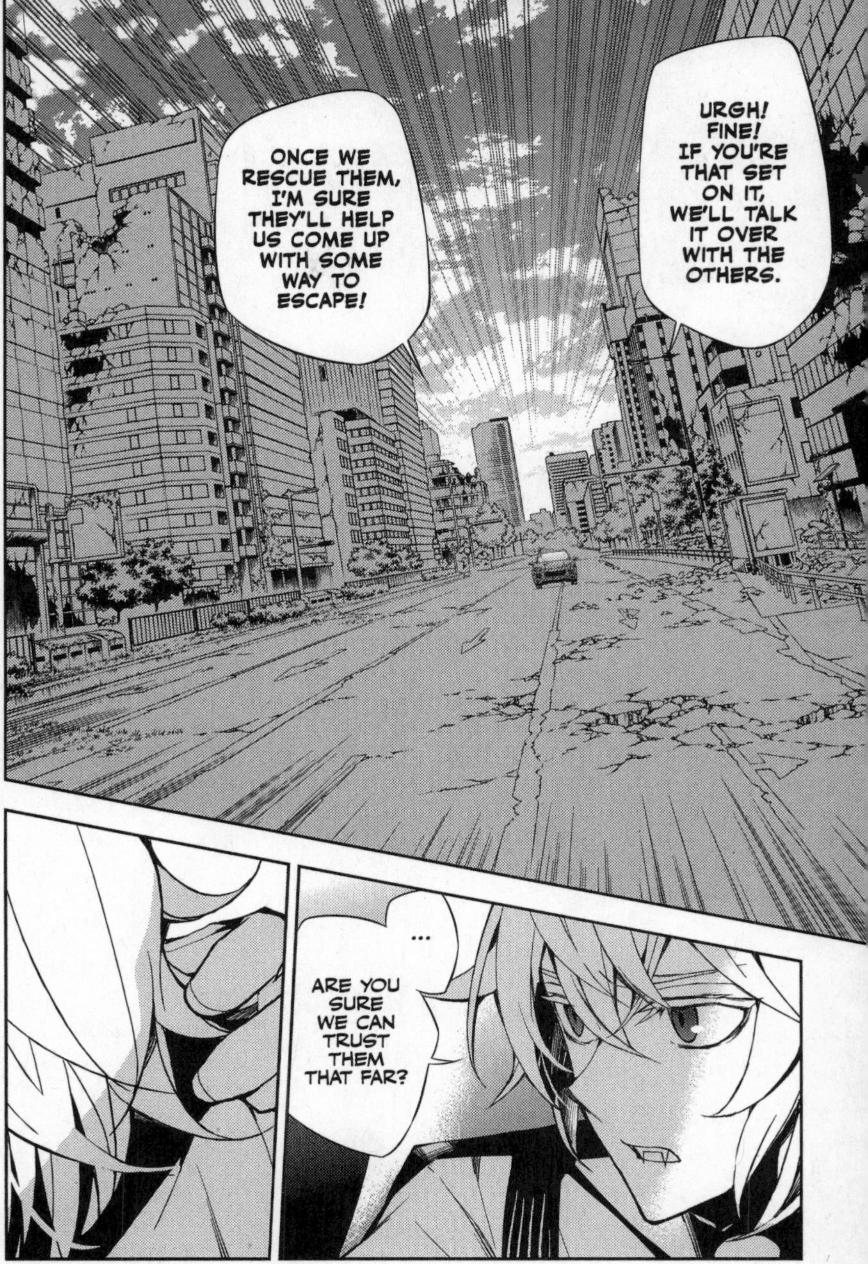
URGH! FINE! IF YOU'RE THAT SET ON IT, WE'LL TALK IT OVER WITH THE OTHERS.
ONCE WE RESCUE THEM, I'M SURE THEY'LL HELP US COME UP WITH SOME WAY TO ESCAPE!
...
ARE YOU SURE WE CAN TRUST THEM THAT FAR?

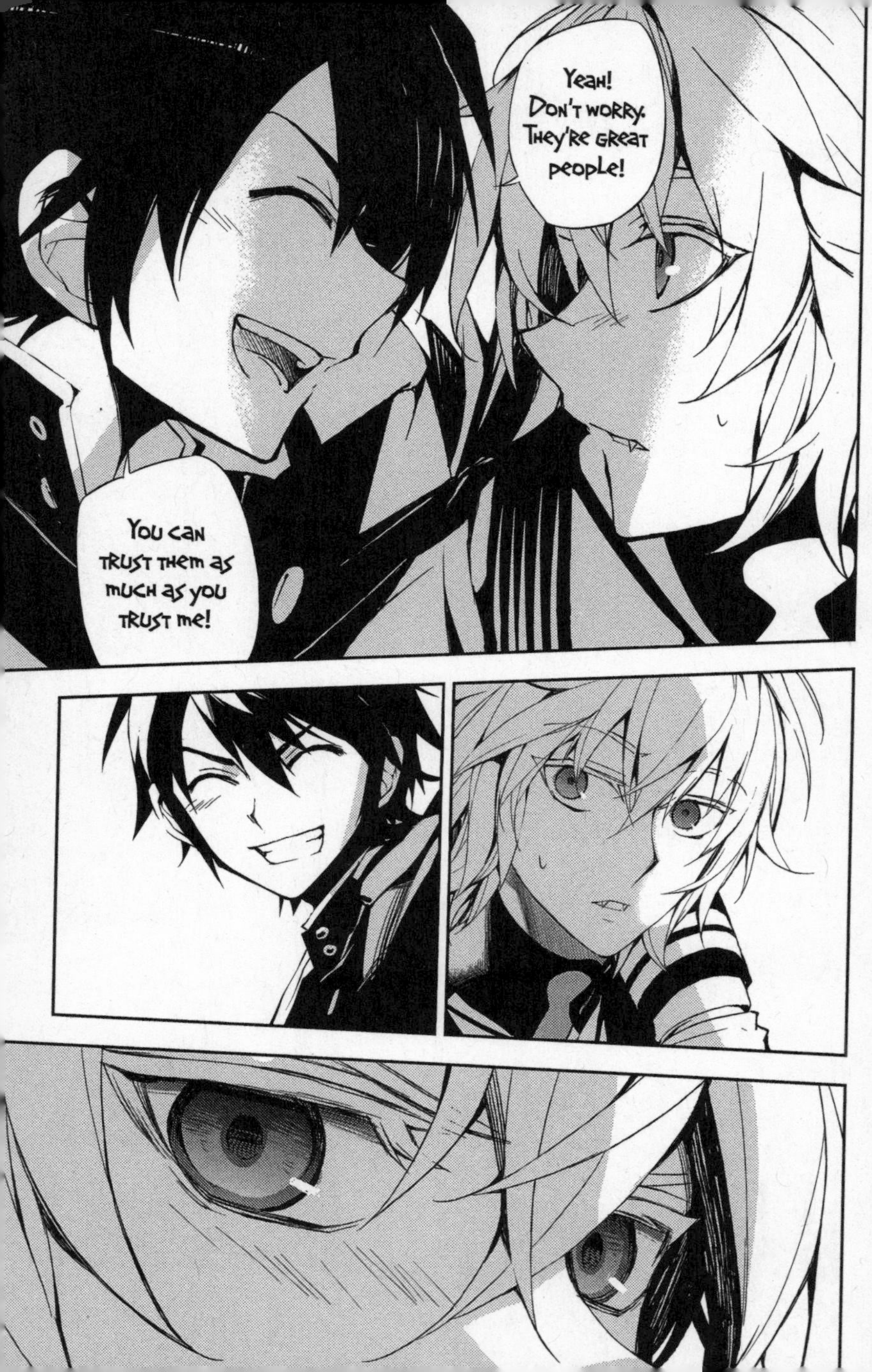
Yeah! Don't worry. They're great people!
You can trust them as much as you trust me!

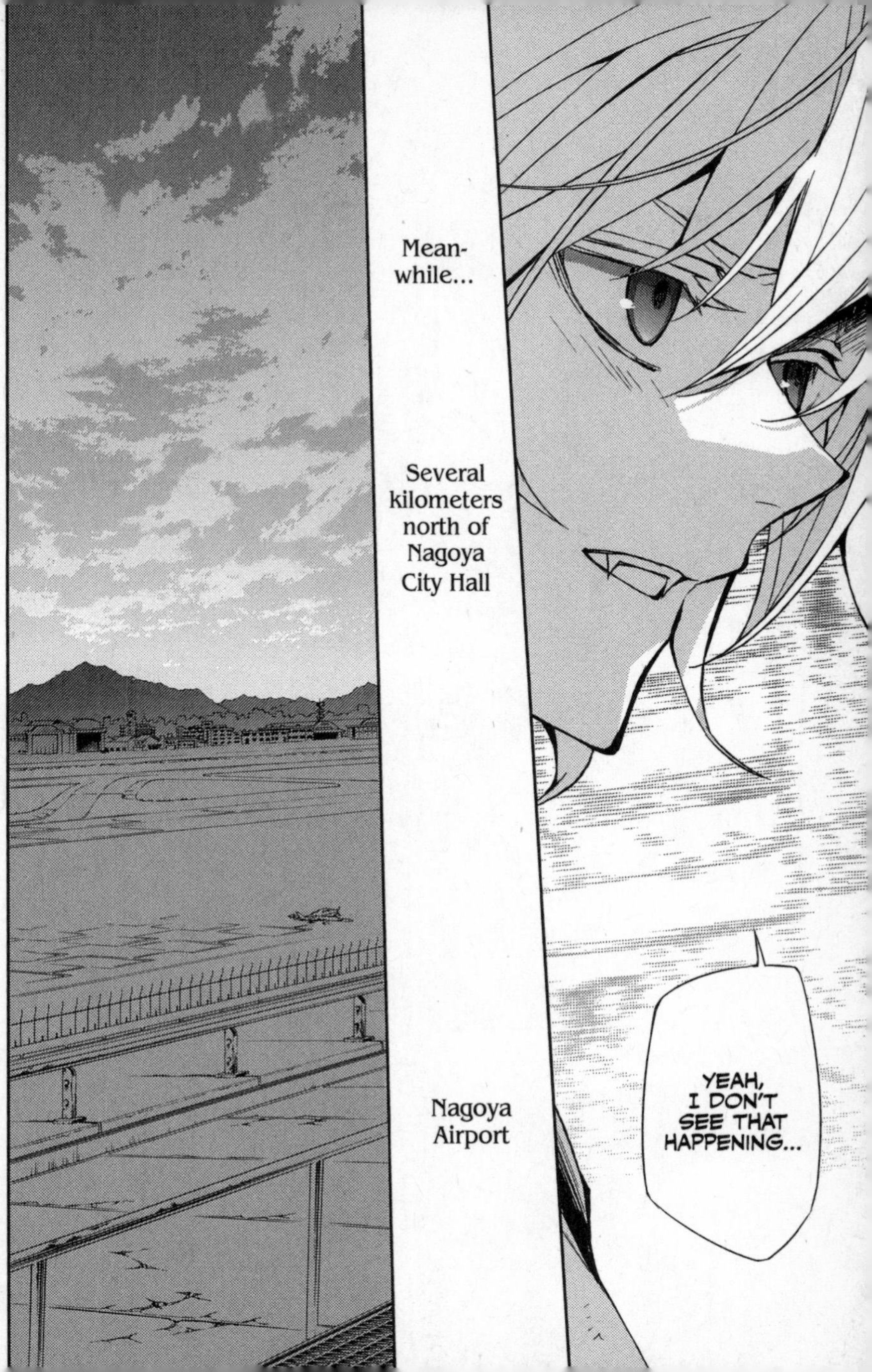
YEAH, I DON'T SEE THAT HAPPENING...
Mean-while...
Several kilometers north of Nagoya City Hall
Nagoya Airport

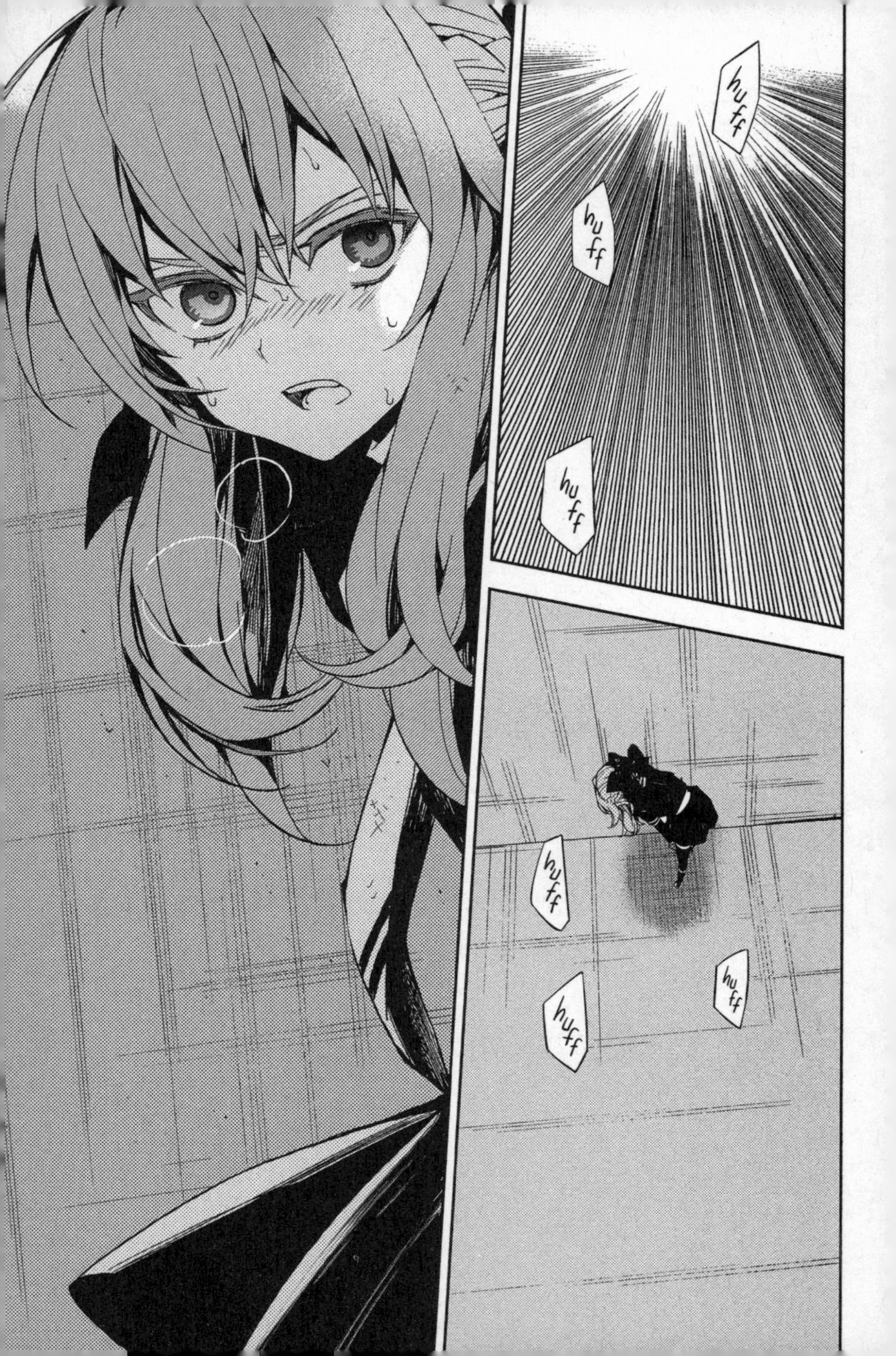
huff
huff
huff
huff
huff
huff

Seraph of the End
VAMPIRE REIGN

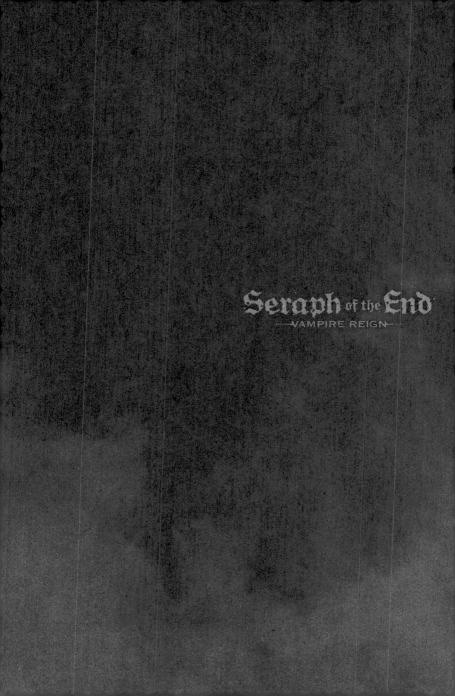

Chapter 38
The Namanari Awakens

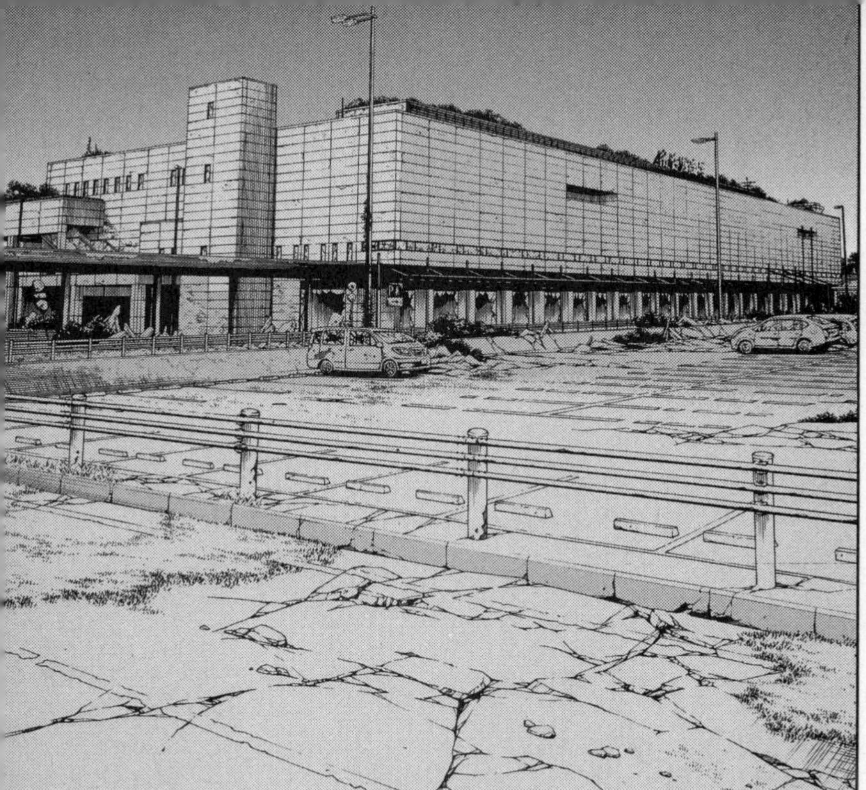

Final Rendezvous Point

Nagoya Airport

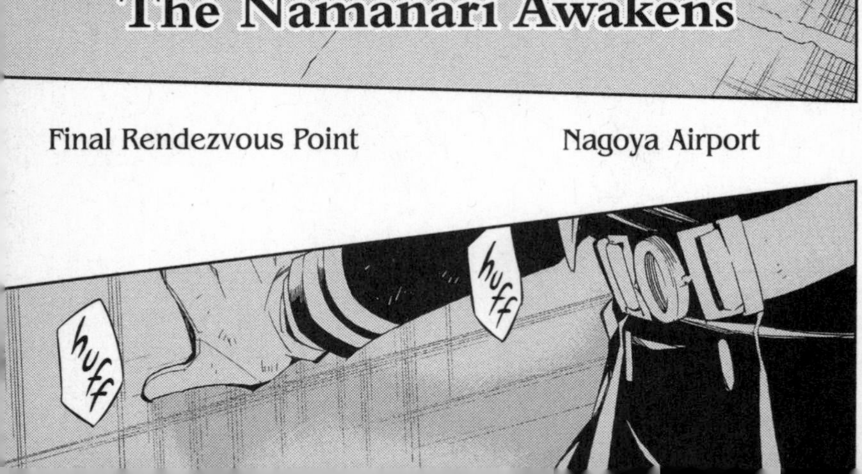
huff
huff

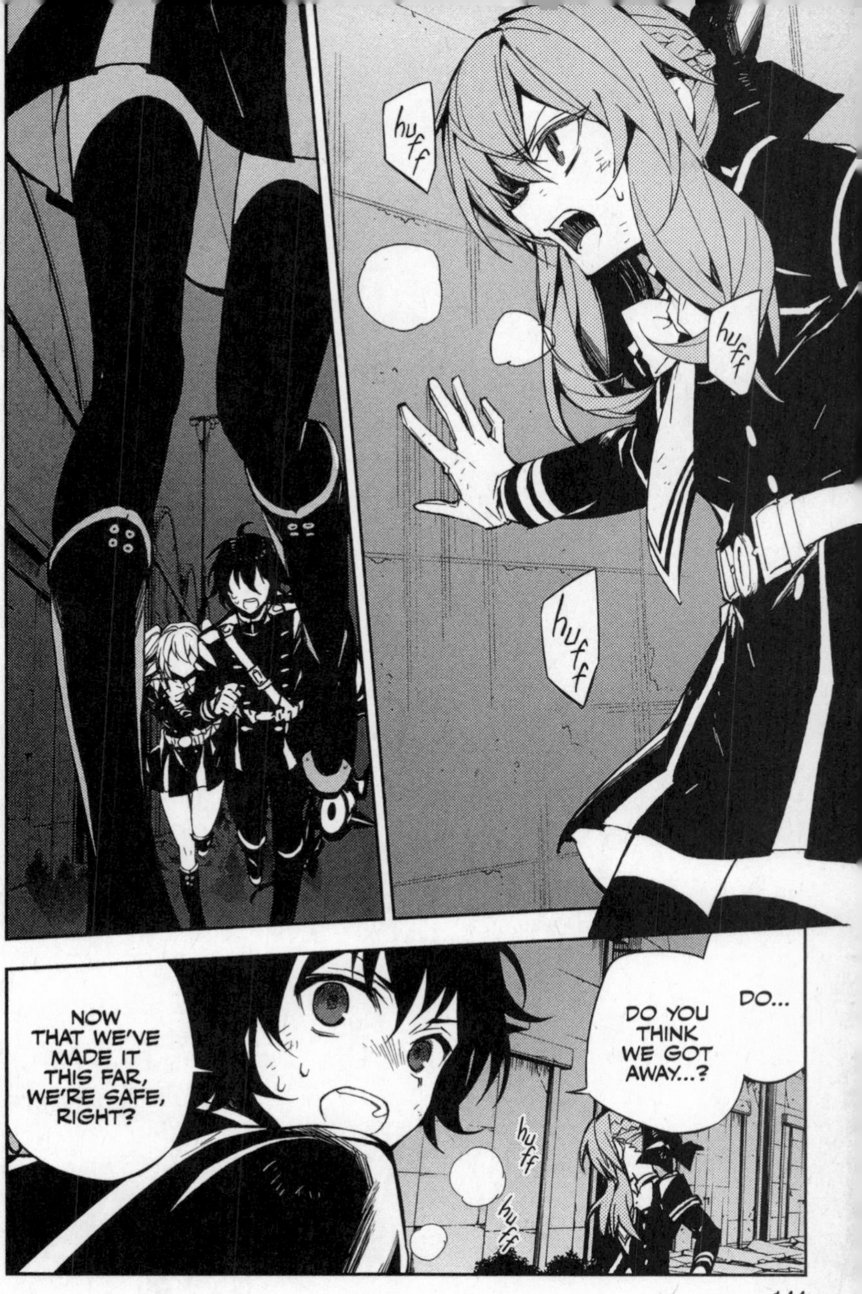
huff
huff
huff
DO...
DO YOU THINK WE GOT AWAY...?
huff
huff
NOW THAT WE'VE MADE IT THIS FAR, WE'RE SAFE, RIGHT?

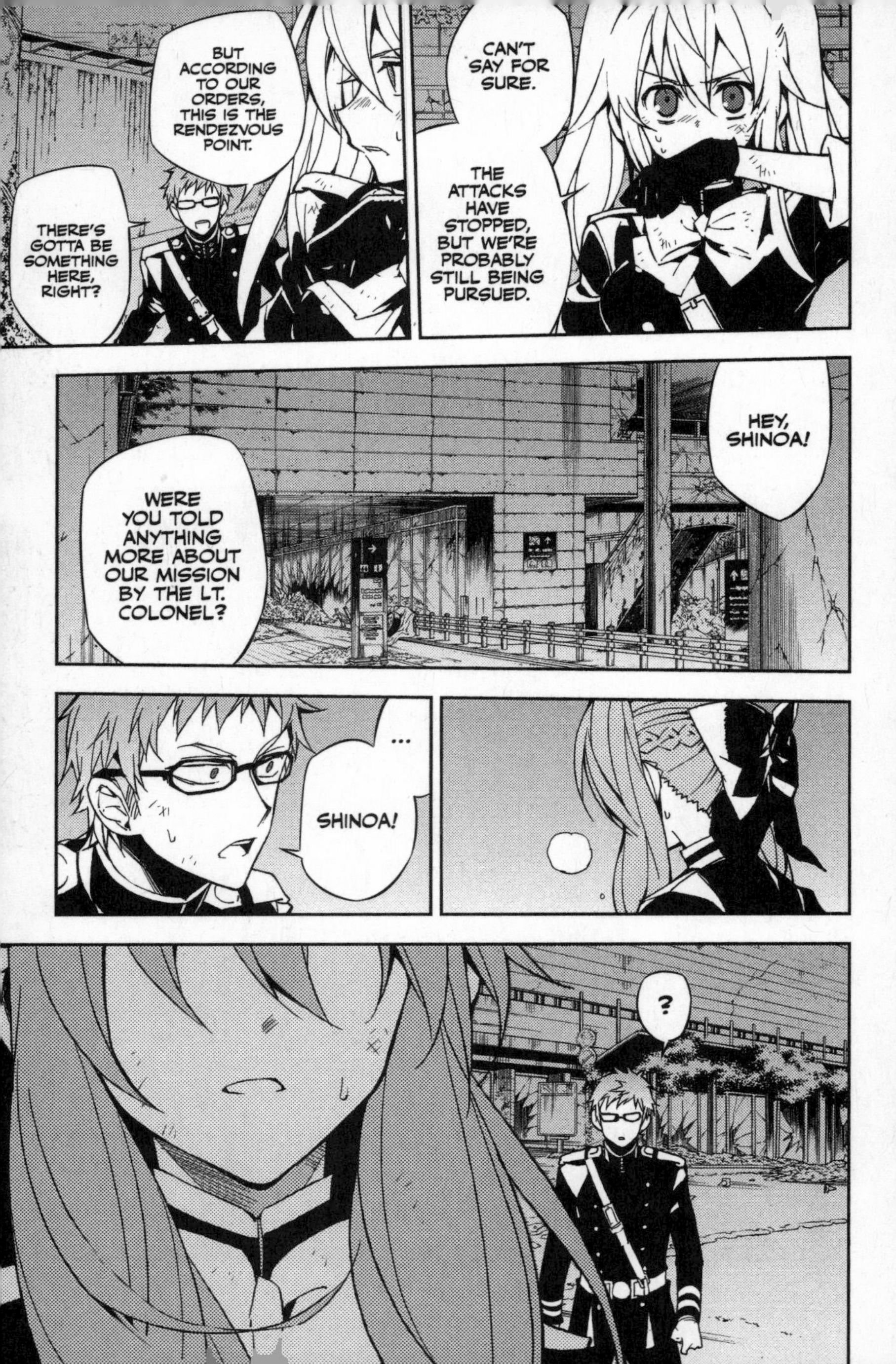
CAN'T SAY FOR SURE.
THE ATTACKS HAVE STOPPED, BUT WE'RE PROBABLY STILL BEING PURSUED.
BUT ACCORDING TO OUR ORDERS, THIS IS THE RENDEZVOUS POINT.
THERE'S GOTTA BE SOMETHING HERE, RIGHT?
HEY, SHINOA!
WERE YOU TOLD ANYTHING MORE ABOUT OUR MISSION BY THE LT. COLONEL?
...
SHINOA!
?

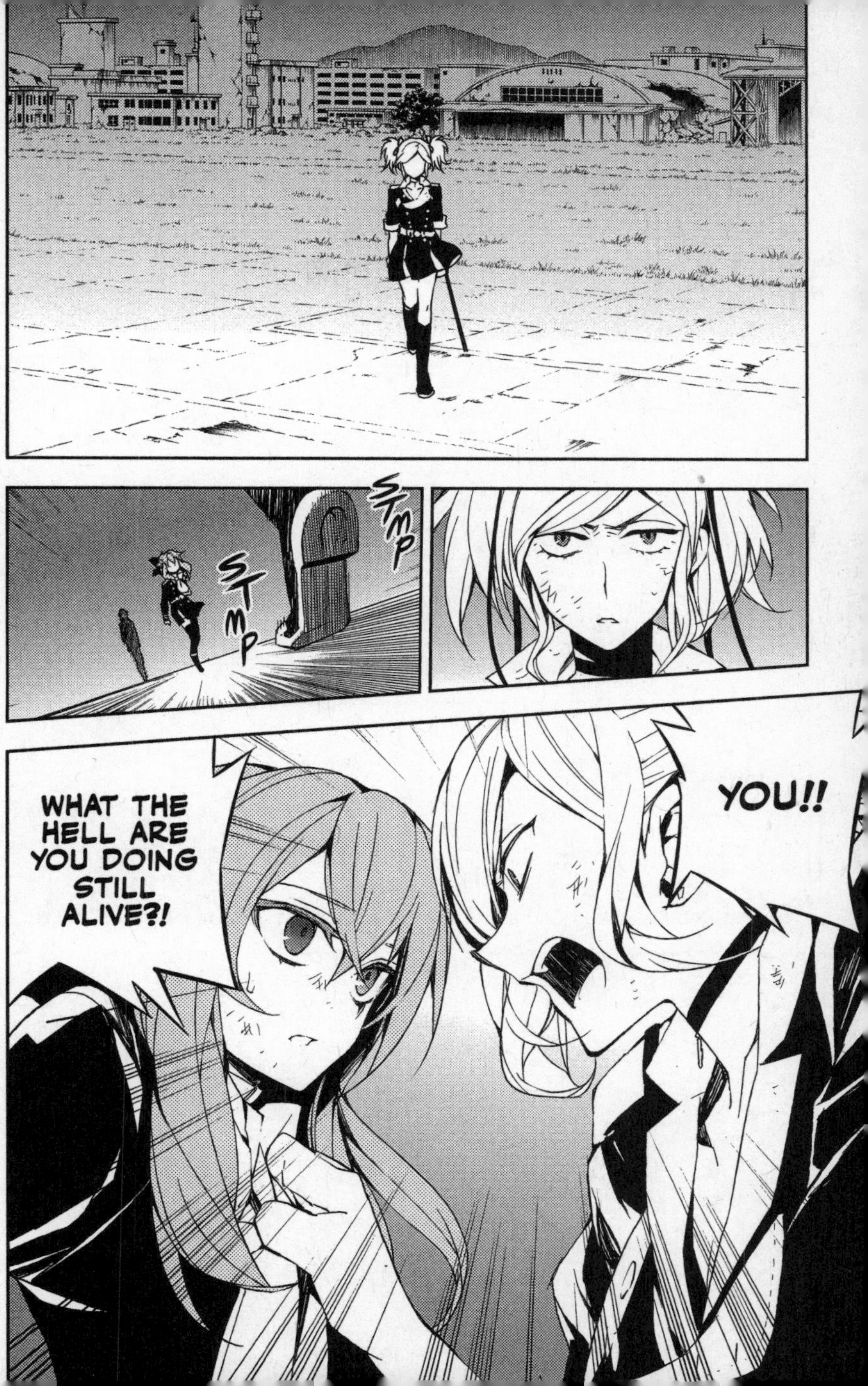
STMP
STMP
YOU!!
WHAT THE HELL ARE YOU DOING STILL ALIVE?!

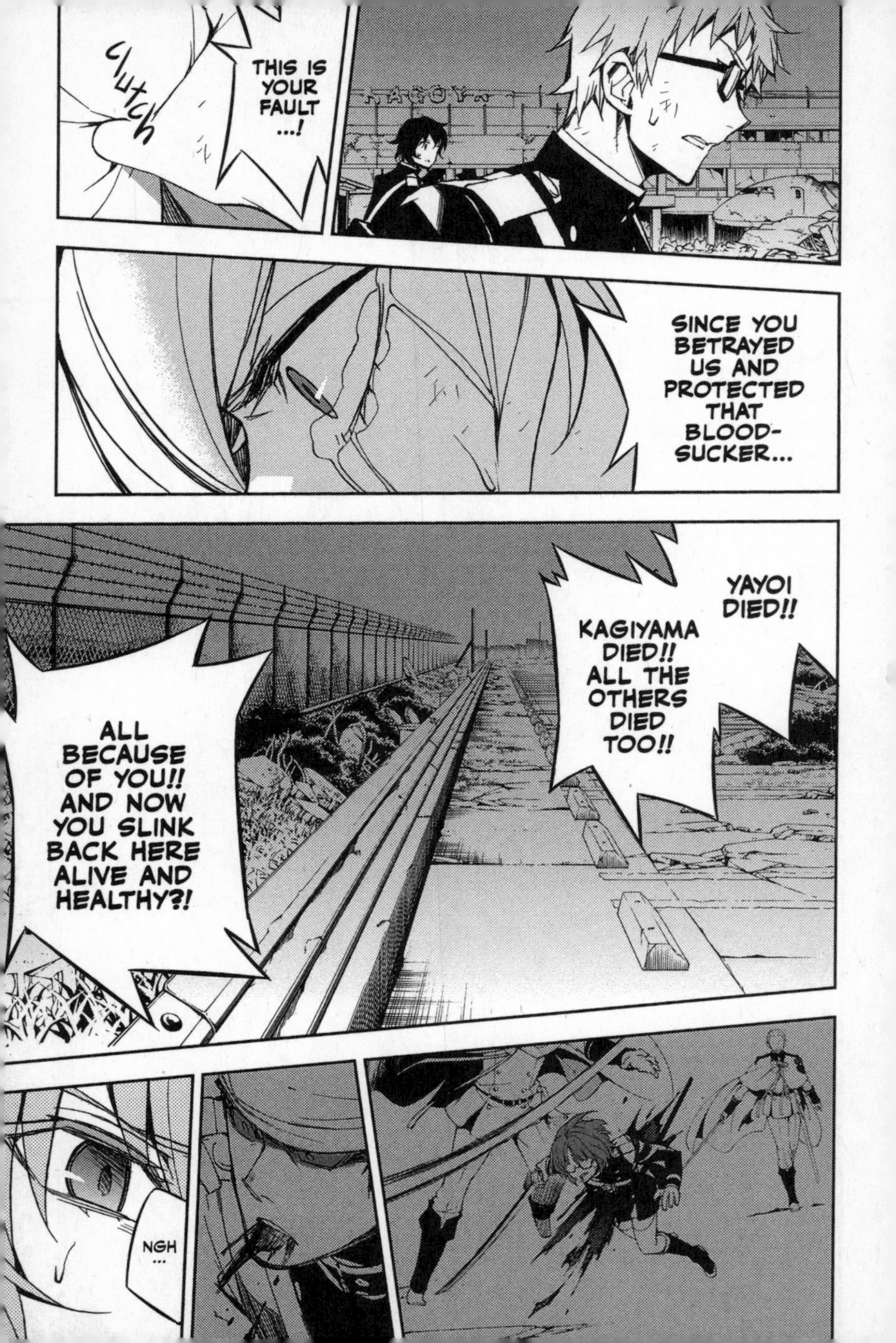
THIS IS YOUR FAULT ...!
clutch
SINCE YOU BETRAYED US AND PROTECTED THAT BLOOD-SUCKER...
YAYOI DIED!!
KAGIYAMA DIED!! ALL THE OTHERS DIED TOO!!
ALL BECAUSE OF YOU!! AND NOW YOU SLINK BACK HERE ALIVE AND HEALTHY?!
NGH ...

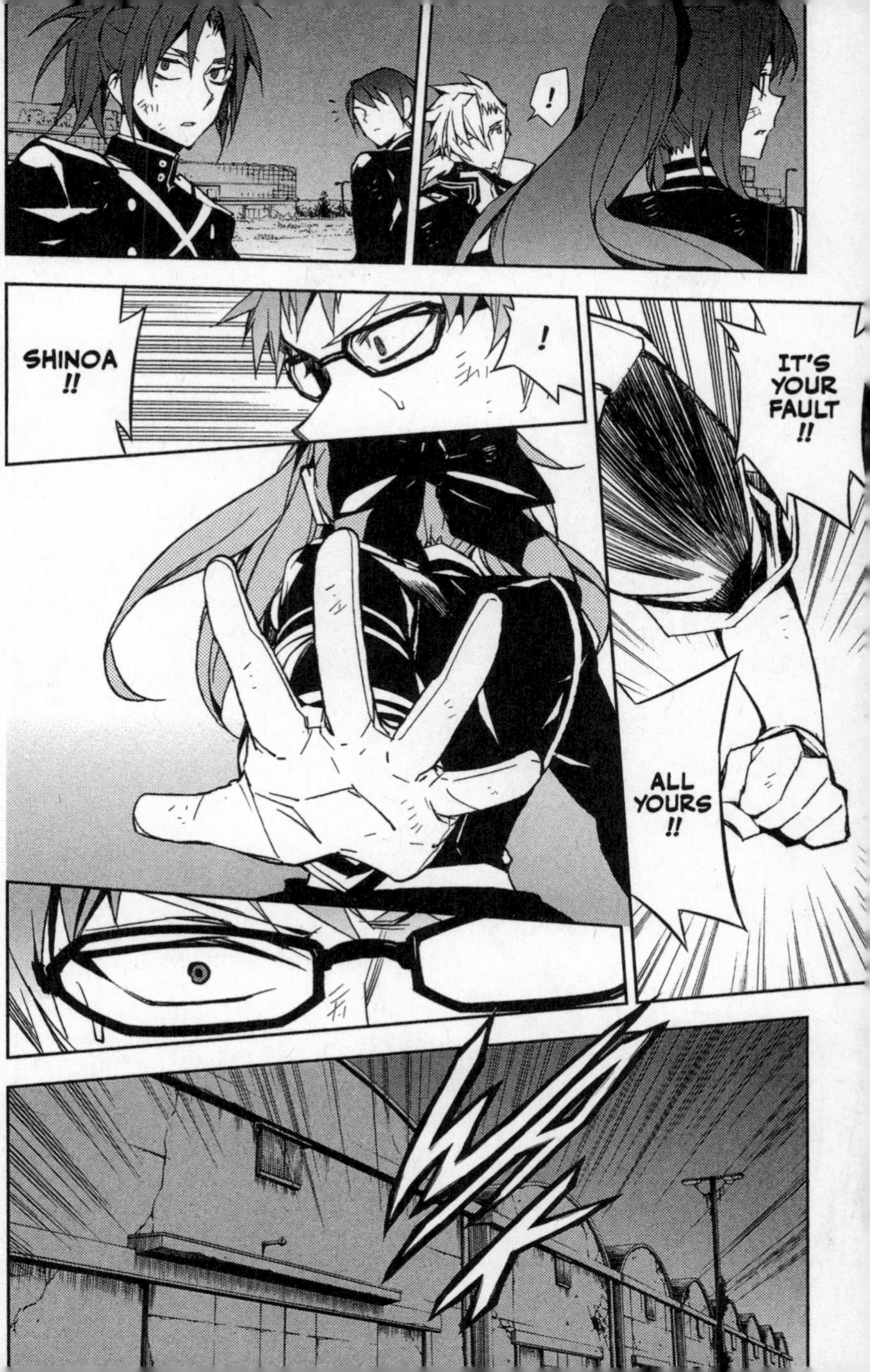
!
IT'S YOUR FAULT !!
ALL YOURS !!
!
SHINOA !!

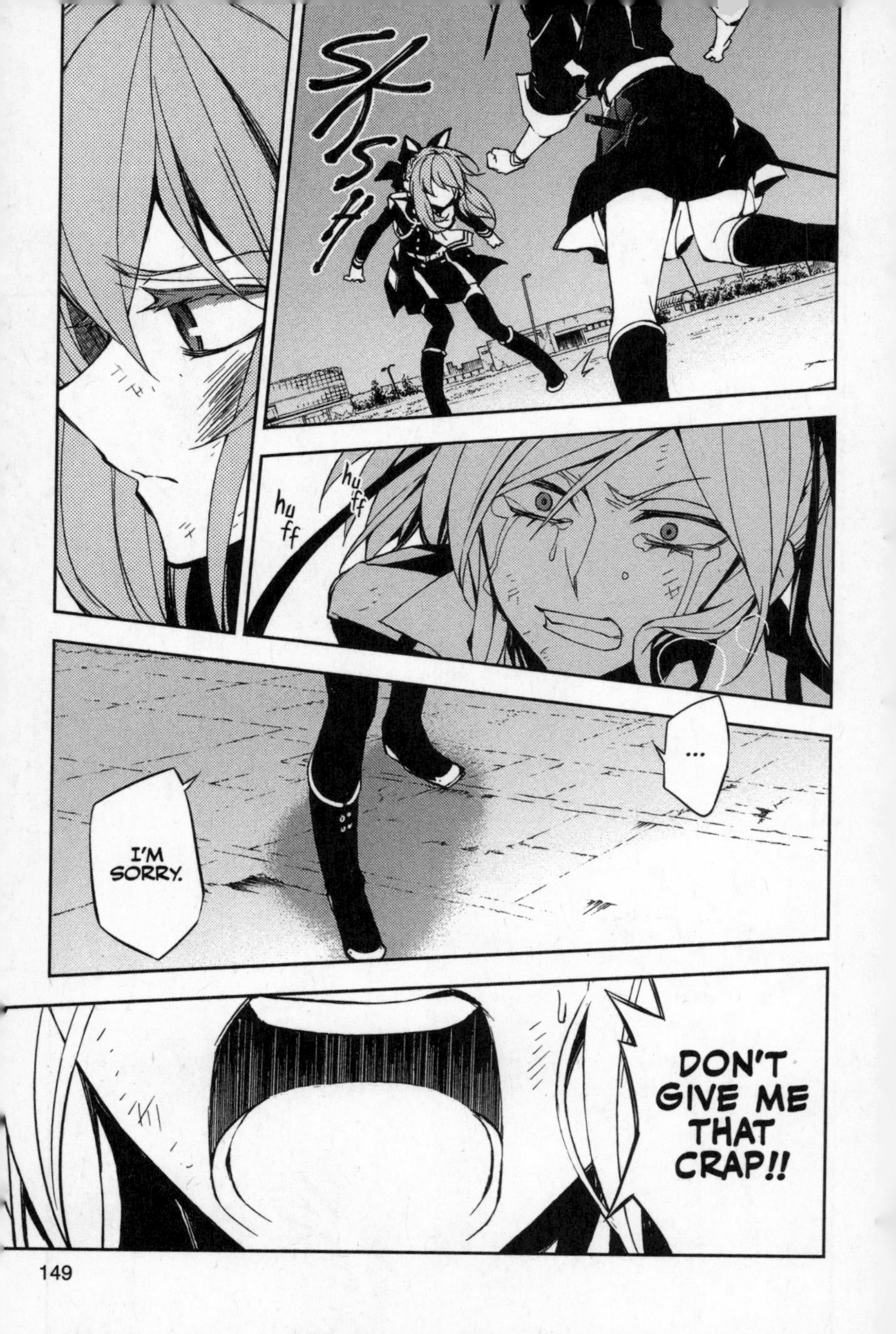
SKSSH
huff
huff
...
I'M SORRY.
DON'T GIVE ME THAT CRAP!!

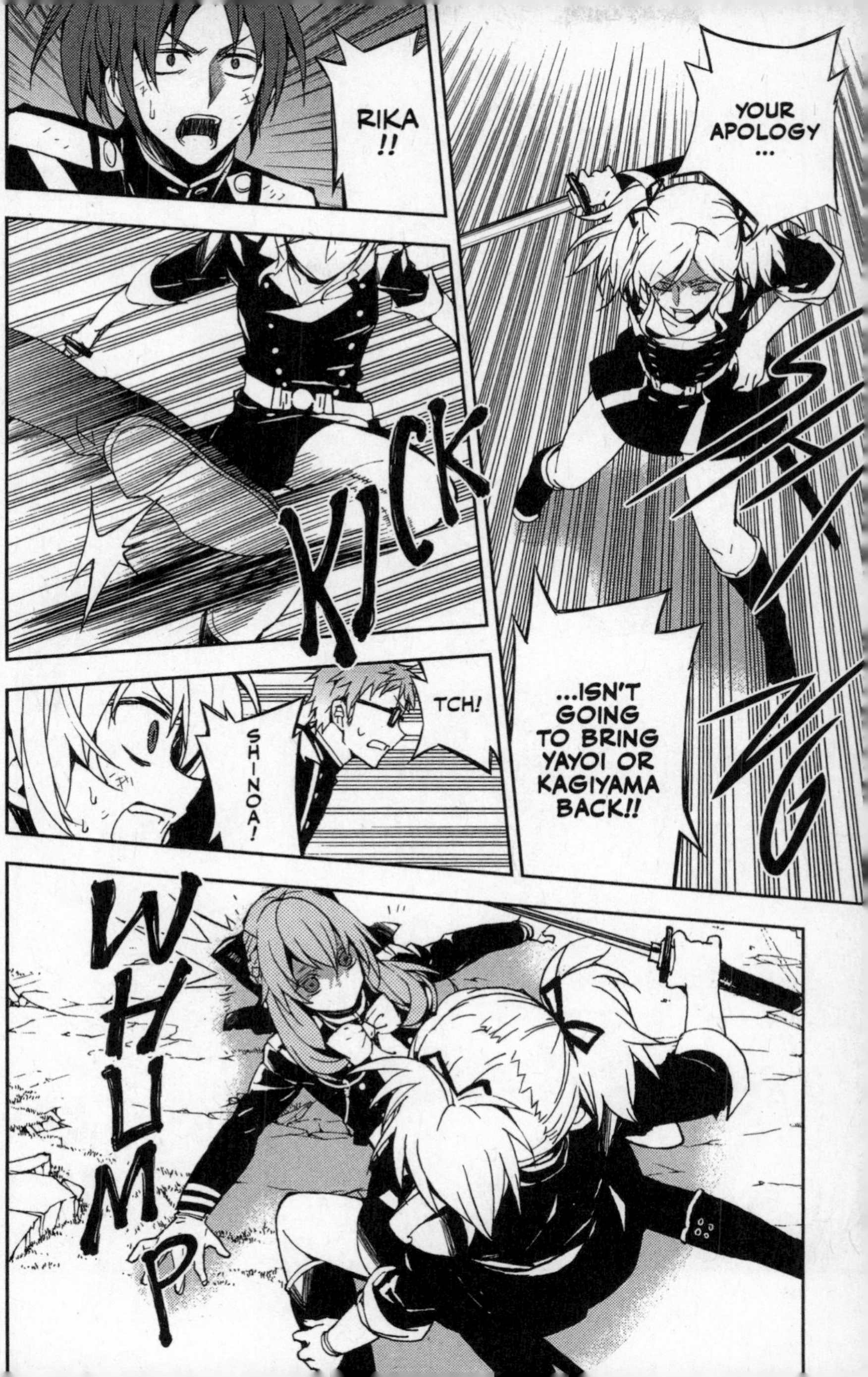
YOUR APOLOGY ...
SHING
...ISN'T GOING TO BRING YAYOI OR KAGIYAMA BACK!!
RIKA !!
KICK
TCH!
SHINOA!
WHUMP

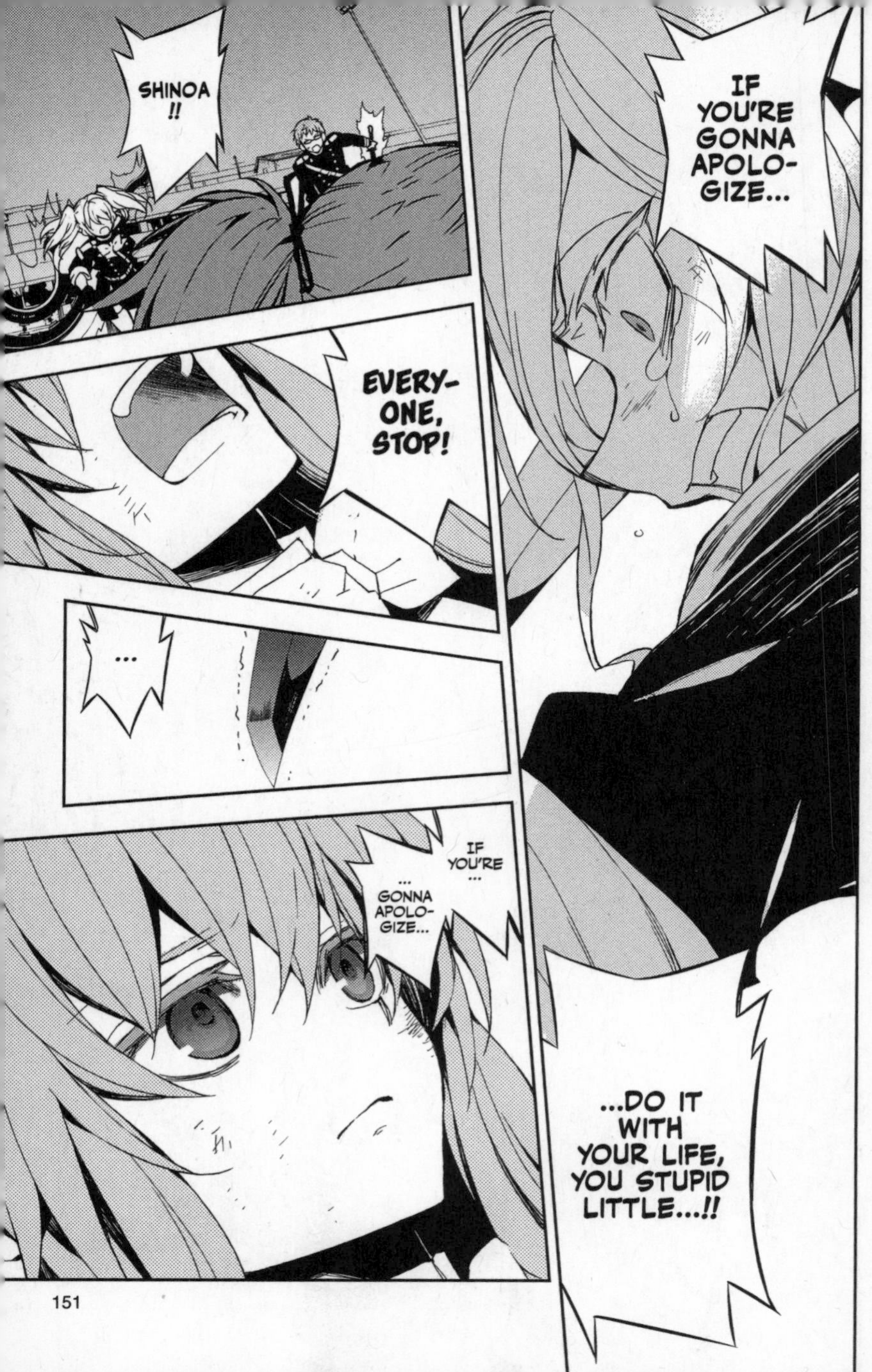
IF YOU'RE GONNA APOLO-GIZE...
...DO IT WITH YOUR LIFE, YOU STUPID LITTLE...!!
SHINOA!!
EVERY-ONE, STOP!
...
IF YOU'RE ...
... GONNA APOLO-GIZE...

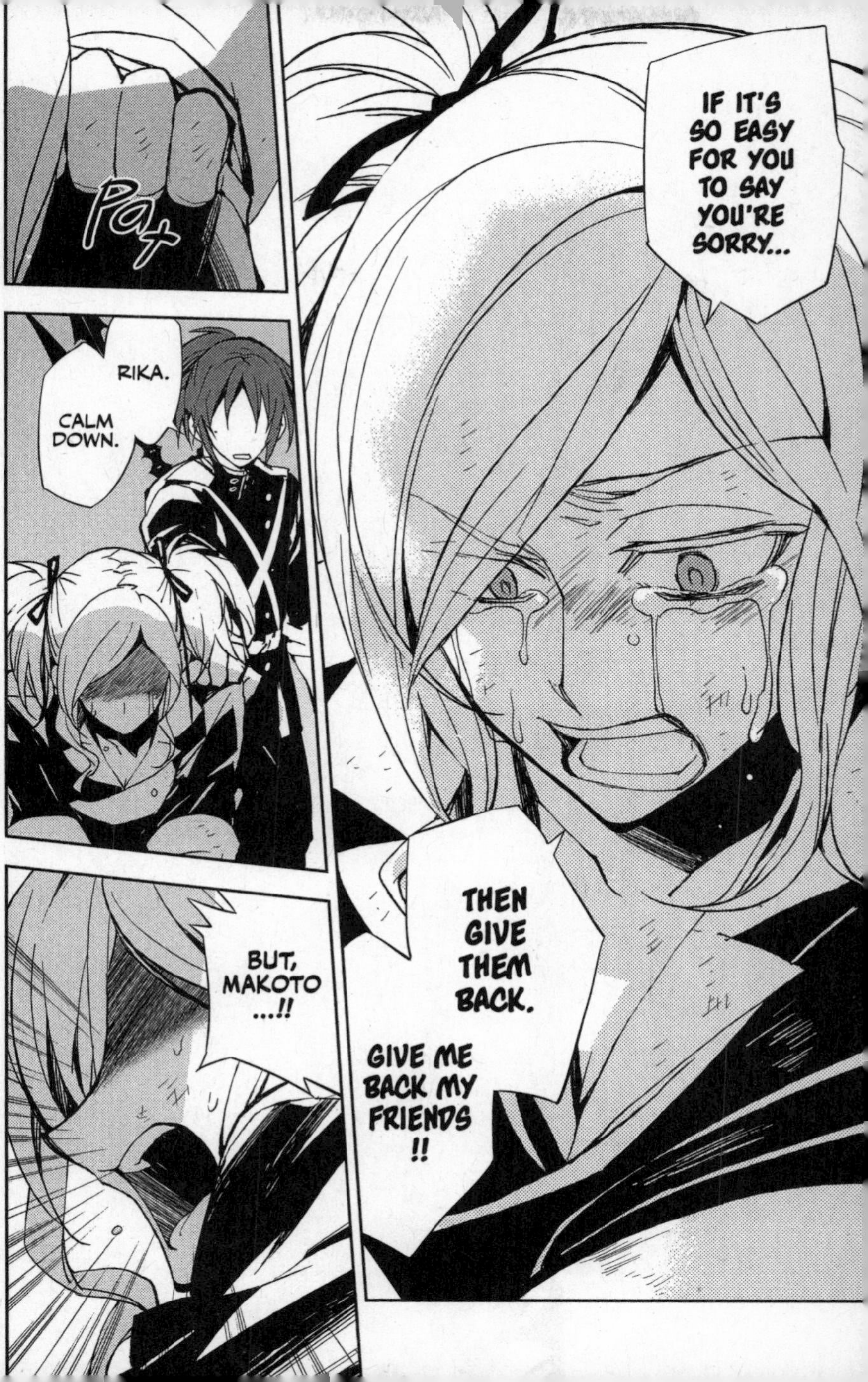
IF IT'S SO EASY FOR YOU TO SAY YOU'RE SORRY...
THEN GIVE THEM BACK.
GIVE ME BACK MY FRIENDS !!
Pat
RIKA.
CALM DOWN.
BUT, MAKOTO ...!!

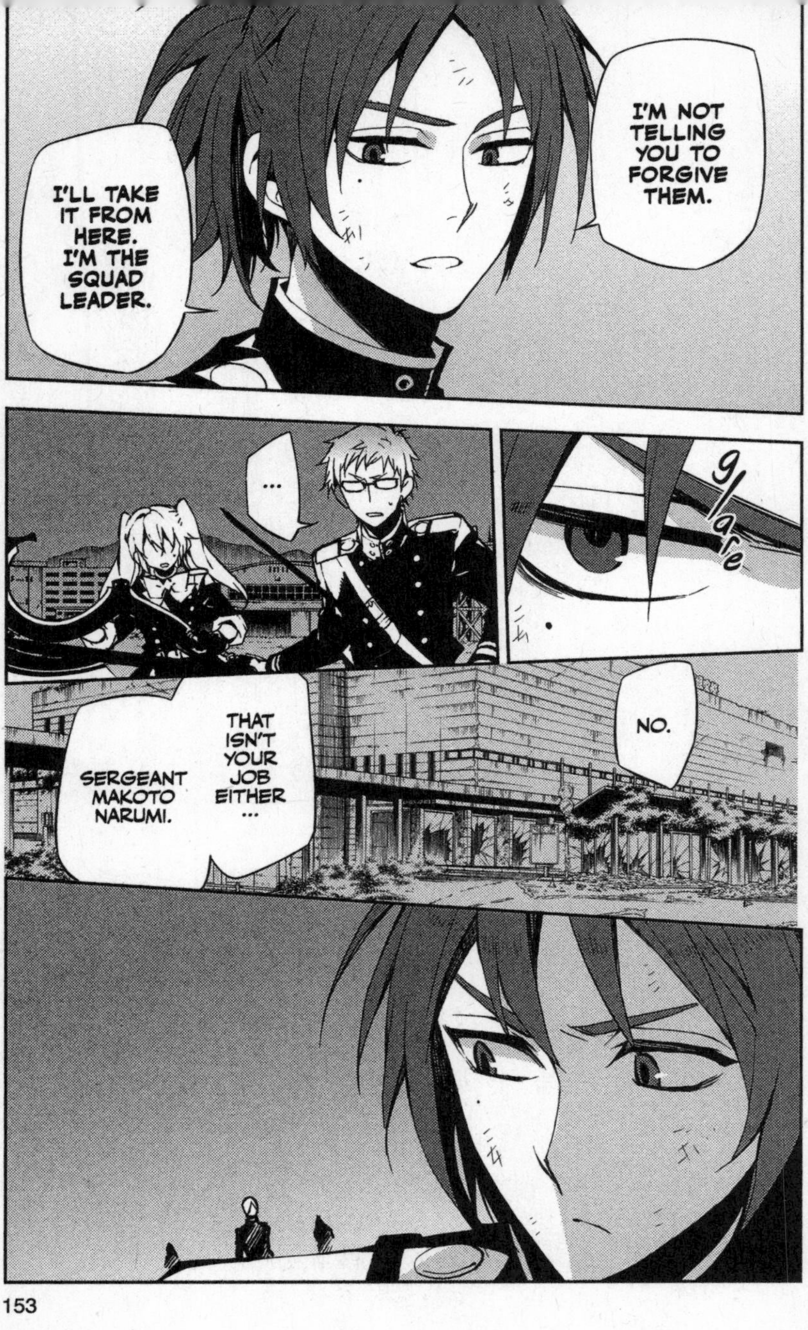
I'M NOT TELLING YOU TO FORGIVE THEM.
I'LL TAKE IT FROM HERE. I'M THE SQUAD LEADER.
glare
...
NO.
THAT ISN'T YOUR JOB EITHER ...
SERGEANT MAKOTO NARUMI.

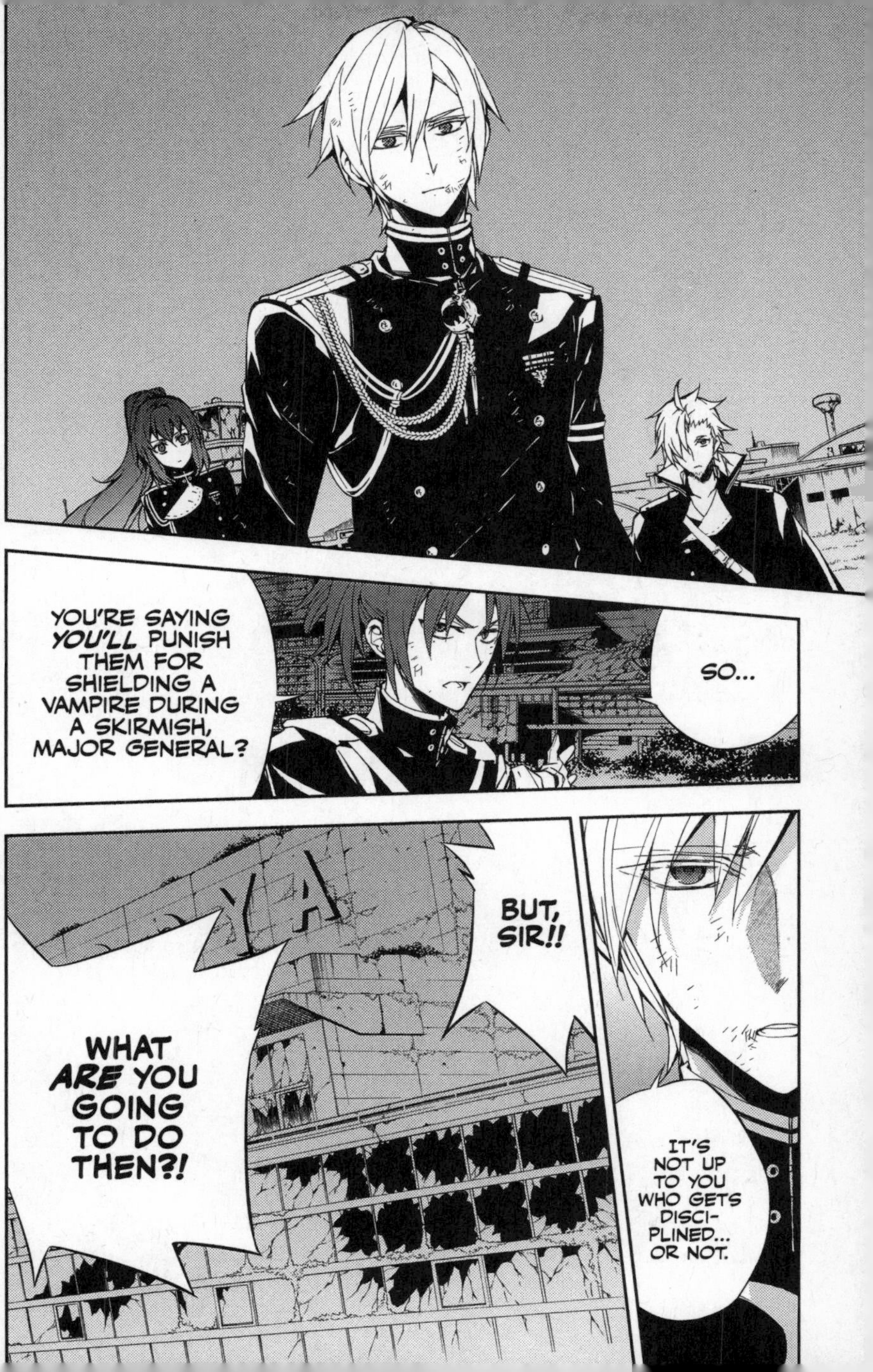

SO...
YOU'RE SAYING *YOU'LL* PUNISH THEM FOR SHIELDING A VAMPIRE DURING A SKIRMISH, MAJOR GENERAL?
IT'S NOT UP TO YOU WHO GETS DISCI-PLINED... OR NOT.
BUT, SIR!!
WHAT *ARE* YOU GOING TO DO THEN?!

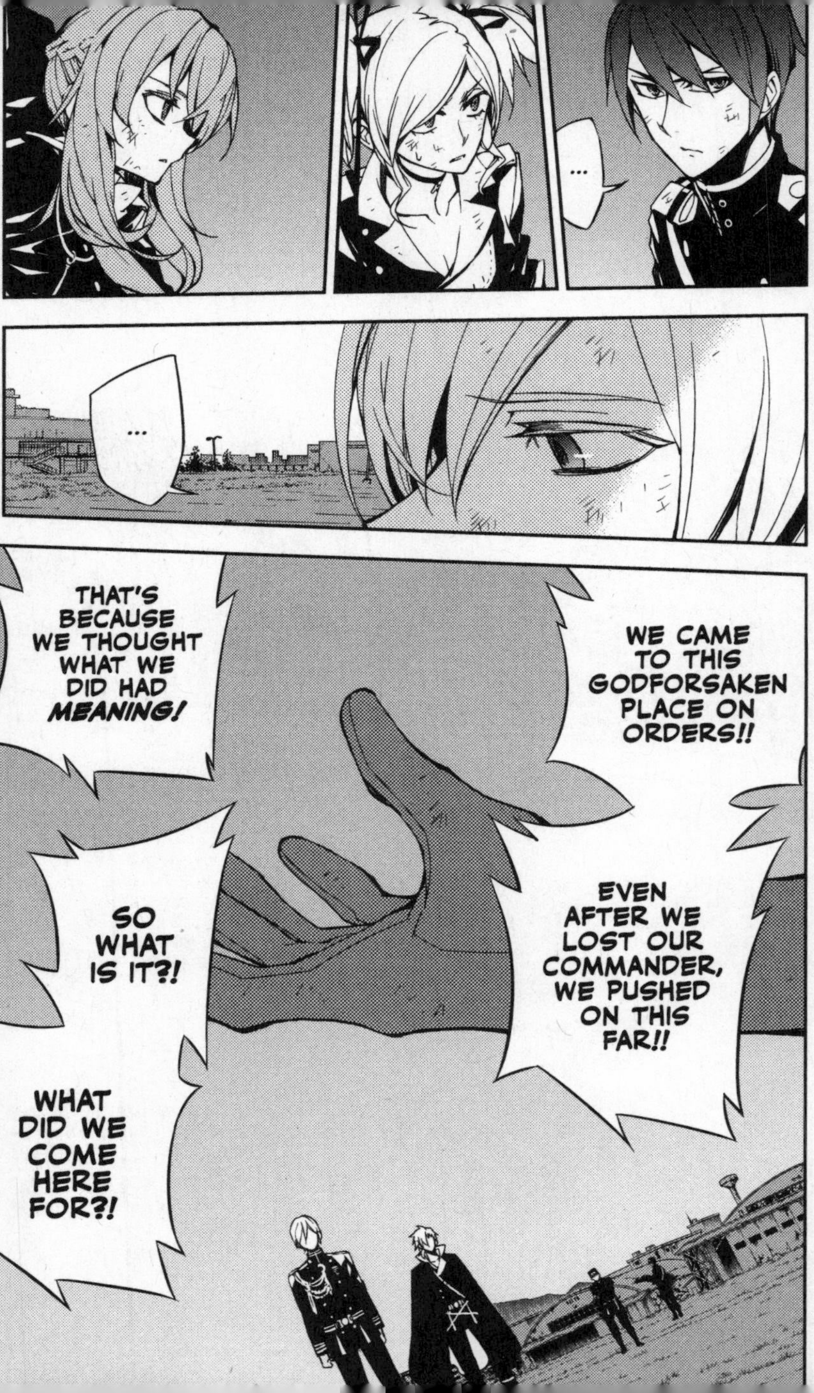
...
...
WE CAME TO THIS GODFORSAKEN PLACE ON ORDERS!!
THAT'S BECAUSE WE THOUGHT WHAT WE DID HAD *MEANING!*
EVEN AFTER WE LOST OUR COMMANDER, WE PUSHED ON THIS FAR!!
SO WHAT IS IT?!
WHAT DID WE COME HERE FOR?!

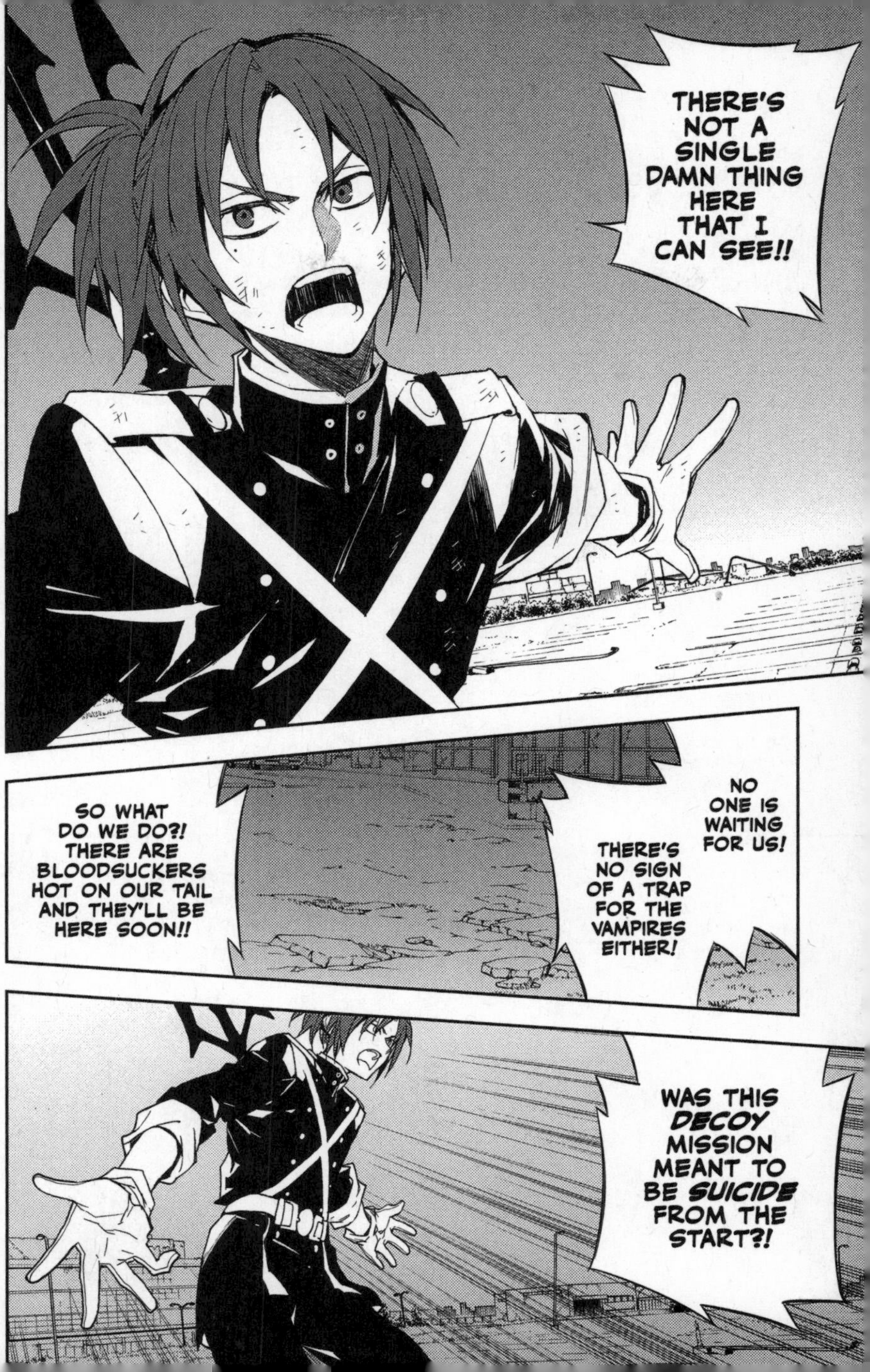
THERE'S NOT A SINGLE DAMN THING HERE THAT I CAN SEE!!
NO ONE IS WAITING FOR US!
THERE'S NO SIGN OF A TRAP FOR THE VAMPIRES EITHER!
SO WHAT DO WE DO?! THERE ARE BLOODSUCKERS HOT ON OUR TAIL AND THEY'LL BE HERE SOON!!
WAS THIS DECOY MISSION MEANT TO BE SUICIDE FROM THE START?!

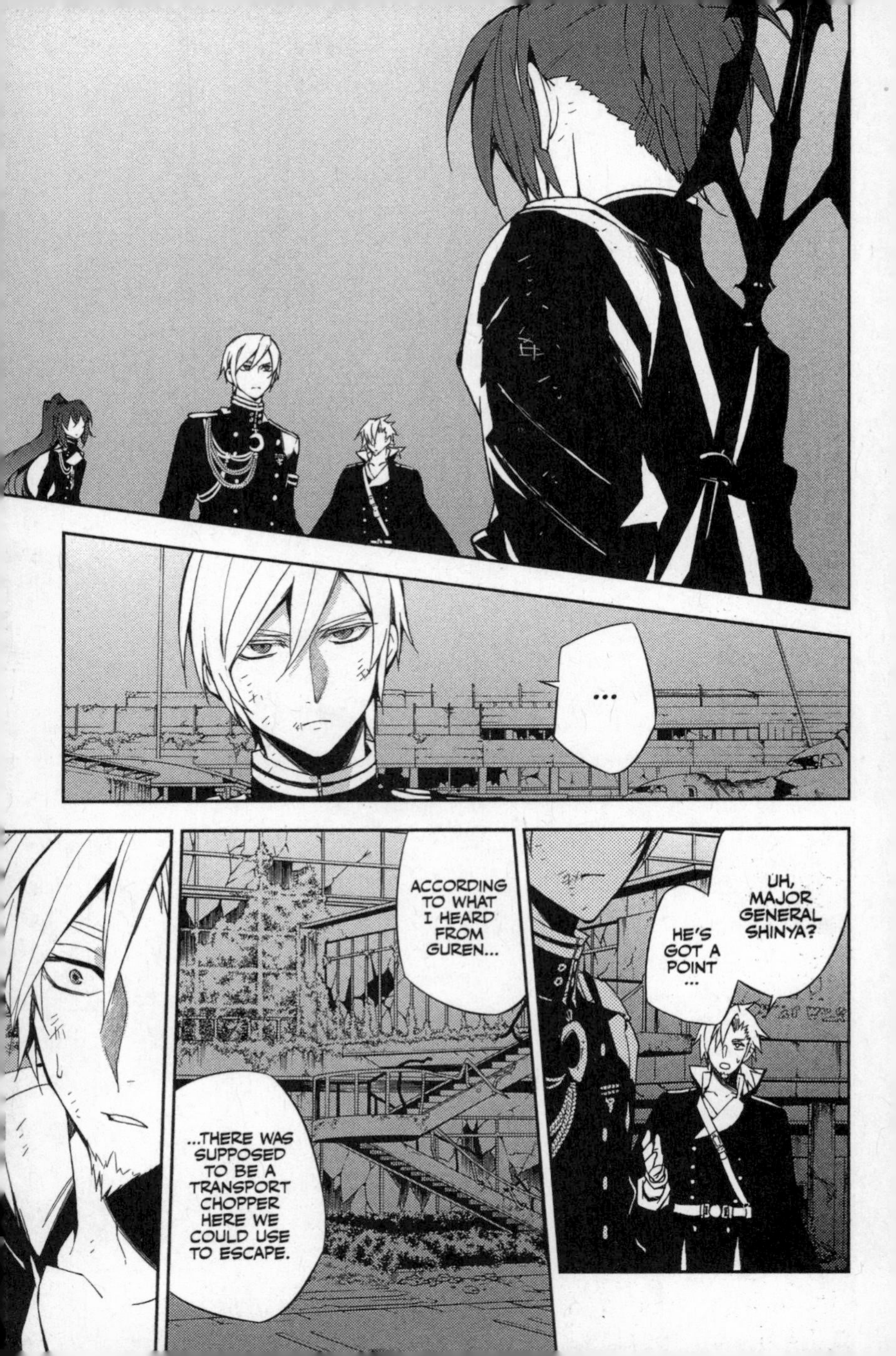
...
UH, MAJOR GENERAL SHINYA?
HE'S GOT A POINT...
ACCORDING TO WHAT I HEARD FROM GUREN...
...THERE WAS SUPPOSED TO BE A TRANSPORT CHOPPER HERE WE COULD USE TO ESCAPE.

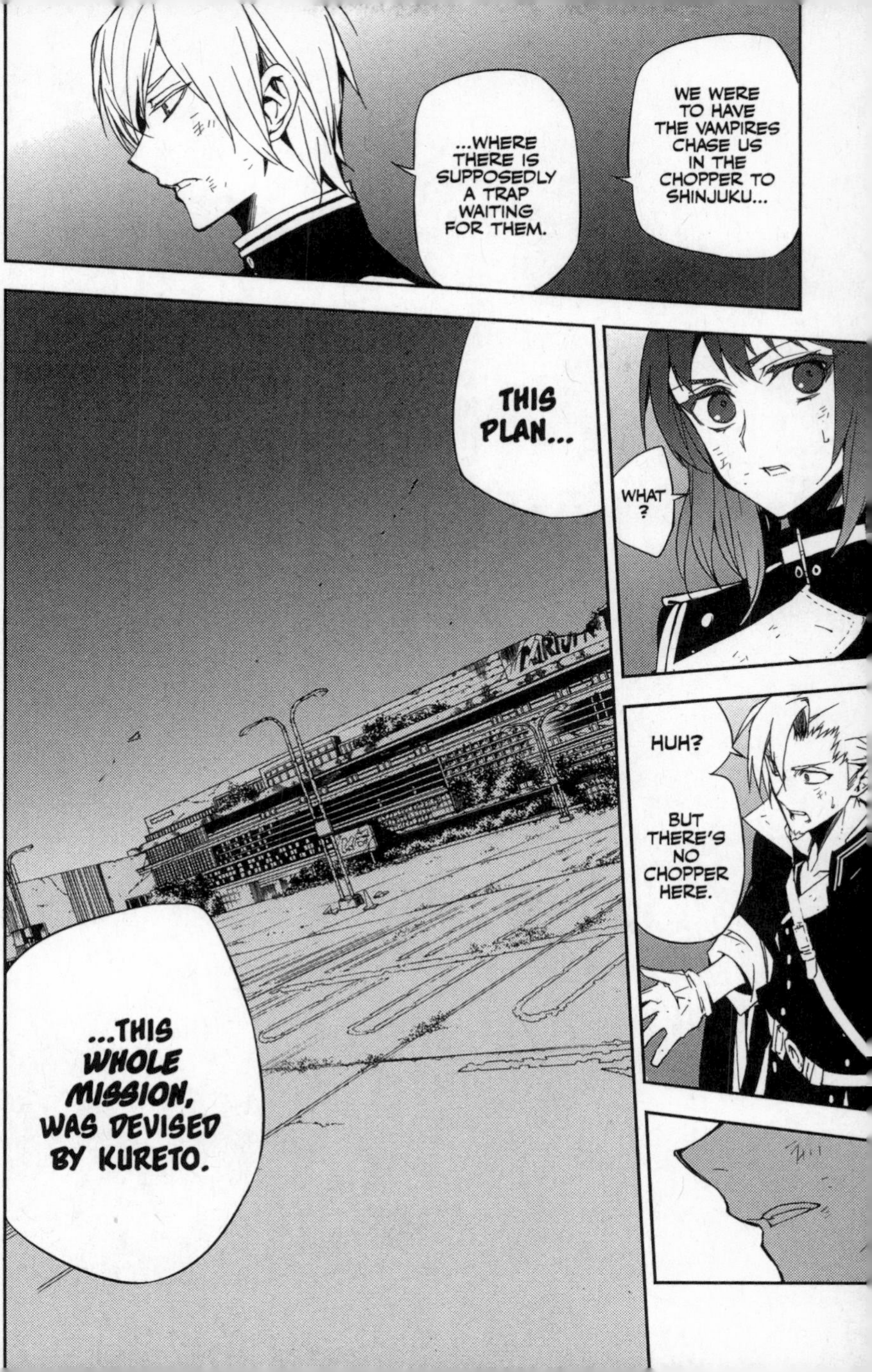
WE WERE TO HAVE THE VAMPIRES CHASE US IN THE CHOPPER TO SHINJUKU...
...WHERE THERE IS SUPPOSEDLY A TRAP WAITING FOR THEM.
WHAT?
HUH?
BUT THERE'S NO CHOPPER HERE.
THIS PLAN...
...THIS WHOLE MISSION, WAS DEVISED BY KURETO.

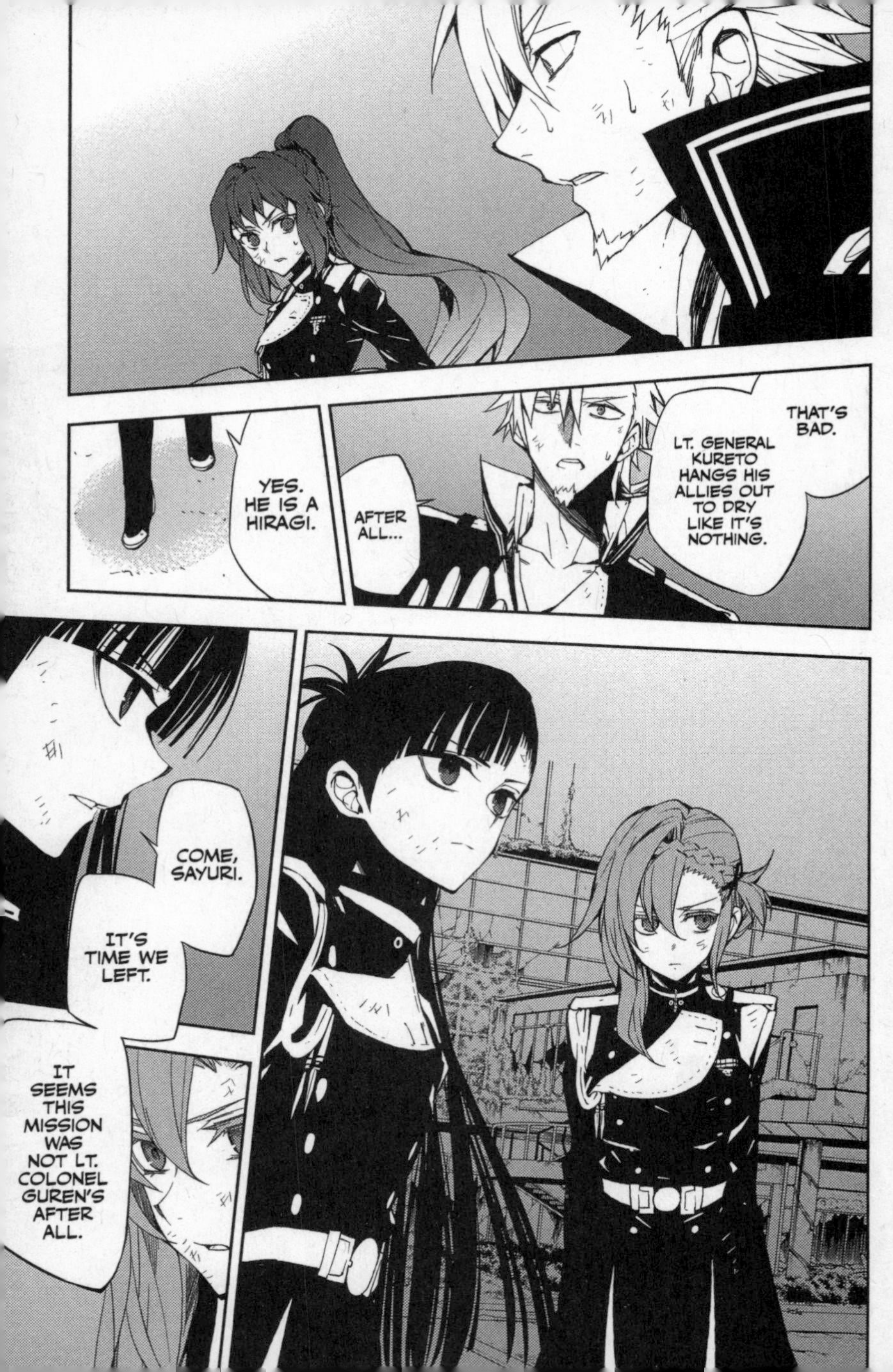
THAT'S BAD.
LT. GENERAL KURETO HANGS HIS ALLIES OUT TO DRY LIKE IT'S NOTHING.
AFTER ALL...
YES. HE IS A HIRAGI.
COME, SAYURI.
IT'S TIME WE LEFT.
IT SEEMS THIS MISSION WAS NOT LT. COLONEL GUREN'S AFTER ALL.

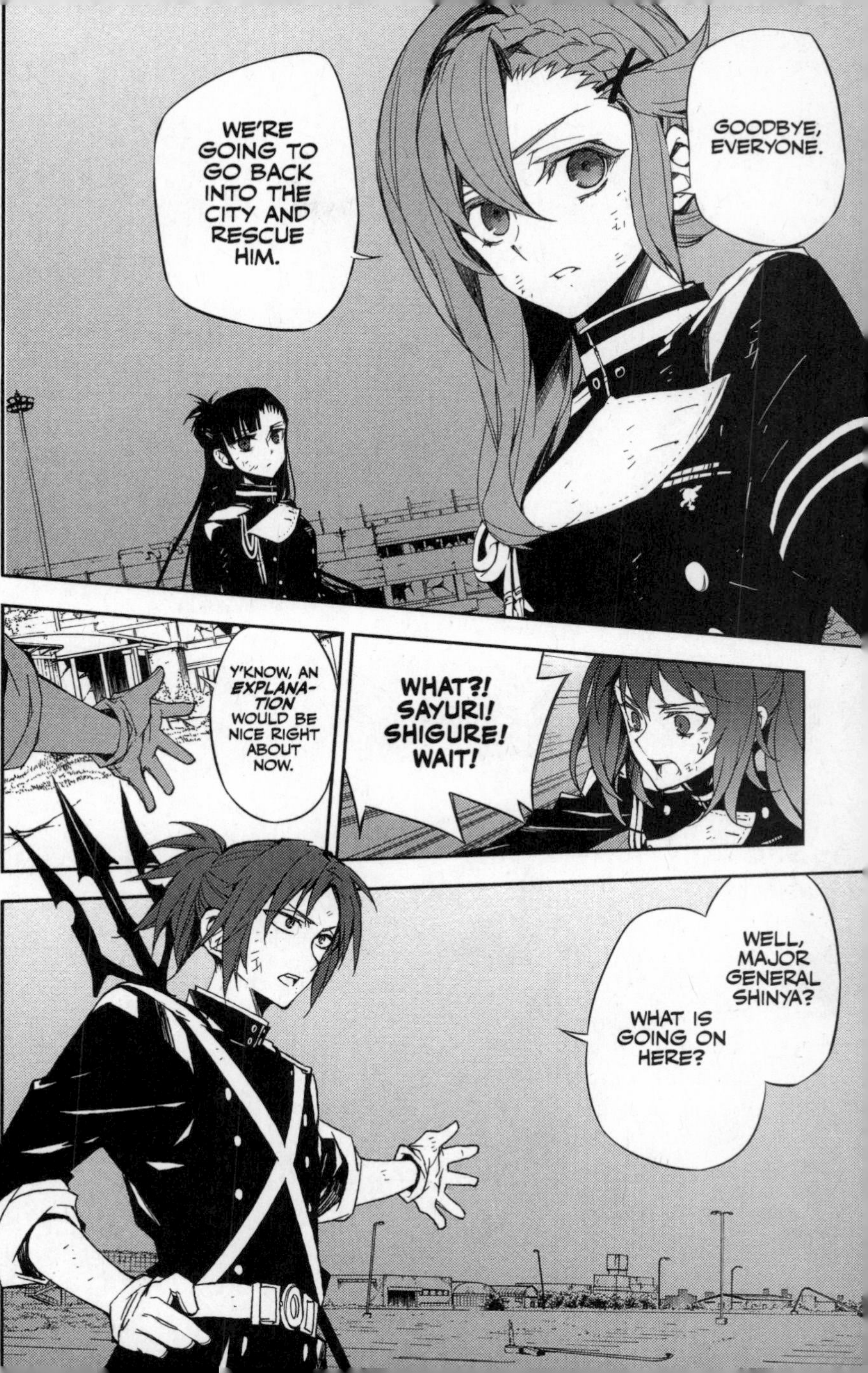
GOODBYE, EVERYONE.
WE'RE GOING TO GO BACK INTO THE CITY AND RESCUE HIM.
WHAT?! SAYURI! SHIGURE! WAIT!
Y'KNOW, AN *EXPLANATION* WOULD BE NICE RIGHT ABOUT NOW.
WELL, MAJOR GENERAL SHINYA?
WHAT IS GOING ON HERE?

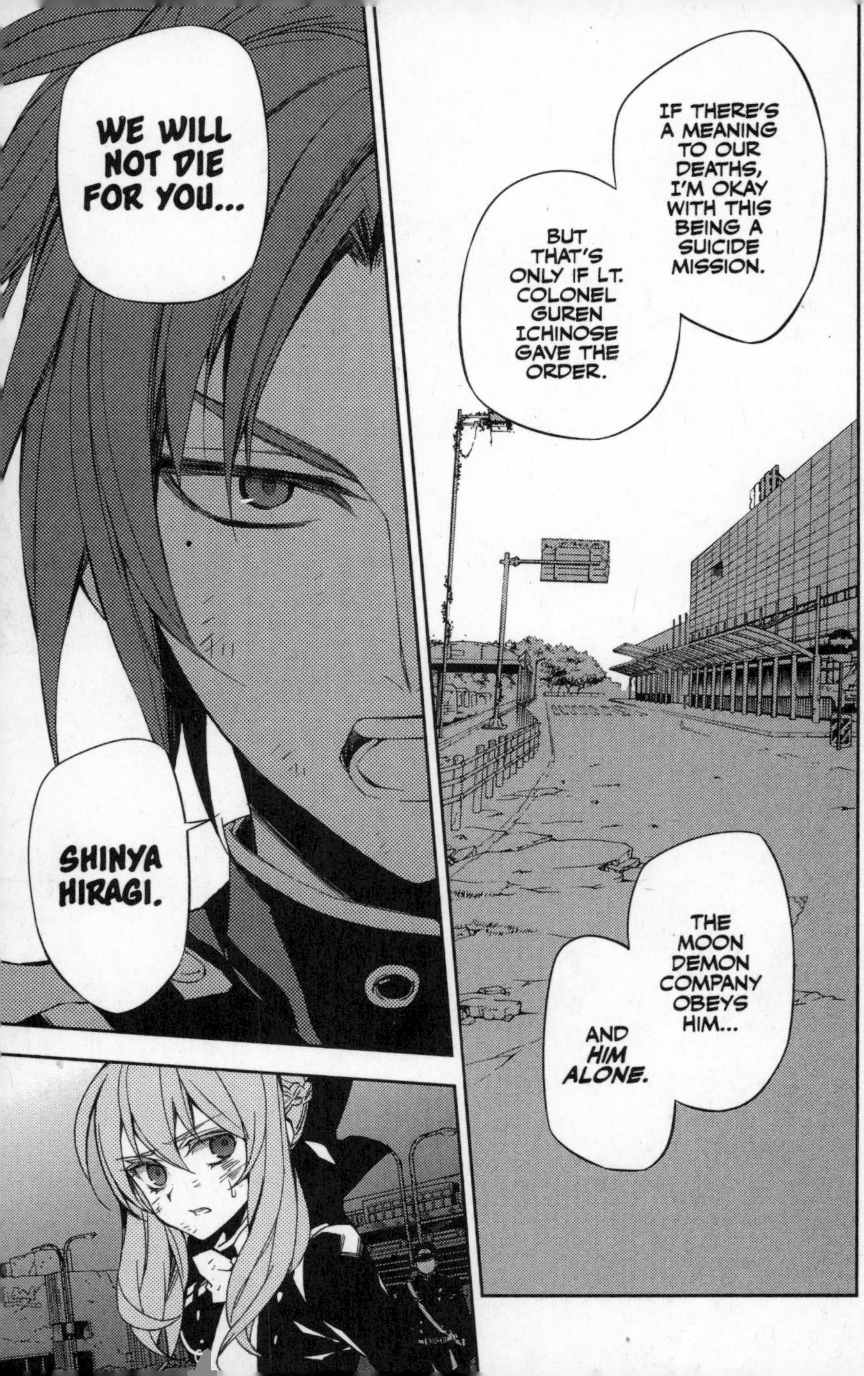
IF THERE'S A MEANING TO OUR DEATHS, I'M OKAY WITH THIS BEING A SUICIDE MISSION.
BUT THAT'S ONLY IF LT. COLONEL GUREN ICHINOSE GAVE THE ORDER.
THE MOON DEMON COMPANY OBEYS HIM...
AND *HIM ALONE*.
WE WILL NOT DIE FOR YOU...
SHINYA HIRAGI.

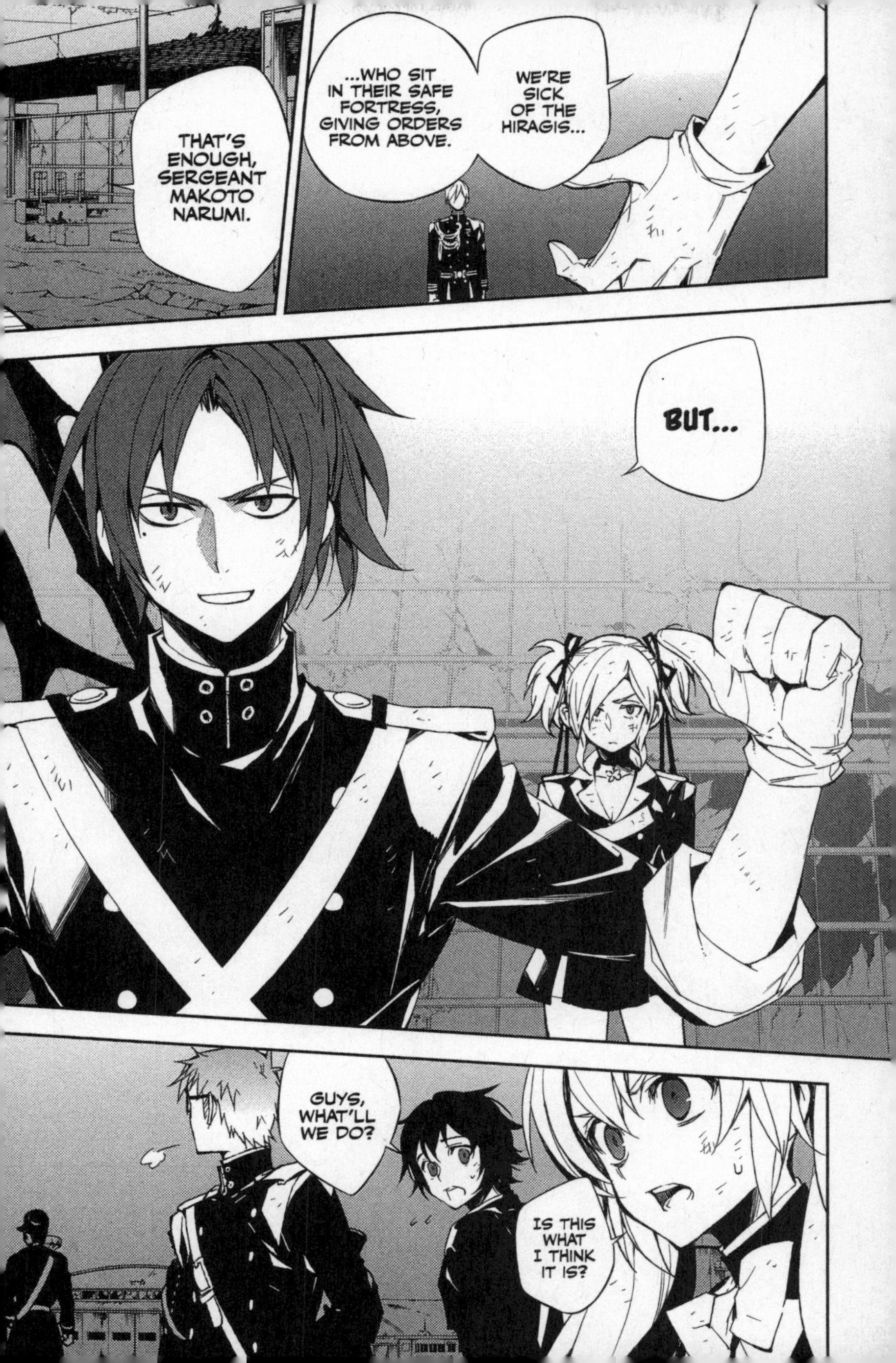
WE'RE SICK OF THE HIRAGIS...
...WHO SIT IN THEIR SAFE FORTRESS, GIVING ORDERS FROM ABOVE.
THAT'S ENOUGH, SERGEANT MAKOTO NARUMI.
BUT...
GUYS, WHAT'LL WE DO?
IS THIS WHAT I THINK IT IS?

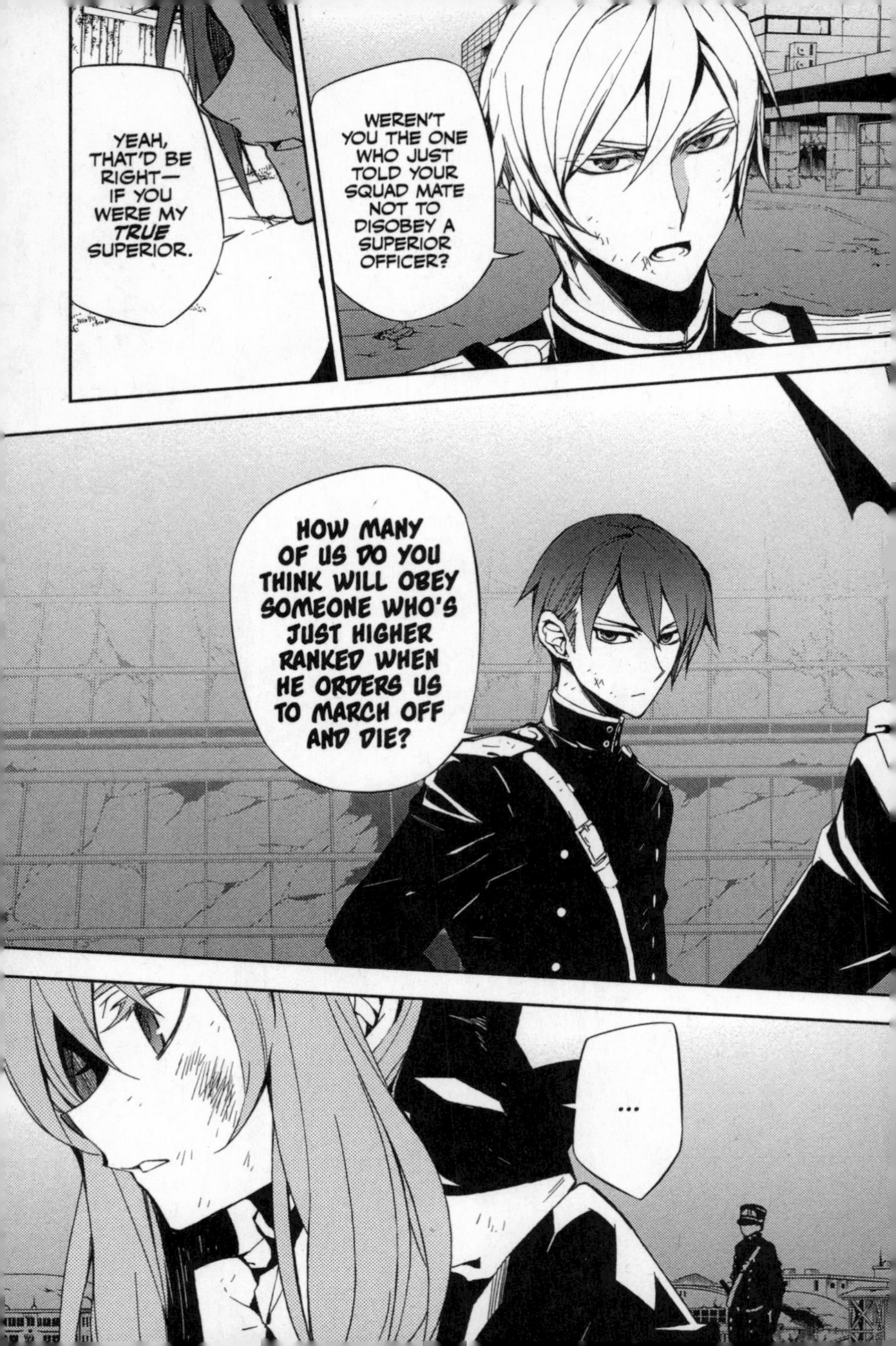
WEREN'T YOU THE ONE WHO JUST TOLD YOUR SQUAD MATE NOT TO DISOBEY A SUPERIOR OFFICER?
YEAH, THAT'D BE RIGHT— IF YOU WERE MY *TRUE* SUPERIOR.
HOW MANY OF US DO YOU THINK WILL OBEY SOMEONE WHO'S JUST HIGHER RANKED WHEN HE ORDERS US TO MARCH OFF AND DIE?
...

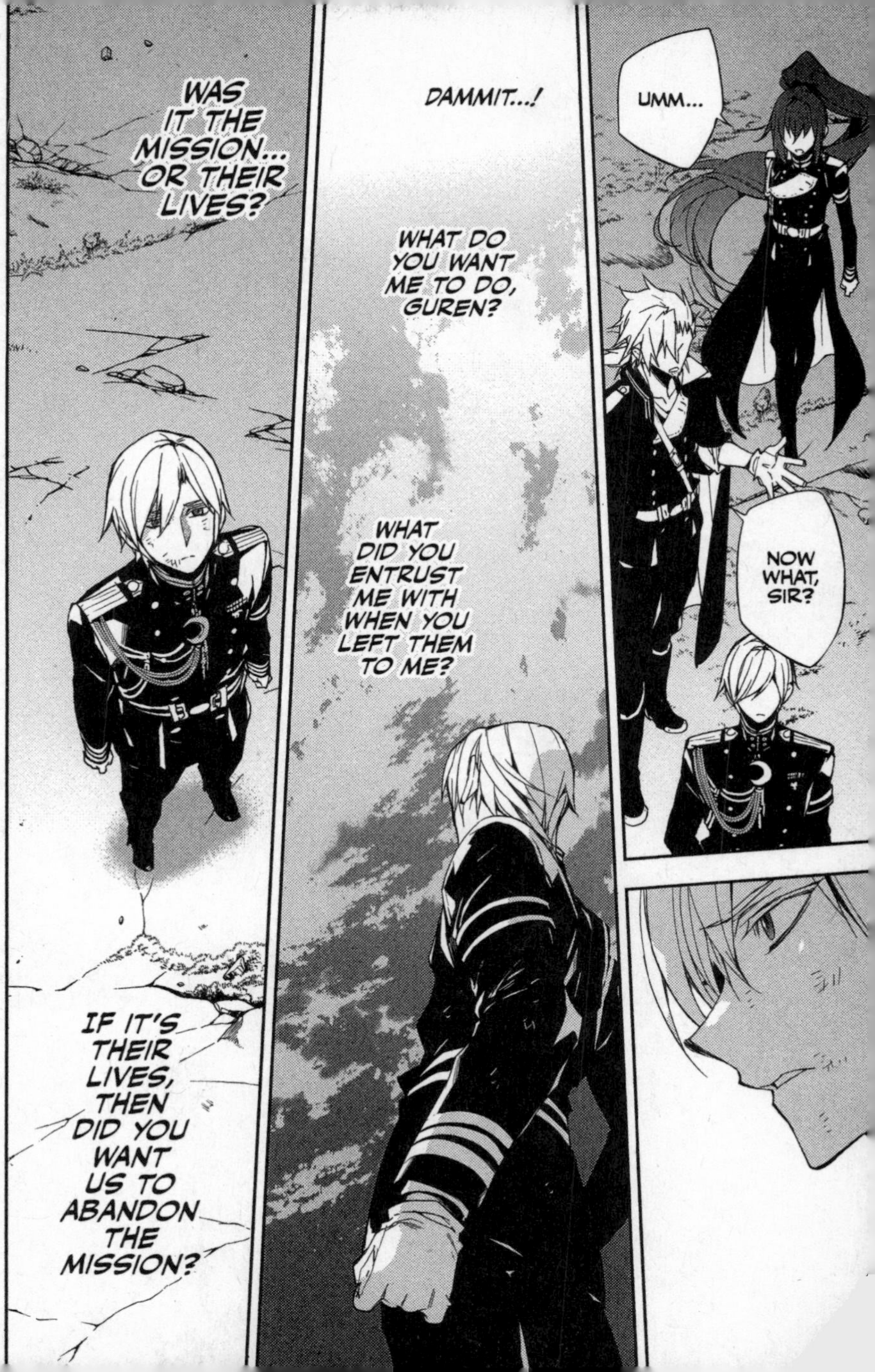
UMM...
NOW WHAT, SIR?
DAMMIT...!
WHAT DO YOU WANT ME TO DO, GUREN?
WHAT DID YOU ENTRUST ME WITH WHEN YOU LEFT THEM TO ME?
WAS IT THE MISSION... OR THEIR LIVES?
IF IT'S THEIR LIVES, THEN DID YOU WANT US TO ABANDON THE MISSION?

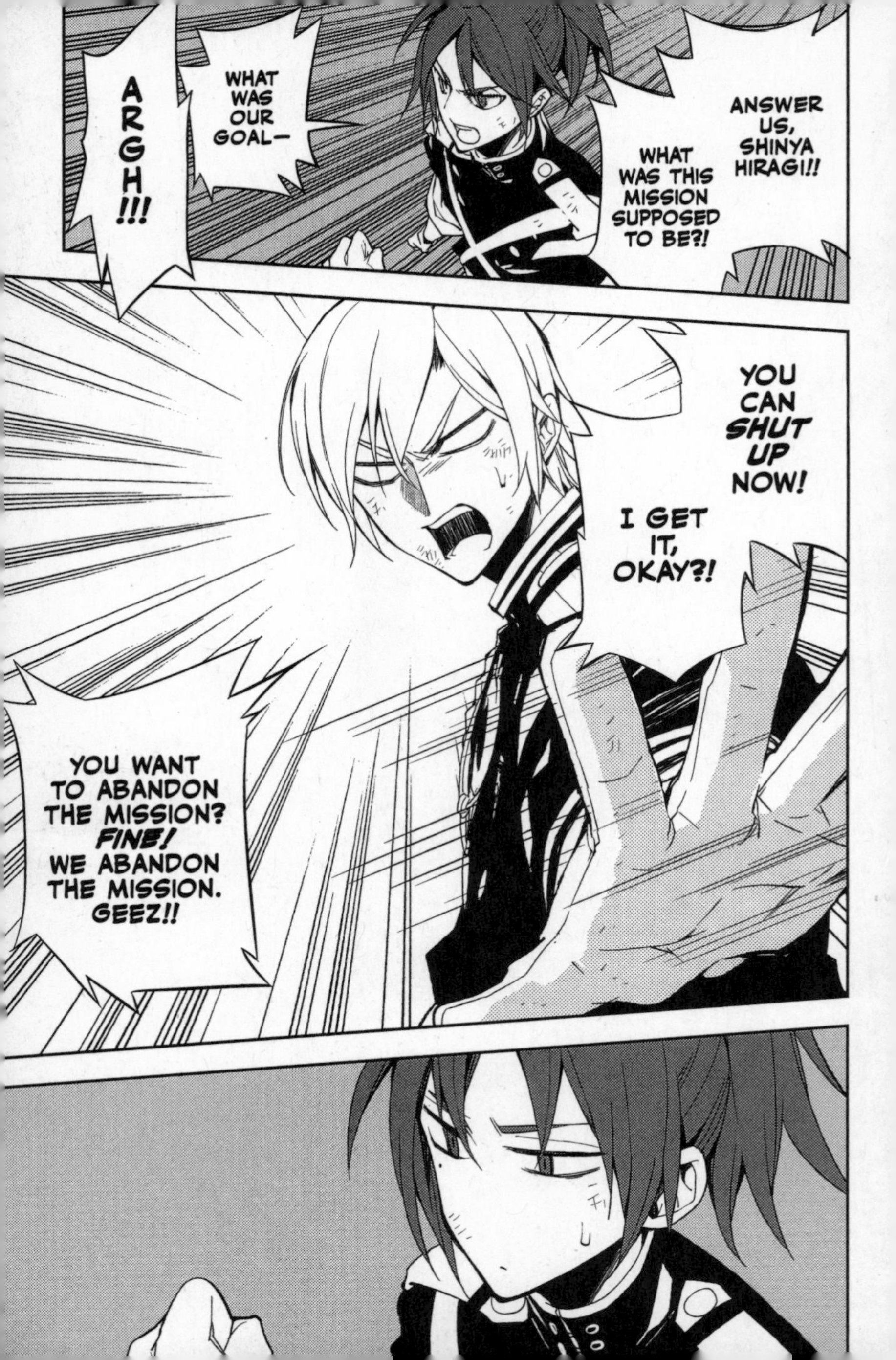
ANSWER US, SHINYA HIRAGI!!
WHAT WAS THIS MISSION SUPPOSED TO BE?!
WHAT WAS OUR GOAL—
ARGH!!!
YOU CAN SHUT UP NOW!
I GET IT, OKAY?!
YOU WANT TO ABANDON THE MISSION? FINE! WE ABANDON THE MISSION. GEEZ!!

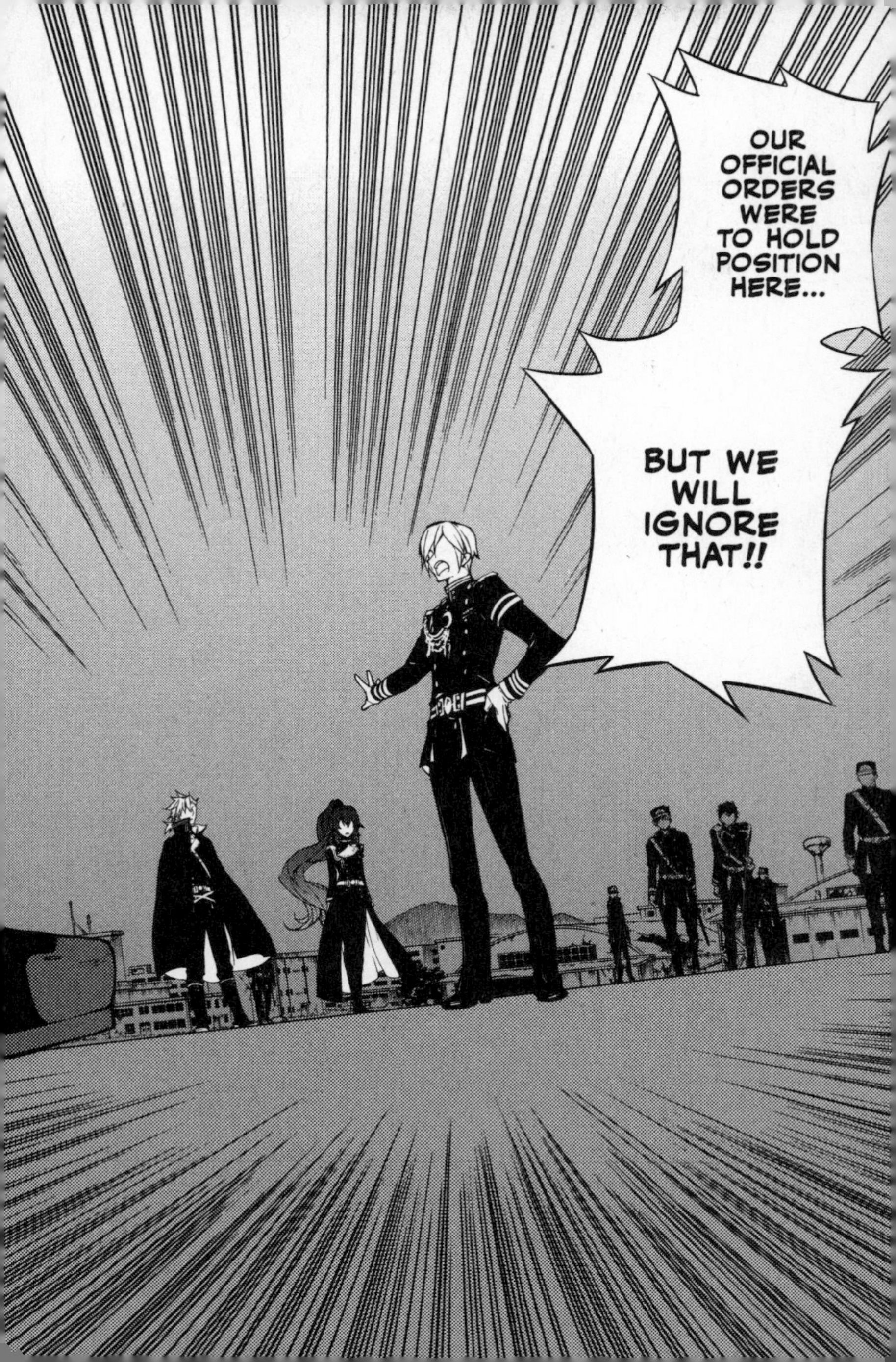
OUR OFFICIAL ORDERS WERE TO HOLD POSITION HERE...
BUT WE WILL IGNORE THAT!!

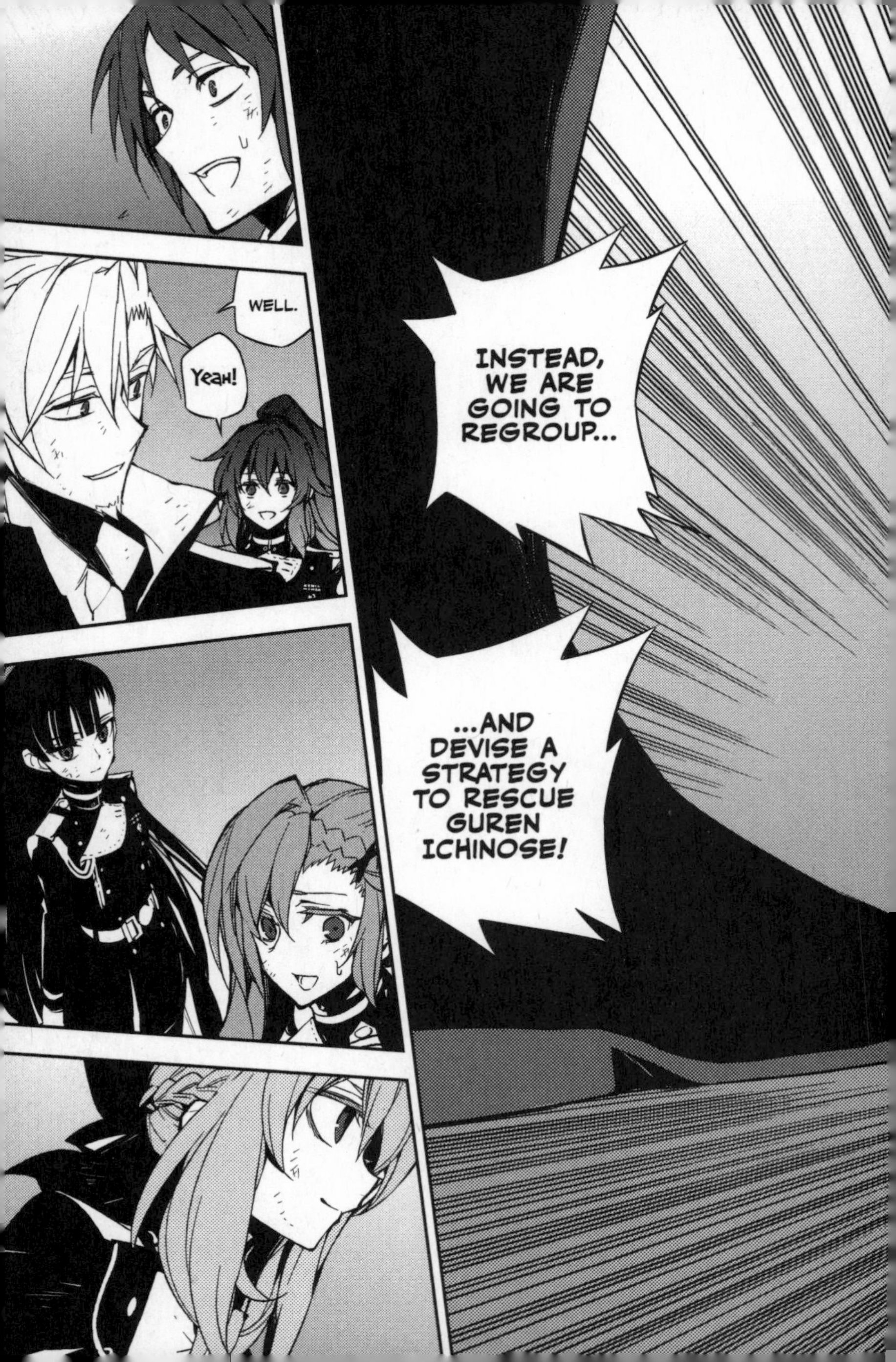

INSTEAD, WE ARE GOING TO REGROUP...
...AND DEVISE A STRATEGY TO RESCUE GUREN ICHINOSE!
WELL.
Yeah!

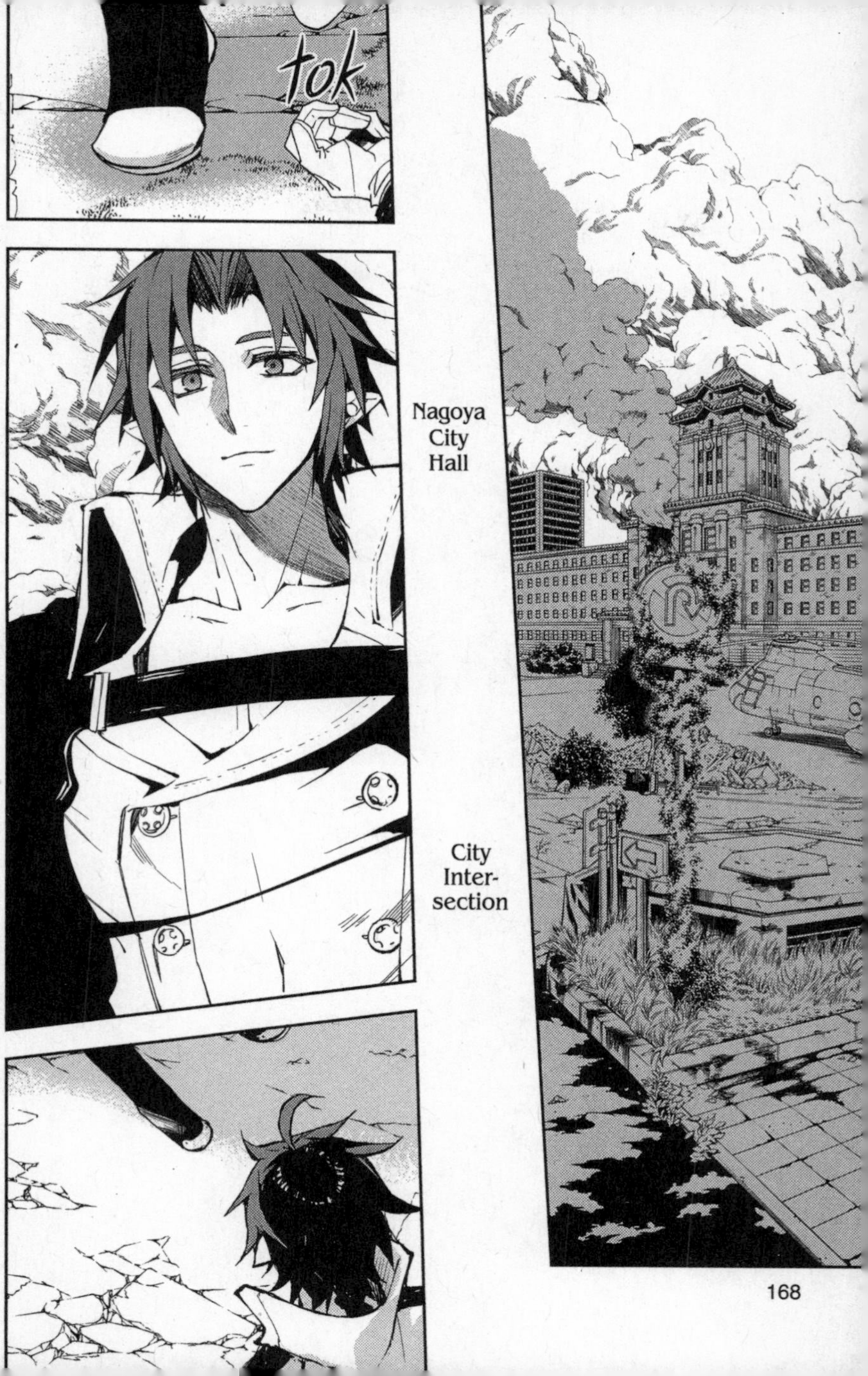

Nagoya City Hall
City Intersection
tok

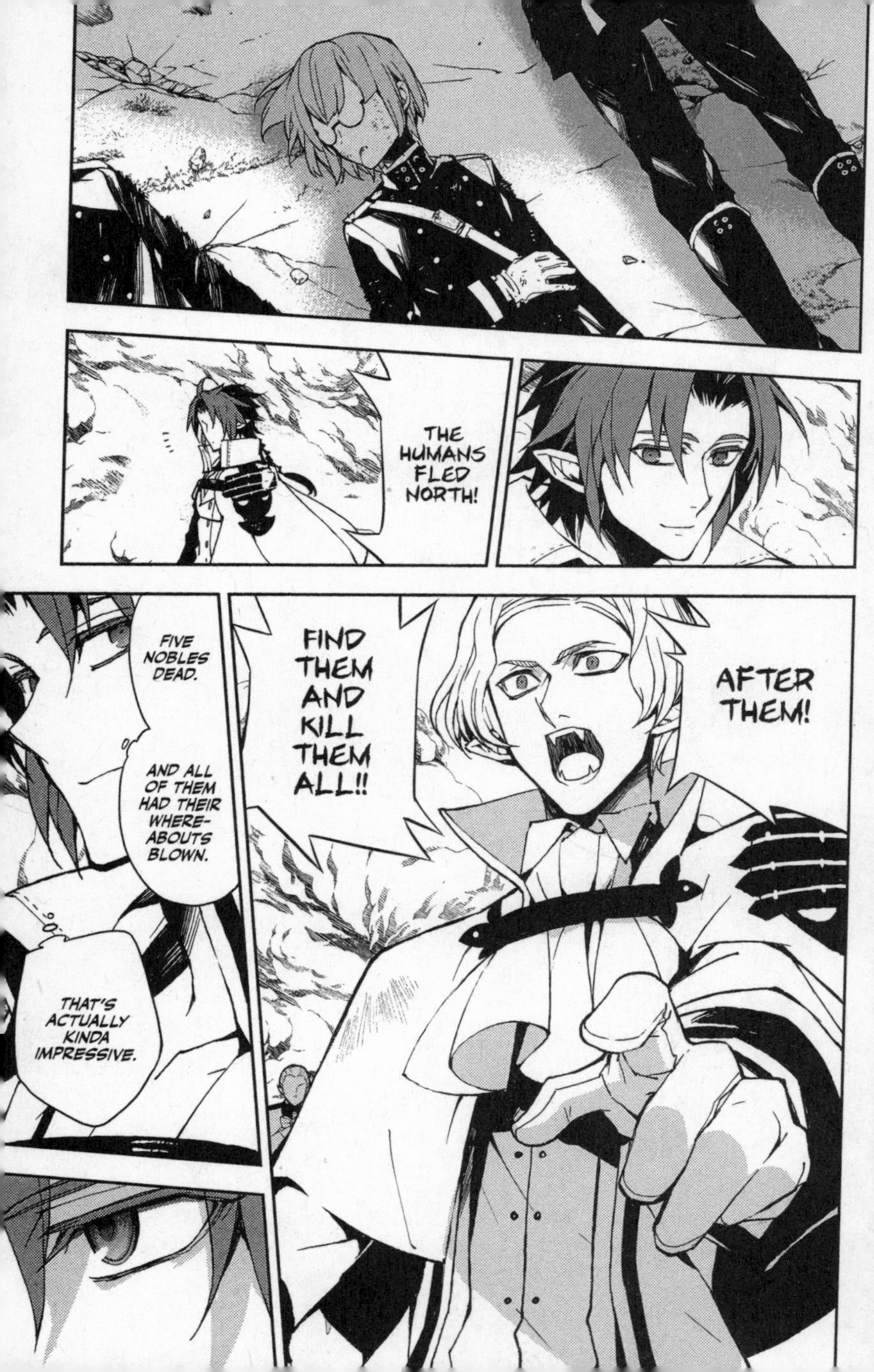
THE HUMANS FLED NORTH!
AFTER THEM!
FIND THEM AND KILL THEM ALL!!
FIVE NOBLES DEAD.
AND ALL OF THEM HAD THEIR WHERE-ABOUTS BLOWN.
THAT'S ACTUALLY KINDA IMPRESSIVE.

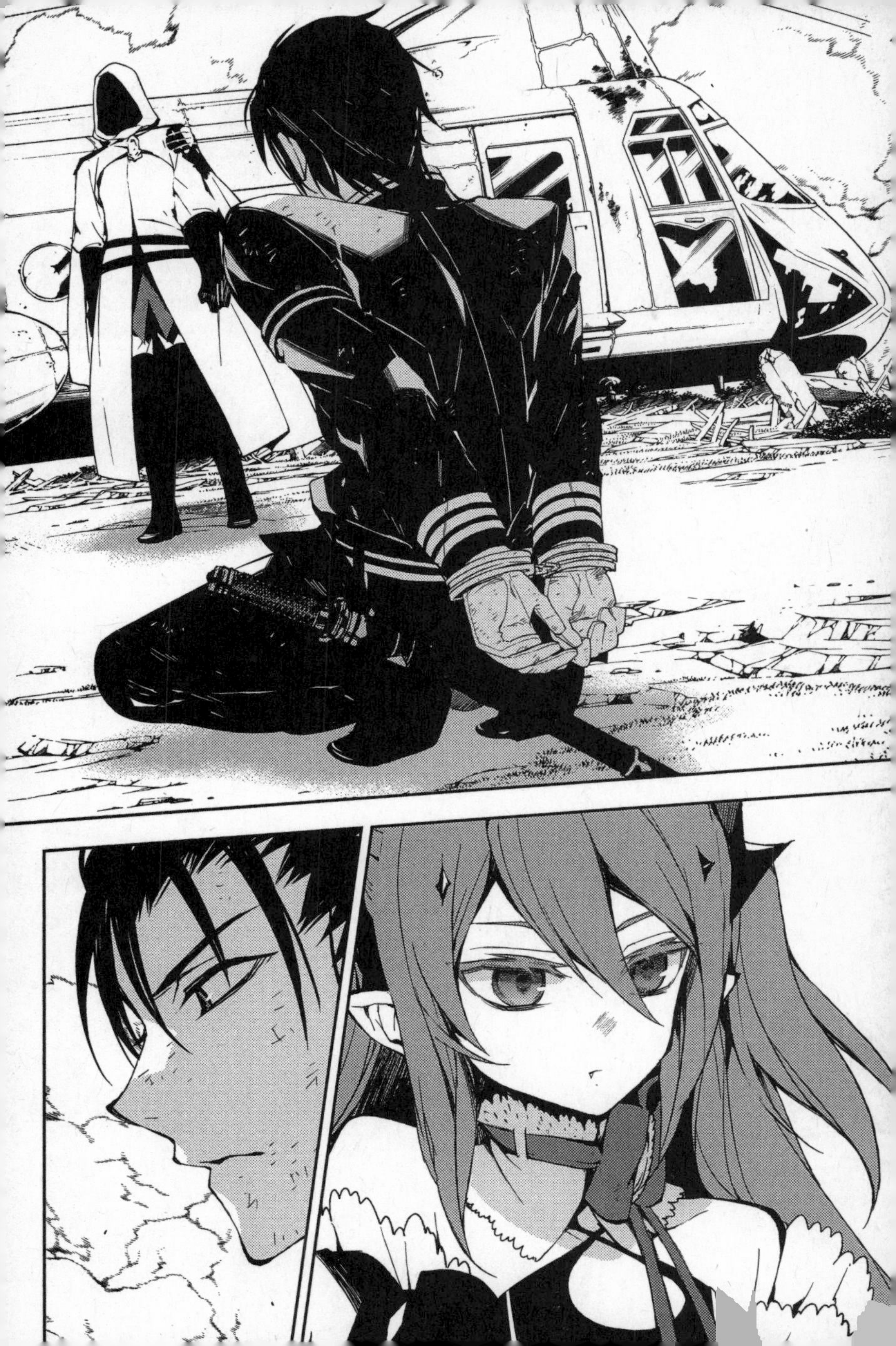

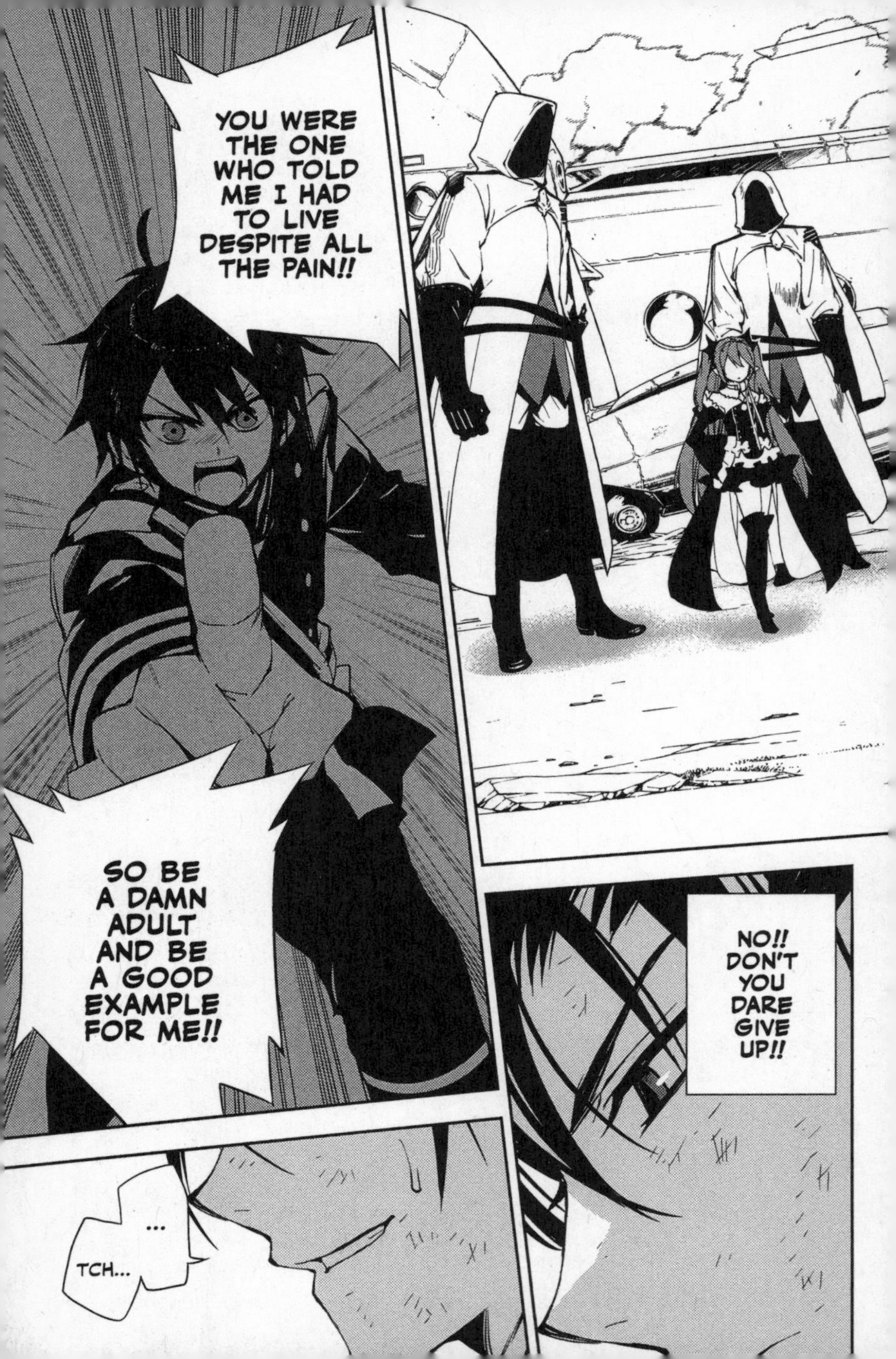
YOU WERE THE ONE WHO TOLD ME I HAD TO LIVE DESPITE ALL THE PAIN!!
SO BE A DAMN ADULT AND BE A GOOD EXAMPLE FOR ME!!
NO!! DON'T YOU DARE GIVE UP!!
...
TCH...

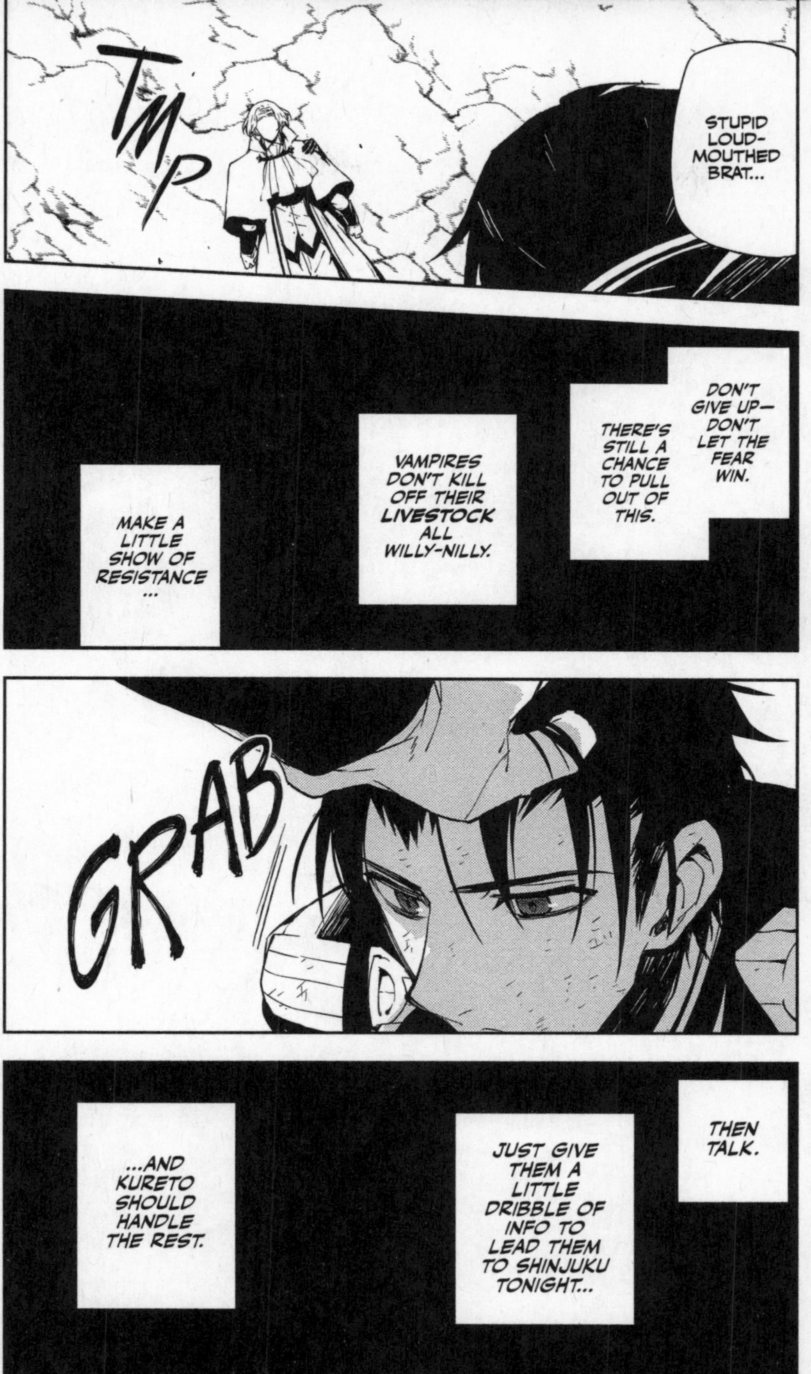

STUPID LOUD-MOUTHED BRAT...
TMP
DON'T GIVE UP—DON'T LET THE FEAR WIN.
THERE'S STILL A CHANCE TO PULL OUT OF THIS.
VAMPIRES DON'T KILL OFF THEIR LIVESTOCK ALL WILLY-NILLY.
MAKE A LITTLE SHOW OF RESISTANCE...
GRAB
THEN TALK.
JUST GIVE THEM A LITTLE DRIBBLE OF INFO TO LEAD THEM TO SHINJUKU TONIGHT...
...AND KURETO SHOULD HANDLE THE REST.

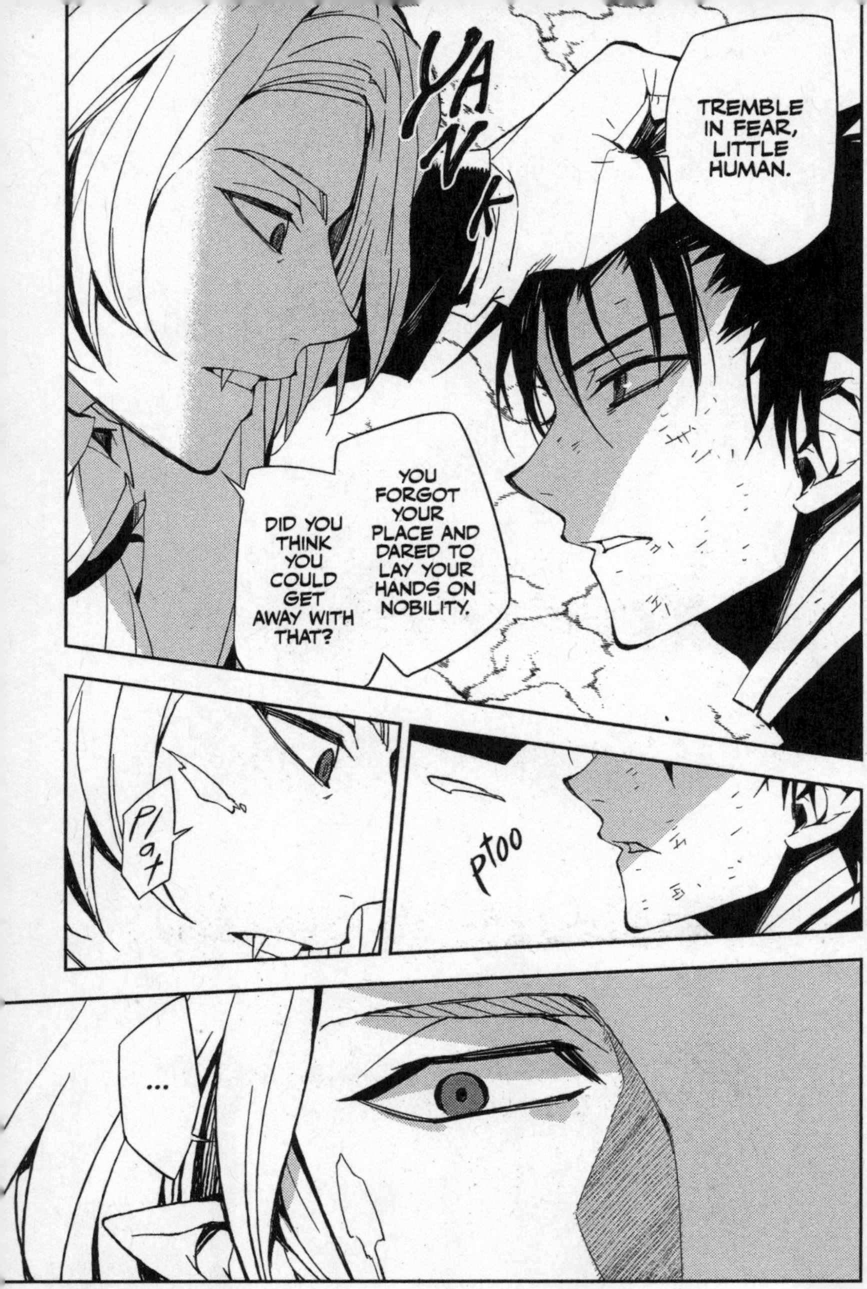
TREMBLE IN FEAR, LITTLE HUMAN.
YANK
YOU FORGOT YOUR PLACE AND DARED TO LAY YOUR HANDS ON NOBILITY.
DID YOU THINK YOU COULD GET AWAY WITH THAT?
ptoo
plax
...

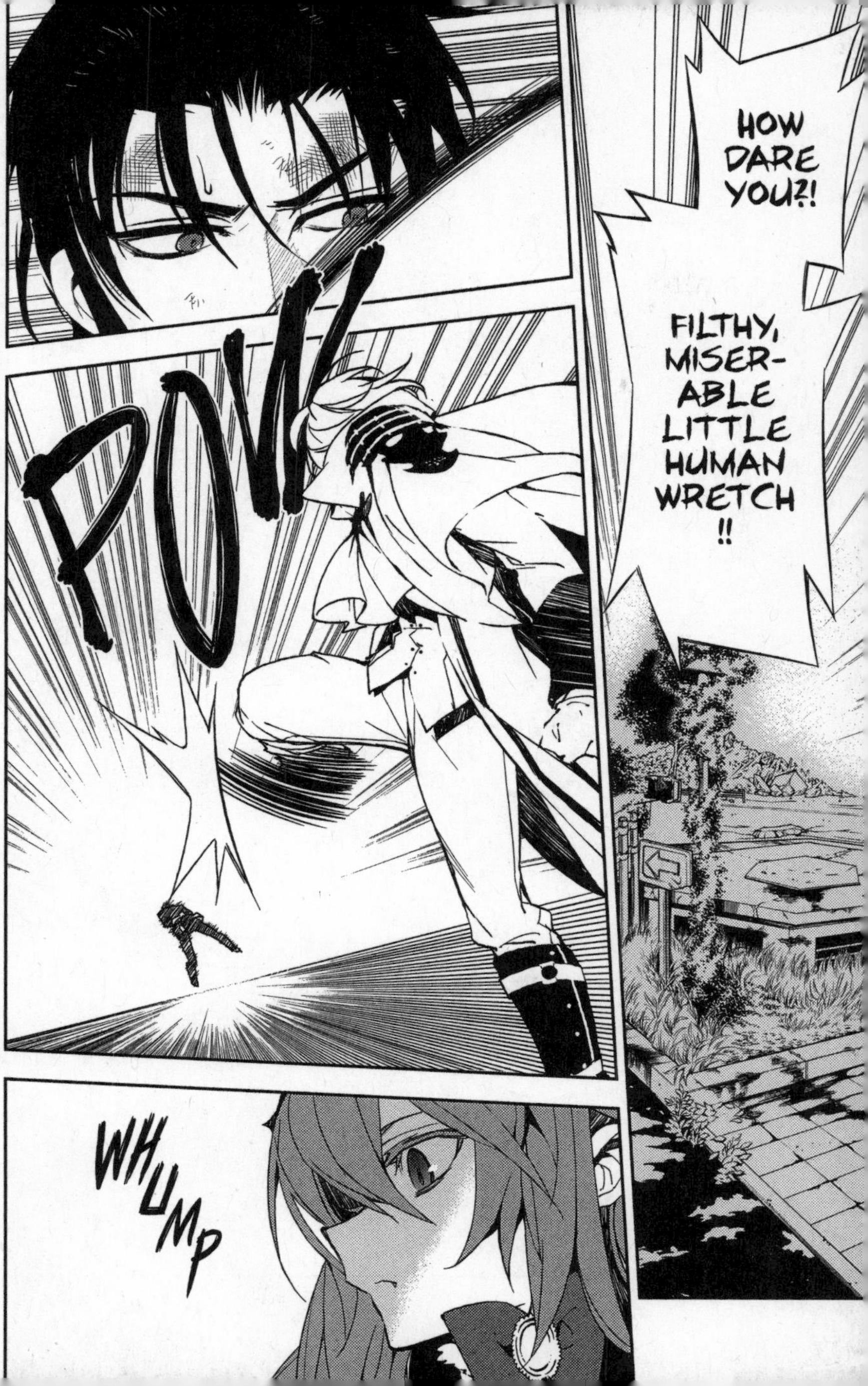
HOW DARE YOU?!
FILTHY, MISER-ABLE LITTLE HUMAN WRETCH!!
POW
WHUMP

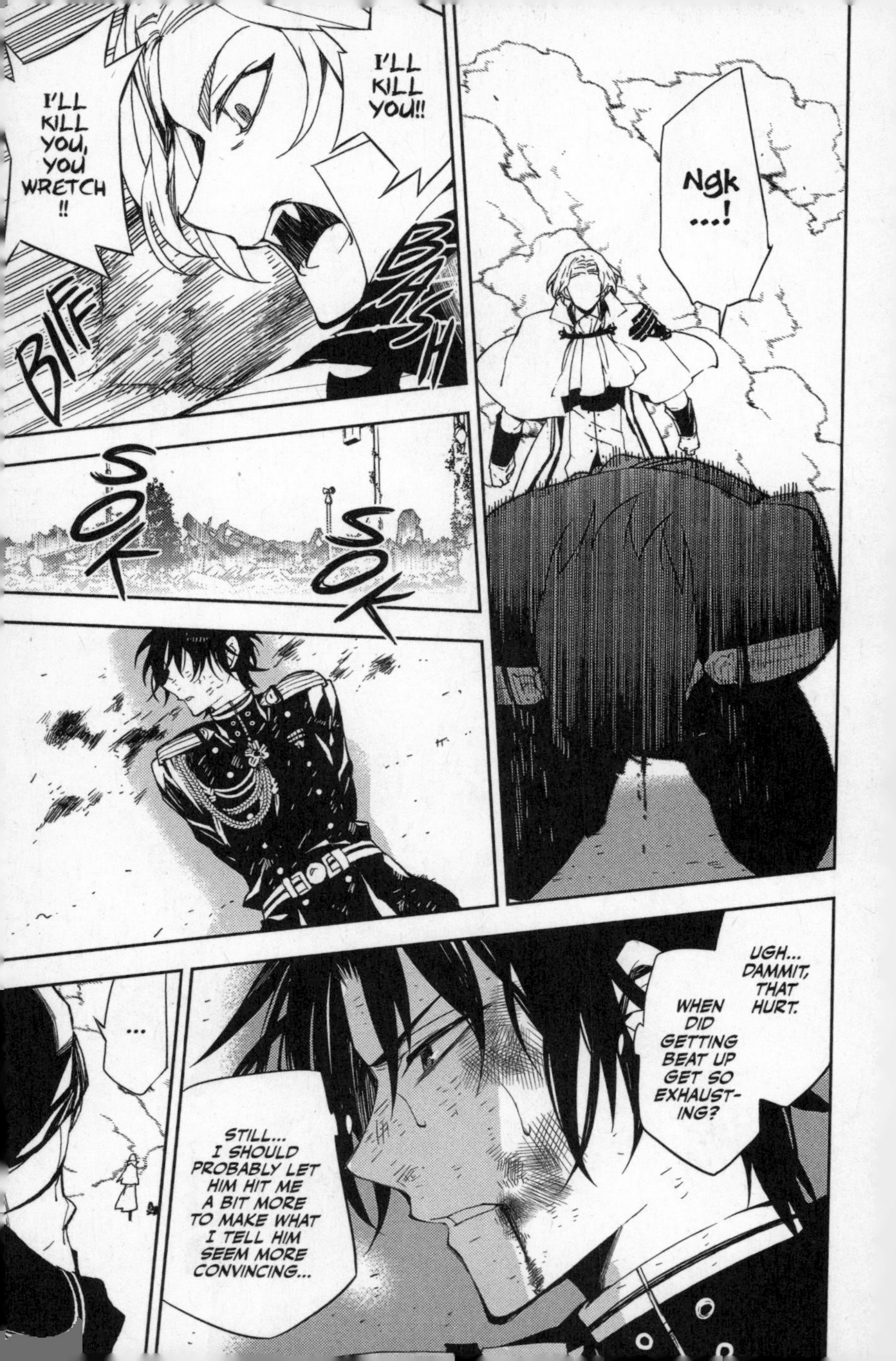
Ngk ...!
I'LL KILL YOU!!
I'LL KILL YOU, YOU WRETCH !!
BASH
BIFF
SOK
SOK
UGH... DAMMIT, THAT HURT.
WHEN DID GETTING BEAT UP GET SO EXHAUSTING?
STILL... I SHOULD PROBABLY LET HIM HIT ME A BIT MORE TO MAKE WHAT I TELL HIM SEEM MORE CONVINCING...
...

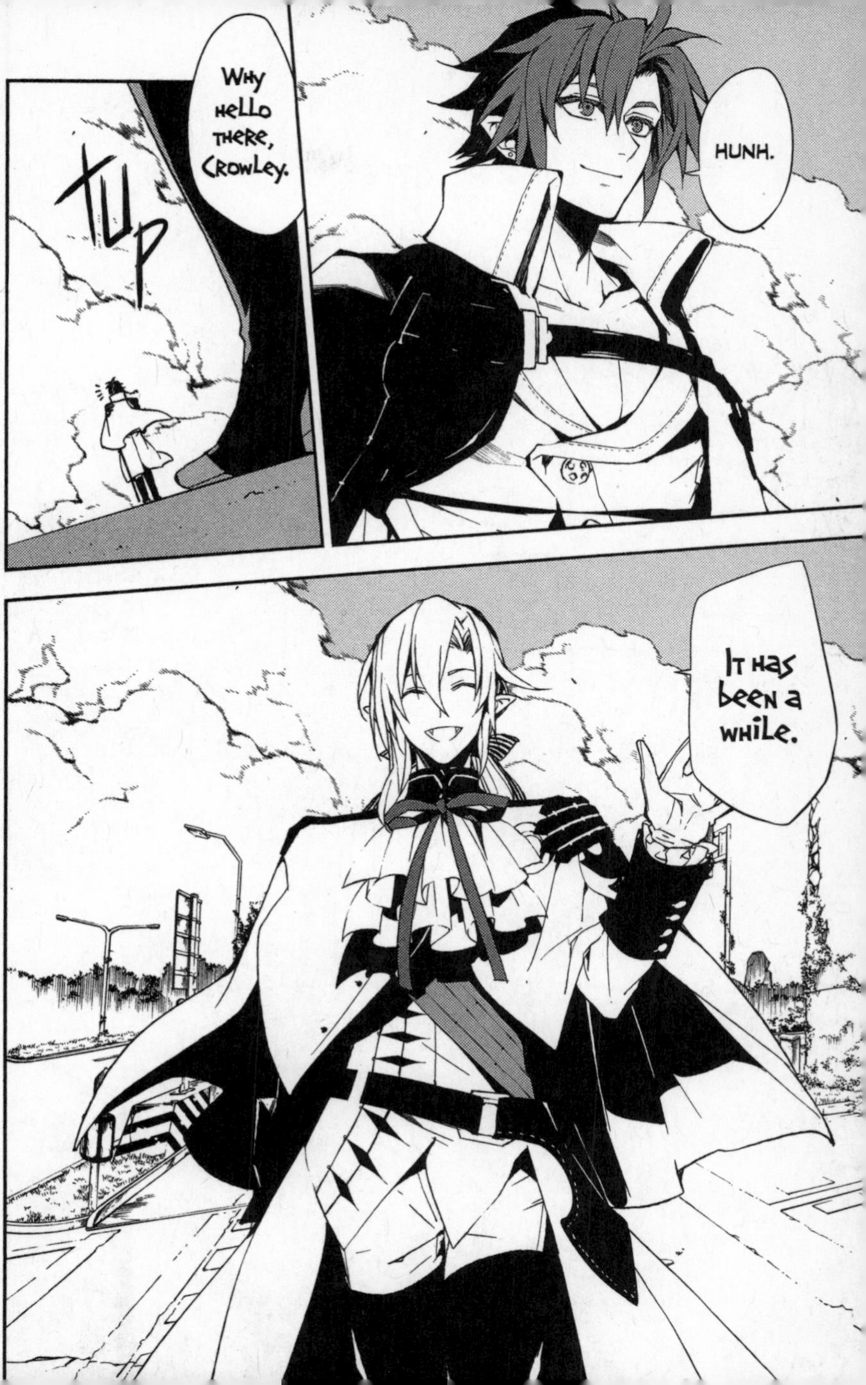
HUNH.
Why hello there, Crowley.
TUP
It has been a while.

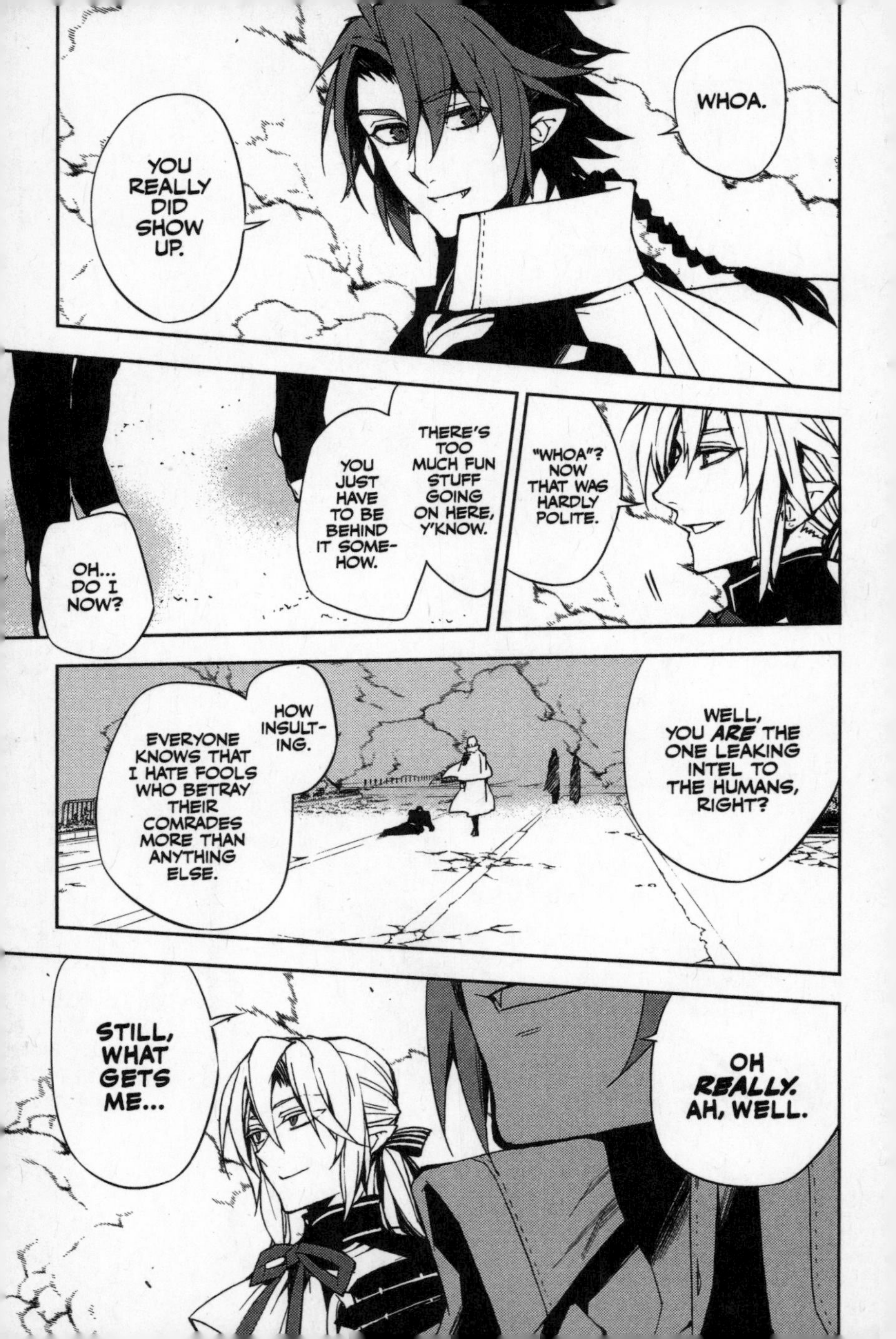
WHOA.
YOU REALLY DID SHOW UP.
"WHOA"? NOW THAT WAS HARDLY POLITE.
THERE'S TOO MUCH FUN STUFF GOING ON HERE, Y'KNOW.
YOU JUST HAVE TO BE BEHIND IT SOMEHOW.
OH... DO I NOW?
WELL, YOU ARE THE ONE LEAKING INTEL TO THE HUMANS, RIGHT?
HOW INSULTING.
EVERYONE KNOWS THAT I HATE FOOLS WHO BETRAY THEIR COMRADES MORE THAN ANYTHING ELSE.
OH REALLY. AH, WELL.
STILL, WHAT GETS ME...

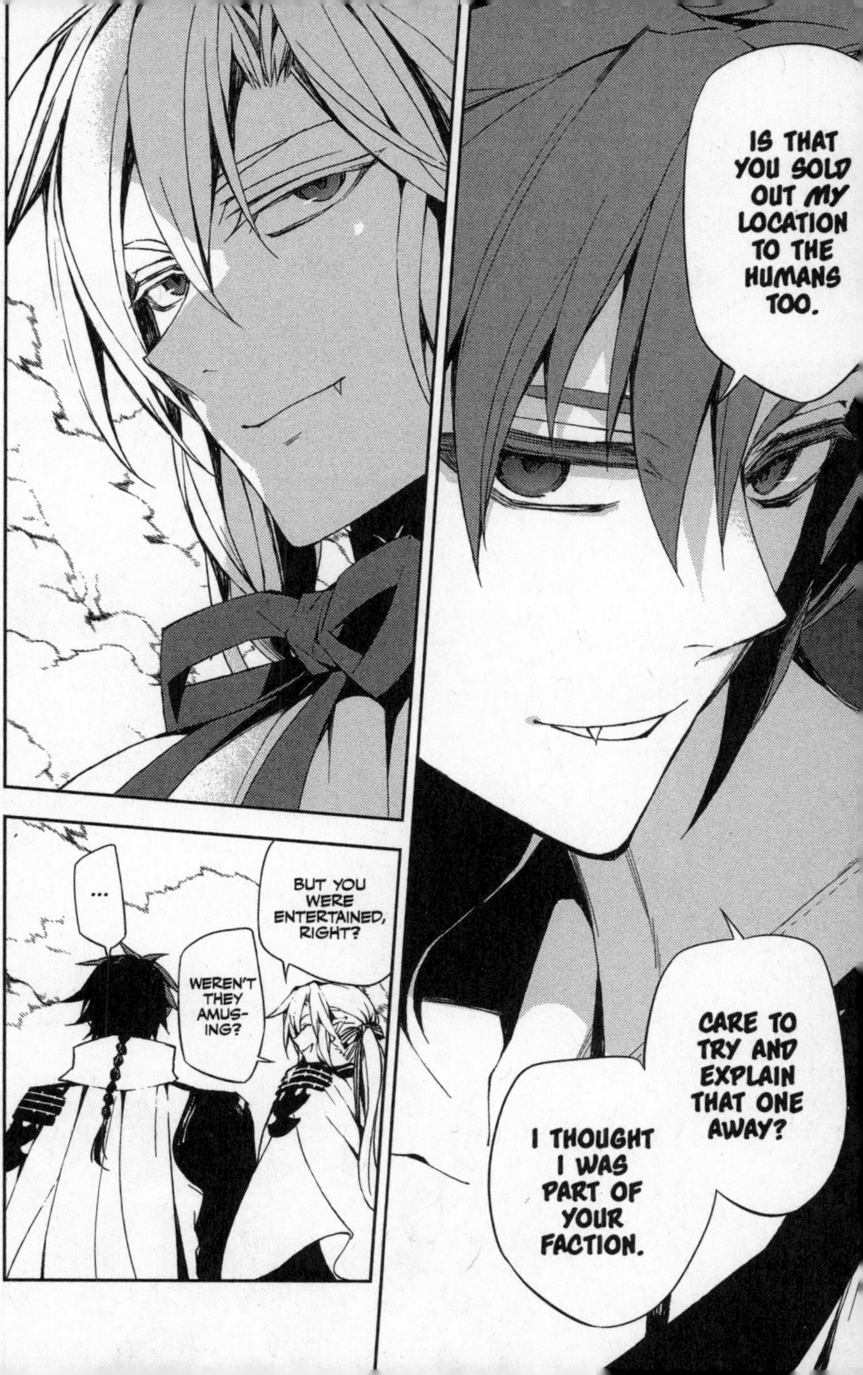
IS THAT YOU SOLD OUT MY LOCATION TO THE HUMANS TOO.
CARE TO TRY AND EXPLAIN THAT ONE AWAY?
I THOUGHT I WAS PART OF YOUR FACTION.
BUT YOU WERE ENTERTAINED, RIGHT?
WEREN'T THEY AMUSING?
...

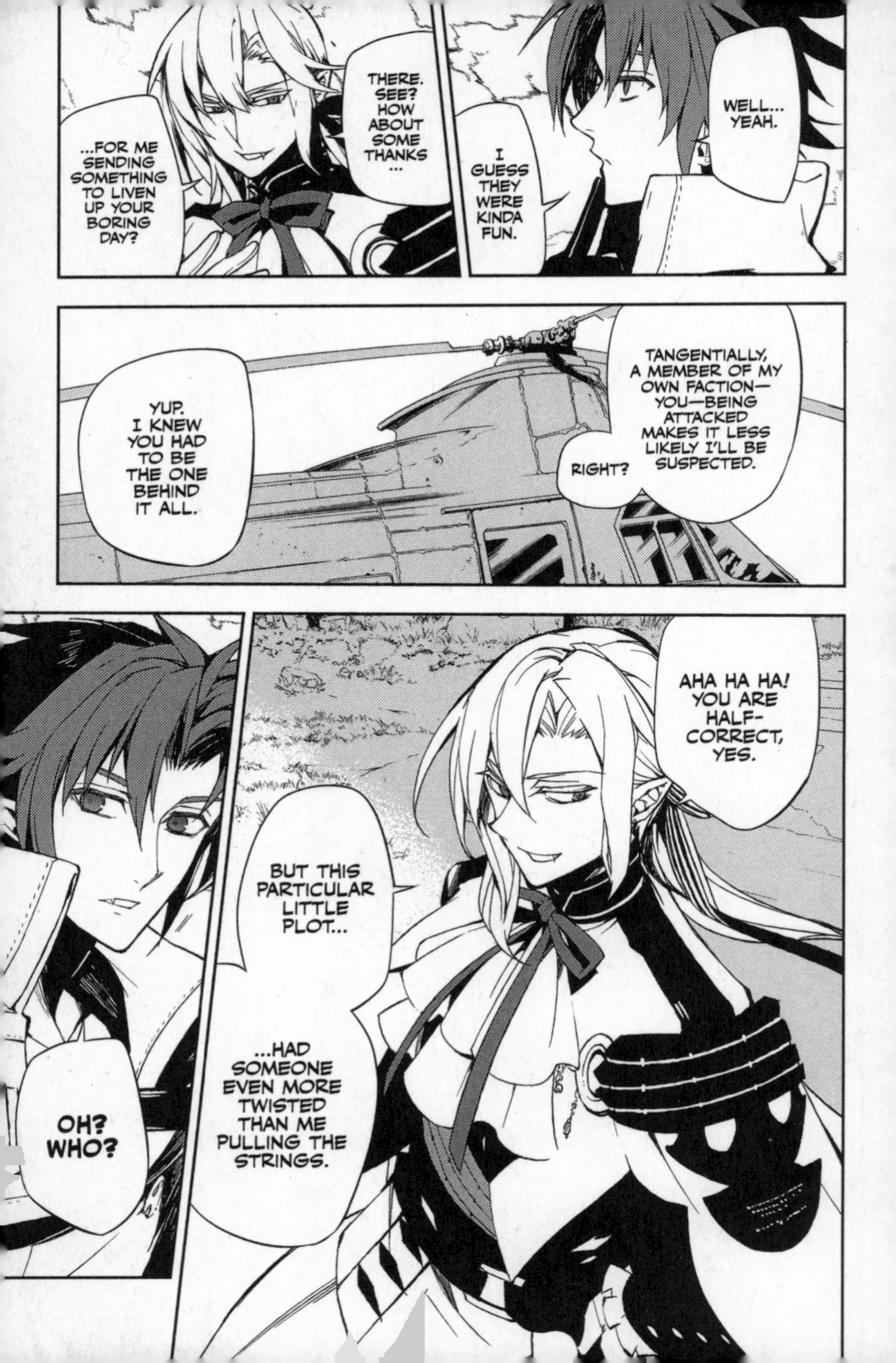
WELL... YEAH.
I GUESS THEY WERE KINDA FUN.
THERE. SEE? HOW ABOUT SOME THANKS...
...FOR ME SENDING SOMETHING TO LIVEN UP YOUR BORING DAY?
TANGENTIALLY, A MEMBER OF MY OWN FACTION—YOU—BEING ATTACKED MAKES IT LESS LIKELY I'LL BE SUSPECTED.
RIGHT?
YUP. I KNEW YOU HAD TO BE THE ONE BEHIND IT ALL.
AHA HA HA! YOU ARE HALF-CORRECT, YES.
BUT THIS PARTICULAR LITTLE PLOT...
...HAD SOMEONE EVEN MORE TWISTED THAN ME PULLING THE STRINGS.
OH? WHO?

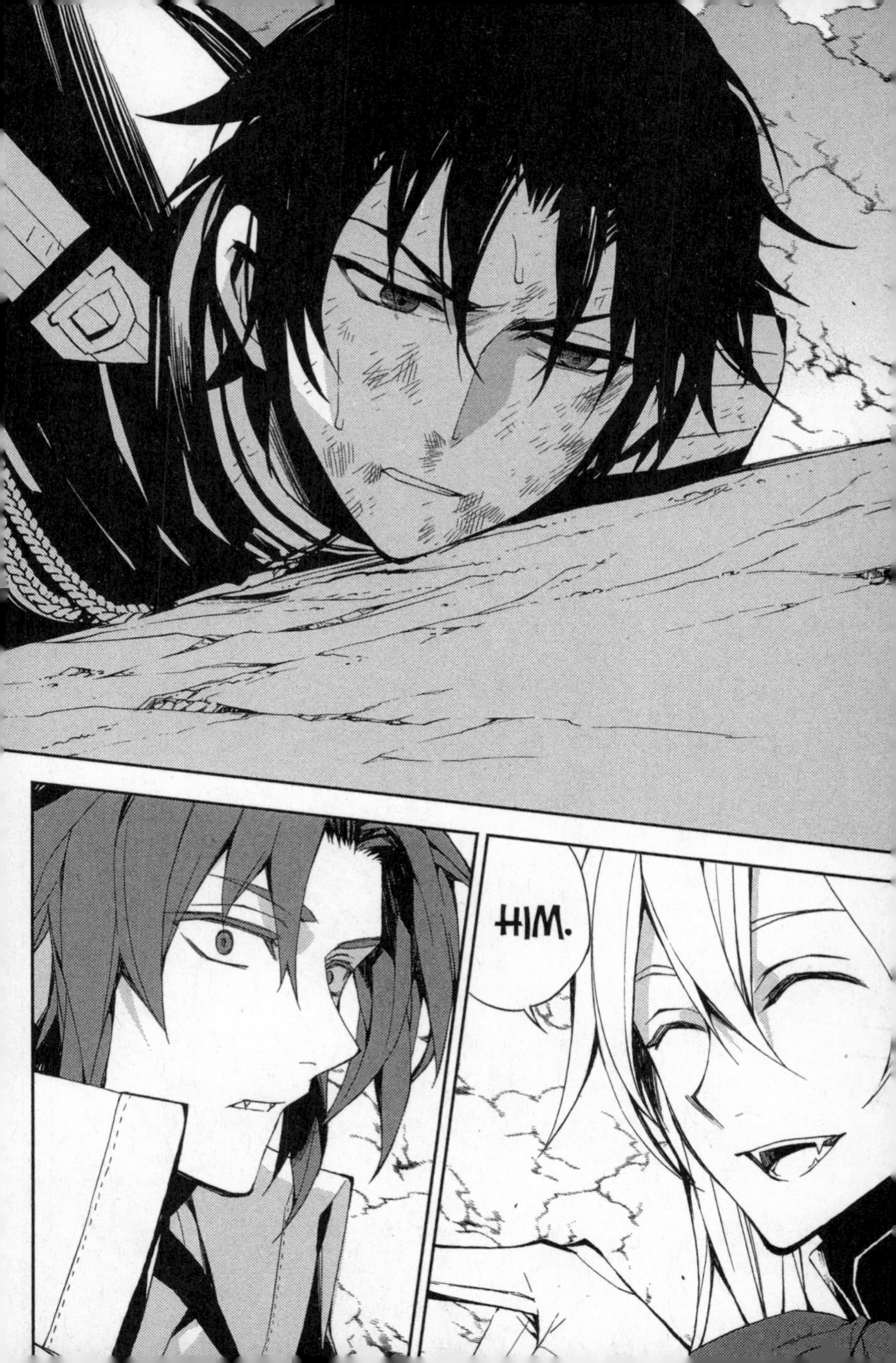
HIM.

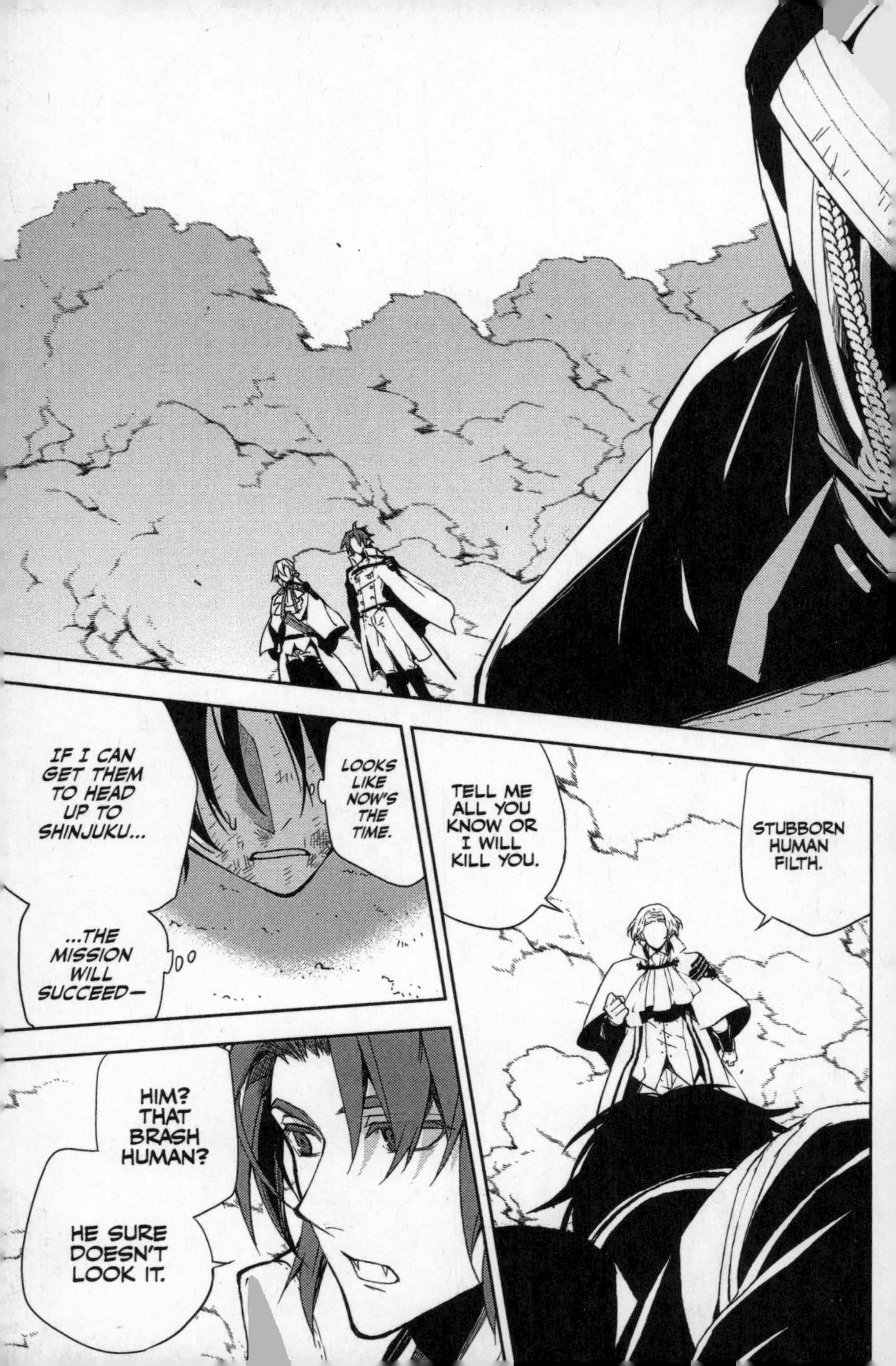
STUBBORN HUMAN FILTH.
TELL ME ALL YOU KNOW OR I WILL KILL YOU.
LOOKS LIKE NOW'S THE TIME.
IF I CAN GET THEM TO HEAD UP TO SHINJUKU...
...THE MISSION WILL SUCCEED—
HIM? THAT BRASH HUMAN?
HE SURE DOESN'T LOOK IT.

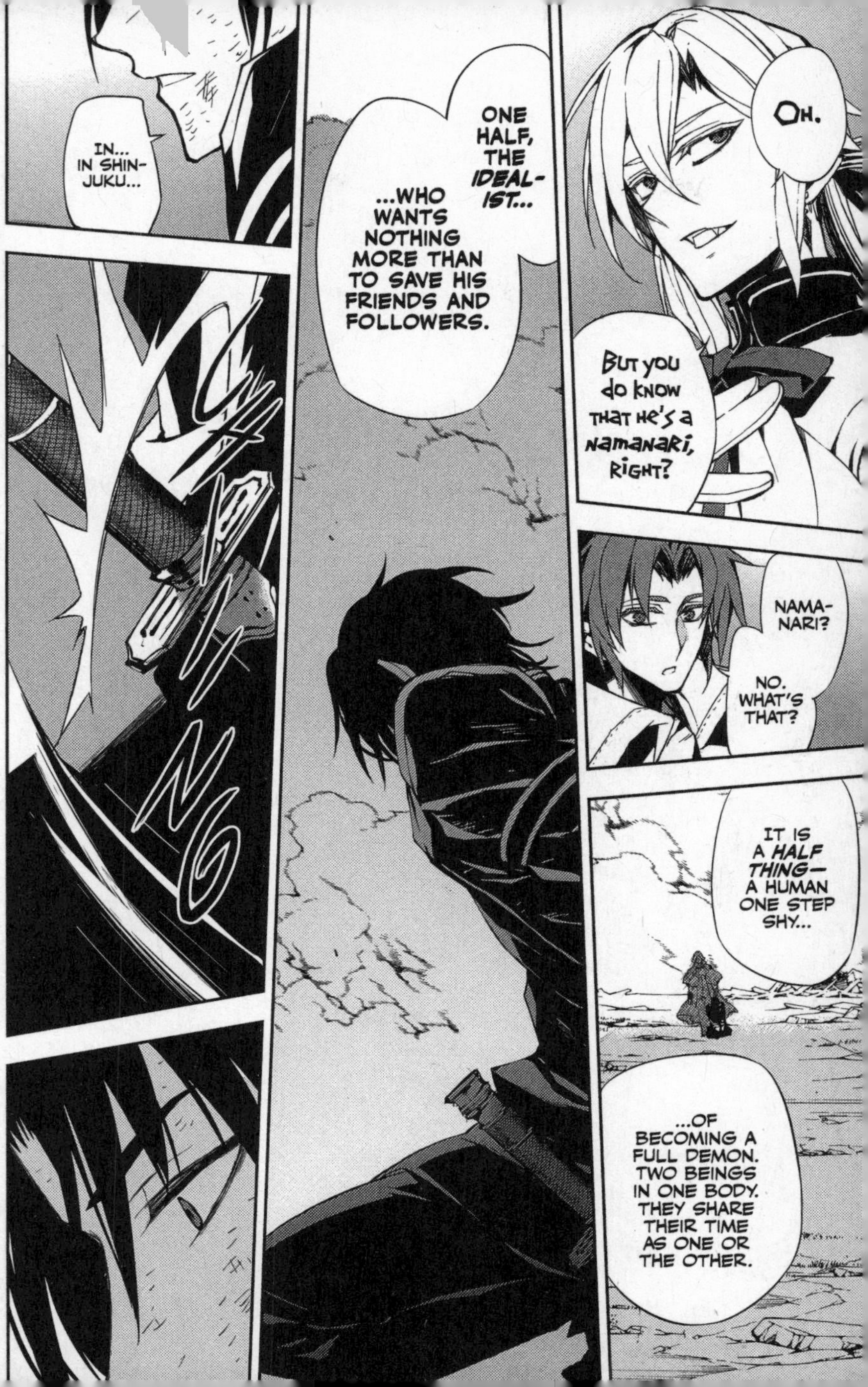

OH.
BUT YOU DO KNOW THAT HE'S A NAMANARI, RIGHT?
NAMA-NARI?
NO. WHAT'S THAT?
IT IS A *HALF THING*— A HUMAN ONE STEP SHY...
...OF BECOMING A FULL DEMON. TWO BEINGS IN ONE BODY. THEY SHARE THEIR TIME AS ONE OR THE OTHER.
ONE HALF, THE *IDEALIST*...
...WHO WANTS NOTHING MORE THAN TO SAVE HIS FRIENDS AND FOLLOWERS.
IN... IN SHIN-JUKU...

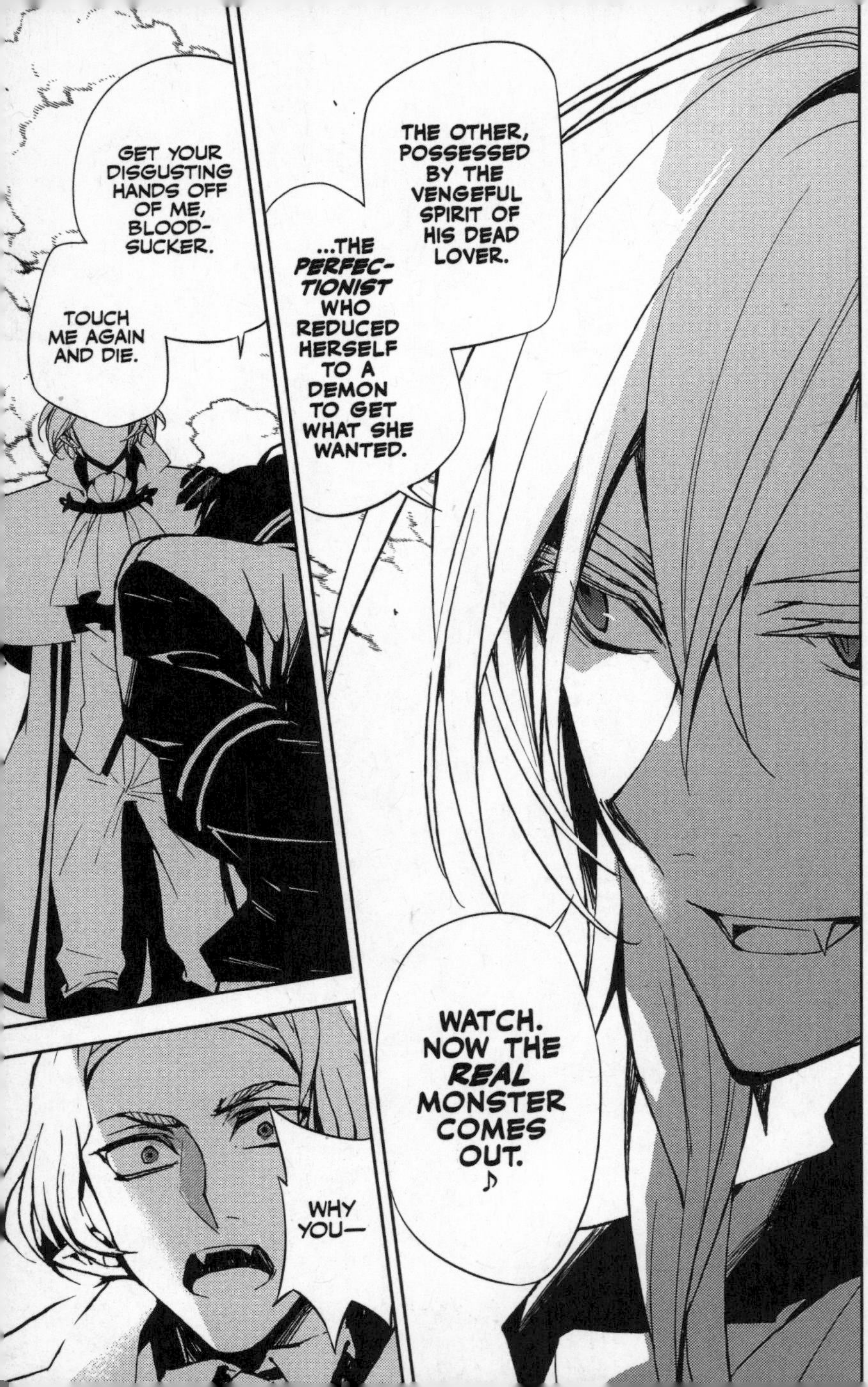
THE OTHER, POSSESSED BY THE VENGEFUL SPIRIT OF HIS DEAD LOVER.
...THE *PERFECTIONIST* WHO REDUCED HERSELF TO A DEMON TO GET WHAT SHE WANTED.
WATCH. NOW THE *REAL* MONSTER COMES OUT. ♪
GET YOUR DISGUSTING HANDS OFF OF ME, BLOOD-SUCKER.
TOUCH ME AGAIN AND DIE.
WHY YOU—

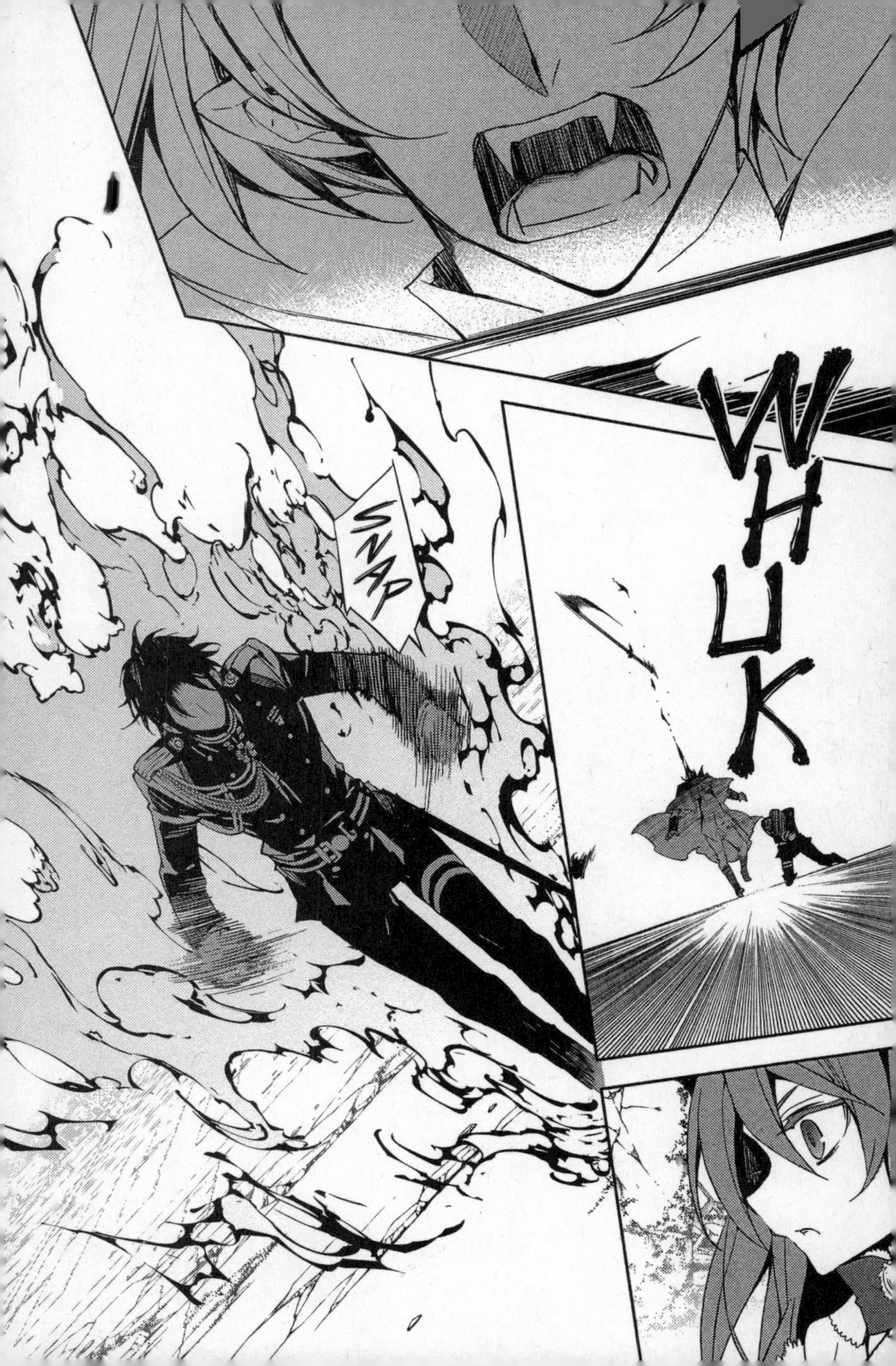
WHUK
SNAP

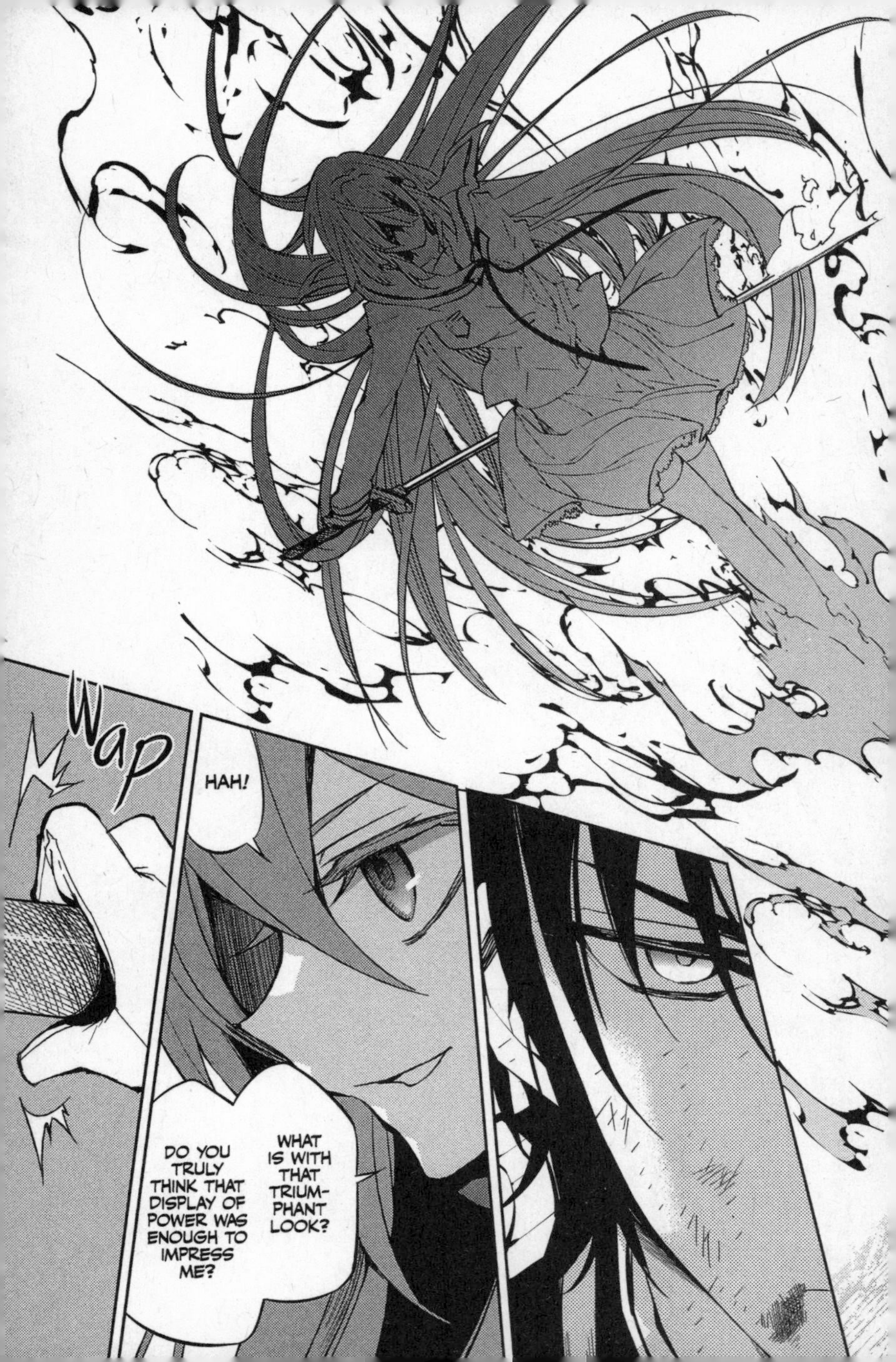
HAH!
WHAT IS WITH THAT TRIUMPHANT LOOK?
DO YOU TRULY THINK THAT DISPLAY OF POWER WAS ENOUGH TO IMPRESS ME?
Wap

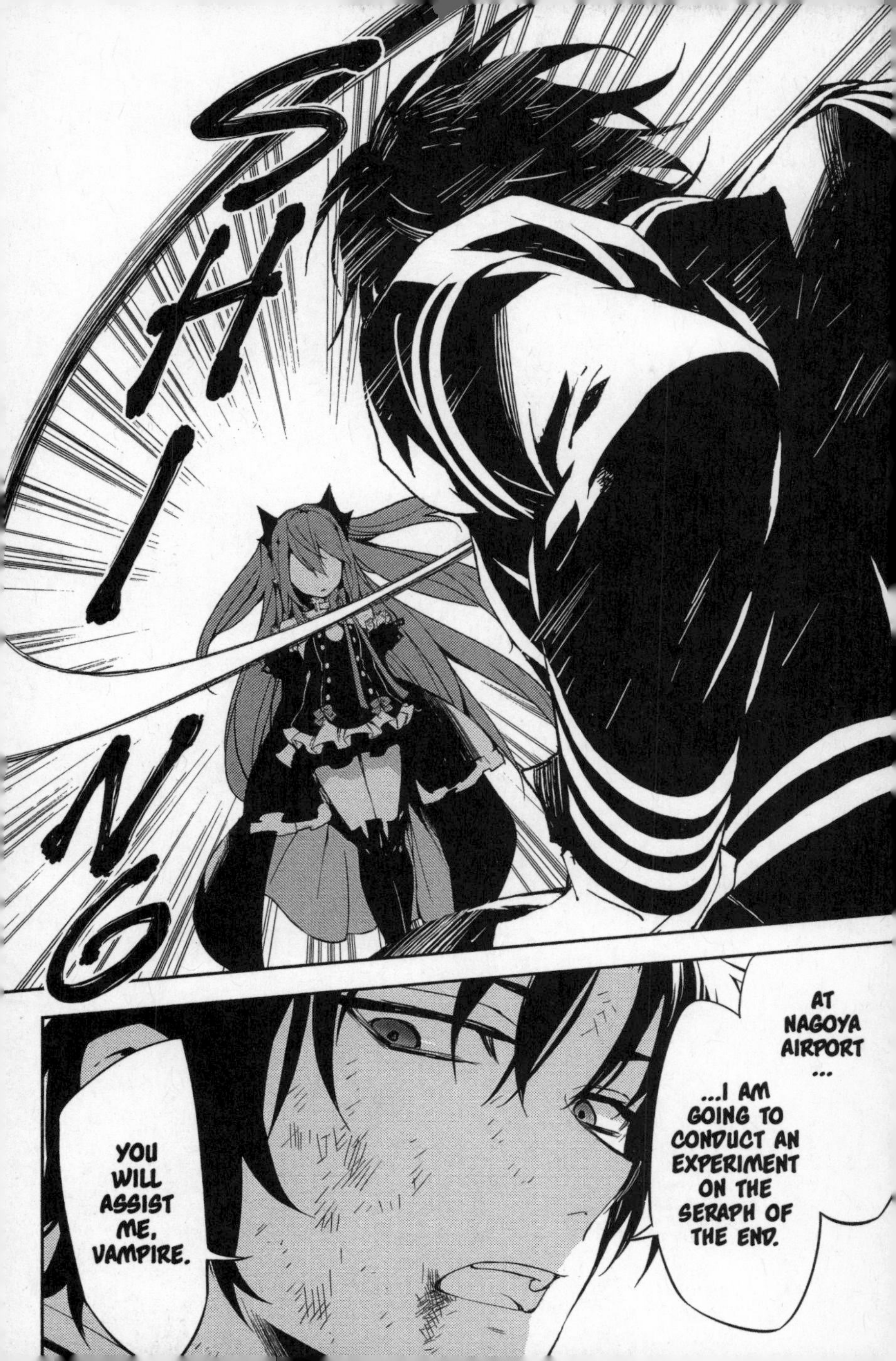
SHIING
AT NAGOYA AIRPORT...
...I AM GOING TO CONDUCT AN EXPERIMENT ON THE SERAPH OF THE END.
YOU WILL ASSIST ME, VAMPIRE.

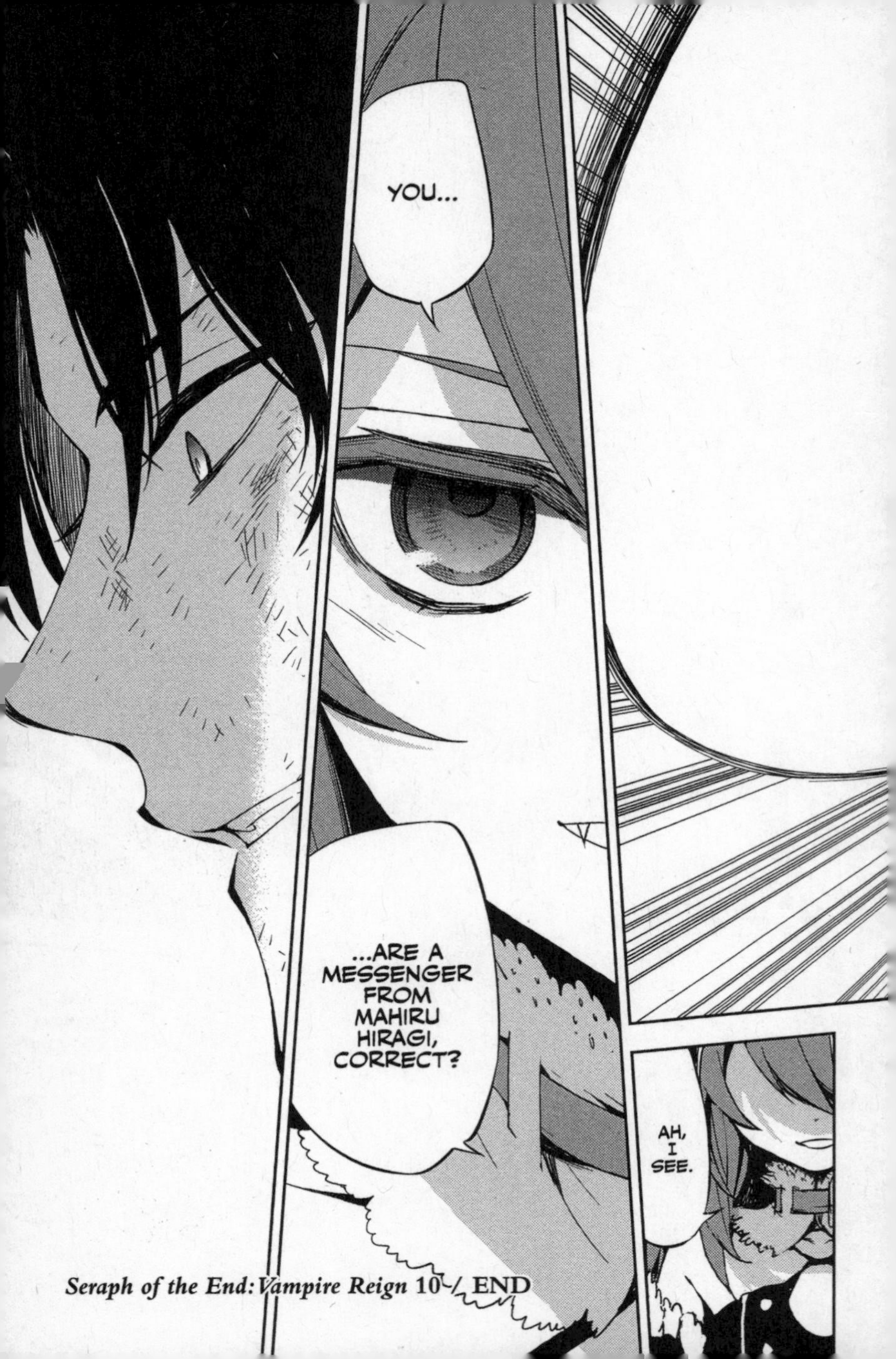
YOU...
...ARE A MESSENGER FROM MAHIRU HIRAGI, CORRECT?
AH, I SEE.

Seraph of the End: Vampire Reign 10 / END

Seraph of the End
VAMPIRE REIGN

Character Materials Collection by Takaya Kagami

MIKAELA
(16 years old)

When a new vampire tastes its first drop of human blood, the last trace of its humanity vanishes and they cease growing, thus becoming a full-fledged vampire. However, in Mikaela's case, even after he was turned, he resisted the urge to drink human blood for years, which is why he continued to grow and mature like a human. In this volume, he finally took his first sip from Yu, and has become a full vampire at age 16.

FERID: "WOW, SO YOU FINALLY DID IT, HUH? YAY! YOU'RE A REAL VAMPIRE NOW!"

MIKA: "..."

FERID: "WE NEED TO CELEBRATE! TODAY IS YOUR NEW BIRTHDAY AFTER ALL."

MIKA: "PLEASE STOP TALKING TO ME."

FERID: "OH, BUT I MUST! HOW ELSE CAN I ASK WHAT SORT OF PARTY YOU WANT FOR YOUR VERY FIRST VAMPIRE BIRTHDAY? DO YOU WANT TO DO A HOT POT PARTY? OOH! THAT'S A GREAT IDEA. I'VE ALWAYS WANTED TO TRY HOT POT. ESPECIALLY THAT ONE WHERE EVERYBODY BRINGS A RANDOM INGREDIENT AND TOSSES IT IN! HAVE YOU EVER HEARD OF THAT, MIKA?"

MIKA: "WHAT THE HECK ARE YOU TALKING ABOUT?"

FERID: "GREAT! THAT'S JUST WHAT WE'LL DO. NOW TO GO AND GET EVERYTHING READY. COME ALONG, CROWLEY. WE NEED TO GO SHOPPING FOR INGREDIENTS!"

CROWLEY: "WHAT? AM I GETTING DRAGGED INTO THIS TOO?"

FERID: "SAYS THE ONE WHO WAS ANXIOUSLY WAITING IN THE WINGS FOR HIS TURN TO COME OUT ONSTAGE."

CROWLEY: "I WASN'T."

FERID: "OH, COME ON! YOU COULD AT LEAST SAY THAT YOU ARE 'SUPER EXCITED' FOR THIS. IT'S A HOT POT PARTY!"

CROWLEY: "I'M REALLY NOT. I'LL SAY IT IF YOU WANT ME TO THOUGH."

MIKA: "CAN I LEAVE NOW?"

FERID: "WHAT, ALREADY? BUT WE STILL HAVE TO TALK ABOUT WHAT YOU WANT IN THE HOT POT."

MIKA: "WHY ARE WE EVEN TALKING ABOUT THIS AT ALL? VAMPIRES ONLY DRINK BLOOD."

FERID: "WHAT? THEY DO?"

MIKA: "THEY DON'T?"

FERID: "YOU HAVE BEEN A FULL-FLEDGED VAMPIRE FOR BARELY A DAY, AND ALREADY YOU THINK YOU CAN TALK TO YOUR SENIORS LIKE A KNOW-IT-ALL?"

MIKA: "..."

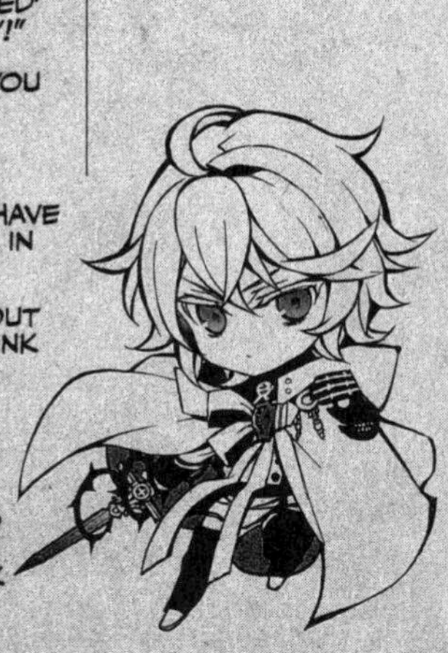

FERID: "HONESTLY! THIS IS WHAT YOU SOUND LIKE: 'DUDE, I'M, LIKE, TOTALLY A REAL VAMPIRE NOW. VAMPIRES, LIKE, ONLY DRINK BLOOD, Y'KNOW. THEY CAN'T HANDLE ANYTHING ELSE.'"

MIKA: "HOLD STILL WHILE I KILL YOU..."

CROWLEY: "CAREFUL. DON'T TAKE HIM SERIOUSLY LIKE THAT OR HE'LL JUST DRAG IT OUT EVEN LONGER."

FERID: "HA! ANYWAY, ALL JOKES ASIDE..."

MIKA: "YOU THINK THAT WAS A JOKE?"

CROWLEY: "DON'T REACT. DON'T REACT. HE'S BAITING YOU."

FERID: "HAVE YOU BOTH HEARD THAT THERE IS GOING TO BE A NEW LIGHT NOVEL SERIES? IT'S ABOUT US VAMPIRES! EVERYONE HAS BEEN SO CURIOUS ABOUT THE SECRETS OF OUR WORLD AND LIVES, YOU KNOW."

MIKA: "..."

FERID: "WHAT? YOU HONESTY HAVEN'T HEARD?"

MIKA: "WHAT ARE YOU TALKING ABOUT?"

FERID: "IT EVEN HAS YOUR NAME IN THE TITLE, *SERAPH OF THE END: VAMPIRE MIKAELA'S STORY*."

MIKA: "IT HAS MY NAME IN THE TITLE?"

FERID: "WHY THEY PICKED YOUR NAME IS A SECRET THOUGH. IT'S A BRAND NEW STORY THAT'S GOING TO TALK ALL ABOUT ONE OF THE BIGGEST MYSTERIES OF THE *SERAPH OF THE END* WORLD. CROWLEY AND MYSELF WILL EVEN BE IN IT, SO YOU KNOW IT WILL BE INTERESTING. ARE YOU SURE YOU HAVEN'T HEARD ABOUT IT BEFORE?"

MIKA: "NOT AT ALL."

CROWLEY: "WHAT'S THE 'BIGGEST MYSTERY' OF OUR WORLD SUPPOSED TO BE ANYWAY?"

FERID: "HOW I MANAGED TO BECOME SUCH A CHARISMATIC AND SUCCESSFUL SUSHI CHEF, OF COURSE—"

MIKA: "I'M LEAVING NOW."

FERID: "HA HA!"

CROWLEY: "AWW, HE LEFT. ANYWAY, SO WHAT IS THAT BOOK GOING TO BE ABOUT? FOR REAL, THIS TIME."

FERID: "OH, LOTS OF THINGS. YOUR LIFE BACK WHEN YOU WERE HUMAN, FOR ONE."

CROWLEY: "REALLY?"

FERID: "PRECIOUS LITTLE YU IS GOING TO BE IN IT TOO."

MIKA: "WHAT?"

CROWLEY: "YOU CAME BACK REALLY FAST..."

FERID: "AS FOR THE REST, YOU'LL JUST HAVE TO READ IN THE AFTERWORD."

CROWLEY: "AWW..."

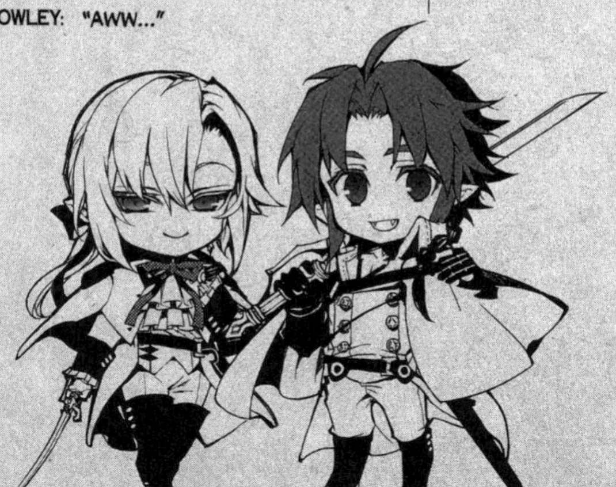

AFTERWORD

HELLO. I'M TAKAYA KAGAMI, AUTHOR AND SCRIPT WRITER FOR THIS SERIES.

I WAS ALREADY WRITING THE STORY FOR BOTH THE MANGA AND THE NOVEL VERSIONS OF *SERAPH OF THE END*, BUT NOW A BRAND NEW LIGHT NOVEL HAS BEEN GREEN-LIT, SO I'M WRITING YET ANOTHER STORY.

THIS TIME IT'S A STORY SET DIRECTLY AFTER THE WORLD ENDED. I WAS ALREADY WRITING A NOVEL ABOUT THE TIME RIGHT BEFORE THE CATASTROPHE. THAT'S THE TALE OF GUREN, SHINYA, MAHIRU AND KURETO'S MISADVENTURES IN *SERAPH OF THE END: GUREN ICHINOSE: CATASTROPHE AT SIXTEEN*. BUT NOW I'M WRITING A SECOND NOVEL SERIES. THIS ONE TELLS THE STORY OF MIKA, OF COURSE, BUT ALSO FERID, CROWLEY AND THE OTHER VAMPIRES AND THEIR GRAND SOCIETY. IT'S CALLED *SERAPH OF THE END: VAMPIRE MIKAELA'S STORY*, PUBLISHED BY JUMP J. BOOKS.

JUST LIKE HOW *VAMPIRE REIGN* AND *GUREN ICHINOSE: CATASTROPHE AT SIXTEEN* ARE NOT MANGA VERSIONS OR NOVEL VERSIONS OF EACH OTHER, I ALSO WROTE THIS STORY TO BE ITS OWN, COMPLETE TALE. I ALSO WROTE IT SO THAT, AFTER READING IT, YOU CAN GO BACK TO THE FIRST NOVEL AND THE MANGA AND SEE ALL THE LITTLE THINGS I SEEDED HERE AND THERE AND GO "OH!!" (AH! I DID STRUCTURE THEM SO EACH IS ITS OWN STAND-ALONE STORY THOUGH. YOU DON'T HAVE TO READ THE OTHERS IF YOU DON'T WANT TO.) BUT IF YOU DO READ ALL OF THEM, I MADE IT SO THEY WOULD ALL BE 16 BILLION TIMES MORE FUN AND INTERESTING. (HAHA)

WHY DO VAMPIRES EXIST IN THIS WORLD? WHAT WAS THEIR SOCIETY LIKE BEFORE THE CATASTROPHE? WHAT WAS CROWLEY LIKE AS A HUMAN AND HOW WAS HE TURNED? WHAT ABOUT KRUL? WHAT WERE MIKA, YU AND GUREN DOING? AND WHAT WAS FERID UP TO?

FERID: "YES, THIS IS WHERE THE GRAND TALE OF HOW I BECAME SUCH A CHARISMATIC MASTER SUSHI CHEF—"

RIGHT, THAT'S ENOUGH THANK YOU. GO AWAY.

ANYWAY! I STRUCTURED THE STORY SO THAT IT BEGINS WITH MIKA AND YU AND THEN SPIRALS OUT INTO A SWEEPING TALE ABOUT VAMPIRE SOCIETY AS A WHOLE. I HOPE YOU WILL GIVE IT A TRY! I EVEN HEARD THAT THE COVER WAS MADE TO GO TOGETHER WITH CROWLEY'S COVER ON THIS MANGA VOLUME! I CAN'T WAIT TO SEE IT.

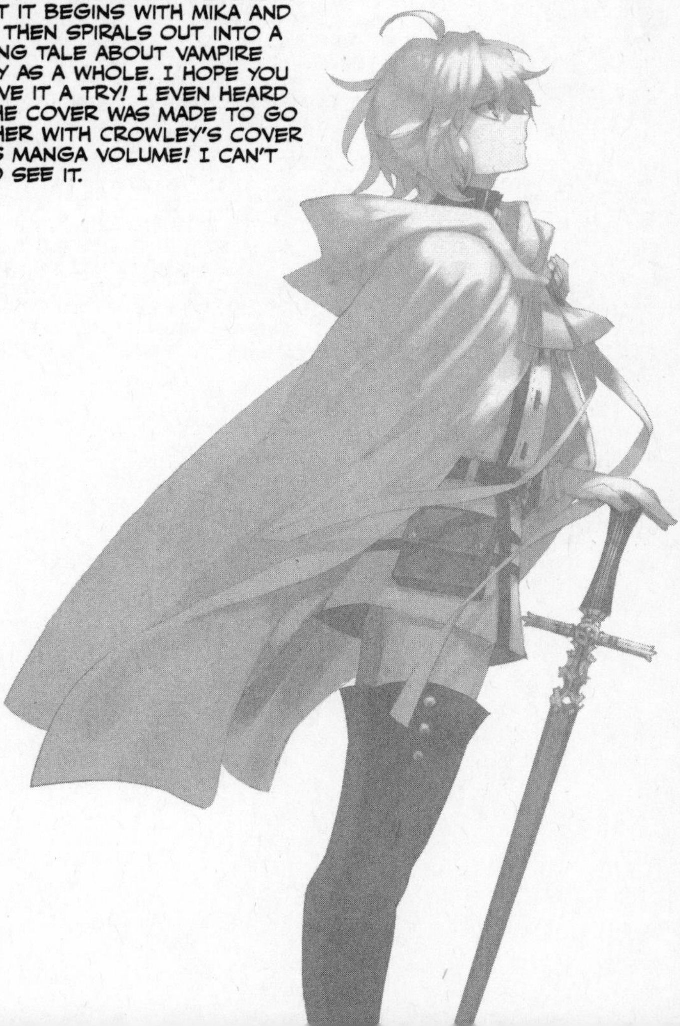

OKAY, NEXT TOPIC! THE SECOND SEASON OF THE ANIME IS AIRING IN JAPAN RIGHT NOW. I HANDED OVER THE OUTLINE OF WHAT WOULD BE HAPPENING TO THE ANIME TEAM ALMOST A YEAR AGO, SO NOW WE GET THE UNBELIEVABLE MIRACLE OF AN ANIME EPISODE AIRING AT ALMOST EXACTLY THE SAME TIME THAT SAME MATERIAL IS SHOWING UP IN THE MANGA. YU AND MIKA WILL FINALLY BE REUNITED IN THE ANIME! IT WILL BE SO FUN TO READ AND WATCH BOTH AND SEE WHAT EACH VERSION DOES DIFFERENTLY FROM THE OTHER. I HOPE YOU ENJOY IT!

BUT DON'T FORGET, EVEN THOUGH THE ANIME IS ENDING, THE STORY STILL GOES ON:

VAMPIRE REIGN.

GUREN ICHINOSE: CATASTROPHE AT SIXTEEN.

VAMPIRE MIKAELA'S STORY.

ALL THREE STORIES ARE GOING TO KEEP GOING, EACH SUBTLY INFLUENCING THE OTHER AND GROWING BIGGER AND BIGGER, SO I HOPE YOU WILL STICK AROUND FOR THE RIDE!

NOW THEN, SEE YOU ALL NEXT VOLUME! WITH VOLUME 11, THE MANGA STORY FINALLY HITS ITS SECOND ARC! (UP UNTIL NOW IT'S BEEN THE VAMPIRE ARC. NOW WE FINALLY GET TO THE SERAPH OF THE END ARC).

I HOPE FOR YOUR CONTINUED SUPPORT!!

—TAKAYA KAGAMI

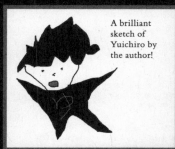

A brilliant sketch of Yuichiro by the author!

TAKAYA KAGAMI is a prolific light novelist whose works include the action and fantasy series *The Legend of the Legendary Heroes*, which has been adapted into manga, anime and a video game. His previous series, *A Dark Rabbit Has Seven Lives*, also spawned a manga and anime series.

66 Since I also write the afterword, I was flailing around not knowing what to write here when I remembered something...this is volume 10! We've finally reached volume 10! This is a historic moment! There are some really exciting things going on in this volume, so I hope you enjoy it. 99

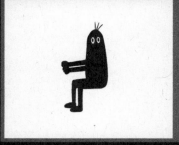

YAMATO YAMAMOTO, born 1983, is an artist and illustrator whose works include the *Kure-nai* manga and the light novels *Kure-nai*, *9S -Nine S-* and *Denpa Teki na Kanojo*. Both *Denpa Teki na Kanojo* and *Kure-nai* have been adapted into anime.

66 Volume 10! We've finally reached double digits. Things are going to keep getting more and more interesting, so I hope you enjoy it. 99

DAISUKE FURUYA previously assisted Yamato Yamamoto with storyboards for *Kure-nai*.

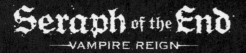

Seraph of the End
—VAMPIRE REIGN—

VOLUME 10
SHONEN JUMP ADVANCED MANGA EDITION

STORY BY **TAKAYA KAGAMI**
ART BY **YAMATO YAMAMOTO**
STORYBOARDS BY **DAISUKE FURUYA**

TRANSLATION **Adrienne Beck**
TOUCH-UP ART & LETTERING **Sabrina Heep**
DESIGN **Shawn Carrico**
EDITOR **Marlene First**

OWARI NO SERAPH © 2012 by Takaya Kagami,
Yamato Yamamoto, Daisuke Furuya
All rights reserved. First published in Japan in 2012 by SHUEISHA Inc., Tokyo.
English translation rights arranged by SHUEISHA Inc.

Printed in the U.S.A.

Published by VIZ Media, LLC
P.O. Box 77010
San Francisco, CA 94107

10 9 8 7 6 5 4 3 2 1
First printing, September 2016

www.viz.com

www.shonenjump.com

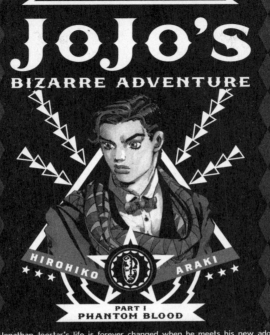
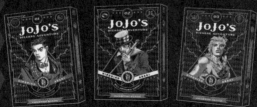

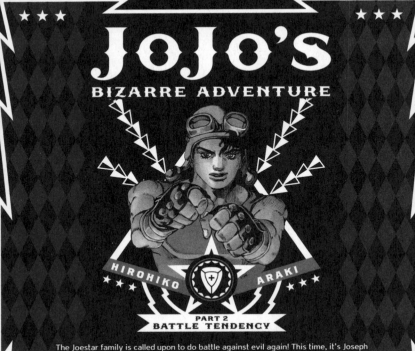
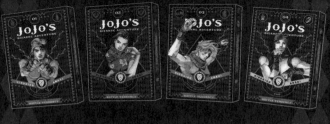

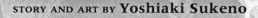

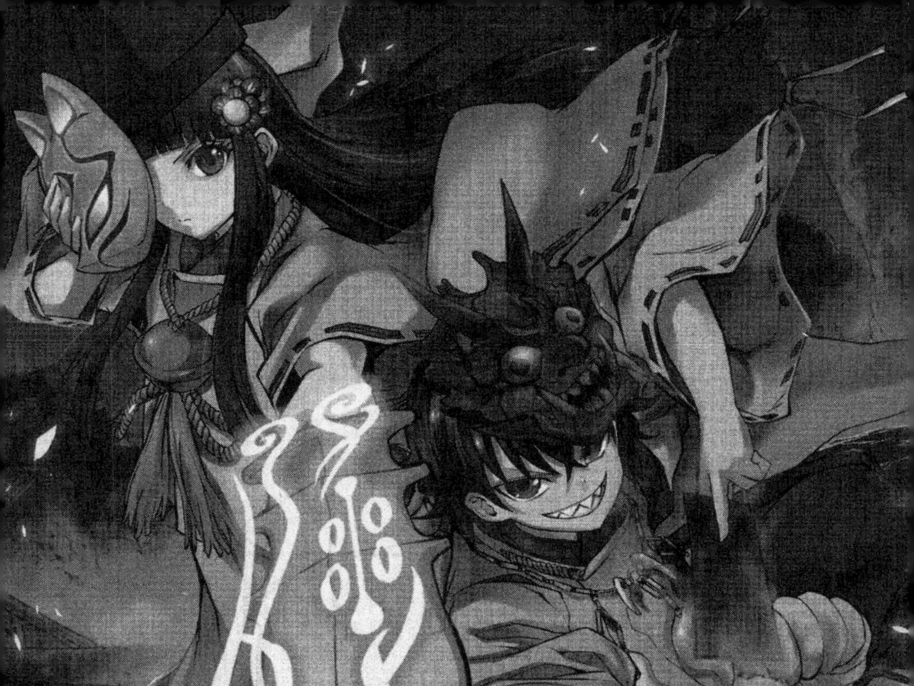

Twin★Star Exorcists

ONMYOJI

STORY AND ART BY Yoshiaki Sukeno

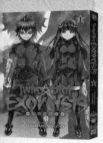

The action-packed romantic comedy from the creator of *Good Luck Girl!*

Rokuro dreams of becoming *anything* but an exorcist! Then mysterious Benio turns up. The pair are dubbed the "Twin Star Exorcists" and learn they are fated to marry...

Can Rokuro escape both fates?

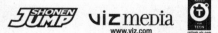

www.viz.com
ratings.viz.com

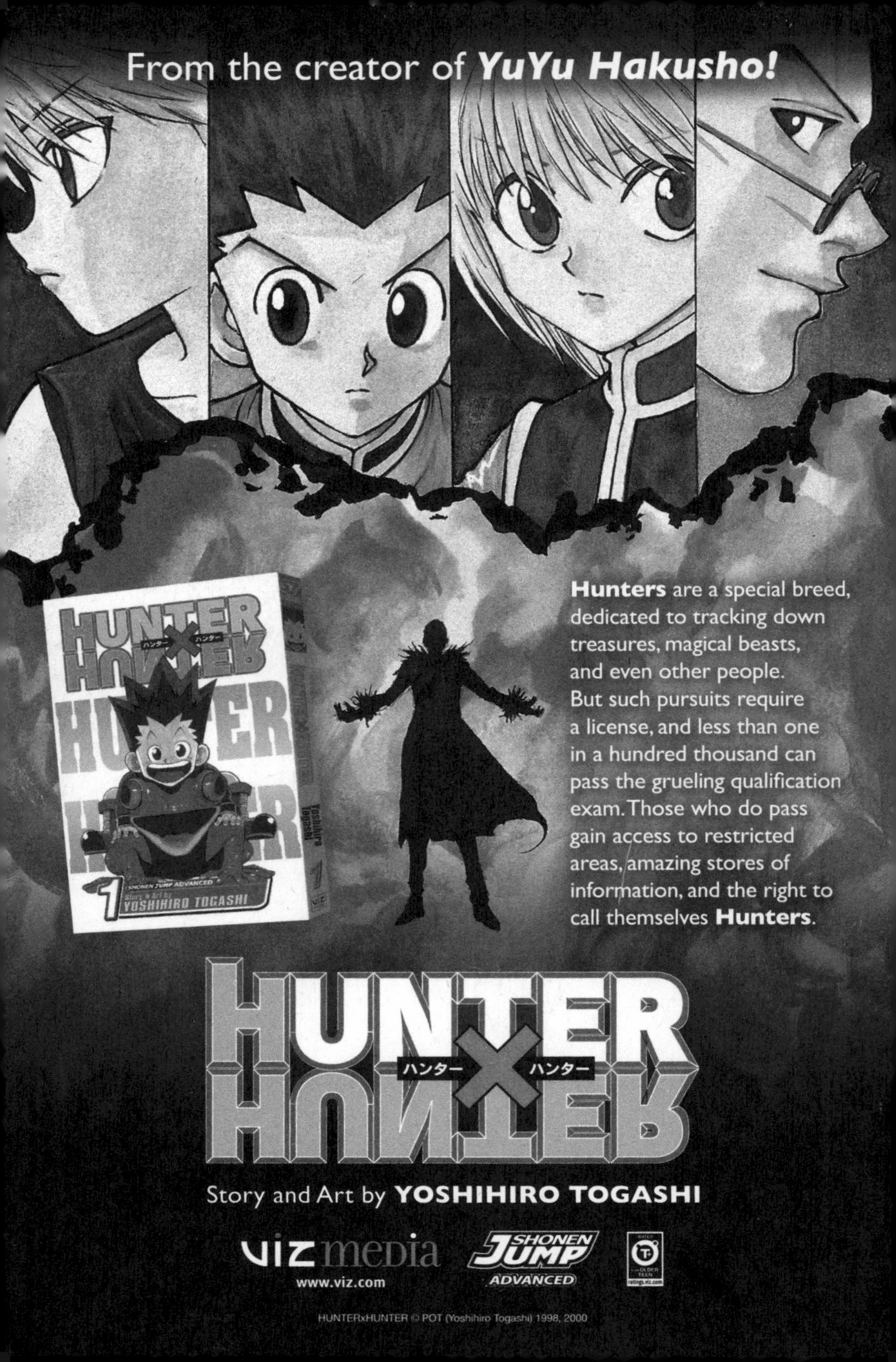
From the creator of *YuYu Hakusho!*
HUNTER × HUNTER ハンター ハンター
SHONEN JUMP ADVANCED
1
Story & Art by YOSHIHIRO TOGASHI
Hunters are a special breed, dedicated to tracking down treasures, magical beasts, and even other people. But such pursuits require a license, and less than one in a hundred thousand can pass the grueling qualification exam. Those who do pass gain access to restricted areas, amazing stores of information, and the right to call themselves **Hunters**.
HUNTER × HUNTER ハンター ハンター
Story and Art by **YOSHIHIRO TOGASHI**
VIZ media
www.viz.com
SHONEN JUMP ADVANCED
RATED T+ FOR OLDER TEEN ratings.viz.com
HUNTERxHUNTER © POT (Yoshihiro Togashi) 1998, 2000

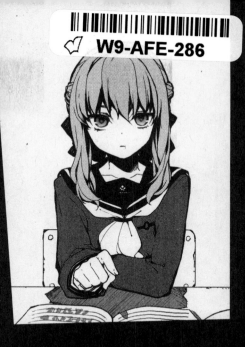

YOU'RE READING THE **WRONG WAY!**

SERAPH OF THE END reads from right to left, starting in the upper-right corner. Japanese is read from right to left, meaning that action, sound effects, and word-balloon order are completely reversed from English order.

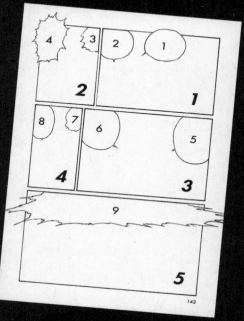

142